Simon Beckett is a freelance journalist and writes for national newspapers and colour supplements. The author of the international bestseller *The Chemistry of Death*, he lives in Sheffield.

Also by Simon Beckett

THE CHEMISTRY OF DEATH

For more information on Simon Beckett and his books, visit his website
at www.simonbeckett.com

WRITTEN IN BONE

SIMON BECKETT

BANTAM PRESS

LONDON • TORONTO • SYDNEY • AUCKLAND • JOHANNESBURG

TRANSWORLD PUBLISHERS
61–63 Uxbridge Road, London W5 5SA
A Random House Group Company
www.booksattransworld.co.uk

First published in Great Britain
in 2007 by Bantam Press
an imprint of Transworld Publishers

A CIP catalogue record for this book
is available from the British Library.

ISBN 9780593055243 (cased)
9780593055250 (tpb)

Addresses for Random House Group Ltd companies outside the UK
can be found at: www.randomhouse.co.uk
The Random House Group Ltd Reg. No. 954009

The Random House Group Ltd makes every effort to ensure that the papers used in its books
are made from trees that have been legally sourced from well-managed and credibly certified
forests. Our paper procurement policy can be found at: www.randomhouse.co.uk/paper.htm

Typeset in 11.5/15pt Bembo by
Falcon Oast Graphic Art Ltd.

Printed and bound in Great Britain by
Mackays of Chatham, Chatham, Kent

2 4 6 8 10 9 7 5 3 1

For Hilary

1

Given the right temperature, everything burns. Wood. Clothing.
People.

At 250° Celsius, flesh will ignite. Skin blackens and splits. The sub-
cutaneous fat starts to liquefy, like grease in a hot pan. Fuelled by it,
the body starts to burn. Arms and legs catch first, acting as kindling
to the greater mass of the torso. Tendons and muscle fibres contract,
causing the burning limbs to move in an obscene parody of life. Last
to go are the organs. Cocooned in moistness, they often remain even
after the rest of the soft tissue has been consumed.

But bone is, quite literally, a different matter. Bone stubbornly
resists all but the hottest fires. And even when the carbon has burned
from it, leaving it as dead and lifeless as pumice, bone will still retain
its shape. Now, though, it is an insubstantial ghost of its former self
that will easily crumble; the final bastion of life transformed to ash.
It's a process that, with few variations, follows the same inexorable
pattern.

Yet not always.

The peace of the old cottage is broken by a footfall. The rotting
door is pushed open, its rusted hinges protesting the disturbance.
Daylight falls into the room, then is blocked out as a shadow fills the

doorway. The man ducks his head to see into the darkened interior. The old dog with him hesitates, its senses already alerting it to what's within. Now the man, too, pauses, as though reluctant to cross the threshold. When the dog begins to venture inside he recalls it with a word.

'Here.'

Obediently, the dog returns, glancing nervously at the man with eyes grown opaque with cataracts. As well as the scent from inside the cottage, the animal can sense its owner's nervousness.

'Stay.'

The dog watches, anxiously, as the man advances further into the derelict cottage. The odour of damp envelops him. And now another smell is making itself known. Slowly, almost reluctantly, the man crosses to a low door set in the back wall. It has swung shut. He puts out his hand to push it open, then pauses again. Behind him, the dog gives a low whine. He doesn't hear it. Gently, he eases open the door, as though fearful of what he's going to see.

But at first he sees nothing. The room is dim, the only light coming from a small window whose glass is cracked and cobwebbed with decades of dirt. In the mean light that bleeds through, the room retains its secrets for a few moments longer. Then, as the man's eyes adjust, details begin to emerge.

And he sees what's lying in the room.

He sucks in a breath as though punched, taking an involuntary step backwards.

'Oh, Jesus Christ.'

The words are soft, but seem unnaturally loud in the still confines of the cottage. The man's face has paled. He looks around, as if fearful he'll find someone there with him. But he's alone.

He backs out of the doorway, as if reluctant to turn away from the object on the floor. Only when the warped door has creaked shut again, cutting off his view of the other room, does he turn his back.

His gait is unsteady as he goes outside. The old dog greets

him, but is ignored as the man reaches inside his coat and fumbles out a pack of cigarettes. His hands are trembling, and it takes three attempts for him to ignite the lighter. He draws the smoke deep into his lungs, a nub of glowing ash chasing the paper back towards the filter. By the time the cigarette is finished his trembling has steadied.

He drops the stub on to the grass and treads it out before bending down to retrieve it. Then, slipping it into his coat pocket, he takes a deep breath and goes to make the phone call.

I was on my way to Glasgow airport when the call came. It was a foul February morning, brooding grey skies and a depressing mizzle driven by cold winds. The east coast was being lashed by storms, and although they hadn't worked their way this far inland yet, it didn't look promising.

I only hoped the worst would hold off long enough for me to catch my flight. I was on my way back to London, having spent the previous week first recovering then examining a body from a moor-land grave out on the Grampian highlands. It had been a thankless task. The crystalline frost had turned the moors and peaks to iron, as breathtakingly cold as it was beautiful. The mutilated victim had been a young woman, who still hadn't been identified. It was the second such body I'd been asked to recover from the Grampians in recent months. As yet it had been kept out of the press, but no one on the investigating team was in any doubt that the same killer was responsible for both. One who would kill again if he wasn't caught, and at the moment that wasn't looking likely. What made it worse was that, although the state of decomposition made it hard to be sure, I was convinced that the mutilations weren't post-mortem.

So all in all, it had been a gruelling trip, and I was looking forward to going home. For the past eighteen months I'd been living in London, based at the forensic science department of a university. It was a temporary contract that gave me access to lab facilities until I found something more permanent, but in recent weeks I'd spent far more time working out in the field than I had in my office. I'd promised Jenny, my girlfriend, that we'd be able to spend some time together after this. It wasn't the first time I'd made that promise, but this time I was determined to keep it.

When my phone rang I thought it would be her, calling to make sure I was on my way home. But the number on the caller display wasn't one I recognized. When I answered, the voice at the other end was gruff and no-nonsense.

'Sorry to disturb you, Dr Hunter. I'm Detective Superintendent Graham Wallace, at Northern Force Headquarters in Inverness. Can you spare me a few minutes?'

He had the tone of someone used to getting his own way, and a harsh accent that spoke of Glasgow tenements rather than the softer cadences of Inverness.

'Just a few. I'm on my way to catch a flight.'

'I know. I've just spoken to DCI Allan Campbell at Grampian Police, and he told me you'd finished up here. I'm glad I've caught you.'

Campbell was the Senior Investigating Officer I'd been working with on the body recovery. A decent man and a good officer, he found it difficult to separate himself from his work. That was something I could appreciate.

I glanced at the taxi driver, conscious of being overheard. 'What can I do for you?'

'I'm looking for a favour.' Wallace clipped the words out, as though each one was costing more than he liked to pay. 'You'll have seen about the train crash this morning?'

I had. At my hotel before I'd left I'd watched the news reports of a West Coast commuter express that had derailed after hitting a van left on the line. From the TV footage it looked bad, the train carriages lying mangled and twisted by the track. No one knew yet how many people had been killed.

10

'We've got everyone we can up there now, but it's chaos at the moment,' Wallace continued. 'There's a chance the derailment was deliberate, so we're having to treat the whole area as a crime scene. We're calling in help from other forces, but right now we're running at full stretch.'

I thought then I could guess what was coming. According to the news reports, some of the carriages had caught fire, which would make victim identification both a priority and a forensic nightmare. But before that could even begin, the bodies would have to be recovered, and from what I'd seen that was still some way off.

'I'm not sure how much help I'd be at the moment,' I told him.

'It isn't the crash I'm calling about,' he said, impatiently. 'We've got a report of a fire death out in the Western Isles. Small island called Runa, in the Outer Hebrides.'

I hadn't heard of it, but that was hardly surprising. All I knew about the Outer Hebrides was that the islands were some of the most remote outposts of the UK, miles from anywhere off the northwest coast of Scotland.

'Suspicious?' I asked.

'Doesn't sound like it. Might be suicide, but more likely to be a drunk or a vagrant who fell asleep too close to a campfire. Dog walker found it at an abandoned croft and called it in. He's a retired DI, lives out there now. I've worked with him. Used to be a good man.'

I wondered if the *used to be* was significant. 'So what else did he say about it?'

There was a beat before he replied. 'Just that it's badly burned. But I don't want to pull resources away from a major incident unless I have to. A couple of the local boys from Stornoway are going out by ferry later today, and I'd like you to go with them and take a look. See if you think it's low priority, or if I need to send a SOC team. I'd like an expert assessment before I press the panic button, and Allan Campbell says you're bloody good.'

The attempt at flattery sat awkwardly with his bluff manner. I'd noticed the hesitation when I'd asked about the body, too, and wondered if there was something he wasn't telling me. But if Wallace thought there was anything suspicious about the death, he'd be sending a Scene of Crime team, train crash or not.

The taxi was almost at the airport. I had every reason to say no. I'd only just finished working on one major investigation, and this sounded fairly mundane; the sort of everyday tragedy that never makes it into the newspapers. I thought about having to tell Jenny that I wouldn't be back today after all. Given the amount of time I'd spent away recently, I knew that wouldn't go down well.

Wallace must have sensed my reluctance. 'Should only take a couple of days, including getting out there. The thing is, it sounds as if there might be something . . . odd about it.'

'I thought you said it wasn't suspicious?'

'It isn't. At least, nothing I've heard makes me think it is. Look, I don't want to say too much, but that's why I'd like an expert such as yourself to take a look.'

I hate being manipulated. Even so, I couldn't deny my curiosity had been aroused.

'I wouldn't ask if we weren't hard pressed right now,' Wallace added, turning the screw another notch.

Outside the rain-smeared taxi window I saw a road sign saying the airport was approaching. 'I'll have to get back to you,' I said. 'Give me five minutes.'

He didn't like that, but he could hardly object. I rang off, biting my lip for a moment before dialling a number I knew off by heart.

Jenny's voice came on the line. I smiled at the sound of it, even though I wasn't looking forward to the conversation we were about to have.

'David! I was just on my way to work. Where are you?'

'On my way to the airport.'

I heard her laugh. 'Thank God for that. I thought you were phoning to say you weren't coming back today after all.'

I felt my stomach sink. 'Actually that's what I'm calling about,' I said. 'The thing is, I've just been asked to go on another job.'

'Oh.'

'It's just for a day or two. In the Outer Hebrides. But there's no one else to do it right now.' I stopped myself from explaining about the train crash, knowing it would sound as though I was making excuses.

There was a pause. I hated the way the laughter had gone from Jenny's voice. 'So what did you say?'

'That I'd let them know. I wanted to talk to you first.'

'Why? We both know you've already made up your mind.'

I didn't want this to develop into an argument. I glanced at the cab driver again.

'Look, Jenny . . .'

'You mean you haven't?'

I hesitated.

'That's what I thought,' she said.

'Jenny . . .'

'I've got to go. I'll be late for work.'

There was a click as she hung up. I sighed. The day wasn't getting off to a good start. *So call her back and say you'll turn it down.* My finger poised over the phone.

'Don't worry, pal. My wife's always giving me a hard time too,' the taxi driver said over his shoulder. 'She'll get over it, eh?'

I made a non-committal comment. In the distance I could see a plane taking off from the airport. The driver indicated for the turn as I keyed in the number. It was answered on the first ring.

'How do I get there?' I asked Wallace.

2

I spend most of my working day with the dead. The long dead, sometimes. I'm a forensic anthropologist. It's a field of expertise, and a fact of life, that most people prefer not to confront until they have to. For a while I was one of them. When my wife and daughter were killed in a car crash, working in a field that reminded me every day of what I'd lost was too painful. So I became a GP, a doctor of medicine tending to the living rather than the dead.

But then events occurred that forced me to take up my original vocation once again. My calling, you might say. Part pathology, part archaeology, what I do goes beyond either. Because even after human biology has broken down, when what was once a life is reduced to corruption, decay and old, dry bones, the dead can still bear witness. They can still tell a story, if only you know how to interpret it. That's what I do.

Coax the dead to tell their story.

Wallace had obviously anticipated that I wouldn't turn him down. A seat had already been booked for me on a flight to Lewis, the main island in the Outer Hebrides. The flight was delayed by almost an hour because of bad weather, so I sat in the departure lounge, trying not to watch as the London flight I should have been on was called, closed, and finally disappeared from the board.

It was a bumpy ride, whose only redeeming feature was that it was short. The day was half gone by the time I caught a taxi from the airport to the ferry terminal at Stornoway, a dour working town still largely dependent on the fishing industry. The dock where I was dropped off was misty and cold, pungent with the usual harbour fug of diesel and fish. I'd been expecting to board one of the big car ferries that belched smoke into the rainy sky above the grey harbour, but the boat I found myself standing before looked more like a small fishing vessel than anything meant to carry passengers. Only the distinctive presence of a police Range Rover taking up most of the deck told me I was at the right place.

A boarding ramp led up to it, rocking queasily in the heavy swell. A uniformed police sergeant was standing on the concrete quayside at the bottom, hands stuffed into the pockets of his coat. His cheeks and nose had the permanent flush of broken capillaries. Pouchy eyes regarded me balefully over a salt and pepper moustache as I wrestled with my bag and flight case.

'You Dr Hunter? I'm Sergeant Fraser,' he informed me, gruffly. There was no first name, and his hands remained in his pockets. He spoke with a hard, almost nasal burr, very different to the mainland Scottish accents I'd heard. 'We've been waiting for you to turn up.'

With that, he went back up the ramp, making no offer to help with my heavy luggage. I hefted the shoulder bag and aluminium flight case and started up after him. The ramp was wet and slippery, rising and falling unevenly with the slap of the waves. I struggled to keep my footing, trying to time my steps with the unsteady motion. Then someone was trotting down the ramp to help. A young uniformed constable grinned as he took the flight case from my hand.

'Here, I'll take that.'

I didn't argue. He went over to the Range Rover strapped to the deck and loaded the case into the back.

'What have you got in here, a body?' he asked, cheerfully.

I put my bag in with the aluminium case. 'No, it just feels like it. Thanks.'

'No problem.' He couldn't have been much older than twenty. He had a friendly, open face, and his uniform looked neat even in the rain. 'I'm PC McKinney, but just call me Duncan.'

'David Hunter.'

His handshake was enthusiastic, as though to make up for Fraser's lack. 'So you the forensic man?'

'Afraid so.'

'Great! I mean, not great, but . . . well, you know. Anyway, let's get out of the rain.'

The passenger cabin was a glassed-in section below the wheel-house. Outside it, Fraser was talking heatedly to a bearded man in oilskins. Behind him a tall teenage boy, face rippled with acne, looked on sullenly as Fraser jabbed the air with a finger.

'. . . waited long enough as it is, and now you're saying you're not ready to go?'

The bearded man stared back impassively. 'There's another passenger. We're not leaving till she's arrived.'

Fraser's already red face had darkened still further. 'This isn't a bloody pleasure cruise. We're already behind schedule, so get that ramp pulled up, OK?'

The other man's eyes stared out above the dark beard, giving him the feral look of a wild animal. 'This is my boat, and I set the schedules. So if you want it pulling up, you'll have to do it yourself.'

Fraser drew himself up to assert himself when there was a clatter-ing from the ramp. A diminutive young woman was hurrying up, struggling under the weight of a heavy-looking bag. She wore a bright red, down-filled coat that looked at least two sizes too big for her. A thick woollen hat was pulled down over her ears. With her sandy hair and pointed chin, it gave her an appealing, elfin appearance.

'Hi, gents. Anyone care to give me a hand here?' she panted.

Duncan had started forward but the bearded man beat him to it. He grinned at the new arrival, white teeth gleaming in the dark beard as he effortlessly took the bag from her.

'About time you showed up, Maggie. We were about to go without you.'

'Good job you didn't, or my gran would have killed you.' She stood with her hands on her hips, regarding them as she caught her breath. 'Hi, Kevin, how's it going? Your dad here still working you too hard?'

The teenager blushed and looked down. 'Aye.'

'Aye, some things never change. Now you're eighteen, you'll have to put in for a pay rise.'

I saw a spark of interest kindle in her eyes as she eyed the police Range Rover.

'So what's going on? Something happened I should know about?'

The bearded man jerked his head dismissively towards us. 'Try asking them. They won't tell us anything about it.'

The young woman's grin faltered when she saw Fraser. Then she recovered, quickly mustering a smile that now held something like defiance.

'Hello, Sergeant Fraser. This is a surprise. What takes you out to Runa?'

'Police business,' Fraser said, flatly, and turned away. Whoever the young woman was, he wasn't pleased to see her.

The ferry captain and his son busied themselves now the late arrival was on board. There was a motorized whine as the ramp was winched up, and the wooden structure of the boat vibrated as the anchor chain was ratcheted into place. With a last, curious glance in my direction, the young woman went into the wheelhouse.

Then, with a belch of diesel, the ferry cast off and chugged out of the harbour.

★

The sea was rough, and what should have been a two-hour crossing took almost three. Once we'd left the protection of Stornoway harbour, the Atlantic lived up to its reputation. It was a turbulent grey plain of angry waves, into which the ferry smacked head on. Each time it would rear up over the crests, then slide sickeningly down the far side before beginning the process again.

The only shelter was in the cramped passenger cabin, where diesel fumes and burning hot radiators made an uncomfortable combination. Fraser and Duncan sat for the most part in miserable silence. I'd tried to draw out Fraser about the body, but he obviously knew little more than I did.

'Just a meat job,' he grunted, sweat beading his forehead. 'Some drunk fell asleep too close to his campfire, most likely.'

'Wallace told me a retired DI had found it. Who is he?'

'That's Andrew Brody,' Duncan piped up. 'My dad used to work with him on the mainland, before we moved to Stornoway. Said he was a damn good police officer.'

'Aye, "was",' Fraser said. 'I was asking about him before we came out. Too much of a loner for his own good, apparently. Didn't like being a team player. I heard he lost it completely after his wife and daughter ran off; that's why he retired.'

Duncan looked embarrassed. 'It was stress, my dad said.'

Fraser waved away the distinction. 'Same thing. Just so long as he remembers he's not a DI any more.' He stiffened as the boat suddenly shuddered and yawed over another mountainous swell.

'Christ, of all the bloody places to get sent to . . .'

I stayed in the cabin for a while, wondering what I was doing on a small ferry in the Atlantic instead of on my way home to Jenny. We'd been arguing more and more lately, and always over the same thing – my work. This wasn't going to help, and with nothing to occupy me I found myself fretting over whether I'd made the right decision, and how I could make it up to her.

Eventually, I left the policemen and went on deck. The wind

blustered against me, peppering my face with rain, but it was a relief after the sour, overheated cabin. I stood in the bow, welcoming the spray on my face. The island was visible now, a dark mass rising from the sea as the ferry chugged towards it. Staring at it, I felt the familiar tightening in my gut, part nerves, part anticipation of what was waiting there.

Whatever it was, I hoped it was worth it.

A flash of red caught the corner of my eye, and I turned to see the young woman unsteadily making her way across the deck towards me. A sudden dip sent her running the last few steps, and I put out my arm to steady her.

'Thanks.'

She gave me a gamine smile as she joined me at the rail. 'It's a rough one. Iain says it's going to be fun trying to dock in this.'

Her accent was a softer, more lilting version of Fraser's. 'Iain?'

'Iain Kinross, the skipper. He's an old neighbour, from Runa.'

'Is that where you live?'

'Not any more. My family moved to Stornoway, except for my gran. We take it in turns to visit her. So you're here with the police, then?'

She asked the question with an innocence I didn't entirely trust. 'More or less.'

'But you're not one yourself? A policeman, I mean?'

I shook my head.

She grinned. 'Thought not. Iain said he heard them call you Doctor. Is there someone injured out here, or what?'

'Not as far as I know.'

I could see that only piqued her curiosity even more.

'So what's a doctor doing coming out to Runa with the police?'

'You'd better ask Sergeant Fraser.'

She grimaced. 'Aye, that'll happen.'

'You know each other?'

'Sort of.' She didn't enlarge.

'So what do you do on Stornoway?' I asked.

'Oh . . . I'm a writer. I'm working on a novel. I'm Maggie Cassidy, by the way.'

'David Hunter.'

She seemed to file the information away. We were silent for a while, watching the island gradually take form in the fading light: grey cliffs rising from the sea, topped with featureless green. A tall sea stack, a natural tower of black rock, thrust up from the waves in front of its cliffs.

'Nearly there,' Maggie said. 'The harbour's just behind Stac Ross, that big rock thingy. Supposed to be the third highest in Scotland. Typical Runa. Its only claim to fame is being third best.'

She stood up from the railing.

'Well, nice meeting you, David. Perhaps see you again before you go.'

She made her way back across the deck to rejoin Kinross and his son in the wheelhouse. I noticed that she seemed much steadier on her feet than she had when she'd come out.

I turned my attention back to the island we were approaching. Beyond Stac Ross, the cliffs fell back into a small harbour. The light was already starting to fade, but I could see a scattering of houses spreading out around it, a small outpost of habitation in the ocean's wilderness.

A sharp whistle came from behind me, carrying even above the wind and the sound of the engine. I turned to see Kinross gesturing angrily.

'Get inside!'

I didn't need to be told twice. The sea was becoming more violent as the waves were funnelled in between the tall cliffs that bracketed the harbour. Now there was no up and down roll, only a nauseating corkscrew motion as the swells jostled each other, sending sheets of spray across the deck.

Grabbing at handholds to steady myself, I made my way back to the overheated cabin. I waited with Duncan and a pale-faced Fraser as the ferry manoeuvred into the harbour, juddering against the impact of the waves. Through the cabin's window I could see them smashing against the concrete jetty, throwing up white clouds of spume. It took three attempts to dock, the entire boat vibrating as the engine revved to hold us in place.

We left the cabin, walking with difficulty on the swaying deck. There was no cover from the wind, but the cold air was wonderfully fresh, with a clean saline tang. Gulls wheeled and cried overhead, while on the jetty men were scurrying about, securing ropes and rubber fenders. Despite the cliffs, the harbour was fully open to the sea, with only a single breakwater jutting out to blunt the force of the waves. A few fishing boats were anchored here, jerking against their moorings like dogs straining at the leash.

Low houses and cottages clung barnacle-like to the steep hillside that dropped down to the harbour. The landscape that spread out behind them was a treeless green vista, windswept and bleak. In the distance, the skyline was dominated by a brooding peak, its tip lost in the mist of low clouds.

The young woman who'd introduced herself as Maggie Cassidy hurried off the ferry as soon as the ramp was lowered. I was a little surprised she didn't say goodbye, but didn't give it much thought. Behind me the Range Rover's engine started up, and I turned to climb into the back. I noticed that Fraser let the young PC drive. The boat was still see-sawing on the swells, and he eased it carefully down the undulating ramp.

A craggy-faced man was waiting for us on the jetty. He was mid-fifties, tall and powerfully built, with the indefinable look of a policeman. I didn't need to be told that this was the retired detective inspector who had found the body.

Fraser wound down the window. 'Andrew Brody?'

The man gave a short nod. The wind ruffled his grey hair as he looked at the three of us inside the car. Behind him, the locals who had helped moor the boat watched curiously.

'This all of you?' he asked, his disapproval obvious.

Fraser gave a stiff nod. 'Aye, for now.'

'What about SOC? When are they coming out?'

'We don't know they are yet,' Fraser retorted. 'That decision's not been taken.'

Brody's mouth tightened at his tone. Retired or not, the ex-DI didn't like being talked down to by a mere police sergeant.

'Then what about CID? They'll have to attend, regardless.'

'A DC's going to follow on from Stornoway after Dr Hunter here has taken a look at the body. He's a forensic expert.'

Until now Brody hadn't paid me any attention. Now he looked at me with more interest. His eyes were sharp and intelligent, and I felt in that brief moment I'd been assessed and judged.

'There's not much light left,' he said, glancing at the darkening sky. 'It's only fifteen minutes' drive, but it'll be dark by the time we get out there. Perhaps you'd like to ride with me, Dr Hunter. I can brief you on the way.'

Fraser bridled. 'I'm sure he's seen burned bodies before.'

Brody regarded him for a moment, as though reminding himself he no longer held rank. Then he turned his steady gaze back to me.

'Not like this.'

His car was parked on the quayside, a newish-looking Volvo saloon. The inside was spotless. It smelled of air freshener and, more faintly, of cigarettes. An old border collie was on a blanket in the back, black muzzle greyed with age. It stood up excitedly when Brody got into the car.

'Down, Bess,' he said, mildly. The dog immediately settled. Brody frowned as he examined the dashboard controls for the heater. 'Sorry, not had it long. Still trying to work out where everything is.'

The headlights of the Range Rover told us Fraser and Duncan were following as we drove out of the harbour. The days didn't last long this far north at this time of year, and dusk was already giving way to darkness. The street lights were on, illuminating a narrow main road barely deserving of the name. It ran up from the seafront through the village: a handful of small shops surrounded by a mix of old stone cottages and newer bungalows that had a temporary, prefabricated look.

Even from the little I could see of it, it was apparent that Runa wasn't the backwater I'd expected. The ruins of a small, roofless church stood by the roadside. But most of the doors and windows in the houses we passed looked new, as though they'd recently been replaced. There was a small but modern school, and a little further out the timber structure of the community hall boasted a new extension that bore a sign saying *Runa Medical Clinic*.

Even the road itself had been resurfaced. It was only narrow, not much more than a single lane with semicircular passing places every hundred metres or so, but the smooth black tarmac would have put most mainland roads to shame. It climbed steeply through the village, then levelled out as we passed the last few houses. On a hilltop over-looking them, silhouetted against the darkening sky, was a tall and crooked standing stone, rising from the grass like an accusing finger.

'That's Bodach Runa,' said Brody, seeing where I was looking. 'The Old Man of Runa. Legend is he went out there to watch for the return of his son, who'd gone to sea. But the son never came back, and the old man stood there so long he turned to stone.'

'In this weather I can believe it.'

He smiled, but it quickly died. After wanting me to ride with him, he now seemed uncomfortable, as though he was unsure where to start. I took out my mobile to check for messages.

'You'll not get a signal out here,' Brody warned. 'If you want to call out you'll have to use either a landline or a police radio. And if we get a good blow even they don't always work.'

I put my phone away. I'd half hoped Jenny might have left a message, though I didn't really expect it. I'd call her from a landline later and try to smooth things between us.

'So what sort of "forensic expert" are you?' Brody asked.

'I'm a forensic anthropologist.'

I glanced at him to see if I needed to explain. Even police officers sometimes had trouble with what I did. But Brody seemed satisfied.

'Good. At least we'll have one person out here who knows what he's doing. How much did Wallace tell you?'

'Just that it was a fire death, and that there was something odd about it. He wouldn't say what, except that it wasn't suspicious.'

His jaw set in disapproval. 'Did he now?'

'Why, are you saying there is?'

'I'm not saying anything,' Brody said. 'You can make your own mind up when you see it. I just expected that Wallace would have sent a full team over, that's all.'

I was starting to have a bad feeling about this. There were strict protocols to be followed if a death was suspicious, and normally I wouldn't get involved until a Scene of Crime team had processed the site. I hoped Wallace hadn't let his preoccupation with the train crash cloud his judgement.

But I also remembered what he'd said about Brody. *Used to be a good man.* Retired police officers often found it hard being out of the loop. Brody wouldn't be the first to exaggerate in order to feel in the thick of things again. I didn't put much credence in Fraser's gossip about his crack-up, but I wondered if similar doubts hadn't coloured Wallace's decision.

'All he wants me to do is take a look,' I said. 'If I see anything that suggests it might not be accidental, then I'll back off until SOC gets out here.'

'That'll have to do, I suppose,' Brody said, grudgingly.

But he still wasn't happy. Whatever he'd told Wallace, the super-intendent clearly hadn't accepted it at face value, and for a one-time detective inspector that was bound to rankle.

'How did you find the body?' I asked.

'The dog caught the scent when I was taking her out for a

24

walk this morning. It's in an abandoned crofter's cottage – a croft's a small farm,' he added, for my benefit. 'You sometimes get kids going out there, but not usually in winter. And before you ask, no, I didn't touch anything. I might be retired, but I know better than that.'

I didn't doubt it. 'Any idea who it might be?'

'Not a clue. Far as I know no one from the island's been reported missing. And there's less than two hundred people live out here, so it'd be hard for anyone to disappear without its being noticed.'

'Do you get many visitors from the mainland or other islands?'

'Not many, but some. The odd naturalist or archaeologist. All the islands are peppered with ruins: stone age, bronze age and God knows what. There are supposed to be burial cairns and an old watchtower on the mountain. And there's been quite a lot of renovation work going on, so we've had builders and contractors coming out. Road resurfacing, houses being done up, that sort of thing. But not since the weather turned.'

'Who else knows about the body?'

'No one as far as I'm aware. The only person I told was Wallace.'

That explained the curious looks of the locals when the police had arrived. Their presence would be big news on an island as small as this. I doubted the reason we were here would remain a secret for long, but at least for the moment we didn't have to worry about sightseers.

'He said it was badly burned.'

Brody gave a grim smile. 'Oh, it's badly burned all right. But I think you'd better see for yourself.'

He said it with both confidence and finality, closing the subject.

'Wallace told me you used to work with him.'

'I did a stint at HQ in Inverness. You know it?'

'I've only travelled through. Runa must have been quite a change after that.'

'Aye, but for the better. It's a good place to live. Quiet. There's time and space to think.'

'Are you from here originally?'

'God, no. I'm an "incomer",' he said. 'Wanted to get away from it all when I took early retirement. And it doesn't get much further away than this.'

There was no disputing that. Once we had left the harbour village, there was hardly any sign of life. The only habitation we'd passed was an imposing old house, set well back from the road. Other than that there had been only the occasional ruined bothy, and sheep. In the gathering twilight, Runa looked beautiful, but desolate.

It would be a lonely place to die.

There was a jolt as Brody turned off the road and bumped down an overgrown track. Ahead of us, the car's headlights picked out a crumbling old cottage. Wallace had said the body had been found at a croft, but there was little left to show this must once have been a working farm. Brody pulled up outside and turned off the engine.

'Stay, Bess,' he ordered the border collie.

We climbed out of the car as the Range Rover drew up behind us on the track. The cottage was a squat, single-storey building that was slowly being reclaimed by nature. Looming up behind it was the peak I'd seen earlier, now only a black shape in the encroaching darkness.

'That's Beinn Tuiridh,' Brody told me. 'It's what passes for a mountain out here. They say if you climb to the top on a clear day you can see all the way to Scotland.'

'Can you?'

'Never met anyone stupid enough to find out.'

He took a Maglite from his glove compartment, and we waited outside the car for Fraser and Duncan to join us. I collected my own torch from the flight case in the Range Rover, then we made our way towards the cottage, torch beams bouncing and criss-crossing in the darkness. It was little more than a stone shack, its walls furred

26

with moss and lichen. The doorway was so low I had to stoop to go inside.

I paused and shone my torch around. The place was obviously long abandoned, a derelict remnant of forgotten lives. Water dripped from a hole in the roof, and the room we were in was cramped, a low ceiling added to the claustrophobic feel. We were in what had once been a kitchen. There was an old range, a dusty cast-iron pan still standing on one of its cold plates. A rickety wooden table stood in the middle of the stone-flagged floor. A few cans and bottles were scattered on the floor, evidence that the place hadn't been entirely untenanted. It had the musty smell of age and damp, but nothing else. For a fire death there seemed remarkably little signs of any fire.

'Through there,' Brody said, shining his torch on another doorway.

As I approached it I caught the first faint, sooty whiff of combustion. But it was nothing like as strong as I would have expected. The door was broken, its rusted hinges protesting as it was pushed open. Watching my step, I went through into the other room. It was even more depressing than the ruined kitchen. The stink of fire was unmistakable now. The torchlight showed ancient, crumbling plaster on the bare walls, in one of which was the gaping mouth of a fireplace. But the smell didn't come from that. Its source was in the centre of the room, and as I shone my torch on it my breath caught in my throat.

There was precious little left of what had once been a living person. No wonder Brody had looked as he did when I'd asked if it was badly burned. It was that all right. Even the white heat of a crematorium isn't enough to reduce a human body to ash, yet this fire had somehow done just that.

An untidy pile of greasy ash and cinders lay on the floor. The fire had consumed bone as readily as it had skin and tissue. Only the larger bones remained, emerging from the ash like dead branches from a snowdrift. Even these had been calcined, the carbon burned from them until they were grey and brittle. Presiding over them all like a broken eggshell was a skull, lying with its jawbone canted off to one side.

And yet, apart from the body, nothing else in the room had been damaged. The fire that had all but incinerated a human being, reduced its bones to the consistency of pumice, had somehow done so without burning anything else nearby. The stone flags below the remains were blackened, but a few feet away a tattered and filthy mattress lay untouched. Old leaves and twigs littered the ground, yet the flames had rejected even these.

But that wasn't the worst of it. What had shocked me to silence was the sight of two unburned feet and a single hand protruding from the ashes. The bones jutting from them were scorched to black sticks, yet they were completely unmarked.

Brody came and stood beside me.

'Well, Dr Hunter? Still think there's nothing suspicious about it?'

3

The wind moaned fitfully outside the old cottage, an eerie background music to the macabre scene before us. From the doorway, I was aware of Duncan's indrawn breath as he and Fraser saw what was lying on the floor.

But I was getting over the shock now, already beginning to assess what I was seeing.

'Is there any chance of getting some more light in here?' I asked.

'We've got a portable floodlight in the car,' Fraser said, tearing his eyes from the pile of bone and ashes. He was trying to sound blasé but the attempt wasn't entirely convincing. 'Go and get it, Duncan. *Duncan.*'

The young PC was still staring at what was left of the body. The blood had left his face.

'You OK?' I asked. My concern wasn't entirely for his sake. I'd worked on more than one body recovery where a green police officer had vomited on the remains. It didn't make anyone's job any easier.

He nodded. His colour was starting to come back. 'Aye. Sorry.'

He hurried out. Brody regarded the remains.

'I told Wallace it was a strange one, but I don't think he believed me. Dare say he thought I'd gone soft after a few years off the job.'

He was probably right, I thought, remembering the doubts I'd harboured myself only a few minutes before. But I couldn't blame Wallace for being sceptical. What I was looking at was freakish enough to flout all apparent logic. If I hadn't seen it for myself I might have thought the report was exaggerated.

The body – what was left of it – was lying face down. Without going any closer, I played my torch on the unburned limbs. The feet were intact from just above the ankle, and what made the sight even more disturbing was that both were still wearing trainers. I moved the torch beam higher, until it shone on the hand. It was the right one, and could have belonged to either a small man or a large woman. There were no rings, and the fingernails were unvarnished and bitten. The radius and ulna protruded from the exposed tissue of the wrist, their bone burned a dark amber close to the flesh and quickly becoming blackened and crazed with heat fractures after that. Just before where they should have joined the elbow, both had burned right through.

It was the same with the feet. The charred shafts of the tibia and fibula emerged from each as if the flames had eaten away everything up to this point, then came to an abrupt halt where the fire had burned them away halfway up the shin.

But other than that the surviving limbs showed little evidence of the fire that had destroyed the rest of the body. The main damage was caused by rodents or other small animals gnawing at the flesh and unburned bone. What soft tissue remained was starting to decompose normally, a marbling effect evident beneath the darkened skin. There was virtually no insect activity – often a vital indicator of how long decomposition has been under way. But given the cold, wintry conditions that was only what I'd expect. Flies need heat and light.

I shone the torch around the room. The remains of a fire lay in the hearth, and at some point a smaller one had been lit on the flagged floor. It was a good six feet from where the body lay, but that didn't signify anything. Unless they were unconscious, no one remained still when they caught fire.

I turned the torch beam on to the ceiling. Directly above the body the cracked plaster was smoke-blackened, but not burned. An oily, brownish deposit coated it. The same fatty residue was also on the floor around the remains.

'What's all that brown stuff?' Fraser asked.

'It's fat. From the body, as it burned.'

He grimaced. 'Bit like you get with a chip-pan fire, eh?'

'Something like that.'

Duncan had returned with the floodlight. He stared wide-eyed at the skeletal remains as he set it on the floor.

'I've read about this sort of thing,' he blurted. He immediately looked embarrassed as we all stared at him. 'Where people burst into flames for no reason, I mean. Without burning anything else around them.'

'Stop talking rubbish,' Fraser snapped.

'It's all right,' I said, turning to Duncan. 'You're talking about spontaneous combustion.'

He nodded eagerly. 'Aye, that's it!'

I'd been expecting this ever since I'd seen the remains. Spontaneous human combustion was generally thought of in the same terms as yeti and UFOs; a paranormal phenomenon for which there was no real explanation. Yet there were well-documented cases where individuals had been found incinerated in a room otherwise untouched by fire, often with hands or lower legs partially intact amongst the ashes. A whole range of theories had been put forward to explain it, from demonic possession to microwaves. But the popular consensus was that, whatever its cause, it had to be some-thing inexplicable to known science.

I didn't believe it for a moment.

Fraser was scowling at Duncan. 'What the hell do you know about it?'

Duncan gave me a sheepish glance. 'I've seen photographs. There was one woman who was burned up, just like this. All that was left was one of her legs, with the shoe still on. They call her the cinder woman.'

'Her name was Mary Reeser,' I told him. 'She was an elderly widow in Florida back in the 1950s. There was almost nothing left of her except for one leg from the shin down, and the foot still had a slipper on it. The armchair she was sitting on was destroyed, and a nearby table and lamp, but nothing else in the room was damaged. Is that the one?'

Duncan looked taken aback. 'Aye. And I've read about others.'

'They crop up now and again,' I agreed. 'But people don't just burst into flames for no reason. And whatever happened to this woman, there was nothing supernatural or paranormal about it.'

Brody had been watching us during the exchange, listening without joining in. Now he spoke up.

'How do you know it's a woman?'

Retired or not, Brody didn't miss much. 'Because of the skeleton.' I shone the torch on to what was left of the pelvis, obscured by ash but still visible. 'Even from what's left, the hipbone's obviously too wide for a man's. And the head of the humerus – that's the ball where the upper armbone fits into the shoulder – is too small. Whoever this was, she was big-boned but definitely female.'

'Like I said, I can't see it being anyone local,' he said. 'I'm sure we'd have noticed if anyone had gone missing. Any idea how long the body might have been here?'

It was a good question. While some things can be gleaned from even the most badly burned remains, an accurate time since death isn't usually one of them. For that you need to trace the extent of decomposition in muscle proteins, amino and volatile fatty acids, all of which are normally destroyed by fire. But the freakish condition of this body meant there was enough soft tissue to run tests that weren't possible for most fire deaths. That would have to wait till I was back in a lab, but in the meantime I could make an educated guess.

'The cold weather will have slowed the rate of decay,' I told him. 'But the feet and hand have started to decompose, so death can't have been too recent. Assuming the body's been here all the time and not moved from somewhere else — and given the way the flagstones underneath it are scorched I'd say that's likely — I'd guess we're looking at around four or five weeks.'

'The contractors had all finished work long before then,' Brody mused. 'Can't be anyone who came out with them.'

Fraser had been listening with mounting irritation, not liking the way the former DI was taking over. 'Aye, well, if it's nobody local I dare say we'll be able to find out who it is from the ferry's passenger list. There can't have been many visitors at this time of year.'

Brody smiled. 'Did it strike you as the sort of service that keeps records? Besides, there are a dozen or so other boats that shuttle between Runa and Stornoway. No one keeps track of who comes and goes.'

He turned to me, dismissing the police sergeant. 'So what now? I assume you'll tell Wallace to send out a SOC team?'

Fraser butted in angrily before I could answer. 'We're not doing anything until Dr Hunter's finished what he came to do. For all we know this was probably just some wino who got drunk and fell asleep too close to the campfire.'

Brody's expression was unreadable. 'So what was she doing on Runa in the middle of winter in the first place?'

Fraser shrugged. 'Could have friends or relatives here. Or could be one of those new-age types, wanting to get back to nature or whatever it is they do. You get them on islands even more remote than this.'

Brody shone his torch on to the skull. It lay face down, tilted slightly to one side amongst the ashes, the back of its once smooth crown marred by a gaping hole.

'You think she might have smashed in her own head as well?'

I intervened before tempers frayed still more. 'Actually, the skull often shatters in a hot fire like this. It's basically a sealed container of fluid and jelly, so when it's heated it acts like a pressure cooker. You get a build-up of gas that eventually makes it explode.'

Fraser blanched. 'Christ.'

'So you still think it could be accidental?' Brody asked, dubiously.

I hesitated, knowing how deceptive fire could be in its effects on the human body. Despite what I'd said, I was also aware of nagging doubts of my own. But Wallace would want facts, not hunches.

'It's possible,' I hedged. 'I know this looks bizarre, but that's not the same as suspicious. I'll need to examine it properly, but there's nothing here that immediately screams murder. Other than the skull, there's no obvious trauma. Or any signs of interference, like if the arms or legs had been tied.'

Brody rubbed his chin, frowning. 'Wouldn't the rope have burned away with everything else?'

'It wouldn't make any difference. Fire makes the muscles contract, so the limbs draw up into a sort of foetal position. It's called the pugilistic posture, because it looks like a boxer's crouch. But if the victim's hands or feet are tied it prevents that from happening, even if the rope burns away.'

I played the torch over the body, letting them see how it had curled up on itself.

'If she'd been restrained, her arms and legs would be straight, not drawn up like this. So we know she wasn't tied up.'

Brody still wasn't satisfied. 'Fair enough. But I was a police officer for thirty years. I saw my share of fire deaths, accidental and otherwise, but never anything like this. Hard to see how this could happen without an accelerant being used.'

Under normal circumstances he was right. But the circumstances here were far from normal.

'An accelerant like petrol couldn't have done this,' I told him. 'It doesn't burn hotly enough. And even if it did, to incinerate a body to anything like this extent would have taken so much that the whole cottage would have gone up. It wouldn't have been a localized fire like this.'

'So what could have caused it?'

I had an idea, but I didn't want to speculate just yet. 'That's what I'm here to find out. In the meantime, let's play safe anyway.' I turned to Fraser. 'Can you tape off a walkway from the doorway, and cordon off the body? I don't want to disturb anything more in here than we have to.'

The sergeant jerked his head at Duncan. 'Go on, go and get the incident tape. We don't have all night.'

He made a point of saying 'incident' tape rather than 'crime scene', I noticed. Brody hadn't missed it, either. His jaw muscles bunched but he said nothing as Duncan headed towards the door.

Before he reached it the room was suddenly lit up as headlights spilled through the small window. We heard the sound of a car engine being switched off.

'Looks like we've got visitors,' Brody commented.

Fraser was already motioning angrily to Duncan. 'Get out there. Don't let anyone in.'

But it was too late. As we hurried from the room a figure was already framed in the front doorway. It was the young woman I'd spoken to on the ferry, her too-big red coat a vivid shout of colour in the depressing sepia of the cottage.

'Get her out,' Fraser snarled to Duncan.

She lowered her torch, shielding her eyes as Fraser shone his in her face. 'Now that's no way to treat a member of the press, is it?'

Press? I thought, dismayed. She'd told me she was a novelist. Duncan had stopped, uncertain what to do. The young woman was already looking behind us, trying to see into the darkened room. Brody tried to close the door, but its rusted hinges seemed to have frozen. They gave an explosive creak, but refused to shut.

Maggie gave him a smile. 'You must be Andrew Brody. Heard about you from my gran. I'm Maggie Cassidy, *Lewis Gazette*.'

Brody appeared unruffled by her sudden appearance. 'What do you want, Maggie?'

'To find out what's going on, obviously. You don't get police coming out to Runa every day.' She grinned. 'Just fluke I came to see my gran when I did. Great timing, eh?'

Now I knew why she'd rushed off the ferry so quickly: she'd gone to get a car. With only one road and the police Range Rover parked outside the cottage, she wouldn't have had much difficulty finding us.

She turned to me. 'Hello again, Dr Hunter. Not got a patient out here, surely?'

'Never mind that,' Fraser said, his face livid. 'I want you out! Now! Before I throw you out on your arse.'

'That'd be assault, Sergeant Fraser. You wouldn't want me to file charges, now would you?' She rummaged in her shoulder bag, emerging with a dictaphone. 'Just a few comments, that's all I'm asking. It's not every day a body's found on Runa. That is what's in there, isn't it? A body?'

Fraser had balled his fists. 'Duncan, get her out.'

She brandished the dictaphone towards us. 'Any idea who it is? Are there any suspicious circumstances?'

Duncan reached out to take hold of her arm. 'Come on, miss . . .' he said, apologetically.

Maggie gave a resigned shrug. 'Ah, well. Can't blame a girl for trying.'

She turned as if to go, but her bag slipped from her shoulder. Duncan automatically bent to pick it up, and as he did she suddenly ducked to one side, peering round him. Her eyes widened as she saw what was in the other room.

'Oh, my God!'

'Right, out!' Fraser pushed past Duncan and grabbed her by the arm. He began herding her firmly towards the door.

'Ow! You're hurting!' She raised the dictaphone. 'I'm recording this. I'm being physically thrown out by Sergeant Neil Fraser . . .'

Fraser took no notice. 'I see you hanging round here again, you'll be under arrest. Clear?'

'This is assault!'

But Fraser had already thrust her out of the cottage. He turned on Duncan.

'Get her in her car and see she leaves. You think you can manage that?'

'Sorry, I—'

'Just do it!'

Duncan hurried out.

'Great!' Fraser fumed. 'Just what we needed, a bloody hack!'

'She seemed to know you,' Brody commented.

Fraser glared at him. 'I'll take your statement now, *Mr* Brody.' The emphasis was deliberately insulting. 'After that we'll not be needing you any more.'

Brody set his jaw, but that was the only sign of annoyance. 'What are you planning on using for a command post while you're here?'

Fraser blinked suspiciously. 'What?'

'You can't leave this place unattended. Not now. If one of you wants to come back to town with me, I've got a camper van you can use. Nothing fancy, but you'll be hard pushed to find anything else on the island.' His eyebrows went up. 'Unless you were planning on staying out here all night in the car?'

The sergeant's expression made it plain he hadn't thought that far ahead. 'I'll send Duncan with you to get it,' he said gruffly.

There was humour in Brody's eyes as he gave me a nod. 'Pleasure meeting you, Dr Hunter. Good luck.'

He and Fraser went out. When they'd gone, I stood in the silence of the small room, trying not to acknowledge the unease I felt now I was alone.

Don't be stupid. I went back into the room where the remains of the dead woman lay. As I started to plan what I had to do, I felt the hairs on the back of my neck begin to prickle. I quickly turned round, expecting to find that Duncan or Fraser had returned.

But, except for the shadows, the room was empty.

4

I sat in the front of the Range Rover as Fraser drove back to the village, drowsy in the stifling heat from the vents and the rhythmic tick of the windscreen wipers. The headlights fastened hypnotically on the road ahead, but beyond their cone of brightness the outside world was reduced to darkness and rain-streaked glass.

I'd done as much as I could for that night. After Brody took Duncan back to town to collect the camper van, I'd used Fraser's radio to brief Wallace while the sergeant taped off the cottage. The superintendent had sounded even more harried than he had that morning as I outlined what I knew so far.

'So Brody wasn't exaggerating,' Wallace said, sounding surprised. The connection buzzed, threatening to break up.

'No.' I took a deep breath. 'Look, you're not going to like this, but you might want to think about getting SOC out here.'

'You're saying you think it's murder?' he asked, sharply.

'No, just that I can't say for certain it isn't. There's no way of knowing what might be hidden under the ashes, and I don't want to risk contaminating a crime scene.'

'But you've seen nothing so far to suggest that's what it is?' he pressed. 'In fact, from what you've said, everything still points to the opposite.'

Except my instincts, and I knew better than to offer them as a reason. 'That's right, but—'

'So sending SOC would be purely a precaution at this stage.'

I could already see what was coming. 'If you want to put it like that, yes.'

He heard the annoyance in my tone and sighed. 'Under normal circumstances I'd have a team out there with you first thing to-morrow. But right now this train crash takes priority. There are still people trapped, and the weather's hampering rescue efforts. And it looks as though the van that was left on the line was stolen and left there deliberately. So as well as everything else, I've got to consider the possibility that this was a terrorist attack. At the moment I can't take SOCOs off that for something that in all likelihood's going to be an accidental death.'

'And if it isn't?'

'Then I'll get a team out to you straight away.'

There was a pause. I could understand his reasoning, but that didn't mean I was happy about it.

'All right. But if I find anything I don't like then I'm backing off until SOC arrive,' I said at last. 'And one more thing. While I'm here I'd like to try to work on getting a tentative ID. Can you send me details from the missing persons database of any young women who fit the dead woman's basic profile? Race, size, age, that sort of thing.'

Wallace said he'd have the missing persons files emailed to me, then ended the call without ceremony. As I hung up I told myself I'd done what I could. And he was probably right. Perhaps I was just being over-cautious.

There wasn't much more I could do that night. The battery-powered floodlight Fraser had brought was a poor substitute for the generator-fed lamps that would normally illuminate this sort of scene, so I'd decided to wait for daylight to carry out any sort of real assessment. Putting my doubts to one side, I took my digital camera from the flight case and began photographing the remains.

There was something oppressive about the derelict cottage, with its sagging ceilings and crumbling walls. As I worked I tried to ignore the irrational unease I felt. It had nothing to do with the pitiful mound of bones and ash in the centre of the room. The dead hold no fear for me. I've seen death in most of its forms, and I don't believe in ghosts. If the dead live on, it's only in our minds and hearts.

At least, that's where mine were.

Yet there was something unnerving about being alone out there. I put it down to tiredness and the mournful circling of the wind; the way the floodlight created dark shadows in every corner. I told myself that the biggest danger was that the remains would be compromised by the cottage's ancient roof. The whole thing looked unsafe, and with the weather getting worse I didn't want a sudden collapse to damage the fragile bones before I'd had a chance to examine them.

I'd just finished taking photographs when Duncan returned with Brody's camper van. It was actually like a small Winnebago, with separate, self-contained living quarters. Inside was relatively cramped, but as scrupulously clean as the ex-inspector's car had been.

'You'll be fine. Nice and cosy in here,' Fraser told Duncan, patting the side of the van. Somehow I wasn't surprised that it would be the young PC who would be staying here overnight. Fraser jerked his head towards the cottage. 'If she comes out to bother you, you've my permission to arrest her.'

'Aye, thanks a bunch,' Duncan said, unhappily.

Fraser gave a wheezing chuckle. Promising to bring him out some supper, he had left Duncan trying to light the van's paraffin heater and offered me a lift back into town. We'd been driving for about ten minutes when I saw something standing out like a lighthouse in the darkness. It was the imposing house I'd noticed on the way to the cottage, now lit up by spotlights.

'Must be nice to have money to burn,' Fraser commented, sourly.

'Who lives there?'

'Guy called Strachan. Locals think the sun shines out of his arse, by all accounts. Came here a few years ago and started chucking money around. Fixed up the roads and houses, paid for a new school and medical clinic. Absolutely loaded. Got his own yacht, and his wife's supposed to be a stunner.' He gave a derisive snort. 'Some people have all the luck.'

I looked at the gaily lit windows, suspended in the darkness, and wondered briefly why life and luck should favour some, and victimize others. Then we rounded a bend in the road, and the house was lost from view.

We reached the village not long afterwards. It was spread out in the darkness ahead of us as the road dropped down towards the harbour, a smattering of bright yellow embers. Soon we were close enough to make out individual houses, their curtains drawn to shut out the winter night.

Fraser turned off the main road before it reached the harbour, cutting off back up a narrow side street. Standing by itself at the top was a tall old building on which was hung a neat sign that said *Runa Hotel*. It looked snug and welcoming, but after where I'd spent the afternoon anything would be an improvement.

We pulled up outside. The rain had eased as I climbed out of the car. Shredded clouds streamed across an ink-black sky, giving glimpses of bright stars and a sickle moon that shone like a broken opal. The night was cold, but the rain-washed air carried a salty freshness. Even here it was so quiet I could hear the sound of the waves crashing on the seafront, invisible in the darkness.

I followed Fraser up the steps and through the double doors. An appealing scent of beeswax and freshly baked bread engulfed me as I found myself in a long, warmly lit hallway. The bare floorboards had been polished to the colour of cinnamon by generations of feet, and the walls and ceiling were clad in old pine panels, so that it was like walking into an old ship. An ancient grandfather clock tocked away steadily against one wall, next to a mahogany-framed mirror whose silver was mottled with age.

A young woman emerged through a swing door at the far end. She looked in her late twenties, tall and slim in jeans and a blue sweater that complemented her dark-red hair. A constellation of freckles dappled her nose and cheekbones, above which were striking sea-green eyes.

'*Feasgar math*. Good evening,' she added for my benefit. I knew Gaelic was still spoken on some Hebridean islands, but I'd only ever heard it used in toasts before. 'I presume you must be Sergeant Fraser and Dr Hunter?'

'Aye,' Fraser answered, but his attention was on the bar visible through an open doorway. An inviting murmur of voices and laughter filtered from inside.

'I'm Ellen McLeod. I wasn't sure what time you'd be here, but your rooms are ready. Have you eaten?'

Fraser reluctantly tore his eyes away from the bar. 'Not yet. Something hot would be welcome when we've dumped our bags.'

'What about Duncan?' I reminded him.

'Oh. Right,' Fraser said, without enthusiasm. 'I've got a PC out on duty going to need feeding as well. Could you sort out a plate of something I can take out to him?'

'Of course.'

Fraser was eyeing the bar again, hungrily. 'Look, you might as well see to Dr Hunter. I'll, er . . . I'll be waiting in here.'

He was already heading for the bar. The broken capillaries in his cheeks and nose hadn't lied, I thought.

'He'll be disappointed if he's wanting a drink. There's only me here,' Ellen said. She gave me a conspiratorial smile. 'I'll show you to your room.'

The stairs creaked as they took our weight, but there was a reassuring solidity to them. The dark-red carpet was worn and faded, but as scrupulously clean as the rest of the house.

A flash of something white caught my eye as I followed Ellen along the first-floor landing. It came from the unlit floor above. I looked up the next flight of stairs and saw the pale face of a little girl watching me through the railings.

I felt my heart stutter.

'Anna, I've told you it's past your bedtime,' Ellen said, sternly. 'Go back to bed.'

The little girl took this as an invitation to come down the stairs. As she emerged from the shadows in her nightgown the shock I'd felt at seeing her was already fading. I could see now that the resemblance to my own daughter was only superficial. Alice had been older, and her hair had been blonde. *Like her mother's.* This little girl was only four or five, her hair the same dark red as the young woman's.

'I can't sleep,' the little girl said, staring at me with open curiosity. 'I'm scared of the wind.'

'Funny, you've never been bothered by it before,' Ellen said, dryly. 'Go on, off to bed, young lady. I'll call in to see you after I've shown Dr Hunter his room.'

With a final look at me, the little girl did as she was told.

'Sorry about that,' Ellen said, continuing down the hallway. 'My daughter's got what I think's called a healthy curiosity.'

I managed a smile. 'Glad to hear it. And the name's David. How old is she? Five?'

'Four. She's big for her age.' There was a quiet note of pride in her voice. 'Do you have children?'

I felt my face stiffen. 'No.'

'Are you married?'

'I used to be.'

She pulled a face. 'Serves me right for asking. Divorced?'

'No. She died.'

Ellen's hand went to her mouth. 'Oh, I'm sorry . . .'

'It's all right.'

But she was looking at me now with realization. 'It wasn't just your wife, was it? That's why you looked so shocked when you saw Anna.'

'They were about the same age, that's all,' I said, as neutrally as I could. I knew she meant well, but seeing her daughter had touched on a rawness that was usually covered over. I smiled. 'Anna looks a lovely little girl.'

Ellen took the hint. 'You wouldn't say that if you saw her when she can't get her own way. She might be only young, but she can be a madam when the mood takes her.'

'And you've still got the teenage years to look forward to.'

She laughed, a good clear sound that made her look not much more than a girl herself. 'I don't even want to think about that.'

I wondered where the little girl's father was. Ellen didn't wear a wedding ring, and from the way she'd spoken earlier it sounded as if she was alone here with her daughter. Not that it was any of my business.

She opened a door at the far end of the hall. 'Here we are. Not very grand, I'm afraid.'

'It's fine,' I told her. And it was. The room was spartan, but clean and comfortable. A single brass bedstead was flanked by an old pine dresser on one side and a wardrobe on the other, its tartan counter-pane neatly turned down to reveal crisp white sheets.

'The bathroom is at the end of the hall. Shared, but only between yourself and Sergeant Fraser. We don't get many guests at this time of year.' There was resignation in the way she said it. 'Well, I'll leave you to sort yourself out. Just come down to the bar when you're ready for supper.'

There was a telephone on the dresser, so at least I'd be able to call Jenny. 'Is there anywhere I can log on to the Internet? I'd like to check my emails.'

'If you've got a laptop you can use the phone line in here. We're not wireless yet, but there's a broadband connection.'

'You've got broadband?' I asked, surprised.

'Did you think we'd still be using smoke signals?'

'No, I just . . .'

She smiled at my discomfort. 'It's all right, I don't blame you. We can still lose power and phones if the weather's bad, so we're not that sophisticated yet. But it works fine most of the time.'

When she'd gone I sat down heavily on the bed. Its springs made a metallic rustling as they took my weight. *God.* I was more tired than I'd thought. The incident on the stairs had struck through the defences I'd painstakingly built up after Kara and Alice had died. It had taken a long time to reach a state of truce with the cold fact that I was still alive, while my wife and daughter weren't. Jenny had played a large part in that, and I was deeply thankful to have been given a second chance.

But every now and then the loss would still hit home with a force that took my breath away.

I rubbed my eyes, fatigue catching up with me. It had been a long day. *And you've not finished yet.*

I took my laptop from my bag and put it on the dresser. I picked up the phone to call Jenny as I waited for it to boot up. She should be back from work by now, at her flat in Clapham where we were unofficially living together. Unofficially because I still had my own flat in east London, although I hardly ever stayed there. When we'd left Norfolk eighteen months ago, while Jenny was still recovering from an abduction that had nearly killed her, we'd both felt it would be good for us to keep some degree of independence. For the most part it had worked out.

It was only recently that the first fault lines had begun to appear in our relationship.

I knew I was largely to blame. When Jenny and I had met I'd been a GP. Technically, I still was, but the work I did now was very different. Not only did it often take me away from home, it was a painful reminder of a time – and an experience – she would rather forget.

It was a conflict I had no idea how to resolve. My work was as much a part of me as breathing, but I couldn't imagine losing Jenny. Yet I was beginning to think that before much longer I'd have to choose between them.

The phone rang for a while before she answered. 'Hi, it's me,' I said.

'Hi.' There was a strained pause. 'So. How are the Outer Hebrides?'

'Cold and wet. How was your day?'

'Fine.'

Jenny was a teacher. Positions were hard to come by in London, but she'd found a part-time post at a nursery school which she enjoyed. She was good at her job, and good with children. I knew she wanted some of her own some day. That was something else I wasn't sure about.

I couldn't bear the stilted awkwardness between us. 'Listen, I'm sorry about earlier.'

'It doesn't matter.'

'No, it does. I just wanted to explain—'

'Don't. Please,' she added, less forcefully. 'There's no point. You're there now. I was just disappointed you wouldn't be coming back today.'

'It'll only be another day or two,' I said, aware it was a feeble olive branch.

'OK.'

The silence stretched on. 'I'd better go,' I said after a while. 'I'll call you tomorrow night.'

I heard her sigh. 'David . . .'

My stomach knotted. 'What?'

There was a pause.

'Nothing. I'm just looking forward to seeing you, that's all.'

I told her the same and reluctantly broke the connection. After I'd hung up I stayed on the bed, wondering what it was she'd been about to say. Whatever it was, I was far from sure I wanted to hear it.

Sighing, I connected my camera to the laptop and downloaded the photographs from the cottage. There were over a hundred shots of the remains, capturing them from every angle. I quickly browsed through them, making sure there was nothing I'd overlooked. Bleached by the flash, the sight of the surviving hand and feet had lost none of its ability to shock. I spent longer studying the images of the broken skull. It looked like countless others I'd seen in the aftermath of fire. An almost textbook-perfect case of a cranial blow-out.

So why did I feel I was missing something?

I stared at the screen so long my eyes began to hurt, without finding anything that rang any alarm bells. Finally, I accepted I wasn't going to. *Wallace is probably right. You're just being over-cautious.*

I backed up the files on to a USB memory stick, then connected the laptop to the hotel's Internet server so I could check my emails. The missing persons files I'd asked Wallace to send hadn't arrived, so I replied to the messages that were most urgent, then lay on the bed and closed my eyes. I could easily have fallen asleep if my stomach hadn't rumbled noisily to remind me that, tired or not, I needed to eat.

I pushed myself off the bed and headed for the door. As I passed the window, I idly glanced out. My own reflection stared back at me from the dark, rain-flecked glass, but for a second I thought I'd glimpsed something – someone – outside.

I went over and looked out. A lonely street lamp stood in the street below, a bright yellow smudge in the darkness. But except for that the night was empty.

Trick of the light, I told myself. Switching off the bedroom light, I went downstairs.

5

The bar was little more than a snug into which a few tables had been squeezed. Like the hallway, it was clad in pine panels, so that the overall impression was of being inside a giant wooden box. Set against one wall was a fireplace made entirely of seashells. A peat block burned in its hearth, filling the air with a rich, spicy scent.

There were fewer than a dozen customers, but it was enough to make the place feel busy without being overcrowded. The voices were a curious blend of lilting Scots and the harsher consonants of Gaelic. I received a few curious looks as I went in. Word had obviously spread about what had been found at the old crofter's cottage, no doubt thanks to Maggie Cassidy. But after the initial glances everyone went back to what they were doing. Two old men were playing dominoes by the window, the clack of the black rectangles a staccato counterpoint to the chink of glasses. Kinross, the bearded ferry captain, was talking at the bar to a huge man with a ponderous gut. A blowsy woman in her forties was with them, her raucous laugh and smoker's voice carrying above the barroom hubbub.

All the tables were occupied. There was no sign of Fraser, so I guessed he had gone to take Duncan's supper out to the camper van.

I hesitated, feeling the usual stranger's exclusion at walking into a closed gathering.

'Dr Hunter.' Brody was sitting at a table by the fire, hand raised to attract my attention. The old border collie was curled asleep on the floor at his feet. 'Won't you join me?'

'Thanks.' I was glad to see a familiar face. I went over, easing my way past the domino players.

'Can I get you a drink?' He had a mug of tea on the table in front of him. I still hadn't eaten, but a drink would be welcome.

'A whisky, thanks.'

He went to the bar as I took the chair opposite him. Kinross gave him a nod as he made room. Cautiously respectful rather than friendly. There was no one serving, so Brody simply poured a measure of whisky into a glass, then chalked it up on a slate hanging by the bar.

'Here you go. Fifteen-year-old Islay malt,' he said, setting the glass in front of me with a small jug of water.

I looked at his tea. 'You don't drink yourself?'

'Not any more.' He raised his mug. 'Slàinte.'

I added a little water to the malt. 'Cheers.'

'So did you get much done after I'd left?' he asked, then smiled ruefully. 'Sorry, shouldn't ask. Old habits and all that.'

'Not much to tell yet, anyway.'

He nodded and changed the subject. 'How are they settling into the camper?'

'All right, I think. At least, Duncan is.'

Brody smiled. 'Drew the short straw, did he? Ah well, he'll stay in worse places before he's finished. That van stood me in good stead when I first retired. Not seen much use since I came out here, though.'

'Duncan was saying you used to work with his father.'

His smile grew reflective. 'Aye. Small world, eh? We served in the Territorial Army together when we were both green PCs. Last time

50

I saw Sandy his lad was still at school.' He shook his head. 'Where's the time go, eh? One minute you're chasing crooks and thinking about promotion, the next . . .'

He broke off, brightening as Ellen came over. 'Can I get you something to eat, Dr Hunter?' she asked.

'That sounds good. And it's David.'

'David,' she corrected herself, smiling. 'I hope Andrew here's not bothering you. You know what these ex-policemen are like.'

Brody wagged a finger, mock-stern. 'Careful, that's slander.'

'Would a slice of home-made apple pie make amends?'

He patted his stomach, regretfully. 'Tempting, but I'd better not.'

'The sky won't fall if you treat yourself for once.'

'You can never be too careful.'

Ellen laughed. 'Aye, I'll remember that next time you sneak sweets to Anna.'

The big man who was with Kinross suddenly raised his voice. 'Another couple of drams here, Ellen.'

'In a minute, Sean.'

'Shall we help ourselves, then? We're dying of thirst.'

It was the woman at the bar who'd spoken. She was drunk, a condition I guessed from the look of her wasn't unusual. A few years ago she might have been attractive, but now her features were puffy and etched with bitterness.

'The last time you helped yourself, Karen, you forgot to chalk it up,' Ellen retorted. There was steel in her voice. 'I'm having a conversation. I'm sure you can survive for a few more minutes.'

She turned back to us, and so missed the anger that clouded the woman's face. 'Sorry about that. A few drinks and some people forget their manners. Now, I was asking you what you wanted to eat. There's mutton stew, or I can make you a sandwich if you'd rather.'

'Mutton stew sounds good. But I don't mind if you serve them first.'

'They can wait. It'll do them good.'

'Ellen . . .' Brody said, quietly.

She sighed, then gave him a tired smile. 'Aye, all right. I know.'

He watched her go to the bar to serve them. 'Ellen can be a little . . . fiery,' he said, but with affection. 'Causes friction sometimes, but the hotel's the only watering hole on Runa, so everyone either abides by her rules or stays home. She's a good cook, too. Did a college course on the mainland. I eat here most nights.'

Even if Fraser hadn't mentioned on the ferry that Brody was estranged from his wife and daughter, I would have guessed that he lived on his own. There was something intrinsically solitary about him.

'Does she run this place by herself?'

'Aye. Not easy, but between the bar takings and the occasional guest, she manages.'

'What happened to her husband?'

His face closed down. 'There wasn't one. Anna's father was someone she met on the mainland. She doesn't talk about it.'

The way he said it made it clear that he wasn't going to either. He cleared his throat and nodded towards the group at the bar.

'Anyway, let me tell you about some of Runa's local colour. Kinross you'll have met on the boat. Surly bugger, but he's had it rough. Wife died a couple of years ago, so now there's just him and his teenage lad. The loudmouth with the beer belly is Sean Guthrie. Used to be a fisherman but lost his boat to the bank. He's got an old one he's trying to patch up, but he scrapes a living now doing odd jobs, and helping Kinross run the ferry sometimes. Harmless enough mostly, but keep clear of him when he's had too many.'

He was interrupted by a raucous laugh from the woman.

'That's Karen Tait. Runs the general store, when she's sober and can be bothered. Got a sixteen-year-old daughter, Mary, who . . . well, she isn't what she should be. You'd think Karen would be at home with her, but she'd rather prop up the bar in here every night.'

His expression made it clear what he thought of that.

A blast of cold air swept into the bar as the outside door was opened. A moment later a golden retriever burst into the bar in a scrabble of claws.

'Oscar! *Oscar!*'

A man came in after it. I'd have put him a year or two either side of forty, with the chiselled good looks of a latter-day Byron. His weatherproof coat was black and obviously expensive. Like its wearer, it looked out of place amongst the scuffed coats and oilskins favoured by the other islanders.

His entrance had silenced everyone in the room. Even the domino players had halted their game. The man casually snapped his fingers at the dog. It trotted back to him, wagging its tail.

'Sorry about that, Ellen,' he said with an easy confidence, the clipped vowels of South Africa evident in his voice. 'He shot straight in as soon as I opened the door.'

Ellen looked unimpressed with both the newcomer and his apology. 'You should keep hold of him, then. This is a hotel, not a kennel.'

'I know. It won't happen again.'

He looked contrite, but as she turned away and walked out I saw him flash a quick smile and wink at the drinkers at the bar. There were grins in reply. Whoever the newcomer was, he was popular.

'Evening, everyone. It's a raw one out there tonight,' he said, shrugging out of his coat.

There was a chorus of '*Feasgar math*' and 'aye's. I had the impression he could have said it was a beautiful evening and they would just as readily have agreed with him. But the newcomer either didn't notice their deference, or accepted it as his due.

'Will you take a drink, Mr Strachan?' Kinross asked, with an awkward formality.

'No, thank you, Iain. But I'll gladly buy a round myself. Help yourselves, and mark it up on my tab.' He gave the woman at the bar a smile that made his eyes crinkle. 'Hello, Karen. I've not seen you for a while. Are you and Mary keeping well?'

She was more susceptible to his charm than Ellen had been. Her blush was visible even from where I sat.

'Yes, thank you,' she said, pleased to be singled out.

Only now did the newcomer turn towards where Brody and I were sitting. 'Evening, Andrew.'

Brody gave a stiff nod in return. His expression was hard as granite. He shifted his legs to put them between his border collie bitch and the golden retriever, which was sniffing around her.

The newcomer swatted the retriever with his gloves. 'Leave her alone, Oscar, you hound.'

The dog came away, wagging its tail. Its owner gave me a grin. For all his self-assurance, there was something engaging about him.

'And you must be one of the visitors I've been hearing about. I'm Michael Strachan.'

I'd already guessed this must be who Fraser had told me about on the way back from the cottage: Runa's unofficial laird, and the owner of the big house. He was younger than I'd expected, somehow.

'David Hunter,' I said, shaking the offered hand. He had a dry, strong grip.

'Can I buy you both a drink as well?' he offered.

'Not for me, thanks,' I said.

Brody rose to his feet, his expression stony. He towered nearly a half-head over Strachan.

'I was just leaving. Nice seeing you again, Dr Hunter. Come on, Bess.'

The dog obediently trotted out after him. Strachan watched him go, mouth curved in a faint smile, before turning back to me. 'Mind if I join you?'

He was already sliding into Brody's seat, casually tossing his gloves on to the table. In his black jeans and charcoal-grey sweater, sleeves pushed back to reveal tanned forearms and a Swiss Army watch, he looked as though he'd be more at home in Soho than the Outer Hebrides.

The golden retriever flopped down beside him, as near to the crackling fire as it could get. Strachan reached down and scratched its ears, looking every bit as relaxed himself.

'Are you a friend of Andrew Brody's?' he asked.

'We only met today.'

He grinned. 'I'm afraid he doesn't approve of me, as you probably noticed. I'm sure he was a good policeman, but God, the man's dour!'

I didn't say anything. I'd been quite impressed by Brody so far. Strachan slouched easily in his chair, casually resting one foot on his knee.

'I gather you're a . . . what is it? A forensic anthropologist?' He smiled at my surprise. 'You'll find it's hard to keep anything a secret on Runa. Especially when we've got a reporter whose grandmother lives on the island.'

I thought back to how Maggie Cassidy had come over to talk to me on the ferry. Stumbling against me, pretending to be a novelist as she'd pumped me for information.

And I'd fallen for it.

'Don't feel too bad,' Strachan said, interpreting my expression. 'It isn't often we get this sort of excitement. Not that we want it, obviously. The last time a body was found here was when an old crofter tried to walk home in the dark after a few malts too many. Got lost and died of exposure. But this doesn't sound anything like that.'

He paused, giving me a chance to comment. When I didn't he went on anyway.

'What was it, some kind of accident?'

'Sorry, I can't really say.'

Strachan gave an apologetic smile. 'No, of course. You'll have to excuse my curiosity. It's just that I've got what you might call a vested interest in this place. I'm responsible for a lot of redevelopment here. It's brought more people to the island than we're used to – contractors and so on. I'd hate to think I'd imported big-town troubles as well.'

He seemed genuinely concerned, but I wasn't going to let myself be drawn. 'You don't sound like a local,' I said.

He grinned. 'The accent's a bit of a giveaway, eh? My family's Scottish originally, but I grew up near Johannesburg. My wife and I moved to Runa about five years ago.'

'It's a long way from South Africa.'

Strachan tousled his dog's ears. 'I suppose it is. But we'd been travelling round a lot, so it was time to put down roots. I liked the remoteness of this place. Reminded me in some ways of where I grew up. Place was pretty depressed back then, of course. No local economy to speak of, population in decline. Another few years and it could have been another St Kilda.'

I'd heard of St Kilda, another Hebridean island that had been abandoned in the 1930s, and lain unoccupied ever since. Now it was a ghost-island, tenanted only by seabirds and researchers.

'You seem to have helped turn it round,' I said.

He looked embarrassed. 'We've still got some way to go. And I don't want to make out it's all down to me. But Runa's our home now. Grace, my wife, helps out at the school, and we do what we can in other ways as well. That's why I worry when I hear about something like this happening. Hello, what's up, Oscar?'

The golden retriever was looking expectantly at the doorway. I hadn't heard anyone come into the hotel, but a moment later there was the sound of the front door opening. The dog gave an excited whine, its tail thumping against the floor.

'I don't know how he does that, but he always knows,' Strachan said, shaking his head.

Knows what? I wondered, and then a woman came into the bar. I didn't need to be told to know that she was Strachan's wife.

It wasn't just that she was beautiful, although she was certainly that. Her white Prada parka was flecked with rain, setting off thick, shoulder-length hair that was raven black. It framed a face whose skin was flawless, with a full mouth it was hard to take your eyes from.

But it was more than that. There was an energy to her, a sheer physical presence that seemed to draw all the light in the room. I remembered Fraser's envious comment earlier: *His wife's supposed to be a stunner.*

He was right.

She'd had a tentative smile as she came into the bar, but when she saw Strachan it bloomed into something dazzling.

'Caught you! So this is where you end up when you go out on "business", is it?'

She had the same faint South African accent as her husband. Strachan rose to give her a kiss.

'Guilty. How did you know I was here?'

'I came to get some things from the store, but it was shut,' she said, taking off her gloves. They were fur-lined black leather, unobtrusively expensive. On her left hand she wore a plain gold wedding band, and a diamond ring whose single stone danced with blue light. 'Next time you want to sneak a drink, don't leave your car outside.'

'Blame Oscar. He dragged me here.'

'Oscar, you bully, how could you?' She fussed the dog, which had started to prance excitedly around her. 'All right, calm down.'

She looked across at me, waiting for an introduction. Her brown eyes were so dark they were almost black.

'This is David Hunter,' Strachan said. 'David, this is my wife, Grace.'

She smiled and held out her hand. 'Pleased to meet you, David.'

As I took it I could smell her perfume, subtle and delicately spiced.

'David's a forensic expert. He's come out with the police,' Strachan explained.

'God, what an awful business,' she said, growing serious. 'I just hope it's no one from here. I know that sounds selfish, but . . . well, you know what I mean.'

I did. When it comes to ill fortune we're all selfish at heart, offering up the same prayers: *not me, not mine. Not yet.*

Strachan had got to his feet. 'Well, nice meeting you, Dr Hunter. Perhaps I'll see you again before you leave.'

Grace arched an ironic eyebrow. 'Don't I even get a drink now I'm here?'

'I'll buy you a drink, Mrs Strachan.'

The offer came from Guthrie, the man with the ponderous gut. I had the impression he'd beaten Kinross and several others to the punch. Beside them, all but forgotten, Karen Tait's blowsy face was pinched with jealousy.

Grace Strachan gave the big man a warm smile. 'Thank you, Sean, but I can see Michael's raring to go.'

'Sorry, darling, I thought you wanted to get back,' Strachan apologized. 'I was planning to cook mussels for dinner. But if you're not hungry . . .'

'Sounds like blackmail to me.' The smile she gave him had become intimate.

He turned to me. 'If you get a chance before you leave, you should take a look at the burial cairns on the mountain. There's a group of them, which is unusual. Neolithic. They're quite something.'

'Not everyone's as morbid as you, darling.' Grace shook her head in mock-exasperation. 'Michael's fond of archaeology. I think he'd rather have old ruins than me, sometimes.'

'It's just an interest,' Strachan said, growing self-conscious. 'Come on, Oscar, you lazy brute. Time to go.'

He raised his hand in response to the respectful goodnights that accompanied them to the door. As they went out they almost bumped into Ellen coming the other way. She checked, almost spilling the steaming plate of stew she was carrying.

'Sorry, our fault,' Strachan said, his arm still round Grace's waist.

'Not at all.' Ellen gave them both a polite smile. I thought I saw a flicker of something else on her face as she looked at the other woman, but it was gone before I could be sure. 'Evening, Mrs Strachan.'

It seemed to me there was a reserve there, but Grace didn't appear to notice. 'Hello, Ellen. Did you like the painting Anna did at school the other day?'

'It's on the fridge door, with the rest of the gallery.'

'She's got real promise. You should be proud of her.'

'I am.'

Strachan moved towards the door. He seemed impatient to leave. 'Well, we'll let you get on. Night.'

Ellen's face was so devoid of emotion it might have been a mask as she set the plate in front of me. She acknowledged my thanks with a perfunctory smile, already turning away. As she went out I reflected that Brody wasn't the only person on Runa who didn't seem overly impressed by the island's golden couple.

'Bitch!'

The word seemed to ring in the quiet of the bar. Karen Tait's mouth was pressed tight with bitterness as she glared at the door, but it wasn't clear which of the two women who'd just left the insult was aimed at.

Kinross levelled a warning finger at her, eyes angry above the dark beard. 'That's enough, Karen.'

'Well, she is. Stuck up—'

'*Karen.*'

She subsided resentfully. Gradually, the ordinary sounds of the bar began to fill the silence. The clicking of the domino players' pieces resumed, and the tension that seemed to have momentarily been present was dissipated.

I took a forkful of the mutton stew. Ellen was as good a cook as Brody had said. But as I ate, I suddenly felt someone's eyes on me. I looked up, and saw Kinross staring at me from across the bar. He held my gaze for a moment, his expression coldly watchful, before he slowly turned away.

When I woke the hotel room was dark. The only light came from the window, where the street light outside lit the drawn curtains with a diffuse glow. There was an unnatural hush. The wind and rain seemed to have stopped, leaving not a whisper in their wake. The only sound was my own breathing, a steady rise and fall that could almost have been coming from someone else.

I don't know when I realized I wasn't alone. It was more a dawning awareness of another presence than a sudden shock. In the dim light from the window, I looked at the foot of my bed and saw someone sitting there.

Although all I could make out was a dark shape, somehow I knew it was a woman. She was looking at me, but for some reason I felt neither surprise nor fear. Only the weight of her mute expectation.

Kara?

But the hope had been nothing more than a waking reflex. Whoever this was, it wasn't my dead wife.

Who are you? I said, or thought I said. The words didn't seem to disturb the cold air of the room.

The figure didn't answer. Just continued its patient vigil, as though all the answers I would ever need were already laid out for me. I stared, trying to fathom either its features or its intent. But I could make out neither.

I jumped as a gust of wind shook the window. Startled, I looked round, then turned back, expecting the shadowy figure to be still at the foot of the bed. But even in the darkness I could see the room was empty. And always had been, I realized. I'd been dreaming. A disturbingly realistic one, but a dream none the less.

For a long time after my wife and daughter had been killed, I'd been no stranger to those.

Another gust shook the window in its frame, driving rain against the glass like handfuls of gravel. I heard what sounded like a cry from outside. It could have been an owl or some other night bird. Or something else. Wide awake now, I got out of bed and went to the window. The street lamp below was visibly shaking in the wind. I caught a flash of something pale flitting on the edge of its yellow corona, then it was gone.

Just something blown on the wind, I told myself, when it didn't reappear. But I continued to stare into the dark outside the window until the cold air sent me shivering back to bed.

6

While I was wondering what I'd seen outside my bedroom window, out at the cottage Duncan wasn't happy. The wind had picked up, buffeting the camper van like a boat in a high sea. He'd already taken the precaution of putting the paraffin heater in a corner to stop it from tipping over. Its blue flame hissed only a few feet from where he sat wedged behind the camper's small table. Still, even though the cabin was cramped, it was better than spending the night either in the Range Rover or huddled in the cottage doorway. Which was where Fraser would probably have put him, he reflected. No, it wasn't having to stay in the van that bothered him.

He just couldn't stop thinking about what lay in the cottage.

It was all well and good Fraser laughing, but he wasn't the one having to stay here. And Duncan had noticed the sergeant hadn't offered to linger after he'd brought out his supper. No doubt in a hurry to get back to the bar, because judging by his breath he'd already made a start on the whisky. Duncan had watched the Range Rover's lights disappear with a feeling he'd not had since he was a kid.

Not that he was afraid of being out here. Not as such, anyway. He lived on an island, and once you were out of Stornoway town there were plenty of places on Lewis where there was no sign of a living soul. He'd just never had to stay out in the middle of nowhere by himself before.

Not with an incinerated corpse lying no more than twenty yards away.

Duncan couldn't get the image of those unburned limbs and baked bones out of his mind. However it had happened, they'd once been a *person*. A woman, according to Dr Hunter. That was what was so shocking about it, that someone who'd once laughed and cried and all the rest could end up reduced to that. The thought was enough to give him the creeps.

Too much imagination, that's your trouble. Always had been. He wasn't sure if it would make him a better or worse police officer. It wasn't enough for him to note down the facts, he always had to get lost in 'what if's. Couldn't help it, it was just the way his mind worked. Like what if the woman *had* been burned by something science didn't know about yet? What if she *had* been murdered?

What if the killer was still here on the island?

Aye, and what if you stopped trying to scare yourself? Duncan sighed and picked up the criminology textbook he'd brought out with him. Fraser could laugh at that as well, but he intended to make detective some day. And if he was going to do something, he wanted to do it as well as he was able. Learn as much about it as possible, and if that meant making a few sacrifices, then so be it. Unlike some people he could mention, Duncan didn't mind hard work.

Tonight, though, he found it hard to concentrate. After a while he pushed the textbook away, restlessly. *Stick the kettle on. At least you can make a cuppa.* Duncan thought he would be sick of tea by the time he'd finished here.

As he got up to fill the kettle at the tiny sink, there was a sudden quietening as the wind dropped, gathering itself for its next assault. In the brief lull Duncan heard another sound from outside. It was drowned out a second later as the gale struck the van again with renewed force, but he was sure he hadn't imagined it.

The sound of a car engine.

He looked out of the window, waiting for the dazzle of headlights that would announce the Range Rover's arrival. But the darkness outside remained unbroken.

Duncan thought for a moment. Even if the sound had come from a car passing on the road, its lights would have been visible. Which meant he'd either imagined hearing an engine . . .

Or someone had turned off their headlights to conceal their approach.

Bit of fresh air will do me good, anyway. He pulled on his coat, then picked up his heavy Maglite and climbed out of the camper van. He nearly switched on the torch, but at the last second decided against it. If there was anyone creeping around here, that would only warn them he was coming. He made his way slowly towards the cottage, depending on the fleeting breaks in the cloud cover to see where he was going. The Maglite's weight was comforting as the black outline of the cottage loomed in front of him. At a foot long, the torch could also double as a substantial club. Not that he'd need it, he told himself, and as he did so there was a flash of light from behind the cottage.

Duncan froze, heart thumping. He reached for his radio to call Fraser, then stopped. There was too much chance that the trespasser would hear him. He started forward again. He could see that the tape sealing the door hadn't been tampered with. Staying close to the wall, he made his way to the corner of the cottage.

He paused, listening. There was a scrape of something brushing against stone, then a swish of movement through the long grass. No two ways about it.

Someone was definitely there.

Duncan gripped the Maglite, tensing himself. *Stay calm.* He took a deep breath, then another. *OK, get ready . . .*

Flinging himself round the corner, he turned the torch full on.

'Police! Stay where you are!'

There was a startled curse, then a figure was sprinting away. Duncan set off after it, the wet grass threatening to snag his legs. He hadn't gone far when the figure suddenly tripped and fell headlong. Seizing it by the shoulder, he pulled it over and shone the torch beam on its face.

Maggie Cassidy glared up at him, squinting against the bright light.

'Get off me! *O mo chreach*, I think I've broken my leg!'

Duncan felt a mix of relief and anticlimax. And guilt. As he helped the reporter to her feet, he realized she barely reached his shoulder.

'You frightened me to death, yelling like that!' she grumbled. 'You'd just better hope my leg's not broken, or I'm suing.'

'What are you doing here?' Duncan asked, trying not to sound defensive.

There was only a second's pause. 'I thought I'd come and see how you were getting on.' Maggie gave him a smile. 'Can't be much fun being stuck out here in this.'

'So why were you looking through the cottage window?'

'There wasn't a light on in the camper van. I thought you might be in there.'

'Aye, course you did.' He noticed her trying to slip something into her pocket. 'What have you got there?'

'Nothing.'

But he was shining his torch on to it, revealing a mobile phone clasped in her hand.

'You'll not have much luck calling anyone from here,' he said. 'You weren't planning on taking any pictures with that, now were you?'

'No, of course not . . .'

He held out his hand.

'Look, I wasn't able to get anything, all right?' she protested.

'Then you won't mind showing me, will you?'

Maggie's shoulders slumped. She let him see the screen.

'They were rubbish anyway,' she muttered, bringing up two blurred and bleached-out images.

As he would explain later, Duncan didn't think they would be any use. Even he couldn't make out what they were. But he made her delete them anyway.

'And the rest.'

'That's it, I told you.'

He just looked at her. With an irritated sigh she showed him the other pictures in the memory.

'Must have forgotten about that one, hey?' he said, cheerfully, as another blurred shot of the cottage appeared.

'Happy now?' she demanded, deleting it. 'So now what are you going to do? Arrest me?'

Duncan had been asking himself the same question. Offhand, he wasn't even sure she'd broken any law. She hadn't actually crossed the incident tape.

Besides, he had to admit there was something he liked about her.

'Will you give me your word you won't try this again?' he asked, in what he hoped was an authoritative voice.

'I won't, honest. Ouch.' She winced as she put her weight on her leg.

'You all right?' Duncan asked.

'I can walk, no thanks to you. So can I go now?'

He hesitated. 'Where's your car?'

She gestured back down the track. 'I left it back near the road.'

'You sure you can manage?'

'Like you care,' she retorted. 'I can manage.'

Grinning to himself, Duncan watched her small figure hobbling off down the track, torch beam bobbing in front of her. When he was satisfied she'd gone, he started back to the camper van. As he went inside, he noticed a patch of mud in the doorway. He hadn't noticed it before. *Bloody Fraser. Too much to ask for him to wipe his feet.*

Thinking about Maggie Cassidy, he went to put the kettle on.

Maggie's car was parked about fifty yards along the track. Her limp had vanished as soon as Duncan was out of sight, but she was still scowling when she reached the old Mini. It was her grandmother's: a tub of junk, but better than nothing.

She flopped down into the driver's seat and examined her mobile phone. Even though she'd deleted the pictures herself, she still couldn't help making sure they were really gone. They were.

'Bollocks,' she said out loud.

Throwing the phone into her handbag in disgust, she took out her dictaphone and starting recording.

'Well, a right waste of time that was,' she said into it. 'And I still didn't manage to get a proper look at the body. Last time I try to play at commandos.'

The scowl faded, replaced by a reluctant smile.

'Still, gave me quite a rush, I have to admit. I've not been that scared since I wet myself playing hide-and-seek at junior school. God, when that young PC jumped out at me! What was his name? Duncan, I think they called him. Keen bugger, but at least he seemed human. Cute, too, come to think of it. Wonder if he's single?'

She was still smiling as she saved the recording and started the car. Its headlights split the darkness as she pulled away in a belch of exhaust. The unhealthy rattle of its engine quickly receded once she reached the road, and, after a final crunch of gears, the night settled back into silence.

For a heartbeat nothing stirred. Then a shadow detached itself from the ground next to where the Mini had stood and slowly headed off into the dark.

7

A grudging daylight was only just seeping into the sky as I showered and shaved next morning. There had been no let-up in the rain overnight, and I hoped the remains were still all right. I knew they'd lain there for several weeks already, and there was no reason to suppose the cottage's crumbling roof wouldn't survive a few more days, even in this weather. Even so, I'd be relieved when they could be moved somewhere safer.

I hadn't slept well after waking from the dream. I felt grainy and tired as I accessed my emails to see if the missing persons files from Wallace had finally arrived. They had, five of them in all. There was no time to look at them now, so after transferring them on to my laptop's hard drive I went down for breakfast.

The bar doubled as the dining room, and I'd nearly finished eating by the time Fraser trudged in. He looked red-eyed and hungover, the smell of unmetabolized alcohol noticeable even across the table. After he'd returned from the cottage the evening before, he'd settled himself in the bar with the air of a man getting down to business. I'd left him there when I'd gone to bed, and judging from his appearance he'd obviously made a night of it.

I tried not to smile as he gingerly sipped his tea. 'I've some aspirin in my bag,' I offered.

'I'm fine,' he growled.

He queasily regarded the plate of fried eggs, bacon and sausage that Ellen set down in front of him. Then, taking up his knife and fork, he set about eating it with the determination of a marathon runner.

'How long will you be?' I asked. I was keen to make a start, conscious of how short the days were up here at this time of year.

'Not long,' he muttered, hand shaking as he forked up a spoonful of dripping egg.

Ellen was clearing my breakfast plate from the table. 'If you want, you can take my car. I won't be using it today.'

'Good idea,' Fraser agreed quickly, through a full mouth. 'There's things I need to do in the village anyway. Start asking round, see if anyone knows who the dead woman is.'

It hadn't been made public yet that the body was a woman's. I glanced at Ellen, and saw the slip hadn't gone unnoticed. She gave me a knowing look as he carried on eating, oblivious.

'If you're ready I'll get you the car keys.'

I followed her from the bar. 'Look, about what Sergeant Fraser said . . .' I began.

'Don't worry, I won't say anything,' she smiled as she went into the kitchen. 'You run a hotel, you learn to keep secrets.'

The kitchen was a single-storey extension, much newer than the rest of the hotel. Heavy saucepans stood on an old gas cooker, blackened with use, while a tall pine dresser was laden with mismatched crockery. A small portable gas fire hissed next to a big wooden table, on which sat a child's colouring book and set of crayons. Ellen rooted in a drawer for the car keys, then led me out through a door into a small yard. Propane gas cylinders stood against the wall in a wire safety cage, looking like upright orange bombs. Parked in the lane just beyond them was an old VW Beetle.

'It's not much to look at, but it's reliable enough,' she said, giving me the keys. 'And I've made a flask of tea and sandwiches for you all. I'd guess you won't want to be running back here to eat.'

I thanked her as I took them. The VW grated and whined when I started it, but it rattled along happily enough. The weather hadn't improved since the day before: grey skies, wind and rain. But at least the village was more alive this morning. There were people in the street, and children were filing through the gate towards the small but new-looking school. I looked for Anna but couldn't make her out amongst the parkas and duffel coats. A man wearing a peaked woollen hat, emaciated-looking even in a thick coat, was ushering them inside. He paused to stare at me as I drove past. When I nodded to him he looked away without acknowledgement.

Then I was leaving the village, passing the hill where Bodach Runa, the ancient standing stone Brody had pointed out, stood watch. The island could never be described as picturesque, but it was starkly impressive: a landscape of hills and dark peat moors, dotted with sheep. The only sign of habitation was the big house I now knew belonged to the Strachans. Lights no longer burned in every window, but it was still by far the most imposing building I'd seen on the island. Its turreted granite walls and mullioned windows had been weathered by the Atlantic winds, but there remained an air of permanence about them.

Brody's Volvo was already parked outside the cottage when I arrived. The ex-inspector and Duncan were in the camper van, a kettle hissing away on the small cooking ring. The cramped cabin smelled of stale bodies and paraffin fumes.

'Morning,' Brody said when I went in. He was sitting on a tattered padded bench that butted up to a fold-down table, his old dog asleep at his feet. Somehow, I wasn't surprised to find him here. He might have retired, but he hadn't struck me as the type who would simply be able to let go after calling this in. 'Sergeant Fraser not with you?'

'He had things to do in the village.'

I saw disapproval register on his face, but he made no comment. 'Don't mind my coming out again, do you?' he asked, as though reading my mind. 'I spoke to Wallace this morning. He said it was your call.'

'In that case it's fine by me.'

Now that Wallace knew that Brody hadn't been exaggerating when he'd reported the body, I guessed he was probably glad the former DI was prepared to stick around. If it came to that, so was I. It might have ruffled Fraser's feathers, but it didn't hurt to have someone with Brody's experience on hand.

Duncan yawned. He looked as though he hadn't slept well, and began unwrapping the bacon and egg sandwich that Ellen had sent with the enthusiasm of a child at Christmas.

'Apparently we had a visitor last night,' Brody told me, giving him a meaningful look.

Through mouthfuls of sandwich, Duncan described Maggie Cassidy's attempt to take photographs of the remains. 'She didn't get any,' he insisted. 'And I made her promise she wouldn't try again.'

Brody raised an eyebrow sceptically, but said nothing. A thick criminology textbook sat on the table in front of Duncan, a bookmark tucked into the first few pages.

'Been studying?' I asked.

He blushed. 'Not really. Just something to read, you know.'

'Duncan was just saying he wants to apply for CID,' Brody added.

'Eventually,' Duncan said quickly, still looking embarrassed. 'I've not put enough time in yet.'

'Doesn't hurt to know what you want to do,' Brody said. 'I've been telling him about a couple of cases I worked with his father, but it doesn't seem to have put him off.'

Duncan grinned. Leaving them to it, I opened the flight case I'd brought with me. Inside was my field kit, the basics I always took with me on a job. A dictaphone to record notes, disposable overalls, shoes and masks, latex gloves, trowels, brushes, as well as two different-sized sieves. And plastic evidence bags. Lots and lots of evidence bags.

I was down to my last few pairs of disposable gloves and overalls, having used most of them on the Grampian job. The overalls were extra-large, so they would fit over my coat. I struggled into them and snapped protective overshoes over my boots, then pulled on the latex gloves over a pair of silk liners. Normally I carried chemical hand warmers for when I worked outside, but I'd already used them all in the Grampians. For the time being I'd just have to put up with cold fingers.

Duncan had been watching me get ready. Now he put down his sandwich.

'Doesn't it bother you? Working with dead bodies, I mean?'

'Don't be impertinent, lad,' Brody said, reprovingly.

The PC looked embarrassed. 'Sorry. I didn't mean . . .'

'That's all right,' I reassured him. 'Someone needs to do it. As for the rest . . . You get used to it.'

But his words stayed with me. *Doesn't it bother you?* There was no easy answer. I was well aware of what many people would regard as the gruesome nature of my work, but it was what I did. What I was.

So what did that make me?

The question was still troubling me as I stepped out of the camper van and saw a sleek silver-grey Saab coming along the track towards the cottage. Drawn by the sound of its approach, Brody and Duncan came out as it pulled up next to Ellen's VW.

'What the hell is he doing here?' Brody asked, irritably, as Strachan climbed out.

'Morning,' he said, as his golden retriever jumped out of the Saab after him.

'Get that dog back in the car!' Brody snapped.

The retriever was sniffing the air intently. Strachan reached to take hold of it, but before he could it suddenly caught a scent and bounded straight for the cottage.

'Bloody hell!' Brody swore, and raced to cut it off.

He was surprisingly fast for a man his size and age. He grabbed hold of the dog's collar as it tried to dodge past, almost yanking it off its feet as he pulled it back.

Strachan ran up, his face shocked. 'God, I'm sorry!'

Brody kept hold of the retriever's collar, suspending its front paws off the ground as it yelped and struggled.

'What the *hell* do you think you're doing?'

'I've said I'm sorry. I'll take him now.'

Strachan held out his hand but Brody didn't relinquish his hold. It was a big dog but the ex-inspector held it without effort, gripping its collar so tightly it was starting to choke as it wriggled to free itself.

'I said I'll take him now,' Strachan repeated, more firmly this time.

For a moment I thought Brody wasn't going to hand it over. Then he thrust the animal at Strachan. 'You shouldn't be out here. You or your bloody dog!'

Strachan soothed his pet, keeping hold of its collar. 'I apologize. I didn't mean to let him out. I just wanted to see if I could do anything.'

'You can get back in your car and leave. This is police business, not yours!'

But now Strachan was starting to grow angry himself. 'Funny, I thought you'd retired.'

'I've got clearance to be here. You haven't.'

'Perhaps not, but that still doesn't give you any legal right to tell me what to do.'

Brody's jaw muscles bunched with the effort of restraint. 'Constable McKinney. Why don't you escort this gentleman back to his car?'

Duncan was looking worried, out of his depth as the two of them confronted each other.

'No need. I'm going,' Strachan said. There were twin patches of colour on his cheeks, but he was more composed now. He gave me a shamefaced smile, studiously ignoring Brody.

'Morning, Dr Hunter. Sorry about this.'

'That's OK. It's just better not to have many people around,' I said.

'No, I appreciate that. But if there *is* anything I can do to help, then please let me know. Anything at all.' He gave the dog's collar an affectionate shake. 'Come on, Oscar, you bad lad.'

Brody watched him lead the dog back to the car, his expression stern and unforgiving.

Duncan began to stammer an apology. 'Sorry, I wasn't sure what I should . . .'

'No need to apologize. Shouldn't have lost my temper like that.' Brody took a packet of cigarettes and a lighter from his pocket, clearly still rattled.

The kettle had started to boil in the camper van. I waited till Duncan had gone back inside to make the tea, then turned to Brody.

'You don't like Strachan much, do you?'

Brody smiled. 'That obvious, is it?' He took a cigarette from the packet and regarded it with distaste. 'Filthy habit. I gave up when I retired. But I seem to have started again.'

'What have you got against him?'

He lit the cigarette and took a long drag, exhaling the smoke as if he resented it. 'I don't approve of his sort. Privileged types who think because they've got money they can do as they like. He didn't even earn it himself, he inherited it. His family made their fortune in gold mining out in South Africa during apartheid. You think they were so keen to share it with their workers over there?'

'You can't blame him for what his family did.'

'Perhaps not. But he's too cocksure of himself for my liking. You saw how he was in the bar last night, buying everyone drinks, turning his charm on for Karen Tait. A wife like that, and he's still got a roving eye.'

I remembered what Fraser had told me about Brody's own wife

leaving him, and wondered if his dislike of Strachan was coloured with envy. 'What about what he's done for the island? From what I've heard, Runa was going the same way as St Kilda before he came here.'

Brody said nothing for a moment. His border collie had come to look out of the camper-van door, back legs stiff with arthritis. He stroked its head.

'There's a story about St Kilda that always makes me wonder if what happened there wasn't for the best anyway. Before the islanders left, they killed their dogs. All of them. But only two were killed by lethal injections. The rest had stones tied round their necks and were thrown into the harbour. Their own *dogs.*'

He shook his head.

'Never could fathom why anyone would do something like that. But I expect they must have had a reason. I was a policeman long enough to know that whatever people do, there's always a reason. And one way or another it's usually self-interest.'

'You can't think that Runa would have been better off abandoned?'

'No, I suppose not. Strachan's made people here more *comfortable*, I'll grant him that. Better houses, better roads. You won't find anyone has a bad word to say about him.' He shrugged. 'I just don't believe in something for nothing. There's always a price to pay.'

I wonder if he wasn't being overly cynical. Strachan was helping the island, not exploiting it. And Brody wouldn't be the first policeman I'd met who'd become so hardened by exposure to the darker face of humanity that he was unable to see there was also a brighter side.

Then again, he might just be a more astute judge of human character than I was. A man I'd once mistakenly regarded as a friend had told me I was better at understanding the dead than the living, and perhaps he'd been right. At least the dead don't lie or betray.

75

Only keep their secrets, unless you know how to decipher them.
'I ought to get on,' I said.

The cottage didn't look any more prepossessing by daylight.
Darkness had at least hidden the full extent of its ruin and squalor.
Its roof was swaybacked and gaping in places, the cracked windows
thick with decades of grime. Behind it rose the imposing bulk of
Beinn Tuiridh, now visible as a misshapen tumble of rocks smeared
with dirty traces of snow.

A corridor of incident tape had been run from the front door into
the room where the burned remains lay. The ceiling above them
looked on the verge of collapse, although as yet no rain had leaked
on to the ash and bones themselves. In the murky light that filtered
through the window, they looked even more pathetic than I remembered.

I stood back and considered them, struck once again by the gruesome incongruity of the unburned hand and feet. Still, gruesome or
not, the decomposing soft tissue was an unexpected bonus for a fire
death. It would allow me to analyse the volatile fatty acids to establish
a time since death, as well as providing fingerprints and DNA to help
identify the unknown woman.

Since this wasn't a crime scene – as Wallace had been at pains to
point out – there was no real reason for me to grid out the remains.
That was usually done to record the position of any evidence that
was found. But I did it anyway. The stone floor prevented me from
hammering pegs into the ground, but I carried drilled wooden
blocks for that purpose.

Arranging them in a square around the body, I placed a peg in
each one. By the time I'd finished stringing a grid of nylon cord
between them my hands were numb and frozen in the thin latex
gloves. Rubbing them to get some feeling back, I used a trowel and
fine brush to begin clearing away the covering layer of talc-like
ash.

Gradually, what was left of the carbonized skeleton was laid bare.

Our lives, and sometimes deaths, are stories written in bone. It provides a telltale record of injuries, neglect or abuse. But in order to find what was written here, first I had to be able to see it. It was a slow, painstaking business. Working on one square of the grid at a time, I carefully removed and sifted the ash, plotting the location of bone fragments and anything else I found on to graph paper before sealing everything in evidence bags. Time passed without my noticing. Thoughts of the cold, of Jenny, of everything, all vanished. The world narrowed down to the pile of ash and desiccated bones, so that I was startled when I heard someone clearing his throat behind me.

I looked up to see Duncan standing in the doorway. He held up a mug of steaming tea.

'Thought you could use this.'

I checked my watch and saw it was nearly three o'clock. I'd worked right through lunchtime without realizing. I straightened, wincing as my back muscles protested.

'Thanks,' I said, stripping off my gloves as I went over.

'Sergeant Fraser's just called in, wanting to know how you were getting on.'

Fraser had put in a brief appearance earlier, but hadn't stayed long, claiming he needed to carry on interviewing the locals. After he'd gone, Brody wondered aloud how many of his conversations would take place in the hotel bar. I thought it might be quite a few, though I didn't say as much.

'Slowly,' I told Duncan, gratefully letting the hot mug warm my frozen hands.

He lingered in the doorway, looking at the remains. 'How much longer do you reckon it'll take?'

'Hard to say. There's a lot of ash to sift through. But I'll probably be done by tomorrow morning at the latest.'

'So have you, you know . . . found anything so far?'

He seemed genuinely interested. By rights I should report to Wallace first, but I didn't see any harm in telling Duncan some of what I'd learned.

'Well, I can confirm it's definitely a woman, under thirty, white and about five feet six or seven.'

He stared at the charred bones. 'Seriously?'

I indicated the hips, now cleaned of the covering of ash. 'If the body's female you can often tell the age from the pelvis. In a teenager or adolescent the pubic bone is almost corrugated. As a woman gets older it starts to flatten out and then erode. This one is pretty smooth, so she was no teenager, but not old enough for any real wear and tear. Which puts her in her late twenties, thirty at the most.'

I pointed at one of the long thigh bones. It had survived the fire better than most of the smaller ones, but its surface was still blackened and covered with the fine lines of heat fractures.

'You can use the length of the femur to get a rough idea of height,' I said. 'As for race, a lot of the teeth have cracked or fallen out, but there are enough left to see they were more or less upright, rather than jutting forward. So she was white, not black. I can't completely rule out yet that she wasn't Asian, but . . .'

'But there's not many Asians in the Hebrides,' Duncan finished for me, looking pleased with himself.

'That's right. So we're probably looking at a white woman in her twenties, about five-seven and big-boned. And I found metal buttons, along with what was left of a zip and bra hook, in the ash. So she wasn't naked.'

Duncan nodded, bright enough to understand what that meant. The fact she'd been dressed wasn't conclusive, but if she'd been naked then the likelihood was that we'd have been looking at sexual assault. And therefore murder.

'Looks like it was definitely an accident, then, eh? She just got too close to the fire, something like that?' He sounded faintly disappointed.

'That's how it looks.'

'Could she have done it to herself? Deliberately, I mean?'

'You mean suicide? I doubt it. She'd have used an accelerant, and as I've said, an accelerant wouldn't have caused this. And there'd be a container somewhere nearby, which there isn't.'

Duncan rubbed the back of his neck. 'What about the, er, you know, the hand and feet?' he asked, almost sheepishly.

I'd been waiting for that. But the light coming through the dirty windowpane was already beginning to dim, and I still had a lot to do.

'I'll give you a clue.' I pointed at the greasy brown residue that clung to the smoke-blackened ceiling. 'Remember what I said about that?'

Duncan looked up at it. 'That it was fat from when the body burned?'

'That's right. That's the key. See if you can work it out.' I drained my mug and handed it back to him. 'Right, I need to get on.'

But once he'd gone I didn't start work right away. Now I'd cleared away most of the covering layer of ash I could start to remove the surviving bones, bagging them for proper examination later. Even though I'd been deliberately thorough, I'd found nothing that pointed to a suspicious death. No visible knife marks on the bone, no other sign of skeletal trauma or injury. I'd even found the hyoid, the delicate horseshoe-shaped bone that so often breaks during strangulation, buried in the ashes. It had been reduced almost to the fragility of powder, so delicate that the slightest nudge might break it, but it was still whole.

So why did I still feel I was missing something?

A wayward gust of wind from the holes in the roof chilled me as I stood looking down at the remains. I went to where the skull lay canted on the floor, crazed with heat fractures. The cranium is made up of separate plates that butt against each other like geological fault lines. The blow-out had left a hole nearly the size of a fist in one of them, on the occipital bone at the back of the crown. Small fragments of bone lay on the floor around it, blown there when the hot gases had made their explosive exit. That was another indication that the damage happened in the fire – if the hole had been caused by an impact the fragments would have been driven inwards, into the skull cavity.

Yet something about the skull bothered me, a sort of nagging neural itch. Almost involuntarily, I found myself starting to examine it again.

As though with malicious timing, the daylight had begun to fade with increasing speed. Last night I'd avoided working at night because I didn't want to make mistakes. Now I felt I would be making an even bigger one if I didn't. I moved the floodlight, but it still wasn't bright enough for what I wanted. Taking out my torch, I set it on the floor so it shone on to the gaping skull cavity.

Light spilled eerily from the empty eye sockets as I turned my attention to the shards of bone that lay on the floor. Most were tiny, no bigger than my thumbnail. I'd already recorded their positions on the graph paper but now, like a ghoulish jigsaw puzzle, I began trying to piece them back together.

It was something I'd normally only attempt in a laboratory, where I had the right clamps, tweezers and magnifying lenses to help me. Here I didn't even have a table, and my progress was made even slower by my cold-numbed fingers. Gradually, though, I fitted the fragments together until I had a sizeable section.

And then I saw it.

A blow forceful enough to break the cranium will cause lightning-like fractures to radiate from the point of contact. Normally they're hard to miss, and I'd seen no evidence of them here. But I'd been looking in the wrong place. The fragments had joined together to reveal a ragged spider's web of cracks. Distinctive, zigzag lines that could only have been caused by a heavy impact, strong enough to fracture the bone without actually breaking it.

The skull had burst in the fire, all right, but in an area where it had been already weakened.

I carefully laid the bone fragments back on the ground. Brody had been right all along. This was no accident.

The woman had been murdered.

8

I barely noticed the wind and rain as I went back to the camper van. It was pitch dark outside, and the light from its window shone out like a beacon. There was a sour taste in my mouth. Someone had killed a young woman and then set fire to her body. Whether Wallace liked it or not, he hadn't any choice now but to escalate this to a full-scale murder inquiry.

I was angry with the superintendent, but far more so with myself. It was no consolation that fire deaths are notoriously difficult; I should have taken notice of my instincts. And there was also something else to consider. It would be a mistake to assume that, just because the dead woman wasn't local, her killer wasn't either. We didn't know what the victim had been doing on Runa, but according to Brody few outsiders came here at this time of year. So the likelihood was that she'd come over either with, or to see, someone who lived here.

Which would mean her killer was still on the island.

That thought stayed with me as I hurried to the camper van. It was almost stiflingly warm after the icy cottage, the air heavy with the fumes from the paraffin heater.

'How's it going?' Duncan asked, getting to his feet.

'I need to talk to Wallace. Can I use your radio?'

'Uh, sure,' he said, surprised. He handed it across. 'I'll, er, I'll be outside, then.'

The police radio was one of the new digital sets, which allowed calls to either landlines or mobiles. But Wallace didn't answer any of his numbers. *Great.* I left messages telling him to call me and started struggling out of my overalls.

'Everything all right?' Duncan asked, coming back in.

'Fine.' He would find out soon enough, but I wanted to speak to Wallace before I told anyone else. 'I'm going back to the village.'

There was no point my staying at the cottage any longer. I wasn't touching anything else till SOC got here, and I needed to calm down and think through the implications of what I'd found. But as I started to go out I hesitated.

'Look, keep an eye out, OK? Anything suspicious, anyone comes out here, call Fraser straight away.'

He looked puzzled and a little offended. 'Aye, of course.'

I went out to the car. It was raining heavily now, and the windows on Ellen's old VW fogged as soon as I got in. Turning the heater on to clear them, I struggled with the unwieldy gear lever and bumped down the track to the road. The wipers screeched as they smeared rain across the windscreen. I sat forward in my seat, peering through the steamed glass. Hardly any cars seemed to use the road, but I'd no desire to hit a sheep that had strayed on to the tarmac.

I was about halfway to the village when a pale shape suddenly darted into the road in front of me. There was just time to see the reflective eyes of a dog gleam in the headlights as I stamped on the brake, and then the car spun out of control. The VW slewed crazily, flinging me against the seatbelt as it lurched to a halt.

The impact took my breath away. I sat back, shaken, rubbing my chest where the seatbelt had bruised it. But I wasn't badly hurt, and the VW's engine was still running. The car had gone off the road and was angled down into a ditch, its headlights shining on to thick hummocks of grass rather than tarmac.

At least I hadn't hit the dog. I'd seen it bounding off as I lost control. It had been a golden retriever, so unless there were two on the island it must have been Strachan's, although God knew what it was doing out here.

The thought that it had all of the island to choose from, yet had managed to run out in front of me, didn't help my temper as I put the gears into reverse and tried to back up on to the road. The wheels churned and skidded, but the car didn't move. I shifted into first and tried to go forward, with the same result.

I switched off the engine and got out to take a look. The car didn't appear to be damaged, but the rear wheels were bogged down in muddy ruts. Putting up my hood, I went to the boot to try to find something to give the tyres purchase. But there was nothing. I got back in the car, the rain glistening like white wires in the headlights as I considered my options. There was no point going back to the camper van, so that left two choices. I could either stay with the car until someone came along, or walk the rest of the way to the village. If I stayed I could be waiting hours. And at least walking would keep me warm.

I swore as I realized that I'd left my torch in my flight case back at the van. I turned on the overhead light and checked the glove compartment, hoping to find one there. But apart from some old maps and scraps of paper it was empty.

I turned off the headlights and waited for my eyes to adjust to the sudden dark. After a while I accepted they were as acclimatized as they were going to get. Night had fallen on Runa, and it was only going to get darker. Still, I felt reluctant to leave the car. I'd just found out there was probably a killer on the island. It was an unsettling thought to find yourself stranded with on an isolated road.

But that was stupid. Even if he was still on Runa, the young woman's killer would hardly be out here. *Come on. No point waiting any longer.*

I got out of the car. As I did, the moon appeared through a break in the clouds. It gave the moors and hills a stark but ethereal beauty, picking out the road with a silvery illumination. My spirits rose as I started walking. *Not so bad after all.* And just as I thought that, clouds shrouded the moon again, and the light was abruptly cut off.

The utter blackness shocked me. I'd lived in the country, and thought I knew how dark a night could be. But this was of a different order to anything I'd experienced before. Runa was a tiny island, miles from the mainland and with no towns or cities to cast even a distant glow. I looked up, hoping to see at least some evidence of lightening in the sky. There was nothing. The cloud bank extinguished any glimpse of stars or moon as effectively as a blanket.

I looked back, hoping to see some reassuring sign of the VW. But the darkness was absolute. Only the sound of my footsteps told me I was still on the road. *It's only the dark. It won't hurt you.* Provided I didn't stray from the road, there was nothing to worry about. Sooner or later it would lead me back to the village.

Even so, as I started walking again my confidence ebbed with every step. The rain was freezing and the wind whittled away at my body heat, making me virtually deaf as well as blind.

But not so deaf that I didn't hear a scuff on the road behind me.

I spun round, heart thumping. I couldn't see a thing except blackness. *Probably just a sheep, or something blown by the wind. Or Strachan's bloody dog.* Turning my back on it, I started walking again. But all my senses were attuned to what might be out there with me, and I was still straining to hear it when I suddenly stepped out into nothing.

I pitched forward, arms windmilling before the ground smacked into me. I tumbled downhill, all sense of up or down lost. Rough grass scratched at my face, and then I jolted to a stop.

Dazed and winded, I lay in the muddy grass, rain bouncing on my upturned face. I knew what had happened. I'd wandered from the centre of the road without realizing it and walked off the edge into a gully. *Idiot!* I started to push myself upright, and cried out as pain exploded in my left shoulder. When it had subsided to a dull ache, I gingerly moved my arm again. The pain lanced back, not quite as severe as before but bad enough to make me gasp out loud.

But at least there had been no sensation of grating bone. I hoped that meant nothing was broken. Swallowing back the bile that had risen in my throat, I felt my shoulder awkwardly with my other hand. Even through my coat I could tell that there was something wrong with the way the joint fitted together. There was a bulge where there shouldn't have been, and as my fingers traced its outline I felt a queasy wave of nausea.

I'd dislocated my shoulder. Badly.

I told myself not to panic. *Deep breaths. Take it one step at a time.* Before I could use my arm again I knew the joint would have to be shot back into place. I reached round with my other hand as far as I could, probing with my fingers to feel where the ball of the humerus had popped out of its socket. I paused, gritting my teeth, and then pushed.

The pain made me almost black out. I yelled as starbursts wheeled across my vision. When they faded I was lying on my back once more, sweat and rain mingling on my face. I wanted to throw up. The spasm subsided but left me weak and shaking.

I didn't bother feeling the shoulder again. I knew it was still out of joint. It was throbbing relentlessly, a bone-deep ache that radiated from the base of my skull right down my arm. I sat up again, weakly. My head spun as I slowly got to my feet. There was no question of walking to the village now. I would have to try to find the car and sit it out, hoping that Fraser or Duncan would come looking for me sooner rather than later.

Climbing back up the slippery bank was hard work. I couldn't see a thing, and could only use one hand to help drag myself up the slope. I had to keep resting, and my shoulder was hurting more than ever now. I wondered if I'd torn any ligaments, but put the thought out of my mind. I couldn't do anything about it if I had.

By the time the slope began to level out I was sweating and exhausted. I hauled myself up the last few feet and then straightened on legs that felt like water. Relief at having made it back to the top swamped out anything else. But then I realized something was wrong.

The road wasn't there.

My relief vanished. I took a few more cautious steps, each time hoping to feel tarmac under my boots. But there was only turf and boggy, uneven ground. I'd obviously been more disorientated by my fall than I'd thought. Instead of climbing back up to the road, I'd clawed my way up another hummock of grass.

I forced myself to stay calm. There was only one thing to do. The road had to be opposite me. All I had to do was retrace my steps, and then go up the other side.

I made my way down the muddy slope, slithering the last few feet on my backside. I groped around, trying to locate the slope I'd fallen down. I couldn't find it. *Come on, it has to be here.* But the terrain at the bottom didn't conform to such neat logic. In the dark it was a maze of humps and gullies. Wandering blind as I was, there was no way of knowing where any of them led.

I knew I couldn't be far from the road, but I had no way of telling which way it was. I looked up, hoping for some glimpse of stars. But land and sky merged into one single, impenetrable darkness. The wind and rain gusted first one way then another, as though trying to confuse me further.

I'd started shivering, from shock as well as cold. Even in my weatherproof outer clothes I knew I could sink into hypothermia if I didn't find shelter. *Come on, think! Which way?* I made my decision and started walking. Even if it was the wrong direction, the exertion would help keep me warm. Staying still now would kill me.

It was hard going. The ground was a treacherous mix of heather and grass, threatening to turn or break an ankle at every step. I stopped dead as something rustled nearby, straining to hear against the gusting of the wind and the rain on my hood. I couldn't see anything except darkness. My heart was racing. *It's nothing. Just a sheep.*

But even as I tried to convince myself, I was recalling the scuff I'd heard behind me on the road. I knew I was being irrational, that even if there was someone else out here, they wouldn't be able to see me any more than I could see them. It didn't help. I was lost and injured, and the dark released all the primitive fears that daylight and the modern world have allowed us to bury.

They weren't buried now.

I carried on walking. The turf underfoot became wetter and more broken as I blundered into a peat bog. My teeth were chattering as I splashed noisily across. Either it had grown colder or my core temperature was dropping despite my efforts. Both, probably.

My shoulder was on fire, lancing me with white heat at every step. I'd lost track of time but I was tiring quickly, becoming careless with fatigue. Another noise came from off to one side, the sound of something moving through the grass. I spun towards it and went crashing down. Agony flared through my injured shoulder as it bore the full brunt of my weight.

I must have passed out. When I came round I was lying face down, the rain pattering hypnotically on my hood. I could taste the loamy stink of peat in my mouth. Still only semi-conscious, I found myself thinking about all the countless dead animals, insects and vegetation it was made from: millennia of rot compressed into a petrochemical sludge. I spat it out and tried to push myself up, but the effort was too much. Water had seeped inside my coat, chilling me to the bone. I was shuddering from the cold, my strength gone. I collapsed back into the mud. *Of all the bloody stupid ways to die.* It was so absurd it was almost funny. *I'm sorry, Jenny.* She'd been mad enough just because I came out here. She was going to be furious when she found out I'd let it kill me.

But the attempt at gallows humour failed miserably. Lying there, I felt anger as well as sadness. *So that's it, is it?* I goaded myself. *You're just going to give up?*

It was then, when it could have gone either way, that I saw the light.

At first I thought I was imagining it. It was only a spark of yellow, dancing in the blackness ahead of me. But when I moved my head the light remained in the same place. I shut my eyes, opened them. The light was still there. I felt a surge of hope as I remembered Strachan's house. That was closer than the village. Perhaps I'd wandered in the right direction after all.

Part of me knew even then that the light was too high to be coming from the house, but I didn't care. It was something to aim for. Without even thinking about it, I crawled to my feet and began to stagger towards it.

The light hung above me, but how far away I couldn't tell. It didn't matter. The yellow glow was the only thing in the universe, drawing me towards it like a moth. It steadily grew larger. Now I could see that it wasn't constant, but flickered to some unheard rhythm. I was barely aware of the ground starting to rise towards it. It climbed still more, became steeper. I was using my one good arm to help pull me uphill, sometimes sinking to a crawl on my knees before stumbling upright again. But the light was closer. I fixed on it, shutting out everything else.

Then it was right in front of me. Not a car, not a house. Just a small, untended fire in front of a ruined stone hut. As disappointment started to filter through my daze, I began to take in what the firelight revealed. All around me were untidy mounds of rocks, and the sight of them stirred some dim connection. They weren't natural formations, I realized.

They were burial cairns.

I could remember both Brody and Strachan mentioning them. And, remembering that, I knew I was even more lost than I'd thought.

I'd wandered all the way out to the mountain.

I swayed on my feet, the last of my reserves gone. As my vision swam, I became aware of movement in the mouth of the ruined hut. I stared, too numb and exhausted to move, as a hooded figure slowly emerged from inside. It stepped into the firelight, eyes reflecting the flames as they stared at me from beneath its hood.

Then the fire seemed to grow dark, and the night spun me off into darkness.

9

There was no wind. That was the first thought that came to me. No wind, no drumming of rain.

Just silence.

I opened my eyes. I was in a bed. Muted daylight filtered through pale curtains, revealing a large, white room. White walls, white ceiling, white sheets. My first thought was that it was a hospital, but then I realized most hospitals didn't run to duvets and double beds. Or en suite glass shower rooms, come to that. And the raffia bedside table looked as if it had come straight from the pages of an interiors magazine.

But just then the fact that I didn't know where I was didn't bother me. The bed was warm and soft. I lay there for a while, my mind running over the last events I could remember. They came back to me surprisingly easily. The cottage. Abandoning the car. Falling in the dark, then heading for the distant fire.

That was where it grew hazy. The memories of stumbling up the mountainside and finding myself at the ancient burial cairns, and of the figure that had emerged from the ruined hut, had the surreal quality of a dream. I had disjointed images of being carried along in pitch blackness, crying out as my shoulder was jolted.

My shoulder . . .

I drew back the duvet, registering that I was naked but more concerned with the sling that strapped my left arm to my chest. A professional job, by the look of it. I cautiously flexed the shoulder and winced as bruised ligaments protested. It hurt like hell, but I could tell it was no longer dislocated. Someone must have put it back, although I'd no memory of it. Which was odd, because having a dislocated shoulder shot back into joint isn't the sort of experience you're likely to forget.

I looked at my wrist and saw that my watch was missing. I'd no idea what time it was, but it was daylight outside. I felt a growing sense of alarm. *Christ, how long had I been out?* I'd still not told Wallace – or anyone – that we were dealing with a murder. And I'd promised Jenny I'd call her the night before. She'd be going frantic wondering what had happened to me.

I had to get back. I threw aside the duvet and was looking around for my clothes when the door opened and Grace Strachan came in.

She was even more striking than I remembered, dark hair tied back to reveal the perfect oval of her face, fitted black trousers and cream sweater revealing a figure that was slim but sensuous. When she saw me she smiled.

'Hello, Dr Hunter. I was just coming to check if you were awake.'

At least now I knew where I was. It was only when her eyes flicked down that I remembered that I was naked. I hurriedly covered myself with the duvet.

The dark eyes were amused. 'How are you feeling?'

'Confused. How did I get here?'

'Michael brought you back last night. He found you on the mountain. Or, rather, you found him.'

So it had been Strachan who'd rescued me. I remembered the figure emerging into the firelight. 'That was your husband I saw out there?'

She gave a smile. 'One of his little hobbies, I'm afraid. I'm glad I'm not the only one who thinks it's odd. Still, good job for you he was.'

I couldn't argue with that, but I was still worrying about how long I'd been asleep. 'What time is it?'

'Nearly half past three.'

The day was more than half gone. I cursed, silently. 'Can I use your phone? I need to let people know what's happened.'

'Already done. Michael called the hotel after he brought you back and spoke to Sergeant Fraser, I think it was. He told him you'd had an accident but that you were more or less in one piece.'

That was something, I supposed. But I still needed to get hold of Wallace. And Jenny, to let her know I was all right.

If she was still speaking to me.

'I'd still like to use the phone, if that's OK.'

'Of course. I'll let Michael know you're awake. He can bring it up with him.' Grace arched an eyebrow, a grin tugging at the corner of her mouth. 'I'll tell him to bring your clothes, as well.'

With that she went out. I lay in bed impatiently, chafed by the thought of the lost hours. But I didn't have to wait long before there was a rap on the door.

Michael Strachan came in, carrying my neatly washed and pressed clothes. My wallet, watch and useless mobile were stacked neatly on top of them. He also had a newspaper tucked under one arm, but he kept hold of that.

'Grace said you might be needing these,' he said, grinning as he set my things on a chair by the bed. He reached into his pocket and took out a cordless phone. 'And this, too.'

I wanted to make the calls straight away, but restrained myself. If not for this man I'd probably be dead. 'Thanks. And thank you for what you did last night.'

'Forget it. I was glad to help. Although I must admit you scared me half to death when you suddenly appeared like that.'

'It was mutual,' I said, dryly. 'How did you get me back?'

He shrugged. 'I managed to prop you upright most of the

way down, but for the last leg I'm afraid it was a fireman's lift.'

'You carried me?'

'Only as far as the car. I don't always take it, but I was glad I had, believe me.' He said it dismissively, as if carrying a grown man even a short distance was nothing. 'So how's the shoulder now?'

I flexed it warily. It was still painful, but at least I could move it without passing out. 'Better than it was.'

'Bruce had the devil of a job popping it back. If not for him, we'd probably have had you airlifted to a hospital. Or stuck you on Iain Kinross's ferry, and I don't think you'd have enjoyed a sea voyage in the state you were in.'

'Bruce . . . ?'

'Bruce Cameron. He's the schoolteacher, but he's also a trained nurse. Looks after the medical clinic.'

'Sounds like a useful combination.'

A look I couldn't quite read crossed his face. 'He has his moments. You'll meet him in a while yourself. Grace called him to say you were awake, so he offered to come out to see how you were. Oh, and your colleagues found Ellen's car this morning and got it back on the road. It isn't damaged, you'll be glad to hear. What happened? Swerve to miss a sheep?'

'Not a sheep, no. A golden retriever.'

Strachan's face fell. 'Oscar? Oh, Christ, you're joking! I'd taken him out with me, but he'd wandered off. God, I'm really sorry.'

'Don't worry about it. I'm just glad I didn't hit him.' Curiosity temporarily got the better of my impatience. 'Look, don't think I'm not grateful, but . . . what the hell were you doing up there?'

He smiled, a little shamefaced. 'I camp there every now and then. Grace thinks I'm mad, but when I was a kid back in South Africa my father used to take me out on safari. You get the same sense of space and isolation on the mountain that I remember from that. I'm not religious or anything, but there's something . . . almost spiritual about it.'

This was a side of Strachan I wouldn't have suspected. 'Pretty lonely, though. And cold.'

He grinned. 'I wrap up, and the solitude's all part of it. Besides, the *broch*'s a good place to think.'

'*Broch?*'

'The stone hut I was in. It's an old watchtower. I love the idea that someone would have been sitting up there by a fire two thousand years ago. I like to think I'm keeping the tradition. And those cairns are even older. The people buried in them would have been lords or clan leaders, and now all that's left is a few piles of stone. Puts things in perspective, don't you think?'

Abruptly, he grew embarrassed.

'Anyhow, so much for my dark secrets. Here, I brought you this.'

He handed me the newspaper he'd brought with him. It was the previous evening's *Lewis Gazette*, folded open on the second page. A headline over Maggic Cassidy's byline announced *Fire Death Mystery on Runa*. The story gave a lurid account of the discovery of the burned body, light on facts but heavy on speculation. Predictably, she'd made reference to spontaneous human combustion, and I was referred to as 'esteemed forensic scientist Dr David Hunter'.

It could have been worse, I supposed. At least there were no photographs.

'It came over on this morning's ferry,' Strachan said. 'I thought you'd want to see it.'

'Thanks.' But the article had rekindled my sense of urgency. 'I hate to ask after all you've done, but could you give me a lift back to the village?'

'Of course.' He paused. 'Is everything all right?'

'Fine. I just need to get back.'

He nodded, but I don't think he was convinced. 'I'll be downstairs. Help yourself to the shower.'

I waited until he'd gone, then grabbed the phone. Wallace's

number was logged in my mobile. I retrieved it and called it on the landline. *Come on, answer,* I urged him silently.

This time he did. 'Yes, Dr Hunter?' he said, with the air of someone with better things to do.

I kept it short. 'She was murdered.'

There was a beat while that registered. Then he swore. 'You're certain?'

'She'd been hit hard enough for the back of her skull to be cracked but not broken. The fire made it blow out at that point, which is why I didn't spot it sooner.'

'Could she have done it in a fall? Panicking when she caught fire, perhaps?'

'A fall could have caused it, but an injury like that would have either killed her outright or at the very least left her unconscious. She wouldn't have been capable of moving afterwards. In which case the body would still be lying on its back, not face down like hers is.'

I heard him sigh. 'There's no way you could have made a mistake?'

I took a moment to reply, not trusting my temper. 'You wanted my opinion, you've got it. Somebody killed her and then set fire to the body. This was no accident.'

There was a pause. I could almost hear him thinking through the logistics of pulling teams away from the train crash and getting them out here.

'All right,' he said, all business now, 'I'll have a support team and SOC out with you first thing tomorrow morning.'

I glanced out of the window. The light was already fading. 'Can't they be here sooner?'

'Not a chance. They'll have to get out to Stornoway first, then go from there to Runa. That's going to take time. You'll just have to sit tight until tomorrow.'

I didn't like it, but there was nothing more I could do. After Wallace had ended the call, I dialled Jenny's mobile. It went straight to voicemail. I left a message telling her I was sorry for not calling, that I was all right, and I'd call her again later. It seemed inadequate and unsatisfying. I'd have given anything to be able to see her just then. But that wasn't going to happen either.

It was only as I put down the phone that I realized I'd automatically called Wallace first instead of Jenny. Wondering uncomfortably what that said about my priorities, I threw back the duvet and went to get ready.

The shower felt wonderful, hot water easing the ache in my shoulder and sluicing away the dirt and stink from the previous night. The sling was semi-rigid, made from Velcro, foam and plastic, so I was at least able to take it off. But dressing with only one hand was harder than I thought. I could barely move my left arm at all, and by the time I'd managed to pull on my thick sweater I felt as though I'd had a hard work-out at the gym.

I went out into the hallway. The big house had been given a thorough makeover. The white walls were newly plastered, the floor laid with coir matting instead of carpet.

At the top of the stairs, a large picture window looked down on to a small, sandy cove. It was flanked by cliffs, and steps ran down to where a sleek yacht was moored at the end of a wooden jetty. Even in the shelter of the cove, its mast rocked violently in the heavy chop. In the failing light I made out two figures standing on the jetty. One of them was pointing out into the cove, the black coat identifying him as Strachan. I guessed the other must be Bruce, the nurse turned schoolteacher.

Downstairs, a huge Turkish rug covered most of the entrance hall floor. On the back wall was a large abstract oil painting, a swirl of purples and blues shot through with indigo slashes that was both striking and subtly unsettling. I'd almost gone past before I noticed that the name at the bottom corner was Grace Strachan's.

The strains of Spanish guitar music were coming from a room at the far end. I went in and found myself in a bright and airy kitchen,

97

redolent with spices. Copper pans hung from the ceiling, while others bubbled on a black Aga.

Grace was next to it, deftly chopping vegetables. She gave me a smile over her shoulder.

'I see you managed to dress OK.'

'Eventually.'

She brushed a strand of dark hair from her eyes with her wrist. Even in a plain black apron she looked almost ridiculously sensual. The effect was all the more powerful because it seemed so unconscious.

'Michael won't be a minute. He's just taken Bruce down to the cove to show him his latest project. Bruce who mended your arm last night?' she said, making it a question.

'Yes, your husband told me. He did a good job.'

'He's a gem. Offered to come up to check on you as soon as school finished. Can I get you a drink, or something to eat? You must be famished.'

It wasn't until then that I realized how hungry I was. I hadn't eaten since the previous day.

Grace seized on my hesitation. 'How about a sandwich? Or an omelette?'

'Really, I don't—'

'An omelette it is, then.'

She poured olive oil into a frying pan and deftly broke three eggs into a bowl as it heated.

'Michael says you're from London,' she said, briskly beating them.

'That's right.'

'I haven't been there in ages. I keep trying to get Michael to go, but he's a terrible stick-in-the-mud. Hates being prised off the island. Won't go any further than Lewis, which isn't exactly a cultural Mecca, let me tell you.'

Stick-in-the-mud wasn't a phrase I'd have associated with her husband. But then, as I'd found out, he was a man of surprises.

'How long have you been here?' I asked.

'Oh, four years, now? No, five. God!' She shook her head, amazed at the swiftness of time.

'Must have taken some getting used to. Living on an island, I mean.'

'Not really. We've always tended to go for fairly out of the way places. You'd think we'd be bored, but we never are. Michael's always busy, and I help out in the school – art classes, mainly.'

'I saw the painting outside. Very striking.'

She gave a dismissive shrug, but looked pleased. 'Oh, it's just a hobby. But that's how we know Bruce so well, through me helping at the school. He was a primary school teacher on the mainland, so he was a real find. And I love children, so it's great being able to work with them.'

A wistfulness briefly touched her face, and then was gone. I looked away, feeling uncomfortably as though I'd had a glimpse of something private. I'd already surmised that she and Strachan didn't have children of their own. Now I knew how she felt about it.

'I saw the yacht in the cove,' I said, hoping to steer back to safer territory. 'Nice boat.'

'She's lovely, isn't she?' Grace beamed, setting a fresh loaf and butter on the table. 'Michael bought her when we first came out here. Only a forty-two footer, but the cove isn't deep enough for anything bigger. And that size, one person can handle her on their own. Michael sometimes takes her to Stornoway, when he has to go over on business.'

'So how did the two of you meet?' I asked.

'Oh, God, we've known each other practically for ever.'

'You mean, as in childhood sweethearts?'

She laughed. 'I know, it's a terrible cliché, but it's true. We grew up near Johannesburg. Michael's older than me, and when I was little I used to follow him around. Perhaps that's why I enjoy it out here. I like to be able to keep him to myself.'

Her happiness was infectious. I found myself envying Strachan his marriage. It made me uncomfortably aware of how much Jenny and I had been drifting apart lately.

'Here you go,' she said, sliding the omelette on to a plate. 'Help yourself to bread and butter.'

I sat down and started to eat. The omelette was delicious, and I'd just finished the last mouthful when the kitchen door opened, letting in a blast of wind and rain. The golden retriever shot in, dripping water, and bounded excitedly over to me. I tried to fend it off one-handed.

'No, Oscar!' Grace ordered. 'Michael, I'm sure David doesn't want muddy paw prints all over him. Oh, and look, you're as bad, you're tracking mud everywhere!'

Strachan had followed the dog inside. With him was the man in the army-surplus peaked cap I'd seen ushering the pupils into the school the day before.

'Sorry, darling, but I still can't find my bloody wellingtons. Oscar, behave yourself. You've blotted your copybook with Dr Hunter enough as it is.' Strachan pulled the dog from me and gave me a grin. 'Glad to see you're up and about, David. This is Bruce Cameron.'

The other man had taken off his hat, revealing a shaved head of ginger stubble, thinning in the classic shape of male pattern baldness. He was short and slight, with the scrawniness of a marathon runner and an Adam's apple so prominent it looked about to break through the skin.

He had been watching Grace since they'd come in. Now he looked at me with the palest eyes I'd ever seen. They were an indefinable non-colour, with the whites visible all the way round, so that he seemed to have a permanent stare.

I saw him take in my empty plate. An expression that could have been anger flitted across his face, then was gone.

'Thanks for taking care of my shoulder last night,' I said, offering my hand. His was thin and bony, and there was no return pressure when we shook.

'I was glad to help.' The voice was a surprise, deep and booming, a stentorian shock coming from such a slight frame. 'I gather you're out here to take a look at the body that's been found.'

'Don't bother asking him anything about that,' Strachan cut in easily. 'I've already had my wrist slapped once for quizzing him.'

Cameron looked as though he didn't appreciate the advice. 'How's the shoulder feeling?' he asked, but without any real interest.

'Better than it was.'

He nodded, managing to seem bored and self-satisfied at the same time. 'You were lucky. You'll need to have it X-rayed when you get back to the mainland, but I don't think there's any serious ligament damage.'

He made it sound as though I'd only have myself to blame if there were. Reaching into his pocket, he took out a small bottle of pills and set them on the table.

'These are ibuprofen. Anti-inflammatories. You might not need them now, but you will when the last of the sedative's worn off.'

'Sedative?'

'You were rambling and your shoulder muscles were badly in spasm, so I gave you one to calm things down a little.'

That explained why I didn't remember him working on my shoulder. And why I'd slept through most of the day.

'What was it?' I asked.

'Don't worry, I'm licensed to prescribe drugs.' He glanced at Grace, with a half-smile I thought was meant to be self-deprecating but just looked smug. He'd made no offer to examine my shoulder, but then I was starting to think I wasn't the real reason for his visit anyway.

'Even so, I'd still like to know what it was,' I said.

I didn't want to seem churlish, but ever since I was almost killed by a deliberate overdose of diamorphine I've never liked being given drugs without knowing what they are. Besides, Cameron's patronizing manner was starting to grate.

For the first time he seemed to fully register my presence. The look he gave me wasn't friendly.

'If you must know, I gave you ten milligrams of diazepam and anaesthetized locally with novocaine. Then I administered a shot of cortisone to reduce inflammation.' He stared at me superciliously. 'Does that meet with your approval?'

Strachan had been listening with amusement. 'Did I mention that David used to be a GP, Bruce?'

He obviously hadn't. Cameron blushed, and I regretted pushing. I hadn't intended to embarrass him. At the same time, I wondered how Strachan knew. Not that it was a secret, but I wasn't sure I liked relative strangers to know so much about my past.

He gave me an apologetic smile. 'I did some checking up on the Internet. Hope you don't mind, but I'm congenitally nosy when it comes to anything that affects Runa. And it is all public record.'

He was right, but that didn't mean I liked his digging into my background. Still, he had taken me into his house the night before. I supposed he was entitled to display some curiosity.

'I've been showing Bruce where the pens are going to be for my new project. Runa's first fish farm,' Strachan went on. 'Atlantic cod. Organic, eco-friendly, and it'll create at least six jobs. More, if it takes off.' His enthusiasm was almost boyish. 'Could be a real boost for the island's economy. I plan to make a start in the spring.'

Grace had begun to debone a chicken, cutting the flesh with the practised ease of a chef. 'I'm still not sure I'm keen on having a fish farm at the bottom of the garden.'

'Darling, I've told you, there's nowhere else sheltered enough on the island. And we've got the sea at the bottom of the garden any-way. It's full of fish.'

'Yes, but they're visitors. These'll be house guests.'

Cameron gave a sycophantic laugh. I saw a flash of irritation on Strachan's face, then the rap of the door knocker came from the hallway.

'We're popular this afternoon,' Grace said. She reached for a towel to dry her hands, but Strachan was already on his way out.

'I'll get it.'

'Perhaps it's one of your policeman friends,' she said to me, as voices carried from the hall.

I hoped so. But instead of Duncan or Fraser it was Maggie Cassidy Strachan had in tow when he returned.

'Look who's turned up,' he said, with the faintest touch of irony. 'You know Maggie, Rose Cassidy's granddaughter, don't you, Grace?'

'Of course.' Grace smiled. 'How is your grandmother?'

'Oh, muddling along, thanks. Hello, Bruce,' Maggie said, receiving a grudging nod in return. She turned to me with a grin. 'Nice to see you still in one piece, Dr Hunter. I heard about your adventure last night. You were quite the talk of the bar.'

I bet I was, I thought ruefully.

'So what brings you out here, Maggie?' Strachan asked. 'Hoping for an exclusive with Dr Hunter?'

'Actually, it was you I wanted to see. And Mrs Strachan as well, obviously,' Maggie added smoothly. She was looking at him with open-eyed candour, the picture of sincerity. 'I'd like to write a feature on you for the *Lewis Gazette*. With Runa being in the news now, it's the perfect time. We can talk about what you've done for the island, take a few photos of you both at home. It'll make a great spread.'

Strachan's good humour had faded. 'Sorry. I take a lousy photo.'

'Oh, come on, darling,' Grace cajoled. 'Sounds like fun.'

Cameron's bass voice rumbled out. 'Yes, I think it's a great idea, Michael. I'm sure Grace is very photogenic, even if you aren't. And it'd be good publicity for the fish farm.'

'That's right,' Maggie said, pushing home her advantage. She gave Strachan the full wattage of her smile. 'And I'll bet you take a great photograph.'

I noticed Grace's eyebrow go up at the reporter's blatant flirting. Although Maggie wasn't conventionally pretty, there was an energy about her that was undeniably attractive.

But Strachan seemed immune. 'No, I don't think so.'

'At least think about it for a day or two. Perhaps—'

'I've said no.' He didn't raise his voice but there was no doubting the finality in it. 'Was there anything else?'

His manner was still polite, but it was obviously a dismissal. Maggie did her best to hide her disappointment.

'Uh . . . no. That was all. Sorry to have bothered you.'

'It's no bother,' he said. 'In fact, could I ask a favour?'

Her face brightened. 'Sure, of course.'

'Dr Hunter needs a lift back to the hotel. It'd save me turning out again if you could take him. Is that OK, David?'

I wasn't delighted at the thought of sharing a car with a reporter who'd already played me for a fool once, but since she was going back to the village it made sense. And I was indebted enough to the Strachans already.

'If Maggie doesn't mind,' I said.

She gave me a look that said she knew what I was thinking. 'I'd love to.'

'You must come out again before you go back,' Grace said, kissing my cheek. Up close her perfume was a dizzying musk. The brief contact of her lips left a lingering memory on my skin. As she stepped back I looked across to find Cameron staring at me with unconcealed jealousy. His infatuation was so naked I didn't know whether to feel embarrassment or pity for him.

Strachan seemed in a better humour again as he showed us into the hall. When he opened the front door a blast of freezing wind and rain greeted us. Outside, a mud-spattered mountain bike was propped against the wall by the door, wide panniers over its rear wheel giving it a cumbersome look.

'Tell me Bruce didn't ride all the way out here in this weather?' Maggie said.

Strachan smiled. 'He says it keeps him fit.'

'Bloody masochist,' she snorted. She held out her hand to Strachan. 'Pleasure to meet you again, Michael. If you change your mind . . .'

'I won't.' He smiled to soften the rejection. There was a glint of mischief in his eye. 'Perhaps if you ask him nicely Dr Hunter will give you an interview instead. I'm sure he enjoyed reading about himself in yesterday's paper.'

Her face coloured. She said nothing as we forged against the wind to where a rust-smeared old Mini was parked, looking like a poor relation next to Strachan's Saab and a black Porsche Cayenne I took to be Grace's.

Maggie was struggling out of her oversized red coat as I climbed into the car. 'The heater's stuck on full, so you'll cook if you keep your coat on,' she said, unceremoniously dumping hers on the back seat. The down-filled red fabric billowed obscenely, like a bag full of blood. I kept mine on. It had taken long enough for me to get it over my sling as it was.

Maggie scowled as she tried to start the car, tugging on the old-fashioned choke. 'Come on, you bloody thing,' she grumbled as the engine coughed and whined. 'It's my gran's, but she never uses it any more. Heap of junk, but handy when I come back.'

The car chugged into life. She scraped into gear and set off down the drive towards the road. I stared through the window at where the windswept moors were already beginning to disappear in the gathering gloom.

'Well, aren't you going to say it?' she said, suddenly.

'Say what?' I'd been so preoccupied thinking about what course the investigation would now take that I hadn't really noticed the silence. But Maggie had obviously misread it.

'That I lied on the ferry. When I told you I was a novelist.'

It took me a moment to realize what she was talking about. The pause seemed to make Maggie even more defensive.

'I'm a reporter, I was just doing my job. I don't have to apologize for it.'

'I didn't ask you to.'

She gave me an uncertain look. 'No hard feelings, then?'

I sighed. Under the brash act there was an appealing vulnerability. 'No hard feelings.'

She seemed relieved. The look of innocence I was coming to suspect spread over her features.

'So, off the record, what do you think happened out at the cottage?'

I laughed despite myself. 'You don't give up, do you?'

She grinned sheepishly. 'I was only asking. It was worth a try.'

The last of the reserve between us disappeared. I didn't have the energy to be angry. And by this time tomorrow she'd find herself with a far bigger story than she'd imagined. I felt a stab of guilt at the secret knowledge of the chaos I'd called down on this remote island. Runa didn't know it yet, but its peaceful existence was about to be shattered.

But even I had no idea just how shattering it would be.

10

After Maggie had dropped me back at the hotel, I'd gone looking for Ellen to apologize for running her car off the road. She'd waved away my apologies.

'Don't worry about that. The main thing is you're all right. More or less,' she'd added with a smile as she looked at my sling. 'Not everyone who gets lost out on these islands is so lucky.'

I didn't feel lucky as I flopped down on my bed. I felt tired and bruised, and my shoulder throbbed like toothache. I took a couple of the ibuprofen that Cameron had given me, and then tried once more to call Jenny on the hotel phone. There was still no answer from either her mobile or her flat.

I left messages on both, giving her the hotel number and asking her to call me. As I hung up I wondered where she could be. She should have been back from work now, and even if she was out she would have had her mobile with her.

Feeling flat and out of sorts, I went online to check my emails. I'd just finished replying to the last one when there was a knock on the bedroom door.

It was Fraser. He was still wearing his heavy coat, soaking wet and radiating cold from outside. He eyed my sling unsympathetically.

'Made it back all right this time, eh?'

There didn't seem much I could say to that. 'Have you spoken to Wallace?' I asked.

He gave a snort. 'The likes of me don't get to speak to superintendents. But he's passed word down the line, let's put it that way.' He regarded me sourly. 'So you're saying it's murder.'

I glanced along the hallway, but there was no one to hear. 'That's how it looks.'

He shook his head in disgust. 'The shit's really going to hit the fan now.'

'Are the remains OK?' I asked. I'd been worried about them lying out in the ruined cottage with only Duncan to watch over them.

'Oh, aye, they're peachy,' Fraser grumbled. 'I've had the station radioing every five minutes, yelling for me to make sure the site — sorry, "crime scene" now — is properly secured. You'd think we were guarding the crown jewels.'

I wasn't in the best of moods to start with, and his carping was beginning to wear thin. 'There've been enough mistakes made already.'

'Not by me,' he retorted. 'I just follow orders. Speaking of which, Wallace wants this kept quiet until the support team gets here tomorrow. So that means Mr ex-DI Brody'll have to be kept in the dark along with everyone else.'

There was a mean satisfaction in his voice. I didn't think there would have been any harm in letting Brody know, but that wasn't my decision. And I supposed everyone would find out soon enough.

Fraser was scowling. 'Going to be a bloody nightmare trying to run a murder inquiry out here. Still, can't see it being hard catching whoever did it.'

'You think so?'

He missed the irony in my voice and rolled his shoulders authoritatively, warming to his theme.

'Place this size, how hard can it be? Someone's got to know

something. And whoever killed her can't be the sharpest tool in the box. Surrounded by bloody sea and moorland, and he burns the body and leaves it where it can be found?' He gave a wheezing laugh. 'Aye, that's some genius, all right!'

I didn't feel so complacent. This had come close to being dismissed as an accidental death. Whether her killer was cunning or just lucky, we couldn't afford to take any more chances.

Duty done, Fraser bad-temperedly stomped off to take Duncan's supper out to the camper van. There was no reason for me to go with him, so I went back to my laptop, hoping to distract myself with work.

But my heart wasn't in it. The bedside cabinet made a poor desk, and the small room had started to crowd in on me like a monk's cell. As I stared blankly at the screen, I caught a faint scent of Grace Strachan's perfume on my clothes, and what little concentration I'd been able to muster vanished.

Closing my laptop with a snap, I took it downstairs. There was no point sitting in my room waiting for Jenny to call. If she did, Ellen would let me know.

It was still early and the bar was almost empty. The two old domino players sat at what was obviously their customary table. They gave cautious nods as I went in.

'Feasgar math,' one of them said, politely.

I said good evening in return, and they went back to their game as though I didn't exist. The only other person there was Guthrie, the big man who Brody had told me was the island's odd-job man, and Kinross's occasional helper on the ferry. He was slumped at the bar, staring morosely into his half-empty beer glass. The flush on his face told me he'd probably been there for some time already.

He gave me a baleful glance as I chalked up a whisky for myself on the slate, then went back to staring into his glass. I took my drink over to the table by the fire that I'd shared with first Brody and then Strachan two nights before.

Opening my laptop, I positioned it so no one else could see the screen, and called up the missing persons files I'd received from Wallace. I'd not had a chance to look at them yet, and though I doubted I'd find anything useful at this stage I'd nothing better to do right then.

Trails of smoke flowed sinuously across the peat slab in the hearth. Its dark surface glowed with traceries of fire, giving off a spiced, earthy fragrance. The heat made me drowsy. I rubbed my eyes and tried to focus my thoughts. But as I was about to open the first file, a shadow fell across the table.

I looked up to find the hulking figure of Guthrie looming over me. His gut hung over the low-slung trousers like a water-filled sack, but he was still a powerful man. The rolled sleeves of his sweater revealed hairless, beefy forearms, and the almost empty pint glass looked tiny in his wind-chapped hand.

''S that you got there?' he slurred. His face was slackened by alcohol, suffused with a beer and whisky blush. He gave off an odour of solder, oil and old sweat.

I closed the laptop. 'Just work.'

He blinked slowly, processing that. I remembered Brody telling me it was best to avoid him when he was drunk. *Too late.*

'Work?' he spat, flecking the table with spittle. He glared disdainfully at the laptop. 'That's not work. Work's what you do with these.'

He held up a balled fist in front of my face. It was the size of a baby's head, the fingers thickened with scar tissue.

'Work's getting your hands dirty. You ever get your hands dirty?'

I thought about sifting through the ashes of an incinerated body, or trying to exhume a corpse from frozen moorland. 'Sometimes.'

His lip curled. 'Bollocks. You don't know what work means. Like those bastards who took my boat. Sat behind their desks in their fucking banks, laying down the law! Never done a fucking day's work in their lives!'

110

'Why don't you sit down, Sean?' one of the old domino players said, gently. It didn't do any good.

'I'm just talking. Get back to your game,' Guthrie muttered sullenly. He glared down at me, swaying slightly. 'You're here with the police. For that body.' He made it sound like an accusation.

'That's right.' I was expecting him to ask who it was or how they'd died. Instead he surprised me.

'So what's on this, then?' he said, reaching for my laptop.

I put my own hand on top of it. My pulse had started to pound, but I kept my voice level.

'Sorry, it's private.'

I kept hold of the laptop, resisting the exploratory pressure he was exerting. Guthrie was easily strong enough to take it from me. He hadn't quite got to that point, but I could see his drink-addled mind turning over the possibility.

'I just want to take a look,' he said, and now the threat was heavy in his voice.

Even if I'd been fully fit I wouldn't have been any match for him. He was a good head taller than me, with the look of a brawler about him. But I was past caring. I'd had a bad enough twenty-four hours as it was.

And this was my work.

I pulled the laptop from his hand. 'I said no.'

My voice was unsteady, but it was from anger more than anything else. Guthrie's mouth had fallen open in surprise, but now it clamped shut. He balled his fists, and I felt my stomach tighten, knowing there was nothing I could do or say that would head off what was about to happen.

'Hey, you big lump, you causing trouble again?'

Maggie Cassidy had appeared in the doorway. She was heading straight for Guthrie, and I felt a moment of alarm as I saw how small she looked against his bulk. Then his face split in a huge grin.

'Maggie! Heard you were back!'

He enveloped her in a bear hug. She looked smaller than ever clutched in Guthrie's embrace.

'Aye, well, I thought I'd better look in and see how you were doing. Come on, put me down, you great oaf.'

They were both grinning now. Guthrie had forgotten about me already, the threat of barroom violence replaced with a childlike enthusiasm. Maggie prodded his bulging stomach, shaking her head in mock-regret.

'You been on a diet, Sean? You're practically wasting away.'

He roared with laughter. 'Pining for you, Mags. Will you have a drink with me?'

'Thought you'd never ask.'

Maggie gave me a quick wink as she led him to the bar, smiling a greeting at the domino players. My hand was trembling slightly as I raised the whisky glass, the adrenalin rush slowly beginning to fade. *Just what I needed to round the day off.*

The place was beginning to fill up now. Kinross and his eighteen-year-old son came in, joining Maggie and Guthrie at the bar. There were more friendly jibes and laughter. I watched how the cruel bumps of acne flared red on Kevin Kinross's face whenever Maggie spoke to him. He hardly took his eyes off her as she chatted to his father, but quickly dropped his gaze when she glanced his way.

Bruce Cameron wasn't the only one who was infatuated, I reflected.

Watching them all, warmly at ease with each other, I was suddenly acutely aware that I didn't belong. These were people who had been born and raised here, who would probably die within this same closed community. They shared an identity and kinship that overrode other ties. Even Maggie, who had left the island years before, was still a part of it in a way an outsider like me – or even 'incomers' like Brody and the Strachans – could never be.

And one of them was a killer. Perhaps even someone in this room. Looking at the faces in front of me, I recalled what Fraser had said about finding the dead woman's murderer. *Place this size, how hard can it be? Someone's got to know something.* But knowing and revealing were different things.

Whatever secrets Runa held, I didn't think it would give them up easily.

I didn't feel like staying downstairs any longer. But as I was about to go back to my room, Maggie caught my eye and excused herself from the group at the bar. I saw Kevin Kinross watching her furtively as she came over to my table. Then he realized I had seen him and hurriedly looked away.

Maggie plonked herself down and gave me a grin. 'You and Sean getting acquainted earlier, were you?'

'That's one way of putting it.'

'He's harmless enough. You must have rubbed him up the wrong way.'

I stared at her. 'How exactly did I do that?'

Maggie counted off on her fingers. 'You're a stranger, you're English, and you're sitting in the bar with a hi-tech laptop. If you wanted to blend into the woodwork you're going the wrong way about it, if you don't mind my saying.'

I gave a laugh. It was close enough to my own thoughts to strike home. 'And here's me thinking I was minding my own business.'

She smiled. 'Aye, well, Sean has been known to get a little tetchy when he's in his cups. But you can't altogether blame him. He used to be a good fisherman until the bank claimed back the loan on his boat. Now he's reduced to odd jobs and trying to fix up some old hulk he salvaged.' She sighed. 'Don't think too badly of him, that's all I'm saying.'

I could have pointed out that I hadn't been the one picking the argument, but I let it go. Maggie glanced at her watch.

'I'd best be off. My gran'll be wondering where I am. I only called in to show my face, and it's probably best if I make myself scarce before Sergeant Fraser shows up.'

She obviously wanted me to ask. And I'd been curious anyway, ever since their exchange on the ferry.

'So what is it between you two? Not an ex-boyfriend, I take it?'

'I'll pretend I didn't hear that,' she said, grimacing. 'Let's say there's a bit of a history between us. A couple of years ago the good sergeant was suspended for assaulting a woman suspect when he was drunk. The charges were dropped, but he was lucky not to be demoted. The *Gazette* found out and ran the story.'

She shrugged, but not as casually as she tried to make out.

'It was my first big story for the paper. So as you can imagine, I'm not exactly top of Fraser's Christmas card list.'

Her smile was part rueful, part proud as she went to rejoin Guthrie and Kinross. As she made her goodbyes, I left the bar and headed up to my room. I hadn't eaten since the omelette Grace had prepared, but I was more tired than hungry. And there was also a sneaking relief that Brody hadn't arrived yet. Wallace was within his rights not to let the retired inspector know about the murder, but after all his help I would have felt uncomfortable keeping it from him.

I felt bone-weary as I made my way upstairs. This trip had been a disaster from start to finish, but I consoled myself that it was about to get back on track. This time tomorrow SOC would be here, and the full machinery of a murder investigation would belatedly be under way. Before much longer I'd be on my way home, and able to put the entire thing behind me.

But I should have known not to take anything for granted. Because that night the storm hit Runa.

11

The storm reached the island just after midnight. Later, I would find out that it was actually two fronts that had collided off the coast of Iceland, playing out their battle as they swept down the North Atlantic from the Arctic. Their assault would be credited as one of the worst the Western Isles had experienced for over fifty years, creating gale force winds that left a trail of roofless houses and flooded roads before battering themselves out against the British mainland.

I was in my room when the storm hit. Tired as I was, I'd found it hard to sleep. Jenny hadn't called, and there was still no answer from either her flat or her mobile. That wasn't like her. I was starting to feel a gnawing anxiety that something could have happened. To make sleep even harder, the wind was booming outside, rattling the window angrily, and my shoulder was aching despite the anti-inflammatories I'd taken. Each time I started to drift off, I would feel myself falling down the gully and jerk awake again.

I was considering whether I should get up and try to work when the bedside phone rang. I snatched up the receiver.

'Hello?' I said, the word rushing out.

'It's me.'

Tension I hadn't even been aware of drained from me at the sound of Jenny's voice.

'Hi,' I said, switching on the bedside light. 'I've been calling you all day.'

'I know. I got your messages.' She sounded subdued. 'I went out with Suzy and a few of the others from work. I turned my mobile off.'

'Why?'

'I didn't want to speak to you.'

I waited, unsure what to say. A gust of wind wrapped itself round the house, its moan rising in pitch. The bedside lamp flickered as though in response.

'I was worried when you didn't call last night,' Jenny said after a moment. 'I couldn't call you on your mobile, and I didn't even know where you were staying. When I got your message this afternoon it was like . . . I don't know, I just felt angry. So I switched off my phone and went out. But then I came in just now and I really wanted to talk to you.'

'I'm sorry, I didn't mean to . . .'

'I don't want you to apologize! I want you here, not out on some bloody island! And I've had too much to drink, and that's your fault as well.'

There was a grudging smile in her voice. I was pleased to hear it, but it didn't displace the heaviness in my chest.

'I'm glad you called,' I told her.

'So am I. But I'm still pissed off with you. I'm missing you, and I've no idea when you're coming back.'

There was a note of fear now. Jenny had recovered from an experience that would have destroyed most people. While she'd emerged stronger from it, it had left a residue of anxiety that still surfaced from time to time. She knew only too well how thin the line was that separated everyday life from chaos. And how easily it was crossed.

'I'm missing you too,' I said.

The silence on the line seemed hollow, broken only by static whispers.

'You're not responsible for everyone, David,' Jenny said at last. 'You can't solve everyone's problems.'

I wasn't sure if it was resignation or regret I could hear. 'I don't try to.'

'Don't you? Seems like you do, sometimes. Other people's anyway.' She sighed. 'I think we need to talk when you get back.'

'What about?' I said, feeling something cold brush against my heart.

A crackle of static cut out her answer. It faded, but not completely.

'. . . still hear me?' I heard her say through it.

'Only just. Jenny? You still there?'

There was no answer. I tried calling her back, but there was no dialling tone.

The line was dead.

As though that had been its cue, the bedside lamp suddenly flickered. It steadied after a few seconds, but its light seemed dimmer than before. The phone lines obviously weren't the only things affected by the storm.

Feeling leaden and frustrated, I put the receiver down. Outside, the wind seemed to roar with triumph, flinging rain in reckless bursts against the window. I made my way over to it and looked out. The gale had shredded the cloud cover, and a full moon bathed the scene with ghostly pale light. The street lamp outside was shaking in the wind.

A girl was standing underneath it.

She seemed frozen, as though the fluctuating power had taken her unawares. Her face tilted up when I appeared in the window, and for a second or two we stared at each other. I didn't recognize her. She looked in her teens, and was wearing only a thin coat that offered no protection against the weather. Underneath it was what looked like

117

a pale nightgown. I saw how the cloth was lashed by the wind, how her wet hair clung to her head. She was blinking the water from her eyes as she stared up at me.

Then she darted into the shadows beyond the street light, heading into the village, and was gone.

Any hope I might have had that the storm would have passed by morning was snuffed out as soon as I woke. The wind shook the window, rain beating against the glass as though frustrated at not being able to break it.

The memory of the unfinished conversation I'd had with Jenny lay heavily on me, but the phone was still dead when I checked it. Until the landlines were repaired, the digital police radios were now our only point of contact with the outside world.

At least the power was still on, although the fitful way the lights were flickering suggested it might not remain so for much longer.

'One of the joys of living on an island, I'm afraid,' Ellen said, when I went down for breakfast. Anna was eating a bowl of cereal at the kitchen table, the portable gas fire filling the extension with pungent warmth. 'The phones are always likely to go off when we get a real storm. Electricity too, if it's a bad one.'

'How long are they usually off for?'

'A day or two, sometimes longer.' She smiled at my expression. 'Don't worry, we're used to it. Everyone on the island uses either oil or bottled gas, and the hotel's got its own back-up generator. We won't starve or freeze.'

'What's wrong with your arm?' Anna piped up, staring at my sling.

'I fell down.'

She thought about that for a second. 'You should watch where you're going,' she said, confidently, going back to her cereal.

'Anna,' Ellen chided, but I laughed.

'Yes, I suppose I should.'

I was still smiling as I went into the bar, my dark mood gone. So what if the phones were down for a day or two? It was an inconvenience, not life or death. Fraser was already eating through his breakfast, devouring a huge plate of fried eggs, bacon and sausage. He looked hungover but less so than he had on the previous mornings. No doubt the prospect of the support team's arrival had cramped his enthusiasm.

'Have you spoken to Duncan yet?' I asked as I sat down. I'd been wondering how the camper van would hold up in this wind. It wouldn't be very comfortable for him, to say the least.

'Aye, he's fine,' he grunted. He slid his radio across to me. 'The super wants you to call him.'

I felt my spirits sink, suddenly certain it wouldn't be good news. It wasn't.

'The storm's buggered everything,' Wallace said bluntly. The radio connection was so bad it sounded as though he were calling from the other side of the world. 'We're not going to be able to get SOC or anyone else out to you in this.'

Even though I'd half expected it, the news was a blow. 'How long before you can?'

His response was lost in a swell of static. I asked him to repeat it. 'I said I don't know. Flights and ferries to Stornoway are cancelled until further notice, and the weather report's not good for the next few days.'

'What about the coastguard helicopter?' I asked, knowing that it was sometimes used to airlift police teams to inaccessible islands.

'No chance. The storm's playing havoc with shipping, and they're not going to pull one from rescue duties for a corpse that's been dead a month already. And even if they could, the updraughts from Runa's cliffs cause problems for helicopters at the best of times. I daren't risk sending one in this. Sorry, but for the time being you're just going to have to sit tight.'

I massaged my temples, trying to ease the nagging headache that had started. Another buzz of static drowned out Wallace's next words.

'. . . given instructions to bring Andrew Brody in on this. I know he's retired, but he was SIO on two murder investigations. Until we can get more men on the ground out there, that sort of experience is going to be useful. Listen to what he tells you.' He paused. 'Do you understand what I'm saying?'

It was clear enough. I wouldn't have wanted Fraser left in charge either. I tried not to look across at the police sergeant as I handed him the radio.

He'd obviously already been told the news. He glowered at me as he stuffed the radio away, as if it were somehow my fault.

'Have you spoken to Brody yet?' I asked.

It was the wrong thing to say. Fraser stabbed his fork into a piece of bacon. 'It can wait till I've finished breakfast. And taken Duncan his.' His moustache worked as he chewed angrily. 'Not as though there's a rush any more, is it?'

Perhaps there wasn't, but I'd prefer Brody to hear sooner rather than later. 'I'll go and tell him.'

'Please yourself,' Fraser said, slicing through his egg as though trying to scar the plate.

He was still eating when I finished my own breakfast, making a point over taking his time. Leaving him to his sulk, I asked Ellen for directions to Brody's house, struggled into my coat and set off.

The wind staggered me as soon as I stepped outside. There seemed an almost hysterical quality to it as it shrieked and gusted, and by the time I reached the seafront my shoulder was hurting from the constant need to brace against it. Beyond the cliffs, the lonely outpost of Stac Ross was nearly obscured by white mist as the breakers dashed themselves against its base. In the harbour itself, boats thrashed against their moorings while the ferry was being flung against the concrete jetty, slamming against the truck tyres hung there with dull, percussive thuds.

Brody lived at the other side of the harbour. Keeping as far away as I could from the stinging spray, I made my way across the seafront. On the far side, the cliffs rose up from a small shingle beach, alongside which was a large corrugated metal shack. Tarpaulin-covered piles of building supplies were stacked nearby, and rotting hulks of old boats littered the yard around it. At one side a decrepit fishing boat was raised up on blocks for repair, its timber hull partly stripped away so that the curved spars of its frame resembled a skeletal ribcage. I guessed this was the old hulk Guthrie was repairing. If it was, he had his work cut out for him.

Brody's house was set well back from the harbour, a neat bungalow that had somehow avoided the uPVC modifications of its neighbours. I wondered if his dislike of Strachan had made him refuse the chance to have it renovated along with the rest.

When Brody opened the door he might almost have been expecting me. 'Come in.'

Inside smelled of cooking and pine disinfectant. The house was small and tidy, with a bachelor's lack of ornament. A gas fire hissed in the lounge's tiled fireplace. A photograph of a woman and girl took centre place on the mantelpiece. It didn't look recent, and I guessed that it was his wife and daughter.

The border collie looked up from its basket and wagged its tail when we walked in, then settled down to sleep again.

'Cup of tea?' Brody asked.

'No thanks. Sorry to call round like this, but the phones are out.'

'Aye, I know.'

He was wearing a thick cardigan. Standing in front of the fire, he tucked his hands into its pockets and waited.

'You were right. It was murder,' I said.

He took the news in his stride. 'You sure you should be telling me this?'

'Wallace wanted you to know.' I explained what I'd found, and what the superintendent had said. Brody smiled.

'Bet that went down well with Fraser.' But he quickly grew serious again. 'An accidental death's one thing, but this changes everything.

I suppose there's a chance that the killer isn't from the island, but it's pretty remote. The victim had to have had a reason for being on Runa, and my guess is he was it. How she got here doesn't matter for now. But I think we've got to assume the killer's local, and that the victim knew him.'

I'd already reached the same conclusion myself. 'I still can't understand why anyone would burn the body and leave it at the cottage instead of burying it or getting rid of it at sea,' I said. Unlike Fraser I couldn't believe the young woman's killer was just incompetent. 'Especially if the killer lives on Runa. Why leave it lying there for weeks until it was found?'

'Laziness or arrogance, perhaps. Or nerves. It takes a lot of guts to go back to a crime scene.' Brody shook his head in frustration. 'Christ, I wish Wallace had sent a full team out here when he had the chance. We might have had an ID on the victim by now. Finding out who killed her would be a whole lot easier if we knew who she was.'

'Isn't there anything we can do?'

He sighed. 'Just wait for the storm to lift, and hope that we can keep a lid on this until then. The last thing we want is for people to find out this is a murder inquiry before the mainland boys get here.'

I'd once been part of a community that had torn itself apart through fear and suspicion, and I'd no desire to repeat the experience. But it still didn't seem right to keep this from the islanders.

'Are you worried how they'll react?' I asked.

'Partly,' Brody agreed. 'Murder or not, island communities like this don't like outside interference. But I'm more worried about what the killer might do. At the moment he still thinks this is being written off as an accidental death, but if he finds out otherwise then all bets are off. And I'd rather not take any chances while there's only two police officers on the island.'

Letting that sink in, Brody absently patted the pockets of his cardigan.

'They're on the mantelpiece,' I told him.

He gave a shamefaced smile as he picked up the packet of cigarettes. 'I try not to smoke in the house. My wife used to hate it, and after fifteen years of marriage you end up ingrained. Like Pavlov's dogs.'

'Is that her and your daughter?' I asked, indicating the photograph.

He looked at it himself, unconsciously turning a cigarette in his fingers. 'Aye, that's Ginny and Rebecca. Becky would be . . . oh, about ten there. Her mother and I split up a year or so later. She ended up marrying an insurance broker.'

He gave a what-can-you-do shrug.

'What about your daughter?'

Brody didn't say anything for a moment. 'She's dead.'

The words were like a punch in the stomach. Fraser had said Brody's daughter had run away, but nothing else.

'I'm sorry. I didn't know,' I said awkwardly.

'No reason why you should. I don't have any proof myself. But I know she is. I can feel it.' He gave me a look. 'Wallace told me a little about you. You were a father yourself, so you know what I mean. It's part of you that's gone.'

I wasn't happy that Wallace had seen fit to tell him about my background. Even now, having other people talk about Kara and Alice's deaths felt like an intrusion. But at the same time, I knew what Brody meant.

'What happened?' I asked.

He looked down at the cigarette in his hand. 'We didn't get on. Becky always was rebellious. Headstrong. Like me, I suppose. I lost touch with her when her mother died. When I took early retirement I started searching for her. Bought the camper van, so I could save on hotel bills. Not that it did any good. I'm a policeman. Used to be a policeman,' he amended. 'I know how easy it is for someone to disappear. But I know how to look for them, as well. There comes a point when you know they aren't going to be found. Not alive, at least.'

123

'I'm sorry,' I said again.

'It happens.' Any emotion he felt was blanked from his face. He raised the cigarette. 'Don't mind, do you?'

'It's your house.'

He nodded, then with a smile put it back in the packet. 'I'll wait till I go out. Old habits, like I say.'

'Look, this might sound a bit . . . strange,' I began. 'But last night I saw a girl outside my hotel room. Must have been after midnight. Early or mid-teens, soaking wet, and just wearing a thin coat.'

Brody chuckled. 'Don't worry, you weren't seeing things. That'd be Mary Tait, Karen's daughter. You know, the loud-mouthed woman from the bar? I think I mentioned her girl's a bit . . . Well, in the old days we'd say "retarded", but I know that's not the word to use now. Her mother lets her run wild. You see her out all times of the day and night, wandering all over the island.'

'And nobody says anything?'

'She's harmless enough.'

'That wasn't what I meant.' Mentally handicapped or not, physically the girl was an adult. She would be easy prey for anyone who was prepared to exploit that.

'No,' Brody agreed. 'I've thought about contacting the social services. But I don't think anyone on Runa would hurt her. They know what'd happen to them if they did.'

I thought about the woman's body out at the cottage. 'Are you sure about that?'

Brody inclined his head. 'Fair point. Perhaps I'd better—'

He broke off as there was a knock on the door. The old border collie pricked up its ears, giving a low growl.

'Shush, Bess,' he said, going to answer it.

There were voices. A moment later Brody returned. With him was Fraser, looking wet and unhappy. The sergeant shook water off his arms.

'We've got a problem.'

★

Duncan was waiting anxiously outside the camper van when we arrived. It was much more exposed out here, away from the shelter of houses and cliffs. The wind seemed to gather pace, flattening the grass as it hurled itself down the side of Beinn Tuiridh and across the dark peat moors.

The constable hurried over to the car as we climbed out. The wind pressed our coats against us, threatening to snatch the car door from my hand when I opened it.

'I radioed as soon as it happened,' he said, having to almost shout to make himself heard. 'I heard it go about half an hour ago.'

By that time we could see for ourselves. The gale had ripped a section of the cottage roof clean off. What was left was hanging precariously, creaking and shifting as the wind tried to finish the job. If the woman's remains were still intact inside, they wouldn't be for much longer.

'I'm sorry,' Duncan said, as though he'd let us down.

'Not your fault, son,' Brody told him, giving his shoulder a pat. 'Call DS Wallace and let him know we've got a situation here. Tell him we've got to get the remains out before the rest of the roof comes down.'

Duncan glanced uncertainly at Fraser, who gave a reluctant nod. As the PC took out his radio, the rest of us headed for the cottage. The incident tape that sealed the doorway was still in place, thrumming in the wind, but the door itself lay on the floor of what had been the kitchen. Shattered roof tiles were scattered everywhere, and rain fell freely through the gaping hole. We all ducked as another tile was ripped away.

Duncan came hurrying back over, shaking his head. 'Can't reach him. I've spoken to the station in Stornoway, and they're going to try to get word through.'

Brody looked at the mess inside the cottage. Rain ran unheeded down his face as he turned to me.

'We don't have any choice, do we?'

'No,' I said.

He gave a nod, then strode forward and began tearing the incident tape from the doorway.

'What the hell are you doing?' Fraser demanded.

'Getting the remains out before the roof comes down,' Brody answered without stopping.

'This is a crime scene! You can't do that without clearance!'

Brody ripped the last of the tape free. 'No time for that.'

'He's right,' I told Fraser. 'We need to salvage what we can.'

'I'm not taking responsibility for this!' Fraser protested.

'Nobody asked you to,' Brody said, going inside.

I went after him, picking my way across the broken tiles that littered the kitchen floor. The inner room where the remains lay wasn't as badly damaged, but almost half of the roof had fallen in. The floodlight lay smashed on its side while the grid was now a tangle of knotted string. Rain had turned the ashes on the floor to a puddle of black slurry.

The evidence bags of ash and bones I'd collected before I'd broken off my examination were sitting in pools of water, but otherwise looked unharmed.

'Let's get the bags out of here,' I told Brody. 'I'll need my flight case from the camper van.'

'I'll get it,' Duncan offered from the doorway.

I hadn't realized he'd followed us in. There was no sign of Fraser.

'Take as many bags with you as you can carry,' I told him. I flinched as a sudden gust of wind made the surviving roof creak above us. 'And hurry.'

As Brody and Duncan took the evidence bags out to the camper van, I turned my attention to the rest of the remains. There was something infinitely sad about a life reduced to this, a few carbonized fragments about to be sluiced away by the elements. At least the photographs I'd taken when I'd first arrived would provide a visual record. It wasn't much, but it was better than nothing.

When Duncan returned with my flight case I wrestled a pair of overalls on over my sling, then pulled on a surgical glove and hurried over to the body. Working as fast as I could, I put the skull and jawbone into evidence bags and began collecting up the fragments of cranium and loose teeth from the floor.

I'd only just finished when the roof gave a groan. A tile fell to shatter on the floor only a few feet from me.

'I think you need to hurry,' Brody said from the doorway.

'I am.'

All at once the wind seemed to still. A sudden quiet descended, broken only by the cascade of rain on to the floor.

'Sounds like it's easing,' Duncan said, hopefully.

But Brody had his head cocked to listen. There was a distant rushing sound, like a train roaring towards us.

'No, it's changed direction,' he said, and then the wind slammed into the cottage again.

I was sprayed with ash and slurry as it seemed to descend right into the room. Above us, the roof responded with a groan of protesting timbers, sending tiles tumbling to the floor.

'Let's go,' Brody shouted above the din, shoving Duncan towards the doorway.

'Not yet,' I yelled. I still hadn't bagged the surviving hand or feet, and we needed those for fingerprint and soft tissue analysis. But before I could do anything there was a loud bang as the roof began to rip free.

'Move!' Brody shouted. I made a grab for the hand as he pulled me to my feet.

'The flight case!' I yelled.

Brody snatched it up without stopping. Debris rained down around us as we ran back through the kitchen. From behind us there was an almighty crash, and for a heart-stopping instant I thought the whole place was coming down. Then we were outside and in the clear.

Breathless, we turned and looked back. The whole of the cottage roof had gone. Part of it had been torn clean off, while the rest had fallen in, bringing down most of one wall as well. The room where we'd been standing only seconds before was now buried under rubble.

Along with the rest of the dead woman's remains.

Fraser and Duncan were standing nearby, their faces shocked.

'Jesus Christ,' breathed Fraser, staring at me.

I looked down at myself. My white overalls were splashed and covered with wet ash. I could feel it on my face, smearing it like a penitent's at Easter. But it wasn't that he'd been staring at.

Still clutched in my fist, like part of a showroom dummy, was the dead woman's hand.

12

We took the evidence bags back to the village. The only other option was leaving them in the camper van, but while the bone and ashes could have been stored there the woman's hand needed to be kept at a low temperature to preserve the decaying tissue. And the camper van didn't have a fridge.

It was Duncan who thought of the medical clinic. We would have to clear it with Cameron, and probably Strachan as well, since he'd funded it. But now we'd had no choice but to remove the remains from the crime scene, it was the obvious place to take them.

Fraser was still grumbling. He made it plain that he was absolving himself of any involvement in what we'd done.

'I didn't say you could do this,' he reminded us, as we loaded the evidence bags into the Range Rover. 'This was your call, not mine.'

'You'd rather we'd left them in there then, would you?' Brody asked, jerking his head towards the roofless cottage. 'Explain to SOC that we'd stood by and watched the body be buried under the rubble?'

'I'm just letting you know I'm not taking the blame for it. You can tell Wallace yourself.'

We still hadn't been able to contact the superintendent. I could almost – though not quite – feel sorry for Fraser. Behind the bluster was a man desperate not to admit he was out of his depth.

'Oh, don't worry. I will.' Brody spoke mildly enough, yet somehow managed to make his contempt plain. 'And seeing how you're washing your hands of it, you might as well relieve Duncan out here. He can clean himself up at my place after he's helped take the bags to the clinic.'

'Stay out here?' Fraser barked, incredulously. 'What for? There's nothing left!'

Brody shrugged. 'It's still a crime scene. But if you want to explain to Wallace why you left it unattended, that's up to you.'

Duncan had been listening, uneasily. 'I don't mind staying.'

'You've been on duty all night,' Brody said, before Fraser could respond. 'I'm sure Sergeant Fraser wouldn't ask a junior officer to do anything he's not prepared to do himself.'

The expression on Fraser's face was poisonous. 'Aye, all right.' He jabbed a finger at Duncan. 'But I want you back no later than six. You'll be staying out here again tonight.'

He shot Brody a triumphant look.

'Can't leave a crime scene unattended, can we?'

I saw the older man's prominent jaw muscles bunch, but he said nothing as Fraser stalked off to the camper van. He gave the still worried-looking Duncan a smile.

'Come on, son. You could do with a shower, if you don't mind my saying.'

I went in the Range Rover with Duncan, while Brody followed in his own car. It was a relief to get out of the wind and rain. My shoulder was hurting, probably jarred as I'd hurried out of the cottage. I put my head back and closed my eyes, and the next thing I knew Duncan was waking me.

'Dr Hunter? Should I stop for her?'

I sat up, blinking. Ahead of us the Porsche Cayenne I'd seen at Strachan's house was pulled to the side of the road. Flagging us down from beside it, unmistakable in her white parka, was Grace.

'Yes, you'd better.'

The wind was whipping her hair as we pulled up alongside. I wound down my window.

'David, thank heavens!' she said, giving me a beaming smile. 'This is a dreadful bore, but I was just on my way to the village and the bloody car's run out of petrol. Would you mind giving me a lift?'

I hesitated, thinking about the evidence bags visible behind the rear seat. By now Brody had pulled up behind us, the road being too narrow to allow him to pass. I considered suggesting she ride with him, but given the frosty relationship Brody had with her husband I thought better of it.

'If it's a problem I'll walk,' Grace said, her smile fading.

'It's no problem,' I said, and turned to Duncan. 'Is that OK by you?'

He grinned. 'Aye, great.' It was the first time he'd seen Strachan's wife. 'I mean, sure, no problem.'

I went to sit in the back, letting Grace have the front seat despite her protests. The delicate musk of her perfume filled the car, and I tried not to smile when I saw that Duncan was sitting noticeably straighter.

Grace gave him a dazzling smile when I introduced them. 'You must be the young man they've got staying in the camper van.'

'Uh, yes, ma'am.'

'Poor you,' she said, sympathetically touching his arm. Even from the back seat I could see Duncan's ears turn crimson. I don't think Grace even realized the effect she had on him. She turned round to talk to me as Duncan tried to concentrate on driving.

'Thanks ever so much for stopping. I feel so stupid, running out of petrol like that. There's no garage on the island, so we have to top up from containers. But I'm sure Michael said he'd filled up the cars last week. Or was it the week before?' She puzzled over it for a second, then airily dismissed it. 'Oh, well. Teach me to check the gauge in future, I suppose.'

'Where would you like us to drop you?' I asked.

'At the school, if that's no bother. I'm taking a painting class this morning.'

'Will Bruce Cameron be there?'

'I should think so. Why?'

Without going into details, I explained what had happened at the cottage, and why we needed to use the clinic.

'God, how gruesome,' Grace said with a grimace. 'Still, I'm sure Bruce won't mind.'

I wasn't so confident, but I couldn't see Cameron refusing her. When we reached the school Grace hurried inside, while I left Duncan guarding the remains and went to tell Brody what was happening.

'This should be interesting,' he said, climbing out of the car.

We went up the path to the school. It was a new building, small and flat-roofed. A few wooden steps ran up to the door, which opened straight into a classroom that took up most of the interior. Computer monitors lined one wall, and desks were arranged in neat lines facing a board at the front.

But at the moment the pupils were all gathered round a large table at the back, busying themselves with pots of paint, brushes and water. There were about a dozen in all, their ages ranging from about four to nine or ten. I recognized Anna amongst them. She smiled shyly when she saw me, then returned to arranging a sheet of paper exactly to her liking.

Grace had already taken off her coat and was busy organizing her class. 'I hope we're not going to have another water-spilling crisis this week, are we? And yes, I'm looking at you, Adam.'

'No, Mrs Strachan,' a young boy with a shock of ginger hair said, smiling bashfully.

'Good. Because if anyone misbehaves, I'm afraid they'll have to

132

have their face painted. And we wouldn't want to have to explain that to your parents, would we?'

There were delighted giggles, a chorus of, 'No, Mrs Strachan.' Grace looked animated and alive, even more beautiful than usual. Cheeks flushed, she turned to us with a smile, motioning with her head to a door at the far side.

'Go on through. I've told Bruce you wanted a word.'

She turned back to the children as we crossed the room, already forgetting about us. The office door was closed, and when I knocked on it there was no answer. I began to wonder if Cameron had slipped out until his bass voice peremptorily drawled a command.

'Come.'

Glancing at Brody, I opened the door and went in. A desk and filing cabinet took up most of the room. Cameron was standing with his back to us, staring out of the window. I wondered if he'd done it for effect, knowing he was backlit. He turned and favoured us with an unfriendly look.

'Yes?'

I reminded myself this would be easier if we had his cooperation. 'We need to use the medical clinic. The storm brought down the cottage roof, and we need somewhere to store what we salvaged.'

The bulbous eyes considered us, coldly. 'You mean you want to keep human remains in there?'

'Only until they can be taken to the mainland.'

'And in the meantime what about my patients?'

Brody spoke up. 'Come on, Bruce. You only hold a clinic twice a week, and the next one isn't for another two days. We should be out of the way long before then.'

Cameron wasn't appeased. 'So you say. But what if there's an emergency?'

'This *is* an emergency,' Brody snapped, losing patience. 'We're not here from choice.'

The teacher's Adam's apple bobbed angrily. 'There must be somewhere else you can take them.'

'If you can think of anywhere feel free to tell us.'

'And if I say no?'

Brody regarded him with exasperation. 'Why should you do that?'

'Because it's a medical clinic, not a morgue! And I don't think you have any right to commandeer it!'

I opened my mouth to object, but before I could Grace's voice came from behind us.

'Is there a problem?'

She stood in the doorway, one eyebrow cocked quizzically. Cameron blushed like a schoolboy caught out by his teacher.

'I was just telling them—'

'Yes, I heard you, Bruce. So did the rest of the class.'

Cameron's Adam's apple worked. 'I'm sorry. But I don't really think the medical clinic should be used for something like this.'

'Why ever not?'

'Well . . .' Cameron was visibly squirming. He gave her an ingratiating smile. 'I am the nurse after all, Grace. I ought to be able to decide what happens in my own clinic.'

Grace regarded him coolly. 'Actually, Bruce, it belongs to the island. I'm sure I don't have to remind you of that.'

'No, of course, but—'

'So unless you can suggest somewhere else they can use, I don't really see that there's an alternative.'

Cameron made an effort to hold on to his tattered dignity. 'Well . . . in that case, I suppose . . .'

'Good. That's settled, then.' Grace gave him a smile. 'Now why don't you run over there and show them where everything is? I'll look after things here until you get back.'

Cameron stared down at his desk as she went back to her class. The flush had gone from his face, leaving him white and tight-lipped. Grace might help him out at the school, but he'd just had a public reminder that it was her husband's money that paid his wages. Wordlessly, he snatched his coat down from where it was hanging and walked out.

'I'd have paid to see that,' Brody said in a low voice, as we went after him.

The medical clinic was a short distance from the school. It was little more than a small extension tacked on to one end of the community centre, with no external door of its own. Cameron had ridden there on his mountain bike, forging against the wind. By the time we arrived he was already going into the glassed-in porch that covered the community centre's entrance. Leaving Duncan in the car with the evidence bags, Brody and I followed him inside.

The community centre looked like a throwback to the Second World War, a long wooden structure with a low asphalt roof and panelled windows. Most of the inside was taken up by a large hall. Our footsteps echoed hollowly on its unvarnished floorboards, on which the ghostly markings of a badminton court had faded almost to invisibility. Posters advertising dances and the now-past Christmas pantomime were pinned to the walls, and old wooden chairs were stacked untidily at one side. The island's redevelopment evidently hadn't extended this far.

'Strachan wanted to build a new community centre, but everyone liked this as it is,' Brody said, guessing what I was thinking. 'Familiarity, I suppose. People like some things to stay the same.'

Cameron had stopped by a new-looking door and was searching irritably through a jangling key ring. While we waited, I went to a scuffed upright piano that stood nearby. The lid was raised, exposing ivory keys that were cracked and yellow with age. When I pressed one a deep, broken note rang out, fading discordantly into silence.

'Would you mind not doing that?' Cameron said waspishly, unlocking the door and going into the clinic.

It was only small, but well equipped, with pristine white walls and shining steel cabinets. There was an autoclave for sterilizing

135

instruments, a well-stocked medicine cabinet and a fridge. Best of all, from my point of view, was the large stainless steel trolley and powerful halogen lamp. There was even a large magnifying lens on an adjustable stand, for examining and stitching wounds.

Cameron had gone to a desk and was making a point of checking that its drawers were locked. Brody and I watched as he did the same with the filing cabinet. That finished, he confronted us with ill-concealed dislike.

'I expect you to leave everything exactly as you found it. I've no intention of cleaning up any mess you make.'

Without waiting for us to answer he started to leave.

'We'll need the key,' Brody said.

Tight-lipped, Cameron unhooked one from the bunch he carried and slapped it down on the desk.

'What about one for the community centre?' I asked.

'We don't keep it locked,' he responded primly. 'It belongs to everyone on the island. That's why it's called the *community* centre.'

'I'd still prefer to have a key.'

He gave a condescending smile. 'Well, that's too bad. Because if there is one I've no idea where it is.'

He seemed to take a petty satisfaction from being able to deny us that much, at least. Brody watched him go out.

'That man is a royal pain in the arse.'

I'd been thinking along the same lines myself. 'Come on, let's get the evidence bags inside,' I said.

I had an unpleasant conversation with Wallace while Brody and Duncan carried the evidence bags of bone and ashes into the clinic. Word had belatedly reached the detective superintendent that we'd been trying to contact him. Unfortunately, he'd called Fraser rather than Duncan, and the sergeant had lost no time in giving his side of events.

Consequently, Wallace was incandescent, demanding to know why we'd violated a crime scene without his permission. In no mood to be shouted at, I angrily pointed out that we'd had no choice, and that none of this would have happened if he'd sent SOC in the first place.

It was Brody who calmed things down, taking the radio to talk to Wallace out of earshot. When he handed it back to me, the superintendent was grudgingly apologetic. He told me to go ahead and continue my examination of the remains.

'I suppose now you've got this far, you might as well see what else you can find out,' he said, ungraciously.

The gesture was little more than an olive branch, as we both knew there was precious little I could do without a properly equipped laboratory. But I said I'd do my best. Before Wallace hung up, I asked what the situation was with the train crash. I'd not heard any news since I'd been on Runa, and I was out of touch.

The superintendent paused. 'It was joyriders. They stalled the van on the line and then panicked and ran off.'

Not a terrorist attack after all, then. People had died, and SOC prevented from coming to Runa, all because some bored teenagers had stolen a van.

I was thinking about that as I returned to the clinic. Duncan was gingerly putting the dead woman's hand into the fridge, holding it out at arm's length. In the plastic of the evidence bag, it looked unsettlingly like a cut of meat for the freezer.

'Still can't get my head round how this happened,' he said, closing the fridge door with relief. 'How the body was burned, I mean. Just doesn't seem natural.'

'Oh, it was natural, right enough,' I said, still brooding over what Wallace had said.

Both Duncan and Brody looked at me.

'You know what caused it?' Brody asked.

I'd known almost from the moment I set eyes on the remains. But I hadn't wanted to commit myself until I'd been able to confirm my theory. Now, though, with the island cut off and half of the evidence buried under the cottage, there didn't seem any reason not to tell them.

'Pretty much,' I said. 'I gave you a clue the other day, Duncan, remember?'

'The fatty stuff on the cottage ceiling, you mean? Aye, but I still haven't been able to work it out.'

He looked embarrassed. Brody was watching me, waiting.

'It comes down to two things. Body fat and what she was wearing,' I explained. 'Have either of you heard of something called the wick effect?'

They both looked blank.

'There are two ways to reduce a human body to ash. You either incinerate it at a very high temperature, which didn't happen here or the entire cottage would have burned down. Or you burn it at a lower temperature, for longer. We've all got a layer of fat just under the skin, and fat burns. Candles used to be made of tallow made from rendered animal fat before paraffin wax was used instead. So what happens is that, in certain conditions, the human body effectively becomes a giant candle.'

'You're joking,' Brody said. For once the ex-policeman seemed rattled.

'No. That's why the residue on the ceiling and ground around the remains was significant. The fat liquefies in the heat and gets carried in the smoke. Obviously, the more body fat a person has, the more fuel there is to burn. Judging from how much was on the ceiling at the cottage, the dead woman had quite a lot.'

'So she was overweight?' Duncan asked.

'I'd say so, yes.'

Brody's forehead was furrowed. 'I don't see where what she was wearing comes in.'

'Because as the fat melts, it soaks into the clothes. They act like a candle wick, letting the body burn for much longer than it would otherwise. Particularly if they're made from a flammable fabric.'

Brody still looked shaken. 'Christ. That's a hell of an image.'

'I know, but it's what happens. Most cases of so-called spontaneous human combustion happen to people who are elderly or drunk. There's nothing suspicious or paranormal about it. They just drop a cigarette on themselves, or brush too close to a fire and set themselves alight, and are either asleep or incapable of putting out the flames. Like Mary Reeser,' I said to Duncan. 'She's the classic case that's always cited as being "inexplicable". But she was elderly, overweight, and a smoker. According to the police report, the last person to see her was her son. She'd just taken sleeping tablets, and was sitting in the armchair in her nightgown – both of which would have acted as wicks – smoking a cigarette.'

Duncan pondered that for a moment. 'Aye, but why wasn't anything else damaged by the fire? And why didn't all the body burn up?'

'Because even when there's a lot of body fat to act as fuel, human tissue doesn't burn particularly hotly. You get a slow-burning fire that's intense enough to consume the body, but not ignite anything else. Again, think of a candle – it melts as the wick burns, but doesn't damage whatever's nearby. As for why the hands and feet sometimes survive . . .'

I held out my hand, pulling back my sleeve to expose my wrist.

'They're mainly skin and bone. There's hardly any fat on them. And they're generally not covered by fabric like the torso, so there's nothing to act as a wick. Hands sometimes get burned just because they're near the body, unless the arms are outflung. But the feet and sometimes the shins are often far enough removed from the fire to survive. Like they were here. She was lying on one hand, so it got burned along with the rest. But the other hand, and her feet, survived.'

Brody rubbed his chin thoughtfully, hand rasping on the whiskers that were already showing through. 'You think this "wick effect" was intentional? That somebody did it deliberately?'

'I doubt it. It's not something you can easily stage. I've never even heard of it happening in a murder before. All the recorded incidents have been with accidental deaths, which was another reason I was slow to chalk this one up as suspicious. No, I think whoever did this probably just wanted to destroy any incriminating evidence they might have left on the body. I'd guess he used a small amount of petrol or some other accelerant to start the fire — not much or the ceiling in the cottage would have been more scorched than it was — then dropped a match on to the body and got out.'

The furrows on Brody's forehead had deepened. 'Why didn't the killer torch the entire cottage?'

'I've no idea. Perhaps he was worried that might attract too much attention. Or he hoped it would look more like an accident this way.'

They were silent as they considered that. Finally Duncan spoke.

'Was she dead?'

I'd spent time wondering about that myself. There had been no sign that the woman had moved around after she was set on fire, no evidence of her trying to put out the flames. The blow that had cracked her skull would at the very least have left her unconscious, and perhaps even comatose. But dead?

'I don't know,' I said.

The walls of the clinic shook under the gale's onslaught. Somehow the sound seemed only to heighten the silence after they'd gone. I pulled on one of my last remaining pairs of surgical gloves. There was an almost full box of them in one of the cupboards, but I didn't want to use them unless I had to. Cameron was tetchy enough without my helping myself to his supplies.

There wasn't much I could do without proper facilities, but now that Wallace had given me permission to examine the remains we'd salvaged there was one thing I wanted to try.

Brody had put his finger on it when he'd said the inquiry was hamstrung until the victim had been identified. Once we knew who she was, it might throw light on who had killed her. Without that information, trying to find her killer would be like groping in the dark.

I hoped I might be able to do something about that.

Taking the skull from its evidence bag, I gently set it on the stainless steel trolley. Blackened and cracked, it lay canted on the cold surface. The empty eye sockets gaped blankly into eternity. I wondered what the eyes they'd once held had looked on not so very long ago. A lover? A husband? A friend? How often had she laughed, unknowing, as the seconds ticked away the last days and hours of her existence? And what had she seen when that realization, finally and irrevocably, made itself known to her?

Whoever she was, I felt an odd sense of intimacy towards her. I knew almost nothing about her life, but her death had pulled me into her orbit. I had seen her history written in her charred bones, noted each year's passing in every bump and scar. She had been laid bare in a way even those who had known her would have never recognized.

I tried to remember if I used to feel like this in the past, on the cases I'd worked before Kara and Alice had been killed. I didn't think so. That seemed an age away now, part of a different life. A different David Hunter. Somewhere along the line, and perhaps due to my own loss, I seemed to have lost the detachment I'd once had. I wasn't sure if that was good or bad, but the truth was I no longer saw the dead woman as an anonymous victim. That was why she'd visited me in my dream, waited expectantly at the foot of my bed. I felt a responsibility towards her. It wasn't something I'd anticipated, or even wanted.

But I couldn't turn away from it.

'OK, tell me who you are,' I said, quietly.

13

For a forensic anthropologist, teeth are a repository of information. They're an enduring bone interface, a bridge between the hidden skeleton and the world beyond the body. As well as revealing race and age, they form a record of an individual's life. Our diet, habits, class, even our self-esteem, can all be gleaned from these chunks of calcium and enamel.

I took the lower jawbone from its evidence bag and laid it on the stainless steel trolley beside the broken cranium. It was as light and fragile as balsa. Under the bright halogen light, the disparate sections of the skull looked like an anatomical pastiche, far removed from anything that had once been alive.

At some point I would have to finish the job I'd tentatively started in the cottage, and piece together the shattered skull fragments I'd managed to salvage. But right now what I needed to do was try to put a face and name to the victim's burned remains.

With luck, her teeth might be the key to that.

Not that I was overly optimistic. While a few back molars remained stubbornly in place in the jawbones, most of the teeth had fallen out when the fire had first burned away the gums, then desiccated the roots. Grey and cracked by the heat, the ones I'd managed to snatch up before the cottage roof collapsed looked like fossilized remnants of something long dead.

I'd found that, even with my arm in the sling, I could still use my left hand to hold or support things. It made life a little easier as I spread a sheet of paper on the table and began arranging the teeth on it in two parallel rows, one for the upper jaw, one for lower. One by one, I laid them out in the order they would have been in the mouth, with the two central incisors in the middle, the lateral incisors next to them, followed by the canines, premolars and then the large molars themselves. It wasn't a straightforward task. As well as damage from the fire, the woman's teeth were so badly eroded it was difficult to determine whether some of them were from the upper or lower jaw, or even what type of tooth they actually were.

Everything outside the clinic ceased to exist as I worked. The world shrank down to the circle of light from the halogen lamp. I took more photographs and sketched out a post-mortem odontogram; a dental chart detailing each crack, cavity or filling in every tooth. Under normal circumstances I would have taken X-rays of the teeth and jaws so that they could be compared with dental records of potential victims. That wasn't an option now, so I did the only thing I could.

I began to fit the teeth back into the empty sockets.

Even using my left hand as much as the sling allowed, it was slow work. I'd lost track of how much time had passed when the lamp suddenly flickered. As though synchronized, a gust of wind rattled against the building, thrumming its structure like a bass note felt rather than heard.

I straightened, groaning as my back muscles protested. God, I ached all over. As though it had only been waiting for me to take notice of it, my shoulder started throbbing. The wall clock told me it was almost five o'clock. It had grown dark outside, I saw. Massaging my back, I looked at the skull and jawbone as they lay on the steel trolley. After a few false starts, I'd fitted most of the teeth back into them. There were only a couple of molars and premolars left, and they wouldn't affect what I had in mind. I was reaching out to turn off the lamp when I heard a noise from the community centre.

The creak of a floorboard.

'Hello?' I called.

My voice echoed in the cold air. I waited, but there was no answer. I went to the door and took hold of the handle. But I didn't turn it.

Suddenly, I felt certain someone was on the other side.

The clinic seemed unnaturally quiet. The door into the community centre had a round window set in it, like a porthole. There was a Venetian blind on my side, but I hadn't bothered to lower it.

Now I wished I had. The hall beyond was in darkness. Anyone in there would be able to see into the clinic, but on my side the window was a circle of impenetrable black. I listened, hearing only the wind rushing outside. The silence was like a solid weight, poised ready to break.

I felt the back of my neck prickle. I looked down at my hand, saw the hairs standing up on it.

This is stupid. There's nothing there. I tightened my grip on the door handle, but still didn't turn it. There was a heavy glass paperweight on the desk. I picked it up, holding it awkwardly as I stooped down to take hold of the door handle with my strapped hand. *Ready . . .*

I threw open the door and pawed for the light switch. I couldn't find it, but then there was a click and the lights came on.

The empty hall mocked me. I lowered the paperweight. The doors to the hall, and the glassed-in entrance porch beyond it, were closed. The noise must have been the building creaking in the wind. *You're turning into a nervous wreck.* I was about to go back into the clinic when I looked down at the floor.

Tracking across it was a trail of wet footprints.

'You're sure you didn't make them?'

Brody was considering the slowly drying puddles on the worn floorboards. The water had run too much to gauge what size shoe or boot had made them, but their path was clear enough. They ran from the community centre entrance across to the clinic door, stopping in front of the glass porthole. A pool had formed below it, where someone had stood while they'd watched me.

'Certain. I hadn't been outside since I arrived,' I told him.

Brody and Duncan had arrived while I'd still been debating what to do about the tracks, the young PC looking fresh-faced after a shave and a shower. Now Brody followed the trail to where it had pooled in front of the clinic door. He stared through the glass panel.

'Somebody got a good look at what you were doing.'

'Cameron, perhaps? Or Maggie Cassidy?'

'It's possible, but I can't see it. And I don't think any of the locals would sneak in like this, either.'

'You think it was the killer?'

Brody nodded slowly. 'I think it's something we have to consider. Bringing the remains here is bound to rattle him, let alone having a forensic expert examining them. What worries me is what he might decide to do about it.'

It wasn't a comforting thought. Brody let it hang there for a few seconds.

'I think I'll feel happier if we could lock the community centre tonight anyway,' he went on. 'The general store sells chain and padlocks. We could get something from there to make this place a bit more secure, at least. Can't see any point in taking chances.'

Neither could I, when he put it like that. Businesslike again, Brody nodded towards where the skull was lying on the steel table.

'Intruders aside, how have you been getting on?'

'Slowly. I've been trying to find some clue as to who she is.'

'Can you do that from what's left?' Brody asked, surprised.

'I don't know. But I can try.'

I went over to where the cranium lay on the trolley, switching on the halogen lamp as Brody and Duncan came to look.

'The condition of her teeth is interesting. They've been cracked by the heat, but they were pretty rotten to begin with. Hardly any of them have fillings, and those that are there are all quite old. She obviously hadn't been to a dentist for years, which suggests she was probably from a deprived social background. You're more likely to look after your teeth if you're middle class. And her teeth weren't just bad; some of them were almost eroded down to the gum. In someone this young, that's a strong sign of heavy drug use.'

'You think she was an addict?' Brody asked.

'I'd say so.'

Duncan looked up. 'I thought most addicts were skinny. Didn't you say this wick effect meant she was overweight?'

It was an astute comment. 'She probably had more body fat than average, yes. But a lot depends on metabolism and how heavily she was using. It doesn't mean she didn't have a drug habit. But there's something else as well. Do you remember why I said her feet hadn't burned?'

'Not enough flesh on them?' Duncan offered.

'And no fabric to act as a wick. She had on training shoes, but no stockings or tights. Or socks, come to that. I'd guess she was wearing something like a skirt and jacket or a short coat. Cheap flammable fabric, probably, that would make a good wick.'

I looked at the remains of the skull, saddened by the brutal way we were dissecting a life. But it was the only way we would catch whoever had done this to her.

'So we've got a young woman who was a serious drug user, who'd let herself go enough for her teeth to rot, and who was skimpily dressed and bare-legged in February,' I went on. 'What does that suggest to you about her lifestyle?'

'She was a prostitute,' Duncan said, this time with more conviction.

Brody rubbed his chin thoughtfully. 'Only one reason a working girl would have come all the way out here.'

'You mean to see a client?' I said.

'I'm hard pushed to think of another reason. Ties in with what we already thought about her knowing her killer. And it'd explain why no one seems to have known she was on the island. Men who pay for sex don't usually advertise the fact.'

But something about that didn't seem quite right to me. 'Even so, it's a hell of a long way for a home visit. And why risk bringing a prostitute out to Runa if you were worried about people finding out? It'd make more sense to go to her rather than bring her out here.'

Brody looked thoughtful. 'There's another possibility. She wouldn't be the first prostitute to try and blackmail a client. Given her drug habit, she might have thought it was worth the trip if there was money to be made out of it.'

It was a plausible theory. Blackmail was a strong enough motive for murder, and it fitted the facts we had so far. Not that there were many of them.

'You could be right,' I said, too tired to try to make sense of it any more. 'But we're just guessing. We don't really know enough to speculate at this stage.'

'Aye, you're right,' Brody agreed, heavily. 'But I'll lay odds that when we find out who she came out here to see – and why – we'll have found her killer.'

Looking at the wet footprints drying on the floor, I wondered if the killer hadn't already found us.

Brody volunteered to stay at the clinic while I went back to the hotel for something to eat, and bought a padlock and chain from the village store.

'You need a break. You look all in,' he said, moving a chair in front of the door and settling down.

I certainly felt it. My shoulder hurt, I was tired and I hadn't eaten since breakfast. Duncan gave me a lift in the Range Rover as far as the store, which Brody thought would still be open. The rain had stopped but the wind still rocked the car as we drove through the village. Brody had told me the phones were still off, so I'd borrowed Duncan's radio to try to call Jenny. Digital or not, the signal was still patchy, and when I finally got through I reached her voicemail yet again. *What did you expect? She's not going to sit around waiting for you to call.*

Disappointed, I gave Duncan the radio back. He took it absently, lost in thought. Except for when I'd explained my findings earlier, he'd been unusually quiet. Almost pensive, in fact, and when he drove past the store I had to remind him to stop.

'Sorry,' he said, pulling over.

He still seemed distracted as I got out of the car, but I put it down to his not relishing another night alone in the camper van.

'No need to wait, I'll walk back from here,' I told him. 'The fresh air will do me good.'

'Dr Hunter?' he said, before I could close the door.

'Yes?' I said, bracing myself against the wind.

But whatever he had been about to say, he'd evidently thought better of it. 'Nothing. Doesn't matter.'

'You sure?'

'Aye. Just me being daft.' He gave an embarrassed smile. 'I better be getting back to relieve Sergeant Fraser. He'll kill me if I'm late.'

I nearly pressed him. But whatever was on his mind, I supposed he'd tell me when he was ready.

I raised my hand in acknowledgement as he drove off, but I don't know if he saw me. I turned to the store. A light still burned inside, and the sign on the door said *Open*. It announced my entry with a tinkle of bells. Inside was a crammed treasure trove of tinned food, hardware and groceries. The smell took me back to my childhood; heady scents of cheese, candles and matches. Behind the worn wooden counter a woman was bending over to unpack tins of soup from a box.

'With you in a second,' she said, and as she straightened I recognized Karen Tait.

I'd forgotten that Brody had said she ran the general store. Without the artificial flush of alcohol she looked more worn down than ever, with only a ghost of a lost prettiness remaining in her puffy features. Her smile was a grudging thing to start with, but it faded altogether when she saw who her customer was.

'Do you have any padlocks?' I asked.

She jerked her chin towards a shelf on the back wall, where there was a selection of ironmongery stacked haphazardly in boxes.

'Thanks,' I said.

She didn't reply. I felt her gaze on me as I sifted through the boxes of bolts, screws and nails, hostile and resentful. But I found what I was looking for; a heavy-duty padlock, and a spool of chain.

'I'll take a metre of this, too, please.'

'The cutters are there as well.'

I wasn't sure I'd be able to cut the chain one-handed, but I wasn't going to give her the satisfaction of asking for help. I hunted around before eventually finding a pair of bolt cutters on another shelf, next to an old wooden yardstick. I measured out the chain, then cut it by bracing one handle of the cutters on my thigh. Putting everything back as I'd found it, I took the length of chain and the padlock over to the counter.

'And I'll take this as well,' I said, selecting a large bar of chocolate from the display.

She rang the items into the till in silence, watching as I took a note from my wallet.

'I'm not changing that.'

The till drawer was open, revealing a selection of coins and smaller notes. She stared back at me, defiantly.

I put my wallet back and rummaged in my pocket. She watched

149

me count out the money, then banged it into the till. I was owed change, but it wasn't worth arguing about. I picked up my buys and headed for the door.

'Think a bar of chocolate will get your feet under that table, do you?'

'What?' I asked, not quite believing I'd heard right.

But she only stared at me sourly. I went out, resisting the temptation to slam the door.

Still fuming, I debated going straight back to the clinic with the chain. But Brody had been adamant I should get something to eat first. I knew he was right, and somehow I didn't think anyone would try anything as long as the old DI was standing guard.

The walk back to the hotel did me good. Windy as it was, at least the rain was holding off, and the air was cold and fresh. By the time I'd reached the side street leading to the hotel my temper had started to subside. Light shone welcomingly from the windows, and the smell of fresh bread and burning peat greeted me when I stepped inside. The grandfather clock clunked majestically as I went down the hallway to find Ellen. The bar was untended, but there were low voices coming from the kitchen.

Ellen's and a man's.

When I knocked on the door the voices stopped. 'Just a minute,' Ellen called out.

After a few moments she opened the door. The yeasty scent of warm bread enveloped me.

'Sorry. Just getting the loaves out of the oven.'

She was alone. Whoever she'd been talking to must have left through the back door. Ellen busied herself turning out the bread from the tins, but not before I'd seen that she'd been crying.

'Is everything all right?' I asked.

'Fine.' But she kept her back to me as she spoke.

I hesitated, then held up the chocolate bar. 'I brought this for Anna. Hope you don't mind her having sweets.'

She smiled, sniffing away the last of her tears. 'No, that's very good of you.'

'Look, are you . . . ?'

'I'm fine. Really.' She gave me another smile, stronger this time.

I came away. I didn't know her well enough to do anything else. But I couldn't help but wonder who Ellen's visitor had been, and why she should want to keep his identity a secret.

Or what he'd done to make her cry.

14

I felt better after a hot shower and a change of clothes. I'd already worn everything I'd packed for the trip to the Grampians, and I made a note to ask Ellen if there was anything I could do about my laundry. My shoulder still hurt, but the shower had helped, and the two ibuprofen I'd taken were starting to kick in as I went downstairs to get something to eat.

Outside the bar, though, I stopped, reluctant to go in. I'd felt like an outsider even before this, but now the extent of my isolation suddenly hit home. Even though I'd already been sure that the woman's killer must still be on the island, might even be someone I'd met, it hadn't seemed to have any direct bearing on me personally. I was there to do a job. Now, though, someone had crept into the community centre to spy on me, and I'd no idea who, or why.

Somehow it seemed that a line had been crossed.

Don't start getting paranoid. And remember what Brody said: until the support teams get here, the best defence is not to let on what we know.

I pushed open the door to the bar. At least the weather seemed to have thinned out some of the customers. Guthrie and Karen Tait were nowhere to be seen, I was relieved to see, and only one of the domino players had turned out. He sat forlornly at their table, the box of dominoes waiting in front of him.

But Kinross was there, staring silently into his pint while his son hunched self-consciously on a bar stool next to him. Fraser was there too, sitting at a table by himself as he attacked a plate piled with sausages and mashed vegetables. He obviously hadn't wasted any time in getting back once Duncan had relieved him at the camper van. A glass of whisky stood next to his plate, announcing that he considered himself off duty, and from the flush on his face I doubted it was his first.

'Christ, I'm starving,' he said, shovelling up a forkful of potato as I sat down at his table. There were flecks of food in his moustache. 'First I've had to eat all day. No joke being out in that camper van this bloody weather, I can tell you.'

He hadn't seemed so bothered when it had been Duncan out there, I thought, wryly. 'Did Duncan tell you we had an intruder?' I said, keeping my voice down.

'Aye.' He waved his fork dismissively. 'Bloody kids, probably.'

'Brody's not convinced that's all it was.'

'I wouldn't pay too much attention to what he says,' he snorted, giving me a glimpse of semi-masticated sausage. 'Duncan says you think the dead woman was a whore from Stornoway. That right?'

I glanced around to make sure no one could hear. 'I don't know where she's from. But I think she was probably a prostitute, yes.'

'And a junkie, by the sound of it.' He washed down his food with a gulp of whisky. 'You ask me she'll have come out here to service the contractors, and one of them got too rough. No great mystery about it.'

'There weren't any contractors out here four or five weeks ago when she was killed.'

'Aye, well, all due respect, but I can't see how anyone can say for sure when that was, not from the bits and pieces that're left. Cold weather like this, they could have been lying out there for months.' He wagged his knife at me. 'You mark my words, whoever killed her'll be back on either Lewis or the mainland by now.'

I revised my estimate of how many whiskies Fraser might have had. But I wasn't going to argue. He'd made up his mind, and nothing inconvenient like the facts was going to change it. Still, I didn't feel like listening to any more of his opinions, and I was considering asking Ellen for some sandwiches to take away with me when the peat slab in the hearth flared from a sudden blast of cold air. A moment later Guthrie stamped into the bar, filling the doorway with his bulk.

I knew straight away that something was wrong. He glared at where Fraser and I were sitting before going to whisper to Kinross. The ferry captain's expression darkened as he turned to stare at us. Then, as his son watched apprehensively, he and Guthrie came over to our table.

Engrossed in his food, Fraser didn't notice until they were standing over us. He looked up irritably.

'Aye?' he snapped, still chewing.

Kinross regarded him in the same way he might something unsavoury and useless caught in a net. 'What do you need a padlock for?'

I kicked myself for not anticipating this. Given our presence at the clinic, it wouldn't take much guessing where the lock was for. And I should have realized that Cameron might not be alone in objecting to our being there.

Fraser frowned. 'Padlock? What the hell are you talking about?'

'I bought one earlier,' I told him. 'For the community centre.'

For a moment he looked aggrieved at not being told sooner, but the lure of food and whisky overcame it. He gestured towards me as he went back to his meal.

'There you go. So now you know.'

Guthrie folded his beefy arms on the shelf of his stomach. He wasn't drunk this time, but he wasn't happy, either.

'And who says you can shut us out of our own fucking community centre?'

Fraser lowered his knife and fork and glowered at him. 'I do. We had an intruder in there earlier, so now we're locking it. Any objection?'

'Aye, you're dead right we have,' Guthrie rumbled, lowering his arms, threateningly. Long and heavily muscled, they gave him the look of an ape as they hung at his side. 'That's our fucking centre.'

'So write a letter of complaint,' Fraser retorted. 'It's being used on police business. Which means it's off limits until we say so.'

Kinross's eyes glittered over his dark beard. 'Perhaps you didn't hear. That's *our* community centre, not yours. And if you think you can come here and lock us out of our own buildings, then you need to think again.'

I broke in before things got out of hand. 'Nobody wants to lock anyone out, but it won't be for long. And we did check first with Grace Strachan.'

I offered a silent apology to Grace for invoking her name, but it had the effect I'd hoped. Kinross and Guthrie glanced at each other, uncertainty replacing the belligerence of a moment ago.

Kinross rubbed the back of his neck. 'Well, if Mrs Strachan said it was OK . . .'

Thank God for that. But my relief was premature. Perhaps it was the whisky, or perhaps he felt his authority had already been undermined enough by Brody. But for whatever reason Fraser decided to have the last word.

'You can consider this a warning,' he growled, levelling a fat finger at Kinross. 'This is a murder inquiry now, and if you try to interfere again then believe me, you'll wish you'd stayed on your bloody ferry!'

The entire bar had fallen quiet. Everyone in the room was staring at us. I tried to keep the dismay off my face. *You bloody idiot!*

Kinross looked startled. 'A murder inquiry? Since when?'

Belatedly, Fraser realized what he'd done. 'That's none of your business,' he blustered. 'Now, if you don't mind, I'd like to finish my supper. This conversation's over.'

He bent over his plate again, but couldn't stop the flush climbing up the back of his neck. Kinross looked down at him, biting his lip in thought. He jerked his head at Guthrie.

'Come on, Sean.'

They moved back to the bar. I stared at Fraser, but he busied himself with his food and refused to meet my eye. Finally, he gave me a sullen glare.

'What? They'll know soon enough when SOC get out here. There's no harm done.'

I was too angry to say anything. The one thing we'd hoped to keep quiet, and now Fraser had needlessly blurted it out. I stood up, not wanting to stay in his company any longer.

'I'd better go and relieve Brody,' I said, and went to ask Ellen to make me some sandwiches.

Brody was still sitting in the hall where I'd left him, guarding the door to the clinic. When I went in he sat forward, poised on the edge of his seat, but relaxed when he saw it was me.

'You've not been long,' he said, getting to his feet and stretching.

'I thought I'd eat down here.'

I'd brought my laptop with me from the hotel. I set it down and took the padlock and chain from my coat pocket. I handed him the spare key.

'Here. You might as well have this.'

He gave me a questioning look as he took it. 'Shouldn't you give the spare to Fraser?'

'Not after what he's just done.'

Brody's mouth tightened as I described what had just happened in the hotel bar.

'Bloody fool. That's just what we didn't need.' He thought for a moment. 'Look, do you want me to stick around for a while? So long as I give Bess her evening walk some time, I've nothing else to do.'

I didn't think he was aware of the loneliness his words implied. 'I'll be fine. You might as well go and get something to eat.'

'You sure?'

I told him I was. I appreciated the offer, but I needed to work. And I could do that better without any distractions.

When he'd gone I wrapped the chain through the handles of the community centre's double doors, then slid the hasp of the padlock through the links and snapped it shut.

Satisfied that the hall was as secure as I could make it, I sat in the chair that Brody had stationed by the clinic door and ate the sandwiches Ellen had made. She'd also given me a Thermos of black coffee, and when I'd eaten I sipped at the scalding liquid, listening to the wind booming outside.

The old building creaked like a ship's timbers in a high sea. The sound was oddly restful, and the food had made me drowsy. My eyelids began to close, but my head jerked back up as a sudden gust of wind rattled the windows. The overhead light dimmed and buzzed indecisively before brightening to life once more. *Time to make a start.*

The skull and jawbone were as I'd left them. Plugging my laptop into a wall socket, I switched it on. Its battery was fully charged, but that wouldn't last long if the power failed. Better to use the island's mains electricity while I could, and trust that the laptop's surge-protection would hold out against it from the fluctuating supply.

Once the laptop had booted up, I opened the missing persons files that Wallace had sent. This was the first time I'd had a real chance to look at them. There were five in all; young women between eighteen and thirty who'd disappeared from the Western Isles or the west coast of Scotland in the last few months. Chances were that they had simply run away, and would turn up at some point in Glasgow, Edinburgh or London, drawn to the chimera of a big city.

But not all of them.

Each file contained a detailed physical description and a jpeg photograph of a missing woman. Two of the photographs were useless, with the subject in one closed-mouthed, and the other a full-body shot that was too low-resolution for me to work with. But a quick glance at the descriptions that accompanied them made it unnecessary anyway. One was black, while the other was too short to be the young woman whose skeleton I'd measured in the cottage.

The other three, though, all matched the physical profile of the dead woman. Their photographs showed them as not much more than girls, caught before whatever event had either caused them to walk away from their lives, or ended them. My laptop had a sophisticated digital imaging program, and I used it to enlarge the mouth of the first picture, zooming in until the screen was filled with a giant, anonymous smile. When it was as large and sharp as I could make it, I began to compare it to those of the skeletal grin.

Unlike fingerprints, which need a minimum number of matching features, a single tooth can be enough to provide a positive ID. Sometimes a distinctive shape, a certain break, is all it takes to reveal an entire identity.

That was what I was hoping for now. The teeth I'd replaced in the skull were crooked and chipped. If none of the women in the photographs showed similar dental flaws, then it would at least rule them out as possible candidates. But if I was lucky enough to find a match, then I might be able to put a name to the anonymous victim.

From the start I knew it wasn't going to be easy. The photographs were only snapshots, hardly intended for the grim purpose I had in mind. Even magnified and cleaned up, the images were grainy and unclear. And the poor condition of the teeth I'd laboriously fitted back into the skull didn't help. If the victim was one of these young women, the photograph had been taken before her drug addiction had eroded them away.

After a couple of hours poring over the images, I felt as though I'd had sand rubbed into my eyes. I poured myself another coffee, rubbing the kinks from my neck. I felt tired and dispirited. Even though I'd known it was a long shot, I'd hoped to find something.

Wearily, I went back to the original images of the three young women. One in particular drew me, though I couldn't have said why. It had been taken on a street, with the young woman standing in front of a shop window. Her face was attractive but hard, with a wariness around the eyes and mouth even though she was smiling. If she was a victim, she wouldn't have been a passive one, I thought.

I studied her photograph more closely. Only the incisors and the upper canines were revealed by her smile. They were every bit as crooked as those I'd replaced in the skull, but none of their characteristics matched. The dead woman's upper left incisor had a distinctive V-shaped chip in it, yet the one on my screen was unmarked. *Give it up. You're wasting your time.*

But there was still something about the picture I couldn't put my finger on. And then I saw it.

'Oh, you've got to be joking,' I said out loud.

I clicked on a simple command. The young woman on my screen vanished and then reappeared, subtly altered. Behind her, the in-complete shop sign could now be made out: *Stornoway Store & Newsag.* But it wasn't what it said that was important, so much as the fact that it was no longer back to front.

The photograph had been the wrong way round.

It was the sort of simple slip-up that usually didn't matter. But at some point, either when it had been scanned from a negative or transferred to the missing persons database, the picture had been inverted. Right for left, left for right.

I'd been looking at a mirror image.

With growing excitement, I magnified the teeth of the young woman in the photograph again. Now her upper left incisor had a V-shaped notch that exactly matched the chip in the skull's. And both lower right canines were crooked, overlapping the tooth next to them to an identical degree.

I'd found a match.

For the first time, I allowed myself to read the description that accompanied the photograph. The young woman's name was Janice Donaldson. She was twenty-six years old, a prostitute, alcoholic and drug addict who had gone missing from Stornoway five weeks ago. There had been no widespread search, no news bulletins. Just one more open file, another soul who had dropped through the cracks.

I looked at her picture again, the electronically frozen smile. She was full-faced, with round cheeks and the beginnings of a double chin. Even given her drug addiction, she was a young woman who was always going to be plump. *Lots of body fat to burn*. It would still have to be confirmed by dental records and fingerprints, but I didn't have any doubt that I'd found the murdered woman.

'Hello, Janice,' I said.

As I was staring at my laptop screen, Duncan was huddled in the camper van, trying to concentrate on his criminology textbook. It wasn't easy. The wind was worse than ever. Even though the van was parked in the lee of the cottage, which took the brunt of the gale's force, it was still being battered mercilessly.

The constant buffeting was unsettling as well as uncomfortable. Duncan had thought about turning off the paraffin heater in case the camper blew over, but he'd decided against it. He'd take his chances on catching fire rather than freeze to death.

So he'd tried to close his mind to the way it was rocking, and done his best to focus on his book as the rain drilled against the metal roof. But when he'd found himself rereading the same paragraph for the third time, he finally accepted it wasn't going to happen.

He closed the book with a sigh. The fact was it wasn't only the gale that was bothering him. He was still fretting over the idea that had occurred to him earlier. He knew he was being stupid, that the notion was completely ridiculous. But now he'd started to wonder about it, he couldn't put it from his mind. That overactive imagination of his again.

The question was, what did he do about it? Tell someone? In which case, who? He'd come close to mentioning it to Dr Hunter earlier, but thought better of it. There was always Brody, of course. Or Fraser. *Aye, right.* Duncan was well aware of the detective sergeant's failings as a police officer. The whisky smell on his breath in a morning was an embarrassment. Disgusting. It was as though he thought people wouldn't notice, or no longer cared. Duncan's father had told him about some officers who'd burned out, their ambition reduced to keeping their nose clean until they could retire with a full pension. He could have been describing Fraser.

Duncan wondered if he'd always been like that, or if he'd gradually sunk into his current state of disillusionment. He'd heard the stories about him, of course; some he'd believed, others he was more sceptical about. But he'd always liked to think there was still a halfway decent police officer buried beneath the alcohol cheeks.

Now, though, he wasn't so sure. Here they were, landed at the sharp end of a murder investigation – *right* at the sharp end – and Fraser still acted as though it were an inconvenience. Duncan didn't see it like that at all. Duncan thought it was the most exciting thing that had ever happened to him.

The recognition made him feel a little guilty. A woman had died, after all. Was it right to feel so keyed up about it?

But this was his job, he rationalized. This was what he'd joined the police for, not filling in parking forms, or sorting out drunken neighbour squabbles. He knew there was evil out there – not in the biblical sense, perhaps, but that was what it amounted to all the same. He wanted to be able to look it in the eye, and make it flinch. Make a difference. *Aye, and I can imagine what Fraser would say about* that.

The smile slowly faded from his face. So what was he going to do?

A flash from outside caught his peripheral vision. He looked out of the window, waiting for it to come again. It didn't. *Lightning?* But there was no accompanying roll of thunder. He turned off the light so that the camper van was in darkness except for the low blue flame of the paraffin heater. He could make out the dark shape of the cottage, but nothing else.

He hesitated. It could have been sheet lightning, he thought. That didn't make any noise, did it? Or perhaps his eyes were just playing tricks.

Then again, it could have been someone outside with a torch.

The reporter again? Maggie Cassidy? He hoped not. Although part of him felt quite keyed up at the prospect, he'd believed her when she'd said she wouldn't try anything again. Naive or not, he'd feel let down if she'd broken her promise. But if it wasn't her, then who? Duncan didn't think there was enough left in the cottage for anyone to bother with, not unless they brought a JCB to dig out the rubble first.

But this was a murder inquiry now. He wasn't going to take the chance. He considered radioing Fraser, but not for long. He could imagine the sergeant's withering response, and he'd no wish to subject himself to it. Not without checking it out first. Pulling on his coat, he picked up the Maglite and went outside.

The force of the wind almost jerked him from his feet. Closing the door as quietly as he could, he paused for a moment, listening. The wind made it impossible to hear. And it was too dark now to see anything without a torch. He switched it on and quickly shone the beam around. It picked out only thrashing grass and the lonely shell of the cottage.

The wind quickly stripped the camper van's heat from him. And he'd forgotten to put on his gloves. Shivering, he approached the cottage, playing the torch beam on its doorway. He'd resealed it earlier — something Fraser hadn't bothered to do — and the tape showed no sign of being touched. He shone the torch inside, satisfying himself that no one was in there, and then began to circle round the ruined walls.

Nothing. Gradually, he allowed himself to relax. It must have been sheet lightning after all. *Aye, either that or your imagination.* He completed his circuit, feet whispering through the thick grass. When he reached the doorway again his main concern was how bloody cold he was. His fingers were going numb on the torch's steel casing.

Even so, he forced himself to shine the beam around one last time before heading back for the camper van. Reaching it, he hesitated, suddenly struck by the thought that someone might be in there waiting.

If they are, I hope they've got the kettle on. Gripping the heavy Maglite, he pushed open the door.

The camper van was empty. The hissing blue glow from the paraffin heater gave out a welcoming heat. Duncan hurried inside gratefully, and shut the door. Rubbing his icy hands to get some feeling back, he switched on the light and lifted the kettle to see if there was enough water in it. There was, but he reminded himself that they'd need to fill the plastic water container tomorrow. Fraser must have spent the entire day drinking tea, he thought glumly.

Duncan put the kettle on the camper van's small gas ring and picked up the box of matches. He took one out and struck it, the sudden flare releasing brimstone smoke.

Someone banged on the door.

Duncan jumped. The sting on his fingertips reminded him he still held the match. He shook it out, released from his surprise.

He almost called out to ask who it was. But a trespasser would hardly walk right up and knock, he chided himself. Even so, he picked up the Maglite again. Just in case.

Then, drawing confidence from the torch's weight, he went to open the door.

15

I was sitting at the desk in the clinic. It was dark, but not so dark that I couldn't see. A dusty twilight seemed to cover everything. The blinds on the window and door were drawn, and the skull and jawbone still sat on the steel trolley. On the desk in front of me was my laptop, its screen dark and dead. The halogen examination lamp was poised over the table where I'd left it, but now it was unlit.

There wasn't a sound. I looked round, taking in my surroundings. And, with the lack of surprise that sometimes accompanies such moments, I knew without thinking about it that I was asleep.

I felt the presence in the corner of the room before I saw it. The figure was lost in shadow, but I could still see her. A woman, heavy-boned and fleshy. A round, attractive face marred by an underlying hardness.

She looked at me, unspeaking.

What do you want? The woman didn't answer. *I've done all I can. It's down to the police now.*

Still looking at me, she pointed to the skull on the table.

I don't understand. What do you want me to do?

She opened her mouth. I waited for her to speak, but instead of words smoke began streaming from her lips. I wanted to look away, but I couldn't. Smoke was pouring from her now, from her eyes, nose and mouth, pluming from her fingertips. I could smell her burning, yet there were no flames. Only smoke. It was filling the room, obscuring my view of her. I knew I had to do something, try to help her.

You can't. She's already dead.

The smoke was getting thicker, starting to choke me. I still couldn't move, but the need to act was overwhelming. I could no longer see the woman, no longer see anything. *Move. Now!* I lurched towards her . . .

And woke up. I was still in the clinic, sitting at the desk where I'd fallen asleep. Now, though, the room was in darkness. A faint glow came from my laptop, where an infinity of stars raced into oblivion. The screensaver had turned itself on, which meant I'd been sleeping for at least fifteen minutes.

The gale thrashed outside as I tried to shake off the effects of the dream. I felt short of breath, and my vision was blurred, as though there were a gauze veil in front of it. And I could still smell the acrid stink of smoke.

I took a deep breath, and immediately started to cough. Now I could taste smoke as well as smell it. I tried the switch for the halogen lamp. Nothing happened. The storm must have finally succeeded in cutting off Runa's electricity. My laptop was running on battery. I hit a key, bringing it out of the powersave mode. Its screen lit up, casting a dim blue light into the clinic. The haze in the air was more obvious now, and as the last vestiges of sleep fell away I realized I hadn't just been dreaming after all.

The room was full of smoke.

Coughing, I jumped up and lunged for the door. I grabbed hold of the handle, but immediately snatched my hand away.

It was hot.

I'd lowered the blind over the glass panel in the door after the intruder's visit that afternoon, but now I yanked it open. The hall beyond was swirling with a sulphurous orange light.

166

The community centre was on fire.

I backed away from the door and quickly looked round the clinic. The only other way out was the small window set high up in one wall. If I stood on a chair I should just be able to squeeze through. I tried to open it, but it wouldn't budge. I saw the window locks and swore. I'd no idea where the key might be, and there was no time to look. I snatched the desk lamp to break the glass but stopped myself at the last second. Even opened, the window would be only just big enough for me to crawl through. If I broke it I'd never fit through the smaller gap. And although the clinic door was shut, the rush of oxygen-rich air from outside might still cause the fire to expand explosively. I daren't risk that.

The smoke had already grown thicker in the room, making it hard to breathe. *Come on! Think!* I snatched my coat off the wall hook and ran to the washbasin. Turning the tap on full I plunged my head underneath, then did the same with my scarf and gloves. Cold water streamed down my face as I struggled into my coat, cursing the sling's clumsiness. Winding the wet scarf round my nose and mouth, I wriggled my right hand into my glove and then pulled up the coat's hood.

Grabbing my laptop from the desk, I spared a glance at the skull and jawbone lying on the steel trolley. *I'm sorry, Janice.*

And at that moment the glass porthole exploded.

The fact that my face was averted meant my hood and scarf protected me from most of the flying shards. I felt a few sting my exposed skin, but the sensation was dwarfed by the sudden blast-furnace wave of heat. I staggered back as smoke and flame billowed into the clinic. Any chance of my climbing from the window had now gone. Even if the fireball caused by breaking it didn't kill me outright, I'd be burned to death before I could wriggle through.

The smoke was already filtering through the scarf, smothering me. Hacking and coughing, I hunched my back against the heat coming through the shattered porthole and grabbed hold of the door handle.

The water on my glove steamed, the heat striking right through the thick fabric, and then I'd yanked the door open and dashed through.

It was like running into a wall of heat and noise. The piano was burning like a torch, discordant notes clamouring out a madman's music as the fire plucked and snapped its wires. I almost retreated into the clinic again, but I knew if I did I would die in there. And now I saw that the community centre wasn't completely ablaze. One half was engulfed in flames, yellow tongues chasing across the ceiling and floor, but the side where the exit was located hadn't yet caught.

Get out! Go! Eyes streaming, I stumbled through the smoke. Almost immediately I was lost and blind. I could smell my coat smouldering, a scorched-wool stink coming from the scarf over my face. Heart pounding from fear and lack of oxygen, I didn't see the stack of chairs until I fell over them.

Pain lanced through my shoulder and the laptop flew from my hands as I tumbled to the floor. But it was falling that saved me. Like suddenly swimming into a thermocline, there was a band of relatively clear air trapped against the floorboards. *Stupid! Should have realized!* I was panicking, not thinking clearly. Keeping my face pressed to the floor, I gulped in greedy breaths as I pawed around for the laptop. I couldn't find it. *Leave it!* I began crawling towards the exit. An eddy in the smoke revealed the double doors right in front of me. Taking a last deep breath, I hauled myself to my feet and tugged at the handles.

And heard the rattle of the padlocked chain.

Shock and fear paralysed me. I'd forgotten all about the padlock. *The key. Where's the key?* I couldn't remember. *Think!* I'd given the spare to Brody, but where was mine? Tearing off my glove with my teeth, I frantically searched my pockets. Nothing. *Oh, Christ, it's still in the clinic.*

Then I felt the thin metal shape in my back pocket. *Thank God!* I fumbled it out, knowing if I dropped it I was dead. The fire clawed at my back. My chest heaved as I tried to fit the key into the padlock, but I daren't take a breath. If I did I'd be inhaling smoke, not air, and the heat would sear my lungs. My hand was clumsy, the lock stubbornly resistant.

Then there was a snick and the hasp slid open.

The chain rasped on the handles as I tore it free. I wrenched open the doors, hoping that the porch would act like an airlock, allowing me to get out before the fresh air fed the fire. It did, but only partly. There was an instant's touch of cold against my face, then I was enveloped in a rush of heat and smoke. I stumbled out with it, eyes squeezed shut, fighting the labouring of my chest to draw breath.

I'd no idea how far I'd gone before I collapsed. But this time it was on to blessedly cold, wet grass. I sucked in one breath after another, tasting cool air that was tainted by smoke, but air all the same.

There were hands on me now, dragging me away from the centre. My eyes were streaming too much to see, but I recognized Brody's voice saying, 'It's all right, we've got you.'

I looked up, coughing and wiping the tears from my eyes. He was supporting me on one side, the even bigger figure of Guthrie on the other. There were people all around, their stunned faces lit by the flames. More were still arriving, flapping overcoats hurriedly thrown on over pyjamas and nightgowns. Someone was shouting for water; a moment later a mug was thrust into my hands. I drank thirstily, the coldness of it wonderfully soothing on my throat.

'Are you OK?' Brody was saying.

I nodded, turning round to look back at the community centre. The whole building was blazing, sending up sheets of flame and sparks that the wind instantly whipped away. The clinic extension, where I'd been only minutes before, was also burning now, gouts of smoke streaming from the shattered window.

'What happened?' Brody asked.

I tried to speak, but another coughing spasm seized me.

'All right, take it easy,' Brody said, urging me to drink again.

Another figure was barging towards us through the gathering crowd. It was Cameron, staring with open-mouthed disbelief at the burning centre. His gaze was manic as he turned it on me.

'What have you done?' he demanded, bass voice quivering with rage.

'For God's sake, give him a chance, can't you?' Brody said.

Cameron's Adam's apple jerked under the skin of his throat like a trapped mouse. 'Give him a *chance*? That's my clinic going up in flames!'

I tried to control my coughing. 'I'm sorry . . .' I croaked.

'You're *sorry*? Look at it! It's gone, the whole place! What the hell did you do?'

The veins in his temples pulsed in a calligraphy of anger. I forced myself to stand, wiping my streaming eyes.

'I didn't do anything.' My throat felt full of gravel. 'I woke up and the hall was on fire. It started in there, not the clinic.'

Cameron wasn't about to back down. 'Oh, so it started by itself, did it?'

'I don't know . . .' I broke off, coughing again.

'Leave him alone, he only just made it out himself,' Brody warned.

A harsh laugh came from nearby. It was Kinross, standing at the front of the crowd. With his dark hair and oilskins he looked like a figure from a wilder, darker age.

'Aye, made sure he was all right, didn't he?'

'Would you rather he'd still been in there?' Brody snapped.

'Do we get a choice?'

I realized that attention was shifting from the fire to us. I glanced round, saw that we'd been hemmed in by the islanders. They were gathered in a circle round us, their faces harsh and unforgiving in the flames.

'It didn't just burn down by itself,' one man muttered.

Other voices began to call out as well, wanting to know why we'd used the centre, who would pay for it to be replaced. I could feel the mood shifting from shock to anger.

170

Then the crowd began to part, making way for a tall figure. With relief I saw it was Strachan. And just like that, the tension subsided.

He strode up to us, hair thrashing in the wind as he stared at the blazing community centre. 'Christ! Was anyone inside?'

I shook my head, trying to stifle the coughs. 'Only me.'

And Janice Donaldson. I looked at the flames wrapping themselves round the building, feeling as though I'd let her down.

Strachan took the empty mug from me. 'Some more water here, please.'

He held it out, not even bothering to see who took it. Almost immediately the mug was refilled and pressed back into my hand. I gulped at the icy water gratefully. Strachan waited until I'd lowered it.

'Any idea how it started?'

Cameron had been watching with barely concealed anger. 'Isn't it obvious? He was the only person in there!'

'Don't talk rubbish, Bruce,' Strachan told him impatiently. 'Everyone knows the place was a fire trap. The wiring was ancient. I should have insisted on tearing down the whole thing when we built the clinic.'

'And that's it, is it? We're supposed to just let it go?' Cameron asked, tight-lipped.

Strachan gave an easy grin. 'Well, you could always lynch Dr Hunter, I suppose. There's a street lamp over there, and I'm sure you could find some rope. But why don't we wait until we know what caused it before we start blaming anyone?'

Turning his back on Cameron, he addressed the gathered islanders.

'I promise we'll find out what happened. And we'll build a new and better clinic and community centre, you have my word on that. But there's nothing more we can do tonight. Everyone should go on home now.'

Nobody moved. Then, as if on cue, what was left of the hall

171

suddenly collapsed in a shower of sparks and flame. Gradually at first, then more steadily, the crowd began to break up, the men grim-faced, many of the women wiping their eyes.

Strachan spoke to Kinross and Guthrie. 'Iain, Sean, will you get a few men together and stay for a while? I can't see that it'll spread, but I'd appreciate your keeping an eye on things.'

It was a deft way of defusing the remaining tension. Kinross and Guthrie looked taken aback, but flattered to have been asked. Strachan turned to Cameron as they moved off.

'Why don't you take a look at David's cuts and burns?'

'There's no need,' I said, before Cameron could respond. Nurse or not, I'd had enough of the man for one night. 'There's nothing I can't see to myself.'

'I still say we should—' Cameron began, but Strachan spoke over him.

'No need for you to stay either, then, Bruce. You're teaching in a few hours. You might as well go home too.'

His tone didn't brook any argument. Cameron stalked off, his expression thunderous. Strachan watched him go, then turned to me.

'OK, so what happened?'

I took another drink of water. 'I must have dozed off. When I woke up the lights were off and the clinic was full of smoke.'

He nodded. 'The power went off all over the island about an hour ago. The blackout must have caused some sort of short.'

For the first time I noticed that the village was in darkness beyond the yellow glow of the flames. No street lamps, no lights showing in windows.

'It's been a hell of a night. Still, it could have been a lot worse.' Strachan paused, a subtle change coming over his manner. 'I heard a rumour earlier. That the police are treating the body that was found as murder. Do you know anything about that?'

Brody spoke up before I could answer. 'You shouldn't take any notice of rumours.'

172

'So it isn't true?'

Brody just stared back at him, stonily. Strachan gave a tight smile.

'That's what I thought. Well, I'll say goodnight, then. I'm glad you're all right, David.'

Brody waited until he was turning away. 'I'm curious. You can't see the village from your house. So how did you know about the fire?'

Strachan faced him. His expression was controlled, but I could see the anger under it.

'There was a glow in the sky. And I'm a poor sleeper.'

The two of them held each other's stare, neither of them giving an inch. Then, with a final nod in my direction, Strachan walked off into the dark.

Brody drove me back to the hotel. Since his house was down by the harbour, he'd rushed up to the community centre in his car when he saw the blaze from his bedroom window.

'I don't sleep much either,' he told me, wryly.

Exhaustion gave me a sense of unreality as we drove through the blacked-out streets. I resisted the urge to lean back against the head-rest and shut my eyes. Reaction was starting to set in, and the cuts and burns I hadn't noticed before had begun to make themselves felt. The stink of smoke and burning clogged my nose and throat. I wound down the window, but the force of the wind made me wind it up again.

'So how do you think it started?' Brody asked, after a while.

'I suppose Strachan could be right.' My throat was still raw. 'The power cut could have caused an electrical short or surge. The centre was a fire trap.'

'Just a coincidence, then, that it burned down a few hours after we'd had an intruder? And after Fraser let slip this was a murder inquiry?'

I felt too shattered to think clearly. 'I don't know.'

He didn't push the point. 'Did we lose everything?'

Most of what mattered, I thought. As well as Janice Donaldson's remains, my flight case and equipment had been in the clinic. My camera, my laptop containing all my notes and files, my tape recorder, all gone up in smoke.

But even as I was thinking that, I was already feeling in my pockets.

'Not quite,' I said, pulling out the USB bar. 'I backed up my hard drive earlier. Force of habit. So at least we've still got a photographic record.'

'Better than nothing, I suppose,' Brody sighed.

'There's something else,' I said. 'I know who she was.'

I told him how the flaws in the skull's teeth had matched those in the photograph of Janice Donaldson, the missing prostitute from Stornoway. Brody gave the steering wheel a little punch of satisfaction.

'Well done,' he grinned, enthusiasm briefly overcoming his natural restraint.

'Well, we've only got the photos of the skull left, so it'll still be better if Forensics can confirm it. With luck they might be able to salvage enough undamaged soft tissue from the cottage to try for a DNA match.'

'If you say you know who she is, that's good enough for me,' Brody said. The implied confidence was flattering. I only hoped Wallace would be as readily convinced.

We were coming to the hotel now. A light on in the hallway told us that Ellen was still up. She'd been woken by the sudden quiet as the blackout had silenced the hotel's constant heartbeat of central heating and refrigerators. Now the steady background vibration announced that the back-up generator was doing its job.

She looked horrified when she saw me. 'Oh, my God, are you all right?'

'I've had better nights,' I admitted. I nodded at the light bulb, slightly dimmer than usual but still working. 'That's a welcome sight.'

'Aye. Provided we're careful, we've enough oil to keep the generator running for three or four days. With luck the power will be back on by then. God willing,' she added dryly.

While Brody went to rouse Fraser, she ushered me into the kitchen and helped me off with my coat. It stank of smoke and was badly scorched, making her wrinkle her nose at the smell.

'Shame it wasn't fireproof as well as waterproof.'

I looked at where the Teflon-coated fabric had charred on the hood and shoulders. I could feel a corresponding sting on my own flesh, but nothing serious.

'I'm not complaining,' I said.

Brody returned a few minutes later with a sleep-bleared Fraser, whisky-breathed and still buttoning his shirt.

'He's not going to like it,' he warned, when I asked him to radio Wallace.

He was right. But the superintendent's anger was mollified to some extent when he learned I had a probable ID for the victim. I'd been going to ask when we could expect help to get here, but the connection was terrible. When it wasn't cutting out altogether, his voice faded in and out of a wash of crackles.

'We'll . . . alk . . . orrow,' I heard him say.

'Modern technology,' Brody sniffed, when I ended the call. 'They replaced the old analogue radios with digital, but they still piggyback the signal off the mobile phone network. Any problems with that and you're liable to lose the lot.'

Fraser made reluctant noises about going to examine the community centre, but there was no real point until the fire had died down. After taking a brief statement from me, he muttered excuses and went back to bed. Ellen had discreetly left the room when I'd called Wallace, but now she returned and began ushering Brody out as well.

'Go and get some sleep. You look nearly as bad as David,' she scolded.

She was right. The ex-policeman was haggard and drawn. He managed a weak smile.

'I'm not sure which of us should be more insulted. But perhaps I will. It's been a long day.'

'We've another tomorrow,' I told him.

'Aye,' he said heavily. But I never doubted for a minute that he'd be there in the thick of it.

After he'd gone, Ellen filled a basin with hot water and brought out antiseptic and cotton wool. 'Right, let's get you sorted out, shall we?'

'It's all right, I can do it myself.'

'I'm sure you can. But you're not going to.' She began to clean the cuts and grazes on my face. 'Don't worry. I used to be the unofficial nurse here before Bruce Cameron arrived.'

The wind moaned outside, but there was an easy silence between us as she worked. I wondered what a young woman like her, a single mother, was doing on a backwater like Runa. Eking out a living somewhere like this couldn't be easy. Brody had told me she'd met Anna's father on the mainland, so she'd obviously left at some point. Yet she'd come back out here. Was that because she actually liked the island's isolation, or was it a retreat from something that had happened out there?

I thought again about the visitor who had been in the kitchen earlier, and who'd left her in tears. There couldn't be many single men on an island this size, so it was hard not to draw conclusions about the reason for her secrecy.

Then again, what did I know? If I'd any sense I'd have been back home with Jenny now. I wished I could talk to her, and regretted not asking to use Fraser's radio when I'd had the chance. I wondered what she was doing, if she was worrying about me. Probably. *You should never have agreed to do this.* What the hell was I doing on a bleak island miles from anywhere, nearly having died of exposure and then being burned to death, instead of getting on with my own life?

Except this was my life, I realized, in a moment of rare clarity. This was what I did. What I was. And if Jenny saw it as a problem, where did that leave us?

Ellen's voice pulled me back to the here and now. 'Is it true what people are saying? About the body?'

'What are they saying?'

She gently swabbed a cut with antiseptic. 'That it was murder.'

Thanks to Fraser, there probably wasn't any harm in confirming what everyone on Runa almost certainly already knew, but I still felt reluctant to talk about it, even with Ellen.

'It's all right, I know I shouldn't ask,' she said, quickly. 'I just can't believe anything like that could happen here. The bar was full of talk about it earlier. No one can think who the victim can be, let alone imagine anyone from here being involved.'

I gave a non-committal murmur. This was exactly what we'd hoped to avoid. Now gossip and rumour would fill the vacuum left by the absence of hard fact, muddying the water and stirring up a silt of mistrust. And the only person to benefit would be the killer.

'So will you be coming back to Runa for your next holiday?' Ellen asked, deliberately lightening the mood.

I started to laugh. It hurt. 'Don't,' I told her, wincing.

She smiled. 'Sorry. But are you always as accident prone as this?'

'Not usually. Must be this place.'

Her smile faded. 'Aye, I can believe it.'

It was too good an opening to miss. 'So what about you? Do you like it out here?'

She suddenly became preoccupied with a cut. 'It's not so bad. You should be here in summer. The nights are glorious. Makes up for days like this.'

'But . . .' I prompted.

'But . . . it's a small island. You see the same faces all the time. A few contractors or the occasional tourist, but that's all. And, financially, it's a struggle keeping your head above water. Sometimes I wish . . . ah, well, it doesn't matter.'

177

'Go on.'

Unguarded, her face showed the sadness I guessed she normally kept in check. 'I wish I could get away from here. Leave this place – the hotel, the island – behind me, and take Anna and just go. Anywhere. Somewhere where there are decent schools, and shops, and restaurants, and people you don't know, who don't know you and your business.'

'So why don't you?'

There was defeat in the way she shook her head. 'It isn't that easy. I grew up on Runa, and everything I've got is here. Besides, what would I do?'

'Andrew Brody told me you'd been to college on the mainland. Isn't that something you could use?'

'Been telling tales, has he?' She looked as though she wasn't sure whether to be angry or amused. 'Aye, I spent a couple of years at catering college in Dundee. That's where I learned first aid, all that Health and Safety nonsense. Fancied myself as a chef at one point. But then my father was taken ill, so I came back. Only temporarily, I thought. But then I found myself with a child to support, and jobs aren't exactly plentiful round here. So when he died I carried on running this place.'

She raised an eyebrow at me.

'Aren't you going to ask?'

'Ask what?'

'About Anna's father.'

'Not when you're putting antiseptic on my cuts, no.'

'Good. Just so you know, let's just say there was never any future there.' Her tone made it clear the subject was closed. She went back to her swabbing. 'So what else did Andrew Brody tell you?'

'Not much. I'd hate to get him barred from the hotel.'

'Not much danger of that,' she laughed. 'Anna's too fond of him. I suppose I am as well, though don't go telling him that, mind. He's protective enough as it is.'

178

She paused. I guessed what was coming.

'Do you know about his daughter?' she asked.

'He told me.'

'He must like you. It isn't something he talks about as a rule. The girl was a bit wild, from what I gather. Still, I can't imagine what it must be like for him, not knowing what happened to her. He tried to track her down after he'd retired, but he never found her. So then he came out here.'

Her expression softened.

'Don't take this wrong. But in a way all this has been good for him. Given him a new lease of life. Some people aren't made for retirement, and Andrew's one of them. I think he must have been a pretty good policeman.'

So did I. I was glad he was here. More so now than ever.

Ellen dropped the bloodied cotton wool into a bowl. 'There you go. Best thing you can do now is have a hot shower and get some sleep. I'll give you some salve to put on your burns.'

A sudden gust of wind struck the hotel, making the entire structure seem to vibrate. Ellen cocked her head, listening.

'Storm's getting up,' she said.

16

The rain started again during what was left of the night, reducing what remained of the community centre to an uneven mound of grey and black ash. Wraiths of smoke rose from it to be whipped away in the wind. One corner remained partially intact, a few feet of scorched wood that petered out to nothing. In places recognizable shapes still protruded through the wreckage: the corner of a fire-buckled steel cabinet, or skeletal chair legs that poked through the ash like dead branches through a grey snowdrift.

It was a dismal scene, made even more depressing by the dark, heavy clouds that obscured the tops of the low hills. The rain was coming down in near-horizontal sheets. And the gale seemed to have worsened, lashing everything in its path with what seemed like deliberate malevolence.

Brody, Fraser and I had gone out to the community centre as soon as it was light. I felt exhausted. I'd had less than four hours' sleep and I ached all over. My shoulder throbbed relentlessly, wrenched during my escape from the fire. I'd hardly recognized myself in the shaving mirror that morning. The skin of my face felt sunburned, peppered with small gashes from the flying glass. My eyebrows and eyelashes had been singed off, giving me a strange, startled expression.

Still, as Strachan had said, it could have been much worse.

Brody and Fraser stood behind me as I studied the smoking wreckage. By rights I should have waited until a fire inspector had made sure that the structure was safe, but there was no telling when that would be. I was under no illusion that Janice Donaldson's remains would have survived this second incineration.

But I had to see for myself.

The rain fell as if the sky were made from water, tamping down the ashes and dampening the outer layer to a black mush. Even so, it hadn't beaten the fire completely. The debris was still smouldering from within. I could feel the heat from it on my face, contrasting the chill against my back.

'Do you think there's a chance anything could still be intact?' Brody asked.

'Not really.' My voice was still hoarse from the smoke.

Fraser gave an irritable sigh. He looked bedraggled and miserable in the rain. 'So why bother?'

'To make sure.'

I could make out one blackened corner of my flight case, protruding from the ashes of what had been the medical clinic. It was open, its contents reduced to so much char. Just beyond it was the stainless steel trolley where I'd worked on Janice Donaldson's cranium. The trolley was lying on its side, half buried under the remains of the roof. The skull and jawbone were nowhere to be seen, but I didn't hold out much hope. The already calcined bones would have been shattered to powder by the impact. A few teeth might have survived, but nothing more. In any event, whatever was left would have to wait until a forensic team arrived to sift through the debris. It would take more resources than I had to carry out a proper search.

I brushed a piece of windblown ash from my face as I carefully picked my way towards the fridge. The dead woman's hand had been inside it, and there was a chance the insulation had protected it. But that hope quickly died when I cleared away the covering of debris.

The fridge's white enamel had been burned black and the rubber seal had melted, letting the door swing open to expose the contents to the flames. Of Janice Donaldson's hand, all that was left was bone, cooked to a dark caramel colour by the heat.

The individual finger joints had fallen away from each other as the connecting tissue had burned from them. They lay in the bottom of the fridge, still hot to the touch. I picked them out, allowing them to cool a little before bagging them. All my unused evidence bags had been in my flight case. They'd gone up in flames with everything else, but I'd brought a box of freezer bags from the hotel to use instead. When I'd collected what was left of the hand in one of them I rejoined Brody and Fraser.

'That it?' Fraser asked, squinting at the bag.

'That's it.'

'Hardly worth bothering with.'

I ignored him and went to where an upright section of charred timber still stood in the ruins of the community centre. The wooden spar was blackened to charcoal. Attached to it were bright copper strands, all that remained of the centre's electrical wiring. The plastic insulation around the copper had been burned away, but the wires themselves were intact, still stapled to the wooden post.

Judging from their position, they would have fed the light switch by the entrance. Seeing them, an idea began to form, too faint even to call a suspicion. I'd only managed to escape from the burning hall because the fire hadn't spread as far as the doors. So it must have started at the far side, opposite where I now stood. I started to circle the wreckage of the centre, making my way round there.

'Now what?' Fraser demanded irritably. Brody said nothing, just watched, thoughtfully.

'There's something I want to check.'

I told myself I was probably wasting my time as I scanned the ashes and wreckage where the back wall had stood. Then something caught my eye. Crouching down, I gently brushed away the ash to reveal what I'd hoped I wouldn't find.

Small metal puddles, gleaming against the charred wood.

The sight sent a chill through me. I'd attended enough fire scenes to know only too well what they meant.

This was no accident.

And then an even worse thought struck me, one I hadn't even considered until now. *Oh, Christ.*

Gripped by a new sense of urgency, I hurried back to Brody and Fraser. But even as I did I heard a car approaching, and saw Maggie Cassidy's battered Mini bumping up the road towards us.

Her timing couldn't have been worse. She climbed out, diminutive as ever in her oversized red coat.

'Morning, gents,' she greeted us, cheerfully. 'I hear somebody had a barbecue last night.'

Fraser was already striding towards her. 'This is off limits. Back in your car. Now!'

The wind flattened her coat around her like a cocoon as she held out her dictaphone, as though to ward him off. There was nervousness in her face, but she did her best to disguise it.

'Aye? Why's that?'

'Because I say so.'

She shook her head with mock-regret. 'Sorry, not good enough. I slept through all the excitement last night, and I'm not missing out on it now. Perhaps if you gave me a few words, oh, say about how there's now a *murder* investigation going on, and how you think the fire started, then I'll be very happy to leave you in peace.'

Fraser balled his fists, glaring at her with such animosity I was worried he'd do something stupid. Maggie gave me a smile.

'How about you, Dr Hunter? Any chance of—'

'We need to talk.'

I don't know who looked most surprised, her or Fraser.

'You're not talking to *her*!'

I caught Brody's eye. 'Let him be,' he told Fraser.

'*What?* You've got to be joking. She's a bloody—'

'Just do it!'

All his years of command cracked into his voice. Fraser didn't like it, but he gave in.

'Aye, fine! Do what you bloody like,' he snapped, walking back towards the Range Rover.

'Don't let him go anywhere,' I warned Brody. 'We need the car.'

Maggie was watching me suspiciously, as though this might be some new sort of trick.

'I need your help,' I told her, taking her arm and leading her back towards the Mini. 'We're going to leave now, and I don't want you to come after us.'

She stared at me as if I were mad. 'What is this, are you—'

'*Listen*. Please,' I added, knowing too much time had already been wasted. 'You want a story, I promise you'll get one. But right now, I need you to leave us alone.'

The incredulous smile slowly died from her lips. 'This is bad, isn't it?'

'I hope not. But I think it might be, yes.'

The wind blew a strand of hair across her face as her eyes searched mine. She gave a nod as she brushed it away.

'All right. But there'd better be a front page story for me in this, all right?'

I hurried back to where Brody and Fraser waited by the Range Rover as she climbed back into her Mini.

'What the hell did you say to her?' Fraser demanded as she drove away.

'It doesn't matter. Have you spoken to Duncan this morning?'

'Duncan? No, not yet,' he said, defensively. 'He hasn't called in yet. But, you know, I was going to take him out some breakfast later . . .'

'Try him now.'

'Now? Why, what's—'

'Just do it.'

He gave me a dirty look but reached for his radio. 'Can't get through . . .' he frowned.

'All right, get in the car. We're going out there.'

Brody had been watching with a worried expression, but said nothing until we were in the car and Fraser was pulling away. 'What is it? What did you find?'

I was staring anxiously through the windscreen as we left the village, scanning the sky ahead of us. 'I checked the wiring back at the community centre. A fire caused by an electrical fault wouldn't have been hot enough to melt the copper core. But there's an area round the back where the wires were melted.'

'So what?' Fraser asked, impatiently.

'It means the fire was hotter there,' Brody said, slowly. 'Oh, Christ.'

Fraser banged the steering wheel. 'Will somebody please tell me what the fuck's going on?'

'It was hotter there because that's where an accelerant was used to start it,' I told him. 'The fire wasn't caused by a short. Somebody set it deliberately.'

He was still trying to work it out. 'What's that got to do with Duncan?'

It was Brody who answered. 'Because if someone wanted to get rid of the evidence, it might not only have been the clinic that was torched.'

I could see from Fraser's face that he finally understood. But even if he hadn't there was no need to explain further.

Smeared across the sky directly ahead was a black trail of smoke.

The meandering terrain prevented us from seeing the source of the smoke. It seemed like every hill and bend in the road conspired to keep the cottage and camper van from view. Fraser put his foot down, tearing along the narrow road much faster than was safe in the atrocious conditions. No one complained.

Then we rounded one final bend, and the old cottage was revealed in front of us. So, too, was the camper van.

What was left of it.

'Oh, no,' Fraser said.

Most of the smoke we'd seen was coming from the cottage. There hadn't been much left to burn, but the thick roof beams and timbers that had fallen in the day before were still smouldering in the ruins. If there had been anything in there that SOC might have salvaged, it had been destroyed now.

But it was the sight of Brody's camper van that transfixed us. It had been reduced to a burned-out shell, tyres melted to misshapen lumps of rubber. The living quarters had been almost completely consumed, walls eaten away by the fire, roof partially blown off when either the gas cylinder or petrol tank had exploded. Thin trails of smoke rose wraith-like from it, only to be whisked away by the wind.

There was no sign of Duncan.

Fraser didn't slow as he went off the road and on to the track, the heavy car slewing on the muddy surface as he stamped on the brakes. He jumped out of the car and ran towards the camper van, leaving the door swinging in the wind behind him.

'Duncan? *Duncan!*' he bellowed, charging across the grass. Brody and I ran behind him, rain whipping into our faces. Fraser lurched to a halt in front of the camper van.

'Oh, Jesus Christ! Where is he? Where the fuck is he?'

He stared round wildly, as though hoping the young PC would suddenly come strolling up. I became aware of Brody's gaze. There was the same awareness in his face that I felt myself, and I knew that he'd seen what I had.

'He's here,' I said quietly.

Fraser followed the direction of my gaze. A boot was sticking out from under a piece of heat-buckled roof, the leather burned away to reveal charred flesh and bone.

He took a step towards the camper van. 'Ah, no, Christ . . .'

Before I could stop him he grabbed hold of the panel and started trying to heave it off.

'Don't,' I began, but as I started forward a hand fell on my shoulder. I looked round at Brody. He shook his head.

'Leave him.'

'It was a crime scene; none of us should touch it. But I understand why Brody didn't try to interfere.'

'I don't really see it making much difference now, do you?' he said, bleakly.

Fraser wrenched the panel free, letting the wind carry it away. It pitched and bounced along the grass like a grounded kite until it came up against the cottage. Fraser continued to tear at the rest of the wreckage like a madman. Even from where I stood, the smell of burned meat was overpowering.

Then he stopped, staring at what he'd uncovered. He stumbled back, as uncoordinated as a broken puppet.

'Oh, Christ. Jesus fucking *Christ*, that's not him. Tell me that's not him!'

The body lay in the centre of the camper van. It wasn't as badly burned as Janice Donaldson's remains had been, but in some ways its scorched humanity made the sight even worse. Its limbs had drawn up, so that it was curled in a foetal position, pathetically vulnerable. Cooked into the flesh round its middle was a charred police utility belt. A fire-blackened baton and handcuffs were still attached to it.

Fraser was weeping. 'Why didn't he get out? Why the fuck didn't he get out?'

I took hold of his arm. 'Come on.'

'Get off me!' he snarled, jerking free.

'Get a grip, man!' Brody told him, harshly.

Fraser turned on him. 'Don't tell me what to do! You're a fucking has-been! You've got no authority here!'

Brody's face was uncompromising. 'Then start acting like a police officer yourself.'

All at once Fraser seemed to sag. 'He was twenty-one,' he mumbled. 'Twenty-one! What am I going to tell everyone?'

'Tell them he was murdered,' Brody said brutally. 'Tell them we've got a killer loose on the island. And tell them if Wallace had sent out a proper inquiry team in the first place, your twenty-one-year-old PC might still be alive!'

There was rare emotion in his voice. And we all knew what he'd left unsaid; that it had been Fraser's slip that had shown our hand about the woman's murder, and perhaps panicked her killer into action. But there was no point in recriminations now, and looking at Fraser I thought he was suffering enough already.

'Take it easy,' I told Brody.

He took a long breath, then nodded, in control of himself again. 'We need to let the mainland know what's happened. This isn't just a straightforward murder inquiry any more.'

Red-eyed, Fraser took out his radio, turning his back to the wind and rain as he stabbed a number into its keypad. He listened, then tried again.

'Come on, come *on*!'

'What's wrong?' Brody asked.

'It's not working.'

'What do mean, it's not working? You called Wallace last night.'

'Well, now there's nothing!' Fraser snapped. 'I thought it was just Duncan's radio before, but I can't raise anybody. See for yourself, there's no bloody signal!'

He thrust it at Brody. The retired inspector took it and tapped in a number. He put the handset to his ear, then handed it back.

'Let's try the one in the car.'

The Range Rover's fixed radio used the same digital system as the handsets. Without bothering to ask Fraser, Brody tried it, then shook his head.

'Dead. The gale must have taken out a mast. If that's happened the whole comms network for the islands could be down.'

I took in the empty, windswept landscape that surrounded us. The low, dark clouds that squatted over the island seemed to shut us in even more.

'So now what do we do?' I asked.

For once even Brody seemed at a loss. 'We keep trying. Sooner or later we'll get either the radios or the landlines back.'

'But what happens until then?'

The rain streaked his face as he looked at the camper van. His mouth set in a hard line.

'Until then, we're on our own.'

17

I volunteered to stay at the croft while Brody and Fraser drove back to the village to find stakes and a hammer. We needed to tape off the camper van, but there wasn't enough of it left to fix the tape to. Moving Duncan's body wasn't an option, even if there'd been anywhere left to take it. With Janice Donaldson's remains we hadn't had a choice, but that didn't apply here. True, it would mean leaving the van and its grisly contents exposed to the elements. But – Fraser's frenzy apart – this time I was determined to preserve the crime scene as we'd found it.

And none of us doubted that it was just that – a crime scene. Someone had torched this deliberately, just as they had the medical clinic. Except Duncan hadn't managed to escape.

Before he and Fraser left, Brody and I stood huddled on the track, bracing ourselves against the gale while the police sergeant tried once more to raise the mainland on the radio. The weather was worse than ever. Rain fell like lead shot, dripping from the scorched hood of my coat in shining strands, and heavy clouds raced overhead, their movement reflected in the rippling of the wind-flattened grass.

But nothing could carry away the stink of burning, or the stark fact of the young policeman's death. It hung like a pall over everything, adding a further chill to the already frigid air.

'You think this was done before or after the community centre?' I asked.

Brody considered the van's blackened shell. 'Before, I'd say. Makes more sense for him to have come out to torch this first, then set fire to the clinic. No point in starting a fire that would alert the entire village until he'd taken care of things here.'

I felt anger as well as shock at the senselessness of it. 'What was the point? We'd already moved the remains to the clinic. Why leave them out here for weeks, and then suddenly do this? It doesn't make sense.'

Brody sighed, wiping the rain from his face. 'It doesn't have to make sense. Whoever this is, he's panicking. He knows he made a mistake leaving the body here, and now he's trying to rectify it. He's determined to destroy anything that might tie him to it. Even if that means killing again.'

He paused, giving me a level look.

'You sure you'll be all right by yourself?'

We'd already discussed this. It made sense for Brody to go back to the village since he knew where to find the materials we needed to seal the site. But someone had to stay out here, and Fraser was in no fit state.

'I'll be fine,' I said.

'Just don't take any chances,' Brody warned. 'Anybody shows up, anyone at all, be bloody careful.'

He didn't have to tell me. But I didn't think I'd be in any danger. There was no reason for the killer to come back here now, not any more.

Besides, there were things I needed to do.

I watched the Range Rover bump down the track to the road. The rain beat a lunatic's Morse code on my coat as I turned back to where the burned-out camper van waited. By now the downpour had tamped down the ashes, so that the wind only plucked off the occasional piece of fly-blown char. Set against the rock-strewn slopes of Beinn Tuiridh, the grey-black hulk seemed almost a part of the barren landscape.

A ring of burned grass surrounded it, where the vegetation had been caught by the fire. Shivering in the freezing wind, I stayed on its edge, trying to visualize the camper van as it had been, forming a picture of how the transformation to its current state had come about.

Then I turned my attention to Duncan's body.

It wasn't easy. The remains I deal with are usually those of strangers. I know them only through their death, not their life. This was different, and it was hard to reconcile my memory of the young constable with what was in front of me.

What was left of Duncan McKinney lay amongst the burned shell of the camper van. The fire had transformed him into a thing of charred flesh and bone; a blackened marionette that no longer looked human. I thought about the last time I'd seen him, how he'd seemed troubled as he'd driven me into the village from the clinic. I wished now I'd tried harder to make him say what was on his mind. But I hadn't. I'd let him drive off, to spend the last few hours of his life alone out here.

I pushed the regret away. Thinking like that wouldn't help me, or him. Rain dripped from my hood as I stared down at the corpse, letting my mind clear of thoughts of who it had been. Gradually, I began to see it without the filter of emotions. *You want to catch whoever did this? Forget Duncan. Put aside the person.*

Look at the puzzle.

The body was lying face down. The clothes had been burned from it, as had most of the skin and soft tissue, exposing scorched internal organs that had been protected by the torso's cocoon. Its arms were bent at the elbows, pulled up as their tendons had contracted. The legs were similarly contorted, throwing the hips and lower body slightly out to one side as they had drawn up in the heat. Part of what remained of the tabletop was visible underneath the body. The feet were nearest the door, the head turned slightly to the right and pointing towards where the small couch had been.

There was nothing left of the couch but a buckled frame and a few blackened springs. Something else was lying amongst them. Leaning forward I recognized the steel cylinder of Duncan's Maglite, blistered and dulled by the fire.

My camera had been destroyed in the clinic along with the rest of my equipment, so I made do with sketching the body's position on a notepad I'd borrowed from the Range Rover. It wasn't perfect, as the sling made drawing difficult, and I had to shield the pad from the rain. But I did the best I could.

That finished, I began to study the body in more detail. Careful not to disturb anything, I leaned as close as I could, until I saw what I'd been looking for.

A gaping hole in the skull, the size of a man's fist.

The sound of a car coming down the track disturbed my thoughts. I looked round, surprised that Brody and Fraser were back so soon. But it wasn't the police Range Rover that was approaching, it was Strachan's gunmetal-grey Saab.

Brody's warning sprang uncomfortably to mind. *Anybody shows up, anyone at all, be bloody careful.* I climbed to my feet, slipping my notepad away, and went to meet him as the car pulled up. He climbed out, staring past me at the camper van, too shocked to raise the hood of his coat.

'Christ! This burnt down as *well*?'

'You shouldn't be here.'

But Strachan wasn't listening. His eyes widened as he saw what was lying in the wreckage. 'Oh, my God!'

He stared, blood draining from his face. Abruptly, he twisted away, doubling up as he vomited. He straightened slowly, fumbling in his pocket for something to wipe his mouth.

'Are you all right?' I asked.

He nodded, white-faced. 'Sorry,' he mumbled. 'Who . . . who is it? The young policeman?'

'Brody and Fraser are going to be back any time,' I said, by way of answer. 'You shouldn't let them find you here.'

'To hell with them! This is my *home*! I've spent the past five *years* getting this place back on its feet, and now . . .' He broke off, running his hand through his rain-flattened hair. 'This can't be happening. I thought the community centre might be an accident, but this . . .'

I didn't say anything. Strachan was recovering from the shock now. He lifted his face to the clouded sky, oblivious to the wind and rain.

'The police won't be able to get out here in this weather. And you're not going to be able to keep this quiet. There are going to be a lot of frightened and angry people wanting answers. You've got to let me help. They'll listen to me more than your police sergeant. Or Andrew Brody, come to that.'

There was a look of determination on the chiselled features as he stared across at me.

'I'm not going to let someone destroy everything we've done here.'

It was tempting. I knew from bitter experience how ugly the mood could turn in a small community like this. I'd felt the brunt of it myself once, and that had been in a community I'd been part of. Out here, cut off from all contact with the outside world, I didn't want to think what might happen.

The question was, how far we could afford to trust anyone? Even Strachan?

Still, there was one way he could help. 'Could we use the radio on your yacht?'

He looked surprised. 'My yacht? Yes, of course. It's got satellite communication as well if you need it. Why, aren't the police radios working?'

I didn't want to tell him we didn't have any means of contacting the mainland at all, but I had to give some reason for asking. 'We lost one of them in the fire. It's just useful to know there's an alternative if Fraser's not around.'

Strachan seemed to accept my explanation. Subdued again, he stared at the camper van.

'What was his name?'

'Duncan McKinney.'

'Poor devil,' he said, softly. He looked at me. 'Remember what I said. Anything you need, anything at all.'

He returned to his car and set off back down the track. As the Saab neared the road, I saw the distinctive shape of the police Range Rover heading towards it. The road's narrowness forced the two cars to slow as they skirted each other, like two dogs warily circling before a fight. Then they were clear, and the Saab accelerated away with a smooth growl.

Keeping my back to the wind, I waited for the Range Rover to pull up. Brody and Fraser climbed out. While Fraser went to open the back, Brody came over, staring at the rapidly disappearing fleck of Strachan's car.

'What was he doing here?'

'He came to offer his help.'

His chin jutted. 'We can manage without that.'

'That depends.'

I told him my idea of using the yacht's radio. Brody sighed.

'I should have thought of that myself. But we don't need Strachan's yacht. Any of the boats in the harbour will have ship-to-shore. We can use the ferry's.'

'The yacht's nearer,' I pointed out.

Brody's jaw worked at the prospect of asking Strachan for a favour. But much as he might dislike the idea, he knew it made sense.

He gave a terse nod. 'Aye. You're right.'

Fraser came over, clutching an armful of rusted steel reinforcing rods, the sort used for concrete foundations.

'There was a pile of those left over from when they built the school,' Brody explained. 'Should do the trick.'

Fraser let the rods fall on to the grass, his eyes red-rimmed. 'This still doesn't sit right with me. Just leaving him out here . . .'

'If you can think of any alternative, then tell us,' Brody said, but not unkindly.

The sergeant nodded, miserably. He went back to the Range Rover and came back with a heavy lump hammer and a roll of tape. He strode ahead of us to the remains of the camper van, his posture rigid and determined. But at the sight of Duncan's body, lying exposed to the elements like a sacrifice, he faltered.

'Oh, Jesus . . .'

'If it's any consolation, he wouldn't have felt any of this,' I told him.

He glared at me. 'Aye? And how would you know?'

I took a deep breath. 'Because he was already dead when the fire started.'

The angry light died from the sergeant's eyes. Brody had come to stand with us.

'You sure?' he asked.

I glanced at Fraser. This wasn't easy for any of us, but it would be hardest for him to hear.

'Go on,' he said, roughly.

I led them through the wet grass until we had a better view of the skull. Scraps of black flesh still clung to the bone, varnished by the rain. The cheeks and lips had burned away, exposing the teeth in a mockery of the policeman's engaging grin.

I felt myself falter. *The puzzle, not the person.* I pointed to the gaping hole in Duncan's skull.

'See there, on the left-hand side?'

Fraser glanced, then looked away. The head was turned slightly, so it was lying partly on one cheek. Its position made it difficult to see the full extent of the damage, but it was unmissable, all the same. The jagged hole overlapped both the parietal and temporal

196

bones on the left side of the skull like the entrance to a dark cave.

Brody cleared his throat before he spoke. 'Couldn't that have happened in the fire, like you thought Janice Donaldson's had?'

'There's no way an injury like that was caused by the heat. Duncan was hit a hell of a lot harder than Janice Donaldson. You can see even from here that pieces of bone have been pushed into the skull cavity. That means the wound was made by an external impact, not cranial pressure. And from the position of the arms, it looks like he just went straight down, without making any attempt to stop himself. He literally didn't know what hit him.'

There was a silence. 'And what did hit him? A hammer or something?' Brody asked.

'No, not a hammer. That would have punched a round hole through the bone, and this is more irregular. From what I can see so far it looks like some sort of club.'

Like a Maglite, I thought. The steel case of Duncan's torch was poking through the ashes near his body. It was the right size and shape, and was heavy enough to have caused the damage. But there was no point speculating until SOC arrived.

Fraser had his fists balled, his eyes drawn to the body despite himself. 'He was a fit lad. He wouldn't have given in without a fight.'

I spoke carefully. 'Perhaps not, but . . . well, from how it looks he had his back turned when he was struck. The body's lying face down, feet towards the door. So he was facing away from it, and pitched forward when he was hit from behind.'

'Couldn't he have been killed outside, and then brought into the van?' Brody asked.

'I don't think so. For one thing, the table's underneath him, which suggests he fell on to it. I can't see anyone lifting his body on to it. And Duncan was hit here, on the side of his head,' I said, tapping my own just above my ear. 'For it to connect there the killer must have swung sideways rather than overhead like you'd normally expect.'

197

Fraser still didn't get it. 'Why does being hit on the side of his head mean he was killed inside the van?'

'Because the ceiling wasn't high enough for an overhead swing,' Brody answered for me.

'It's only guesswork at this stage, but it fits,' I said. 'The killer was standing behind Duncan, between him and the door. That points to him being left-handed, because the impact wound is to the left-hand side of the skull.'

The rain squalled around us as they stared down at Duncan's body, playing it out for themselves. I waited, wondering which one of them would say it first. Surprisingly, it was Fraser.

'So he let them in? And then turned his back?'

'That's how it looks.'

'What the hell was he thinking? Christ, I *told* him to be careful!'

I somehow doubted that. But if the police sergeant needed to revise his memory to ease any guilt he might be feeling, I wasn't going to stop him. There was a more important point here, one I could see from Brody's expression that he hadn't missed, even if Fraser had.

Duncan hadn't thought he was in any danger when he let his killer in.

Brody reached out and took the tape from Fraser.

'Let's get this over with.'

18

The police tape snapped and twisted, strung out between the steel rods that Fraser had hammered into the ground. With only one hand, there was little I could do to help. Brody had held the rods in place while Fraser knocked them in with the lump hammer, positioning them every few yards to form a square perimeter round the van.

'You want to take a turn?' the sergeant panted, halfway through.

'Sorry, you'll have to do it. Arthritis,' Brody told him, rubbing his back.

'Aye, right,' Fraser muttered, pounding the steel rod into the turf as though venting his anger and grief.

Which was perhaps what Brody had intended, I thought.

I stood nearby, hunched against the cold and damp as they ran the tape between the rods. It was only a symbolic barrier, but I still wished there was more I could do as they fought against the wind to secure the whipping ends of the tape.

Finally, it was done. The three of us stood, taking one last look at the camper van behind its flimsy barricade. Then, without a word, we headed back for the Range Rover.

Our priority now was to let the mainland know what had happened. While Wallace still wouldn't be able to send any support until the storm eased, the murder of a police officer would escalate this to a whole new level. And until help arrived, it was more important than ever for us to maintain contact with the outside world. Particularly for Fraser, I thought, watching him trudge ahead of us on the track, his broad shoulders slumped. He looked the picture of abject defeat.

Beside me, Brody suddenly stopped walking. 'Have you got any bags left?'

He was looking down at a tuft of wiry grass, rippling and bent in the wind. Something dark was snagged against it. I reached in my pocket for one of the freezer bags I'd brought from the hotel and passed it to him as Fraser came back.

'What is it?' he wanted to know.

Brody didn't answer. Putting his hand into the bag as though it were a glove, he bent down and picked up the object that had been snared by the grass. Then, reversing the bag so it was inside, he held it up to show us.

It was a large, black plastic screw cap. A thin strap that would once have fastened it to a container stuck out from it, snapped clean after an inch or so.

Brody put his nose to the open top of the bag. 'Petrol.'

He handed it to Fraser, who took a sniff himself. 'You think the bastard dropped this last night?'

'I'd say it's a fair bet. Wasn't here yesterday, or we'd have seen it.'

Fraser's expression was furious as he tucked it into his coat pocket. 'So somewhere on this godforsaken island there's a petrol container with a broken strap but no lid.'

'If it hasn't been chucked off a cliff by now,' Brody said.

The drive to Strachan's house passed in subdued silence. When we turned up the long driveway leading to the house we saw that Grace's Porsche Cayenne had gone, but Strachan's Saab was parked outside.

I couldn't see Strachan's house being without its own generator, but despite the day's gloom there were no lights in any of the windows. Rain dripped from Fraser's fist as he banged the cast-iron door knocker. We could hear Strachan's dog barking inside, but there was no other sign of life. Fraser gave the heavy door a thump, hard enough to rattle it on its hinges.

'Come on, where the fuck are you?' he snarled.

'Probably off on one of his walkabouts,' Brody said, standing back to look up at the house. 'I suppose we could always just go down to the yacht ourselves. It's an emergency.'

'Aye, and what if it's locked?' Fraser asked. 'We can't just break in.'

'People here don't usually lock their doors. There's no cause.'

There might be now, I thought. But I was against it for another reason.

'If we get down there and find it's locked we've wasted even more time,' I said. 'And does anyone know how to use a satellite radio anyway? Or a ship-to-shore, come to that?'

The silence that greeted the question told me neither of them did.

Fraser slammed his hand against the door. 'Shit!'

'Let's go and find Kinross. We'll use the ferry's,' Brody said.

Kinross lived by the harbour. When we reached the outskirts of the village, Brody told Fraser to take a short cut down a narrow cobbled street that bypassed the main road. The ferry captain's bungalow had a prefabricated look to it, and like most of the other houses on Runa it had new uPVC doors and windows.

But the rest of the building had a run-down, uncared-for look. The gate was missing from the bottom of the path, and the small garden was overgrown and strewn with rusting boat parts. A fibre-glass dinghy lay overgrown with dune grass, its bottom holed and splintered. Brody had told me Kinross was a widower who lived alone with his son. It showed.

Brody and I left Fraser brooding in the car while we went up the path. The door bell chimed with a cheery electronic melody. No one

201

answered. Brody rang it again, then hammered on the door for good measure.

The muted sounds of movement came from inside, then the door was opened. Kevin, Kinross's teenage son, stood in the hallway, eyes briefly making contact before darting off again. The angry red mounds of acne scarred his face in a cruel topography.

'Is your father in?' Brody asked.

The teenager gave a shake of his head, not looking at us.

'Know where he is?'

He shuffled uncomfortably, narrowing the gap in the doorway until only a thin strip the width of his face remained open.

'Down at the boatyard,' he mumbled. 'In the workshop.'

The door snicked shut.

We went back to the car. The harbour was a turmoil of crashing waves and churning boats. Out on the jetty, the ferry pitched and rolled at its berth. The sea churned wildly, the spume so thick it was indistinguishable from the rain.

Fraser drove down to the corrugated shack on the seafront that I'd passed on my way to Brody's the previous day. It was set close to the foot of the tall cliffs that encircled the harbour, and which protected it from the worst of the weather.

'The yard's communal,' Brody said as we climbed out of the car and hurried over, having to fight against the wind. 'Everybody with a boat chips in to the running costs, and if they need repairs everyone pitches in.'

'Is that Guthrie's?' I asked, indicating the dilapidated fishing boat hauled up on blocks that I'd noticed the day before. It appeared in even worse condition up close. Half of its timber hull was missing, giving it the skeletal look of some long-dead prehistoric animal.

'Aye. Supposed to be making it seaworthy again, but he doesn't seem in any hurry.' Brody shook his head in disapproval. 'Rather spend his money in the bar.'

Skirting the covered piles of building supplies stacked nearby, we hurried for the workshop entrance. The wind threatened to wrench the door from its hinges when we opened it. Inside, the workshop was stiflingly hot, thick with the smell of machine oil and sawdust. Lathes, welding torches and cutting gear littered the floor, while the walls were covered with shelves of tools, stained black with ancient grease. A radio was playing, the tinny melody fighting against the chug of a generator.

About half a dozen men were inside. Guthrie and a smaller man were crouched over the dismembered remains of an engine that was spread out on the concrete floor. Kinross and the others were playing cards at an old Formica table, on which stood half-drunk mugs of tea. A tin foil pie case doubled as an ashtray, overflowing with cigarette stubs.

They had all broken off what they were doing to stare at us. Their expressions weren't exactly hostile, but neither were they friendly. They regarded us blankly. Waiting.

Brody stopped in front of Kinross. 'Can we have a word, Iain?'

Kinross shrugged. 'I'm not stopping you.'

'I mean in private.'

'It's private enough here.' To emphasize his point he opened a pouch of tobacco and began rolling a cigarette with oil-stained fingers.

Brody didn't bother to argue. 'We need to use the ferry's radio.'

Kinross ran the tip of his tongue along the edge of the cigarette paper, then smoothed it down. He nodded towards Fraser.

'What's wrong with his? Don't the police have radios these days?'

Fraser glared back without answering.

Kinross plucked a piece of tobacco from his mouth. 'Fucked, are they?'

I could hear the sergeant's heavy adenoidal breathing, like an angry bull's, as he started forward. 'Aye, and so will you be if—'

'We're asking for your help,' Brody cut in, laying a restraining hand on Fraser's shoulder. 'We need to get in touch with the mainland. It's important, or we wouldn't ask.'

Kinross unhurriedly lit the roll-up. He shook out the match and tossed it into the overflowing ashtray, then considered Brody through a plume of blue smoke.

'You can try, for what it's worth.'

'Meaning what?' Fraser demanded.

'You won't be able to transmit from the harbour. The radio's VHF. Has to have line-of-sight, and the cliffs block the signal to the mainland.'

'What if you need to send a Mayday?' Brody asked, incredulous.

Kinross shrugged. 'If you're in the harbour, you wouldn't need to.'

Fraser had bunched his fists. 'So take the bloody boat out to sea, where you can transmit.'

'You want to try going out in this, go ahead. But not on my ferry.'

Brody kneaded the bridge of his nose. 'How about the other boats?'

'All VHF, the same.'

'There's Mr Strachan's yacht,' one of the card players suggested.

Guthrie laughed. 'Aye, that's got communications coming out of its arse.'

I saw Brody's face close down. 'Look, can we try the ferry anyway?'

Kinross took an indifferent drag of his roll-up. 'If you want to waste your time, it's up to you.' He nipped out the glowing end of his cigarette and put it in his tobacco pouch as he rose to his feet. 'Sorry, lads.'

'I was losing, anyway,' one of the card players said, throwing in his cards. 'Time I went home.'

Guthrie wiped his hands on an oily cloth. 'Aye. I'm off for something to eat.'

The other card players were already throwing their cards down on the table, reaching for their own coats as Kinross pulled on an oilskin and went out, letting the doors swing back on us as we followed. Rain and spray filled the air with an iodine tang as he strode bareheaded along the harbour to the jetty, oblivious to the breaking waves. The ferry was bucking against its moorings, but he walked up the gangplank without hesitation.

The rest of us were more cautious, holding on to the gangplank's railing as it tipped and swayed. It was barely any better once we were on board, the slippery deck pitching unpredictably. I looked up at the ferry's aerial, bent and quivering in the wind, then at the cliffs surrounding us. I could see now what Kinross meant. They hemmed the small harbour in on three sides, rising up like a wall between us and the mainland.

Kinross was already fiddling with the radio set when we crammed into the claustrophobic bridge. I braced myself against the wall as the deck pitched queasily underfoot. A medley of discordant hums and squeaks came from the radio set as Kinross spoke into its handset, then waited vainly for a response.

'Who are you calling?' Brody asked.

Kinross answered without turning round. 'Coastguard. They've got the biggest radio mast on Lewis. If they can't hear us no one else will.'

We waited as he spoke into the handset, receiving only a hollow hissing in return.

Fraser had been watching the ferry captain with an expression of sullen dislike. 'You remember bringing any strangers across on the ferry about four or five weeks ago?' he asked suddenly.

Brody gave him an angry look, but he took no notice. Kinross didn't turn round.

'No.'

'No what? No you didn't bring anyone, or no you don't remember?'

Kinross stopped what he was doing and turned to stare at him. 'This to do with the murder?'

'Just answer the question.'

Kinross's smile threatened violence. 'And if I don't?'

Brody cut in before Fraser could respond. 'Take it easy, Iain, no one's accusing you of anything. We just came out here to use the radio.'

Deliberately, Kinross lowered the handset. He leaned back against the swaying bulkhead, folding his arms as he regarded us.

'Are you going to tell me what this is about?'

'It's police business,' Fraser growled.

'Aye, and this is my ferry, and my radio. You want to use it, you can tell me what's so urgent.'

'We can't yet, Iain,' Brody interposed, smoothly. 'But it's important. Trust me on that.'

'This is our island. We've a right to know what's going on.'

'I know, and you will, I promise.'

'When?'

Brody sighed. 'Tonight. But right now we need to contact the mainland.'

'Now listen—' Fraser began, but Brody spoke over him.

'You've got my word.'

Kinross stared at him, his expression giving nothing away. Then he got up and headed for the door.

'Where are you going?' Brody asked.

'You wanted me to try the radio, I have.'

'Can't you keep trying?'

'No. Anyone could hear, we'd know by now.'

'What about other ships? Someone could relay a message back to the mainland for us. The cliffs wouldn't block that.'

'Maybe not, but they're still going to funnel the signal, and the set's range is only thirty miles. You want to waste your time pissing in the wind, that's up to you, but you can do it by yourselves.' He indicated the handset. 'Press the switch to talk, let go to receive. And switch it off when you've finished.'

With that he walked out. As the door banged shut behind him, Fraser turned on Brody, angrily.

'What the hell do you think you're doing? You've no authority to tell them anything!'

'We don't have any choice. We need these people's help. You're not going to get it by yelling.'

Fraser's face was crimson. 'One of those bastards killed Duncan!'

'Aye, and antagonizing everyone's not going to find out who did it.' Brody stopped, restraining himself. He took a deep breath. 'Kinross is right. There's no point wasting any more time here when Strachan's yacht has a satellite comms system. We can call into the school on the way and see if Grace is there.'

'And if she's not?' Fraser demanded, truculently.

'Then we'll wait at the house until one of them gets home,' Brody grated, clearly not happy himself at having to ask anything of Strachan. 'Unless you've any better ideas?'

Fraser hadn't. We drove up through the village from the harbour, but when we reached the school Grace's black Porsche wasn't outside. The small building was unlit and empty.

'They must have sent the kids home early because of the power cut. We probably missed her when we detoured to see Kinross,' Brody said, his frustration evident.

There was nothing to do but head for Strachan's house and hope she was there. Fraser drove in moody silence. I couldn't help but feel sorry for him. He wasn't an easy man to like, but Duncan's death had hit him hard. And he'd been out of his depth even before his colleague was murdered.

We were approaching the big house when the sergeant suddenly tensed.

'What the hell's he doing?'

Strachan's Saab was tearing down the road directly towards us. Fraser swore and swerved into the side, stamping on the brake as the Saab skidded to a halt just a few feet away.

'Bloody idiot!' Fraser cursed.

Strachan had jumped out and was running towards us, not even bothering to close his car door. Fraser angrily wound down the window and yelled at him.

'What the hell are you playing at?'

Strachan didn't seem to hear. His face was shockingly pale, his eyes wide and scared as he bent to the open window.

'Grace is missing!' he gasped.

'What do you mean, missing?' Fraser demanded.

'I mean she's *missing*! She's gone!'

Brody had climbed out of the Range Rover. 'Slow down and tell us what's happened.'

'I've told you! Christ, are you all bloody deaf? We have to *find* her!'

'We will, but you're going to have to calm down and tell us what you know.'

Strachan made an effort to compose himself. 'I got back a few minutes ago. Grace's car was here, and there were lights on and music playing, so I thought she was in the house. She'd left a cup of coffee going cold in the kitchen, but when I called she didn't answer. I looked in every room, but there's no sign of her!'

'Couldn't she have gone for a walk?' Fraser asked.

'Grace? In this weather? Look, why are we just standing here, we've got to *do* something!'

Brody turned to Fraser, automatically assuming command. 'We need to organize a search. Go back to the village and bring as many people back as you can.'

'What about you?' Fraser asked, not liking being told what to do.

'I'm going to go up to the house and take a look.'

'I've told you, she isn't there!' Strachan almost yelled.

'We'll take another look anyway. Dr Hunter, do you want to come with me?'

I'd been about to suggest it anyway. If Grace was hurt I'd be more use here than rounding up a search party in the village. We hurried over to the Saab as Fraser drove off in the Range Rover.

'What do you think?' I asked Brody, in a low voice.

He just shook his head, his expression grim.

Strachan had left the Saab's engine running. He barely waited for us to get in before he set off, reversing back up the road and up the driveway before screeching to a halt next to Grace's black Porsche SUV. Without waiting to see if we followed, he ran into the house shouting his wife's name. The only response was a frenzied barking from the dog in the kitchen.

'See, she's not here!' he said, pushing his hand through his hair distractedly. 'And Oscar was running around outside when I got back. If Grace had gone anywhere she wouldn't have just left him outside like that!'

There was a knot of tension in my gut as I heard the catch in his voice. I knew what he was going through. I'd once gone to Jenny's house and found the same terrible absence myself. There had been a killer loose then as well, and being here now, seeing the fear in Strachan's eyes, gave me a terrible sense of déjà vu.

But Brody remained calm as we carried out a quick search of the house. There was no sign of Grace.

'We're just wasting time!' Strachan said as we finished, his panic nearing the surface.

'Did you look in the outbuildings?' Brody asked.

'Yes! There's only the barn, and she's not in there!'

'What about the cove?'

Strachan just stared at him. 'I . . . No, but Grace never goes down there, not without me.'

'Let's take a look anyway, shall we?'

Strachan led us into the kitchen. A half-drunk cup of coffee stood on the table, a book opened but face down next to it, as though Grace had merely stepped out for a moment. Impatiently pushing the retriever aside, Strachan went out through the back door and rushed for the steps leading down to the cove.

I'd been half afraid we'd see Grace's broken body lying on the shingle below us. But except for the yacht moored at the short jetty, the cove was empty. It was a beautiful boat, its hull squeaking against the rubber fenders as the sea threw it about, tall mast swinging back and forth like the arm of a broken metronome.

Strachan hurried along the jetty towards it. He bounded up the gangplank and ran to the cockpit. I was slower to board, struggling for balance with one arm strapped up. As I stepped on to the deck Strachan threw back the cockpit hatch and suddenly froze.

When I reached him I saw why.

Like the rest of the yacht, the cockpit was beautifully equipped; teak panels, stainless steel fittings, and an elaborate instrument console. Or what was left of it. The radio and satcom had been smashed to pieces, the deck below them littered with torn wires and broken circuitry.

Strachan stared at it for a moment, then rushed through the cockpit to the main cabin.

'Grace? Oh, God, *Grace!*'

She lay on the cabin's floor. Her head and shoulders were covered with a sack, but below that Grace's white parka was clearly visible. She lay curled on her side, arms pulled behind her and tied behind her back.

From the waist down she was naked.

Or almost. Her feet hadn't been bound, but her jeans had been left pulled down around her ankles, tethering them as securely as a rope. Her pants were around her knees, as though her attacker had been interrupted in the act of removing them.

She looked obscenely vulnerable lying there, her long legs bare and blue-white with the cold. She wasn't moving. I thought we were too late, but then Strachan touched her and she suddenly began to thrash around.

'Hold her, don't let her hurt herself!' I warned, trying to catch her feet.

'It's all right, Grace, it's me! It's me!' Strachan said, yanking the sacking from her head.

Underneath it her hair was a tangled mess, obscuring her face. A piece of dirty cloth had been crammed into her mouth. Above it her eyes were wide and terrified, but then they fixed on Strachan and she immediately stopped struggling.

'It's all right, I'm here, it's all right!' he chanted, easing the gag from her mouth. She sucked in a breath, sobbing.

'Michael, oh, thank God, Michael!'

Her face was flushed and puffy, the skin imprinted with the rough hessian pattern of the sack. Her right cheek was discoloured by a livid bruise, and her mouth was swollen and bloody. But other than that there were no obvious injuries I could see.

'Are you all right? Are you hurt?' Strachan was asking her, his voice cracked.

'No, I . . . I don't think so.'

'Did he sexually assault you?' Brody asked bluntly.

'Oh, for God's sake!' Strachan exploded. Even I was shocked at the question.

But Grace was shaking her head. 'No . . . no, he didn't . . . I wasn't raped.'

Thank God, I thought. At least she'd been spared that. And it was probably better to deal with the issue now and get it out of the way. Perhaps Brody wasn't being insensitive after all.

Tears were running down Strachan's face as he tenderly brushed the hair from his wife's face. 'Who did it? Did you see him?'

'I don't know, I . . . I . . .'

He hugged her. 'Shh, it's all right, it's over now. It's over.'

Brody and I gave them as much privacy as we could while Strachan drew up Grace's underwear and jeans. I tried to unfasten the rope binding her wrists, but it had been tied too tightly for me to manage with one hand. The skin was chafed and abraded, her hands white from restricted circulation. Brody had to search for a

211

knife to cut it, then we stood back as Strachan helped Grace to her feet.

'Help me carry her,' Strachan said to Brody, their feud temporarily forgotten.

'I can walk,' Grace said.

'I don't think—'

'I'm all right, I can walk!'

She was still crying, but there was none of the hysteria I'd feared. Brody and I stayed a discreet distance behind them as Strachan supported her along the jetty. Grace huddled against him, the two of them so oblivious to anyone else that I felt like an intruder.

As we climbed the steps out of the cove, the seagulls' lonely cries sounded like mocking laughter on the wind.

19

I cleaned and dressed Grace's wounds while Fraser took her statement. He'd arrived with a convoy of cars from the village shortly
after we'd taken Grace back to the house. Strachan had objected to
his wife being questioned so soon, but I'd suggested that it was best
to get it over with. She would have to tell her story again when the
mainland police arrived, but meanwhile it was better for her to
describe what had happened while the memory was still fresh. Not
only could early debriefing help avoid psychological trauma in
assault victims, at least this way I'd be able to make sure Fraser didn't
push her too hard.

Somehow I didn't think he'd be the most sensitive of interviewers.

Strachan had sent everyone who'd come to help search for Grace
back home again, after he'd distractedly thanked and reassured them
that she wasn't badly hurt. Shock and anger was visible on all their
faces. Even though news of Duncan's death hadn't yet spread, by now
everyone had heard that the body found at the cottage had been
murdered. But shocking as that might be, what had happened to
Grace was even more so. The murder victim was unknown to them,
whereas Grace was the wife of Runa's benefactor, respected and well
liked. An attack on her struck right at the heart of the community.

Kinross and Guthrie had been amongst those who'd come out to help with the search. As he'd prepared to leave, the look on the ferry captain's face promised slaughter.

'Whoever did this, he's a dead man when we find him,' he'd vowed to Strachan.

I didn't think it was an empty threat. Emotions were running high all round. Given his infatuation with Grace, it was no surprise that Cameron had also rushed out to help with the search. He'd been the last to leave, stridently insisting that he had to see her. His protests had carried from the hallway into the kitchen where Brody and Fraser waited as I cleaned Grace's wounds.

'If she's been injured I need to examine her,' Cameron boomed, indignantly.

Strachan's voice remained unmoved. 'There's no need. David's doing that.'

'Hunter?' Cameron fairly spat the word. 'With all due respect, Michael, if anyone's going to treat Grace it should be me, not some . . . some ex-GP!'

'Thanks, but I'll decide who's going to look after my wife.'

'But Michael—'

'I said no!' There was a shocked pause. When Strachan spoke again it was with more restraint. 'Go home, Bruce. If I need you, I'll let you know.'

'I seem to be causing trouble,' Grace said, ruefully, as we heard the front door close. She had been stoically enduring my one-handed attempts to dab antiseptic on her injuries.

'I expect he just wants to help,' I said, putting down the wad of cotton wool. 'Excuse me.'

Leaving her with Brody and Fraser, I went out of the kitchen to intercept Strachan as he came back across the large hall.

'I heard what Cameron said,' I told him. 'He's got a point. He'll have more experience at treating wounds than I do.'

The events of the last hour had taken their toll on Strachan. He looked better than he had, but the chiselled features were drawn, and some of the vitality had drained from him.

'I'm sure you're more than capable of putting a dressing on,' he said tiredly.

'Yes, but he's the nurse . . .'

His face hardened. 'For the time being.'

I didn't say anything. Strachan glanced at the kitchen doorway and lowered his voice. 'You must have seen how he looks at Grace. I've put up with it in the past, because I thought he was harmless. But after this . . .'

I'd wondered how Strachan felt about Cameron's feelings for his wife. Now I knew.

'You don't think it was him who attacked her?' I said, doubtfully.

'Somebody did!' he flashed. But the vehemence soon passed. 'No, I'm not saying it was Bruce. I just . . . well, I'd rather he didn't go near her right now.'

He gave an embarrassed smile.

'Come on, let's get back. They'll think we're plotting something.'

We joined the others in the kitchen. Fraser was waiting with his notepad, while Brody sat staring into his cooling mug of tea with a faint frown. The old DI had been unusually quiet since we'd come back to the house, apparently content to let Fraser ask most of the questions.

Strachan sat beside Grace, holding her hand as I finished treating her wounds. None were serious, mainly cuts and abrasions. The worst was the darkening bruise on her face where she'd been hit. It was on her right cheek, which meant whoever had struck her was probably left-handed.

The same as Duncan's killer.

I began to dab the broken skin with antiseptic as she told Fraser what she could remember.

'I'd not been back from school long. I'd just made myself a coffee.' Her hand trembled as she held a glass of brandy and water I'd given

215

her in lieu of any other sedative. There was a faint quaver in her voice, but otherwise she seemed to be coping well with her ordeal.

'When was this?' Fraser asked, writing ponderously in his notebook.

'I don't know . . . about two, two thirty, I think. Bruce decided to close the school early because of the power cut. We'd got heating but no lights.' She broke off to speak to her husband. 'Michael, we really need to see about getting a back-up generator for the school as well, you know.'

'I know, we will.'

Strachan smiled, but he still looked awful. He seemed to blame himself for what had happened, for not being there when she'd needed him.

Grace took a sip of brandy and gave a shudder. 'Oscar was barking at the kitchen door. He wouldn't shut up, and as soon as I opened it he shot off for the cove. I didn't want him going on the jetty in this weather, so I went after him. When I got down there he was barking like a mad thing at the yacht, and I saw the cockpit hatch was open. Even then, I didn't think anything about it. It's never locked, and I thought Michael must have forgotten to close it. I started to go into the cockpit, but there was no light on and I couldn't see. Then . . . then something hit me.'

She faltered, her hand going to the bruise on her right cheek.

'You don't have to talk about it if you don't want to,' Strachan told her.

'I'm fine. Really.' Grace gave him a small smile. She looked shaken, but there was a determination about her as she continued. 'Everything got a bit blurry then. I realized I was on the floor and my hands had been tied behind me. There was something over my head, as well. I thought I was going to suffocate. The sack or what-ever it was stank of fish and oil, and a horrible piece of cloth had been stuffed in my mouth. I could feel cold air on my legs, and realized I didn't have my jeans on. I tried to yell or kick out, but I couldn't. Then I felt . . . I felt my pants being pulled down . . .'

She broke off, her control slipping.

'I just can't believe it must have been someone I *know*! Why would anyone *do* something like that?'

Strachan turned angrily to Fraser. 'For God's sake, can't you see this is upsetting her?'

'It's all right, really. I'd rather finish.' Grace wiped her eyes. 'There's not much more to tell anyway. I sort of passed out again after that. The next thing I knew was when you arrived.'

'But you say you weren't raped?' Fraser asked, tactlessly.

She looked at him levelly. 'No. I can remember that much.'

'Thank God,' Strachan said, fervently. 'The bastard must have heard us shouting for you and cleared out.'

Fraser was laboriously making notes. 'Can you remember anything else? Anything about who attacked you?'

Grace thought for a while, then shook her head. 'Not really.'

'Was he tall, short? Was there any sort of smell about him? Aftershave, anything like that?'

'I'm afraid all I could smell was rotting fish and oil from the sack.'

I finished cleaning the graze on Grace's cheek. 'Is there another way out of the cove?' I asked.

'Apart from the sea, you mean?' Strachan shrugged. 'If you climb over the rocks at the base of the cliff there's a shingle beach that runs halfway back to the village. Towards the end of it there's a path leading up to the cliff top. It'd be a bit hairy in this weather, but not impossible.'

That explained how the attacker had managed to get away without our seeing him. For all we knew he could have simply hidden until we'd gone into the house. We'd been more concerned with making sure Grace was all right than searching for whoever had assaulted her.

Fraser didn't have many more questions after that. I thought Brody might want to ask something himself, but the old DI remained silent as Grace excused herself. Strachan wanted to run a bath for her, but she would hear none of it.

'I'm not an invalid,' she smiled, with a touch of exasperation. 'You stay here with our guests.'

She came and kissed my cheek, the musk of her perfume distinctive even under the reek of antiseptic.

'Thank you, David.'

'Glad to help.'

There were dark shadows under Strachan's eyes, and a haunted look in them, as he watched her go out.

'She'll be all right,' I told him.

He nodded, unconvinced. 'Christ, what a day,' he muttered, passing a hand over his face.

Brody spoke for the first time since bringing Grace into the house. 'Tell me again what happened.'

Strachan looked taken aback. 'I've already told you. I came home and she wasn't here.'

'And where had you been, exactly?'

His tone wasn't quite accusatory, but it didn't leave much doubt why he was asking. Strachan regarded him with growing anger.

'I'd gone for a walk. Up to the cairns, if you must know. I came home after I'd seen David at the cottage, but I was still upset over what had happened to the young constable. Grace was at the school, so I left the car here and went out again.'

'To the mountain.'

'Yes, to the mountain,' Strachan said, his temper barely in check. 'And believe me, I wish to Christ I hadn't! So if that's all, Brody, thanks for your help, but I think it's time you went now!'

The atmosphere in the kitchen fairly crackled. I was surprised at Brody myself. Even though there was no love lost between the two of them, that was no reason to imply that Strachan might have attacked his own wife.

Getting to my feet, I broke the tense silence. 'Perhaps we should all be going.'

Strachan still looked angry, twin patches of colour on his face. 'Yes, of course.' But he hesitated. 'Actually . . . I'd appreciate it if you'd stay for a while, David. Just to make sure that Grace is all right later.'

I'd have expected him to want to be alone with his wife. I glanced at Brody. He gave an almost imperceptible nod.

'There's nothing for you to do back at the village. We can meet up at my place later to talk things through.'

I waited in the kitchen as Strachan showed the other two out. The front door closed. When he came back he seemed ill at ease. Almost embarrassed. But I realized that today had been traumatic for him too. Perhaps he wanted someone to reassure him that Grace would be all right, that what had happened wasn't his fault. Or perhaps he just wanted company.

'Thanks for staying. Just for an hour or so, until Grace goes to bed, then I'll run you back to the hotel.'

'Will she be all right left on her own?' I asked.

That didn't seem to have occurred to him. 'Well . . . You can always stay here, I suppose. Or take my car. It's an automatic, so you should be able to drive it one-handed.'

I'd already had one accident on Runa, and the prospect of trying to drive in my sling didn't appeal. But I'd cross that bridge when I came to it.

'Anyway, I'm forgetting my manners,' Strachan went on. 'Can I get you a drink? I've a bottle of twenty-year-old malt waiting to be opened.'

'Don't open it on my account.'

He grinned. 'It's the least I can do. Come on, let's go into the sitting room.'

He led me out across the hallway into a large sitting room. It displayed the same restrained taste as the rest of the house. Two black leather sofas faced each other across a smoked glass coffee table, and the parquet floor was covered with thick rugs. There was another abstract oil painting of Grace's above the fireplace, flanked on either side by floor to ceiling bookshelves. A glass case of flint tools and arrowheads stood against one wall, and there were other archaeological artefacts – fragments of ancient pottery, stone carvings – placed strategically around the room, each subtly picked out by a concealed light.

I browsed the bookshelves while Strachan opened a black lacquered drinks cabinet. Most of the titles were non-fiction. There were a few biographies of explorers such as Livingstone and Burton, but most were academic texts on archaeology and anthropology. There were several on primitive burial traditions, I noticed. I took down one called *Past Voices, Past Lives* and started leafing through it.

'The chapter on Tibetan sky burials is interesting,' Strachan said. 'They used to take their dead up on mountains and feed them to the birds. Thought they'd carry their spirits to heaven.'

He set a bottle of malt on the coffee table with two thick tumblers and sat down on one of the leather sofas.

'I didn't think you drank,' I said, putting the book back and going to the other sofa.

'I don't. But right now I feel like breaking my rule.' He poured the whiskies and handed one to me. '*Slàinte.*'

The malt was peaty but mellow. Strachan took a drink and began to cough.

'Christ! Is it any good?' he asked, eyes watering.

'Very.'

'That's all right, then.'

He took another drink.

'You could do with getting some rest yourself,' I told him. 'Today's been rough on you as well.'

'I'll cope.'

But his words couldn't disguise his exhaustion. He put his head back on the sofa, resting the nearly empty glass on his chest.

'My father always used to say that it's the things you never see coming you have to watch out for.' He gave a rueful smile. 'Now I know what he meant. You think you're finally in control of your life, and then – bam! Something you never expected suddenly blindsides you.'

'That's just life. You can't guard against everything.'

'No, I suppose not.' He stared broodingly into his glass. I had the feeling he was about to broach the real reason he'd asked me to stay. 'This assault . . . do you think Grace'll be all right? I don't mean physically. Do you think there'll be any . . . I don't know. Psychological scars?'

I chose my words carefully. 'I'm not a psychologist. But I'd say she's handling it pretty well so far. And she strikes me as being pretty resilient.'

He still seemed troubled. 'I hope you're right. It's just that . . . Well, a few years ago Grace had a breakdown. She'd been pregnant, and she miscarried. There were complications. The doctors told her she couldn't have any children. It hit her hard.'

'I'm sorry.' I thought of the wistfulness I'd seen on his wife's face when she'd talked about children the other day. And the way she loved working at the school. *Poor Grace. And poor Strachan*, I thought. I'd envied them their relationship, forgetting that tragedy was no respecter of wealth or glamour. 'Did you ever consider adopting?'

Strachan gave a quick shake of his head and took another drink of whisky. 'It wouldn't be right for us. It's fine, though, really. She's OK. But that's why we left South Africa and did so much travelling. We wanted a fresh start. That's why we settled here. Runa seemed like a sort of . . . of sanctuary. Somewhere we could pull up the drawbridge and feel safe. And now this happens.'

'It's a small island. Whoever did it won't get away.'

'Perhaps not. But Runa won't feel the same. And I worry what it'll do to Grace.'

He was slurring his words slightly, fatigue and reaction

221

compounding the effect of the alcohol. He drained his glass and reached for the bottle. 'Another?'

'No thanks.'

I was starting to think that I should be going. He needed to be with his wife, not down here getting drunk and maudlin with me. And driving one-handed would be hard enough without two whiskies inside me.

I was saved from having to say anything by the sound of someone hammering on the front door. Strachan frowned and put the bottle of whisky back down.

'Who the hell's that? If it's bloody Bruce Cameron again . . .' He stood up, swaying. 'Now I remember why I don't drink.'

'Shall I see who it is?' I offered.

'No, I'll go.'

Still, he didn't object when I went with him into the hallway. The events of the last few hours had rattled everyone. I hung back as he opened the door, and it was only when I recognized Maggie Cassidy's red coat and relaxed that I realized how keyed up I was myself.

But Strachan wasn't pleased to see her. 'What do you want?' he asked without inviting her in.

The rain blustered through the open doorway as Maggie stood framed in it. Her elfin face looked tiny inside the hood of her out-sized coat. She gave me a glance that was almost furtive, then addressed Strachan.

'Sorry to disturb you, but I heard about what happened. I just wanted to see how your wife was.'

'We've nothing to say, if that's why you're here.'

She shook her head earnestly. 'No, I . . . I brought this.' She held up a cloth-covered basin. 'It's chicken soup. My gran's speciality.'

That obviously wasn't what Strachan expected. 'Oh. Well . . . thank you.'

Maggie gave an embarrassed smile as she held out the soup. It

222

reminded me of the way she'd smiled at Duncan just before she'd tricked him by dropping her shoulder bag, and I suddenly knew what was about to happen. I opened my mouth to warn him, but as Strachan started to take it from her the basin slipped between their hands. Soup and broken crockery went everywhere as it shattered on the floor.

'Oh, God, I'm sorry . . .' Maggie stammered. She avoided looking at me as she fumbled in her pocket for a tissue. Pale splashes of soup dotted the bright red of her coat as well as Strachan's clothes.

'Leave it, it doesn't matter,' he said, irritably.

'No, please, let me clean it up . . .'

Her face had gone almost the same colour as her coat, but I wasn't sure if that was because of what had happened, or because she was conscious of me watching her. Strachan crossly took hold of her wrists as she began dabbing ineffectively at the front of his shirt.

'Michael? I heard something breaking.'

Grace was coming downstairs, wrapped in a thick white towelling bathrobe. Her hair was piled loosely on top of her head, the ends of it still damp.

Deliberately pushing Maggie's hands away, Strachan stepped back from her. 'It's all right, darling.' He gestured ironically at the mess. 'Miss Cassidy here just brought you some soup.'

Grace gave a wry smile. 'So I see. Well, don't keep her standing outside.'

'Actually, she was just leaving.'

'Don't be silly, not when she's come all this way.'

Reluctantly, Strachan moved aside to let Maggie in. As he closed the door behind her, she finally acknowledged me.

'Hello, Dr Hunter,' she said, with a look of studied innocence, before quickly turning back to Grace. 'I'm really sorry, Mrs Strachan. I didn't mean to bother you.'

'It's no bother. Come on through into the kitchen while I get a cloth for the mess. Michael, darling, why don't you see to

Maggie's coat? There's a sponge you can use in the utility room.'

'At least let me clean the floor . . .' Maggie protested. She was convincing, I'd give her that.

'Nonsense, Michael can see to that as well. He won't mind, will you, Michael?'

'No,' Strachan said stonily.

Maggie shrugged out of her coat and gave it to him. Without its bulk she looked even tinier than before, yet she still seemed to fill the room with an energy that belied her size.

She didn't look at me as we went into the kitchen. Grace started to fill the kettle.

'I feel really bad about this,' Maggie said to her. 'Especially at a time like this. Being attacked like that . . . it must have been awful for you.'

It was time I intervened. 'Grace, you really should be taking it easy. Maggie and I will be fine by ourselves for a few minutes. Won't we, Maggie?'

Maggie gave me a look of daggers. 'Well . . .'

'Actually, I do feel a little washed out,' Grace said. And it was true she was looking pale. She gave a wan smile. 'If you're sure you don't mind keeping Maggie company, David, I'll see how Michael's doing, and then I think I'll go to bed.'

I told her I didn't mind at all. Maggie watched her go, then her shoulders slumped. She turned to me, angrily.

'Happy now? I was only being sociable!'

Instead of answering I went to the sink and pulled a sheet of kitchen paper from a roll. 'You've got soup on your jeans,' I said, handing it to her. I watched as she angrily started to wipe it off. 'Your gran's name isn't Campbell, by any chance?'

'Campbell? No, she's a Cassidy, same as . . .'

Her face fell as she realized.

'I practically lived on the stuff when I was a student,' I told her. 'Cream of chicken was my favourite. It's the sort of smell you never forget.'

'All right, so my gran didn't make it. So what? It's the thought that counts.'

Her defiance was wafer-thin, but before either of us could say anything else we heard Grace scream. I ran out into the hallway to find her staring towards the open front door, anxiously hugging herself.

A few seconds later Strachan came back inside.

'It's all right, David. False alarm,' he said, closing the door.

Grace wiped her eyes and gave a tremulous smile. 'Sorry. I'm jumping at my own shadow.'

'Can I do anything?' I asked.

Strachan had gone to put his arms round his wife. 'No. I'll be with you in a minute.'

'Actually, we were just leaving,' I said. 'Maggie's offered to drive me back to the hotel. Haven't you, Maggie?'

The reporter managed a strained smile. 'Aye. I'm a regular bus service.'

Neither of us spoke as Strachan helped Grace upstairs, then came back down and collected Maggie's coat from the utility room. There were darker patches of red where he had sponged the soup from it.

'Thank you,' Maggie said in a small voice. She looked down at the floor, where the shards of broken crockery lay amongst the spatters of soup. 'I'm sorry about the mess. And I'm really glad your wife is all right.'

Strachan gave her a cold nod. I told him I'd call out the next day to check on Grace, and ushered Maggie outside. Night had fallen as we hurried to the Mini, leaning into the wind as the rain was driven against us in sheets. It was still warm inside the car, and I belatedly remembered her warning about the broken heater. But that was the least of my concerns as I slammed the car door and turned to her angrily.

'So are you going to tell me what you thought you were doing back there?'

Maggie was struggling out of her coat and thrusting it on to the back seat. 'Nothing! I told you, I just came out to—'

'I know why you came, Maggie. Christ, Grace was *attacked*! She might have been killed, and you pull a trick like that? Just so you can get your name on the front page?'

Maggie was on the verge of tears as she rammed the car into gear and headed for the road. 'OK, so I'm a cow! But I can't just sit at my gran's pretending nothing's happening. Whatever's going on here, a story like this could be a big deal for me! All I want is a few words from one of them.'

'Is that all this is? Just a career opportunity?'

'No, of course it isn't! I was born here, I know these people!' Her chin came up. 'And I left you alone when you asked me to this morning, didn't I? I could have followed you, but I didn't. Give me that much credit, at least!'

Her small face was pinched and intense. I still didn't like what she'd done, but her need to be believed seemed genuine. And she was right; she had kept her word that morning. The wind shook the Mini as I debated what to do. If I could trust her. *What do your instincts say?*

I just hoped I could trust them, as well.

'This is in confidence, Maggie. Strictly off the record, OK? People's lives are at stake.'

She nodded, quickly. 'Aye, of course. And I know I shouldn't have come out to see Grace . . .'

'This isn't just about Grace . . .' I paused, uncertain even now. But it was going to come out soon anyway. Better to tell her now than have her keep snooping around. And perhaps getting herself – or someone else – hurt because of it.

'Duncan, the young constable, was murdered last night.'

Her hand went to her mouth. 'Oh, my God!' She stared through the windscreen as it sank in. 'I can't believe it. I mean, he was . . . What the hell's going on? This is *Runa*, for God's sake, things like that don't happen here!'

'Apparently they do. Which is why you need to stop pulling stunts like this. Two people have been killed already. This afternoon it could easily have been three. Whoever's doing this doesn't care who he hurts, Maggie.'

She nodded, chastened. 'Does anyone else know? About Duncan, I mean?'

'Not yet. Kinross knows something's going on, and so do some of the others. Brody or Fraser will probably have to tell people before much longer. But until they do, I'd appreciate it if you kept it to yourself.'

'I won't say anything. I promise.'

I believed her. For one thing, she couldn't get word out to her newspaper, but for another Maggie looked stunned. She still seemed shell-shocked as the headlights picked out a shape on the side of the road ahead of us. It was blurred by the squeaking windscreen wipers, then resolved into a figure crouched in a reflective yellow raincape.

'Looks like Bruce has had an accident,' Maggie said.

As she slowed I could see it was Cameron, white face caught in the headlights as he worked over the chain of his mountain bike. There was mud smeared on the yellow fabric of his cape.

'Don't tell me he cycled out here in this?' I said, realizing he must still be on his way back from Strachan's house.

'Aye. I passed him on the way out. Prides himself on being out in all weather. Bloody *amadan*.'

I didn't have to understand Gaelic to know an insult when I heard one. Cameron shielded his eyes against the car's lights as we pulled up, a spanner still clutched in his hand. Maggie wound down the window and leaned out, screwing her face up against the rain.

'You want a lift yet, Bruce?' she called.

The reflective cape thrashed around him in the wind, moulding to his skinny frame like a live thing and threatening to blow him off balance. No wonder he'd come off his bike, I thought. He looked frozen and soaked, but when he saw me in the car his expression hardened.

'I can manage.'

'Suit yourself,' Maggie muttered. She closed the window and pulled away. 'God, but that man seriously gets up my nose. Got all snotty the other day when I asked to do a story about him. Just human interest stuff because he's a teacher and male nurse, but he acted like I was scum for suggesting it. I wouldn't have minded, but he could hardly keep his eyes off my boobs. Randy bugger.'

Cameron's feelings for Grace evidently didn't stop him ogling other women, I thought. And then I realized something else, something that hit me so hard I felt winded.

He'd been using the spanner with his left hand.

I turned to look back through the rear window. But the darkness and rain had swallowed him up.

20

'Cameron's an awkward sod. But I don't see him as a killer,' Brody said, putting the kettle on the cooker and lighting the gas under it.

We were in his small kitchen, sitting at his spotlessly clean table while he made tea. I'd had Maggie drop me off at the hotel, but only stayed long enough to collect Fraser. The Range Rover had been parked outside, and I'd expected to find him in the bar. Instead he'd been in his room, and when I'd knocked I could hear him noisily blowing his nose before he came to the door. When he opened it his room was in darkness, and his face was blotched and red. But his manner was as gruff as ever as I said we needed to talk to Brody.

'I'm not saying he is,' I said, as the old DI shook out the match he'd used to light the gas. 'But he was using the bike spanner with his left hand. We know that whoever killed Duncan was left-handed. And Grace was hit on her right cheek, which suggests the same thing about her attacker.'

Fraser sniffed dismissively. 'How can you be sure Strachan's wife wasn't given a backhand?'

'I can't,' I admitted. 'For all I know it could be two different people who attacked them, come to that. But Duncan was hit hard enough to punch a hole in his skull, and send impact fractures halfway across it. You can't get that sort of force behind a backhanded swing.'

Fraser's mouth turned down so far the tips of his moustache touched either side of his chin. 'Cameron's a prick, I'll grant you that. But I can't see a runt like him getting the better of Duncan.'

'Duncan was hit from behind. He didn't get a chance to defend himself,' I reminded him. 'We already know that Cameron's got a thing about Grace, and he also fits the blackmail theory. He's the schoolteacher, so he'd hardly want it known if he was using a prostitute. If Janice Donaldson threatened to tell he might have killed her to keep it quiet.'

Brody dropped tea bags into a pot. 'Perhaps. But assuming you're right, how did he get from the school to the yacht in time to attack Grace?'

'For all we know he could have left before her. He could have taken his mountain bike along the coastal path that Strachan told us about. Dangerous in this weather, but he might have chanced it if he was desperate.'

The kettle set up a mournful whistling as steam began to trail from the cap on its spout. Brody turned off the flame and poured the boiling water into the teapot. With his right hand, I noticed.

I was getting obsessive.

He brought the teapot and three mugs over to the table. 'It's possible. But let's forget Cameron for now and look at what else we've got,' he said, setting the pot down on a place mat and putting cork coasters in front of each of us for the mugs. 'The body of a murdered prostitute turns up, badly burned. Whoever killed her was apparently unconcerned about it being found, until word gets out it's being treated as a murder inquiry.'

He didn't look at Fraser as he spoke, but he didn't have to.

'The killer panics and decides to get rid of the remains properly this time, as well as whatever other evidence might be left. In the process he kills a police officer, and very nearly the forensic expert as well.' He stirred the teapot, then replaced the lid and looked questioningly at us. 'Any comments?'

'Bastard obviously gets off on fire,' Fraser said. 'Pyromaniac, or whatever it's called.'

I wasn't so sure. 'Have there been any other arson attacks or fires on the island?' I asked Brody.

'None that I know of. Not since I've been living here, anyway.'

'So why now? I'm no psychologist, but I don't think people just turn into fire-starters overnight.'

'Could just be a way for him to hide his tracks,' Fraser suggested.

'Then we come back to why Janice Donaldson's body was left in the cottage instead of being buried or thrown off a cliff. Chances are it would never have been found then. We're missing something here,' I insisted.

'Or just complicating things when there's no need,' Fraser countered.

Brody looked thoughtful as he poured the tea. 'Let's go back to the attack on Grace. My feeling is that it was opportunistic. That she walked in on somebody as they were smashing the yacht's comms system. So whoever it was, it had to be someone who knew we can't use the police radios.'

'That rules out Cameron,' Fraser said, spooning sugar into his tea. 'None of us told him. Had to be someone from the boatyard, if you ask me. Kinross or one of those other bearded bastards. They all knew our radios weren't working. One of them could have legged it up to the yacht while we were on the ferry. They'd just about have time to smash up the comms and do the business with Strachan's wife before they were disturbed.'

He put the wet spoon down on the table. Without a word, Brody picked it up and took it to the sink, then brought a cloth over to wipe up the tea stain.

'Could be,' he said, sitting back down. 'But we can't just assume it was one of them. We don't know who else they might have told. And let's not forget there's someone else who knew we wanted to use the yacht's radio.'

I could guess what was coming. 'You mean Strachan?'

He nodded. 'You asked him about it when he came out to the cottage. He's not stupid; he'd have put two and two together.'

I'd come to respect Brody's instincts, but I was starting to think he was letting his animosity cloud his judgement where Strachan was concerned. I'd seen his reaction when he'd realized Duncan was dead. Even if his shock had been feigned, I didn't think anyone could make themselves throw up to order, no matter how good an actor they were.

Fraser obviously shared my doubts. 'No way. We all saw the state he was in. The man was in bits. And why the hell would he attack his own wife and then come running for help? Doesn't make sense.'

'It does if he wanted to divert suspicion from himself,' Brody said, mildly. Then he shrugged. 'But you could be right. For all we know it could have been someone else entirely, who trashed the yacht's communications just to be on the safe side. I just don't think we can afford to rule anyone out at the moment, that's all.'

He was right, I realized. Duncan had already died because too much had been taken for granted.

'I still don't understand what was gained by smashing the yacht's radio anyway,' I said. 'Even if we could contact the mainland, no one can get out to us until the weather improves. So what was the point?'

Brody took a drink of tea and placed his mug carefully back on the coaster. 'Time, perhaps. As far as the mainland's concerned, this is still about a month-old murder. Important, but not life and death. Even the fact we can't get in touch won't worry them overmuch, because they'll know the phones and radios aren't working. If they knew a police officer had been killed, there'd be a helicopter on standby ready to lift off the minute the weather permits. But as things are they'll wait till it clears before they start things moving. So as long as we've no means of communication, the killer's got a clear window to get off the island before anyone even starts looking for him.'

'And go where? Even if he takes a boat, we're in the middle of nowhere.'

Brody smiled. 'Don't be fooled. There's a hundred and fifty miles of islands and coastline out here for someone to lose themselves. Then there's the British mainland, Norway, the Faroes and Iceland all within striking distance.'

'So you think the killer's planning to make a run for it?'

His dog came up and rested its head on his knee. Brody stroked it, fondly. 'I'd say it was likely. He knows he can't stay here any more.'

'So what do we do about it?' Fraser demanded.

Brody gave a shrug. 'Watch our backs. And hope the weather clears.'

It was a depressing thought.

The three of us took the Range Rover back to the hotel shortly afterwards. We hadn't eaten since that morning, and while none of us had much appetite we still needed to eat. The rain had eased, but the gale showed no sign of abating as we made our way back along the harbour and through the village. The island was still without power, and the unlit streets seemed eerily deserted in the car's head-lights as we drove up the steep hill to the hotel.

It was only when we got out of the car that we became aware of the hubbub coming from inside. Brody frowned, his chin lifting as though he'd scented something.

'Something's up.'

The small bar was packed to overflowing, people crowding the hallway round its doorway. Heads turned towards us, the conversations abruptly dying to silence as word spread that we'd arrived.

'Now what?' Fraser muttered.

There was a ripple of movement as the people standing in the doorway shifted in response to some movement inside the bar. A

233

moment later Kinross emerged, the hulking figure of Guthrie just behind him.

Kinross's ice-chip eyes brushed on Fraser and me before fixing on Brody.

'We want some answers.'

With everything else that had happened, I'd forgotten about Brody's promise to explain what was going on. Fraser began to draw himself up, shoulders bunched aggressively, but Brody cut him off.

'Aye, I dare say you do. Just give us a minute here, will you?'

Kinross seemed inclined to argue. Then he gave a short nod. 'You can have two.'

He and Guthrie went back into the bar. Fraser turned on Brody, angrily jabbing a finger at him.

'You're not a bloody inspector any more! I told you before, you've no authority to tell them anything!'

Brody kept his voice level. 'They've a right to know.'

Fraser's face had darkened. The shock of Duncan's death – and perhaps his sense of guilt – had been building up all day. Now he was looking for somewhere to vent it.

'A police officer's been murdered! As far as I'm concerned nobody on this island has a *right* to anything!'

'Two people are dead already. You want to risk anyone else being killed because you didn't warn them?'

'He's right,' I said. I'd been in a situation once before where the police hadn't released information, and people had died as a result. 'You've got to tell them what we're dealing with. If not you're putting more lives at risk.'

Fraser had a cornered look about him, but he wasn't giving in. 'I'm not taking votes on it! I'm not telling anybody anything without proper orders, and neither is anyone else!'

'No?' A muscle was ticking in Brody's jaw, but that was the only outward sign of any emotion. 'That's one good thing about being retired. I don't have to worry about red tape.'

Fraser grabbed hold of his arm as he started towards the bar. 'You're not going in there!'

'What are you going to do? Arrest me?'

He looked at the police sergeant disdainfully. Fraser dropped first his gaze, and then his hand.

'I'm not having anything to do with this,' he mumbled.

'Then don't,' Brody said, and walked away.

I went with him, leaving Fraser standing in the hallway. We had to ease through the crush in the bar. People shuffled aside as we went in, the murmur of conversation dying to a pin-drop silence. It was a small enough room to begin with, not meant for this sort of number. Ellen was serving behind the bar, looking flustered. I spotted Cameron, cleaned up and standing by himself in a corner. He'd obviously made it back after coming off his bike, but the look he gave me was no warmer than before. Maggie was there too, standing with a group that included Kinross and Guthrie, a look of anticipation on her face.

But other than that most were people I didn't recognize. There was no sign of Strachan, although that was hardly surprising. Even if he'd been told about the meeting he wouldn't have wanted to leave Grace by herself in order to come.

I hoped we wouldn't need him to calm things down this time.

Brody made his way to the fireplace and calmly surveyed the room.

'I know you're all wondering what's going on,' he said, his voice carrying without effort. 'By now I'm sure you're all aware that Grace Strachan was attacked this afternoon. And most of you will have heard that the police are treating the body found in the old cottage near Beinn Tuiridh as a suspicious death.'

He paused, looking round the room. I noticed that Fraser had come into the bar. He stood in the doorway, listening sullenly.

'What you don't know is that some time last night, the police officer who was on duty there was murdered. Whoever killed him also torched the community centre and medical clinic, and almost killed Dr Hunter here as well.'

His words provoked an uproar. Brody raised his hands for quiet, but no one took any notice. There were angry shouts of surprise and protest. I could see Ellen looking nervous behind the bar, and found myself wondering if this was a mistake after all. Then a voice was bellowing above the rest.

'Quiet, everyone! I said *QUIET!*'

The clamour died down. It was Kinross who'd shouted. In the silence that followed, the ferry captain stared across at Brody.

'Are you saying it was somebody from the island? One of us?'

Brody stared back without flinching. 'That's exactly what I'm saying.'

There was a rumble of discontent, growing in volume. But it stilled as Kinross made himself heard again.

'No.' He shook his head emphatically. 'No way.'

'I don't like it any more than you do. But the fact is that somebody on this island has killed two people and assaulted another.'

Kinross folded his arms. 'Well, it's not one of us. If there was a killer here, don't you think we'd know it?'

There were muttered 'ayes' and murmurs of agreement. As Brody tried to make himself heard above the rising volume, Maggie squirmed her way to the front. She thrust out her dictaphone, as though this were a press conference.

'The body that was found at the cottage. Do you know who it is?'

Brody paused. I knew he was making a judgement as to how much he should say.

'It hasn't been formally identified yet. But we think it might be a missing prostitute from Stornoway.'

I was watching Cameron as Brody spoke. But if the news meant anything to him he didn't show it. And now other people were shouting their own questions.

'What the hell was a tart from Lewis doing out here?' Karen Tait called out. Her voice was already slurred.

Guthrie grinned. 'Take a guess.'

No one laughed. The big man's smirk slowly died. But I was more interested in another reaction. Kinross's son Kevin had given a start at the mention of the dead woman. His mouth opened in a shocked 'o' before he realized I was watching him.

He quickly dropped his gaze.

Everyone else's attention was still on Brody. 'The police are going to be sending teams out here as soon as the weather allows. I'll ask you all to cooperate with them when they arrive. Until then, we need you all to help us out. The cottage is a crime scene now, so please don't go out there. When Scene of Crime get here, they don't want to waste time chasing false leads. I know you're going to be curious, but please keep away from it. And if any of you think you might have any information, you need to tell Sergeant Fraser over there.'

All eyes instinctively went to Fraser. He looked briefly surprised, then straightened almost imperceptibly, squaring his shoulders as he met the stares. It was a clever touch from Brody, a way of handing some self-respect back to Fraser, and reminding the islanders that there already was a police presence on Runa.

I thought the meeting would end there, but Cameron had other ideas. He'd been quiet so far, but now his orator's voice filled the small room.

'And meanwhile, are we expected to just sit tight and behave ourselves?' He stood with his legs planted and his arms folded. He flicked Maggie a look of supercilious distaste as she pointed her tape recorder at him.

'Unfortunately, there's not much else we can do until the mainland police get here,' Brody answered.

'You tell us there's a murderer loose on the island, practically accuse one of us, and then calmly tell us to do nothing?' Cameron gave an incredulous snort. 'Well, I for one don't—'

'Shut up, Bruce,' Kinross said, without even bothering to look at him.

Cameron's cheeks coloured. 'I'm sorry, Iain, but I hardly think—'

'Nobody here cares what you think.'

'Well, excuse me, but who are you to . . .'

Cameron faltered to silence as Kinross's icy stare swivelled to him. His Adam's apple bobbed as he closed his mouth, swallowing whatever he had been about to say. I almost felt sorry for him. One way and another, the schoolteacher's pride had taken a battering in recent days.

But no one was taking any notice of him now anyway. People were turning away, subdued conversations springing up again as they discussed what they'd just heard. Maggie lowered her dictaphone and gave me a troubled look before making her way out of the bar.

I looked over to where Kevin Kinross had been standing. But at some point the teenager had slipped away too.

We found an empty table when the bar started to thin out after the meeting. Fraser insisting on buying malts for himself and me and a tomato juice for Brody.

He raised his glass. 'To Duncan. And to the bastard who killed him, *Gonnadh ort!*'

'Oh, he'll suffer, all right,' Brody said, softly.

Solemnly, we toasted. Then I told them about Kevin Kinross's reaction to the news that the murdered woman was a prostitute from Stornoway. Perhaps still smarting from his earlier loss of face, Fraser was dismissive.

'Could be just excited at the thought of a prossie. A face like that, he's probably still a virgin.'

'Worth following up, even so,' Brody mused. 'Perhaps we should have a word with him tomorrow, if the support team still aren't here.'

Fraser looked morosely into his glass. 'I hope to Christ they are.'

So do I, I thought. *So do I.*

I made my excuses not long after that. I'd still not eaten, and on an empty stomach the alcohol made me feel light-headed with exhaustion. All at once the events of the past forty-eight hours seemed to catch up with me. I could hardly keep my eyes open.

Ellen was still serving behind the bar as I made my way out, struggling to cope with the unexpected demand. I didn't think she'd seen me, but then I heard her call as I started up the stairs.

'David?' She hurried out of the bar. 'I'm really sorry, I've not had chance to get you anything to eat.'

'That's all right. I'm going to get some sleep.'

'Do you want me to bring something up? Soup, or a sandwich? Andrew's minding the bar for me.'

'I'm fine, really.'

There was a creak on the landing above us. We looked up to see Anna. She was in her nightdress, her face pale and bleary with sleep.

'What have I told you about coming downstairs?' Ellen scolded, as her daughter came down the rest of the way.

'I had a bad dream. The wind took the lady away.'

'What lady, sweetheart?'

'I don't know,' Anna said querulously.

Ellen cuddled her. 'It was just a dream, and it's gone now. Did you thank Dr Hunter for the chocolate he bought you the other day?'

Anna considered, then shook her head.

'Well, go on, then.'

'But I've eaten it now.'

Ellen raised her eyes at me over her daughter's head, suppressing a smile. 'You can still say thank you.'

'Thank you.'

'That's better. Now come on, young lady. Back to bed.'

The little girl was half asleep already. She slumped against her mother's legs. 'I can't walk.'

'And I can't carry you. You're too heavy.'

239

Anna lifted her head enough to regard me with a sleepy eye. 'He can.'

'No he can't, madam. He's got a poorly arm.'

'It's OK. I can manage,' I said. Ellen looked doubtfully at my sling. 'I'd be happy to. Really.'

I hoisted Anna up. Her hair smelled cleanly of shampoo. She snuggled down against my shoulder, just as my own daughter used to. The small, solid weight of her was upsetting and comforting at the same time.

I followed Ellen back to the attic floor, where there were two small private rooms. Anna barely stirred as her mother pulled back the sheets and I lowered her into her bed. I stood back as Ellen covered her again and smoothed her daughter's hair before we crept out and went back downstairs.

She paused when we reached my floor, hand resting on the wooden banister as she looked at me. Her penetrating gaze was concerned.

'Are you OK?'

She didn't have to say what she meant. I smiled.

'Fine.'

Ellen knew enough not to push. With a final goodnight she went back down to the bar. I went into my room and sank down on the mattress fully clothed. I could smell the stink of smoke on my clothes, but it seemed like too much effort to get into bed. I could still feel the phantom weight of Anna. If I closed my eyes I could almost pretend it was Alice's. I sat there, thinking about my dead family as I listened to the wind howl outside. More than ever, I wished I could call Jenny.

But that was something else I couldn't do anything about.

My head jerked up as there was a rap on the door. I'd started to drift off, I realized. I looked at my watch and saw it was after nine o'clock.

'Just a second.'

Rubbing my eyes, I went to the door. I thought it might be Ellen, determined to feed me after all. But when I opened it I found Maggie Cassidy standing in the corridor.

She was holding a tray, on which was a bowl of soup and two thick chunks of home-made bread. 'Ellen said if I was coming up anyway I had to bring you this. Said to tell you that you'd got to eat something.'

I took the tray and stepped back to let her in. 'Thanks.'

She smiled, but there was a hesitancy about it. 'Soup again. Been quite a day for it, eh?'

'At least you didn't drop it this time.'

I set the tray down on the cabinet. There was an awkwardness between us at finding ourselves alone in this context. Neither of us looked at the bed that dominated most of the room, but we were both conscious of its presence. I leaned against the windowsill while Maggie sat on the room's only chair.

'You look bloody awful,' she said at last.

'That makes me feel a lot better.'

'You know what I mean.' She gestured to the tray. 'Go ahead, you might as well start.'

'It's all right.'

'Ellen'll kill me if you let it get cold.'

I didn't have the energy to argue. I was still too tired to feel hungry, but the first mouthful changed that. Suddenly I was famished.

'Quite a meeting tonight,' Maggie said, as I tore off a hunk of bread. 'I thought for a moment Iain Kinross was going to deck Cameron. Still, you can't have everything, eh?'

'You didn't come here just to talk about that, did you?'

'No.' She toyed with the edge of the chair. 'There's something I want to ask you.'

'You know I can't tell you anything.'

'One question, that's all.'

241

'Maggie . . .'

She held up a finger. 'Just one. And strictly off the record.'

'Where's your tape recorder?'

'God, you're a suspicious bugger, aren't you?' She reached into her bag and took out her dictaphone. 'Turned off. See?'

She tucked it back into her bag. I sighed.

'All right, one question. But I'm not promising anything.'

'That's all I ask,' she said. She seemed nervous. 'Brody said the dead woman was a prostitute from Stornoway. Do you know her name?'

'Come on, Maggie, I can't tell you that.'

'I'm not asking what it is. Just if you know it.'

I tried to see the trap. But provided I didn't give any specifics, there wasn't any harm in answering.

'Not officially.'

'But you've a pretty good idea who she is, right?'

I let my silence answer that. Maggie bit her lip.

'Her first name . . . It wouldn't be Janice, would it?'

My face must have been confirmation enough. I put the tray aside, my appetite gone.

'Why do you say that?'

'Sorry, I can't reveal sources.'

'This isn't a game, Maggie! If you know something you've got to tell the police.'

'You mean Sergeant Fraser? Aye, right, that's going to happen.'

'Andrew Brody, then! There's more at stake than a newspaper story, you're playing with people's lives!'

'I'm doing my job!' she flashed back.

'And if someone else gets killed, what then? Chalk it up as another exclusive?'

That hit home. Maggie looked away.

'You said yourself you're from Runa,' I pushed. 'Don't you care what happens here?'

'Of course I bloody do!'

'Then tell me where you got the name from.'

I could see conflicting emotions warring in her. 'Look, it's not like it sounds. The person who told me . . . It was in confidence. And I don't want to make trouble for them. They're not involved.'

'How do you know?'

'Because I *do*.' She looked at her watch, then stood up. 'Look, I've got to go. This was a mistake. I shouldn't have come.'

'But you did. You can't just walk away.'

Maggie's face was still uncertain, but she shook her head.

'Give me till tomorrow. Even if the police still can't get out, I promise I'll tell either you or Brody then. But I need to think it through first.'

'Don't do this, Maggie.'

But she was already heading for the door.

'Tomorrow, I promise.' She gave me a quick, embarrassed smile. 'Night.'

After she'd gone I sat on the bed, wondering how the hell she could have known the dead woman's name was Janice. I'd told only Brody and Fraser, and I couldn't see either the dour ex-inspector or the police sergeant confiding anything to Maggie.

I tried to puzzle it out, but I was too tired to think straight. And there was nothing I could do about it tonight anyway. The soup had gone cold, but I was no longer hungry. I undressed and washed as much of the smoke stink from myself as I could. Perhaps tomorrow I would see if the hotel's generator would run to a hot shower. For now, though, all I wanted to do was sleep.

This time unconsciousness came like flicking a switch.

I woke once, just before midnight, jerking, gasping from a dream where I was chasing something and being pursued myself at the same time. But I couldn't remember what I was running to or from. All that remained was a lingering sense that, however fast I ran, it wouldn't make any difference.

I lay in the darkened room, listening as my heart rate gradually returned to normal. It seemed that the wind didn't sound quite so bad, and as I drifted off again I allowed myself a faint stirring of optimism that perhaps the storm had peaked, that tomorrow the police would finally be able to make it out here.

I should have known better. Because the weather, like Runa itself, was just saving the worst till last.

21

Three o'clock in the morning is the dead time. It's the time when the body is at its lowest ebb, physically and mentally. The time when defences are lowest, when the promise of morning seems impossibly distant. It's when worst imaginings seem inescapable, darkest fears about to be realized. Usually it's just a state of mind, a biorhythmic trough we emerge from with the first paling of dawn.

Usually.

I surfaced from unconsciousness reluctantly, knowing I would find it hard to sleep again once I was fully awake. But as soon as I thought that, of course, it was too late. The bed springs squeaked under me as I looked at the clock. *Just after three.* I could feel the night-silence of the hotel all around me. Sinister creaks and groans as the building shifted and settled, like an arthritic old man. Outside the wind still blustered. I lay staring up at the ceiling, feeling sleep retreat further without knowing why. Then I realized what was different.

I could see the ceiling.

The room wasn't dark. A faint glow was coming through the curtain. My first thought was that it was from the street lamp outside the hotel, that the power must be back on. I felt a surge of relief, thinking that if the electricity had been restored, then perhaps the phones had been too.

But even as I was thinking that I noticed how the light coming through the window wasn't constant. It had a febrile, flickering quality, and when I saw that my relief died.

I hurried to the window and pulled back the curtain. The rain had stopped, but the street lamp outside was dead and dark, quivering in the wind like a limbless tree. The light I'd seen was coming from the harbour, a sickly yellow glow that reflected from the wet rooftops of the houses, growing brighter every second.

Something was on fire.

I quickly pulled on my clothes, wincing as my injured shoulder complained. I hurried down the hall and banged on Fraser's door.

'*Fraser!* Wake up!'

There was no answer. If he'd stayed in the bar all night as I'd expected, trying to drown his guilt and grief over Duncan, there was no way I'd raise him.

Leaving him, I ran downstairs. I expected Ellen to have been woken by the commotion, but there was no sign of her. The wind tried to rip my coat from me as I rushed outside, struggling to fasten it over my arm. Further down the hill people were emerging from houses and banging on doors, their voices calling urgently to each other as they hurried towards the harbour.

As I passed the lane that ran behind the hotel, I noticed that Ellen's old Beetle wasn't there. I guessed she'd already gone to investigate the blaze, but there was no time to give it much thought. The glow in the sky was brighter now, shining on the rain-slick street. I thought it might be the ferry that was burning, but when I reached the quay-side I saw it was still moored safely out on the jetty, caught in the dancing light from the shore.

The fire was in the boatyard.

Guthrie's derelict fishing boat was ablaze. Its stern was already engulfed, the small wheelhouse on its deck burning fiercely. Flames were flowing over its half-timbered hull with a sinuous grace, hiding it behind fluid black smoke. Figures were scurrying about, snatching up buckets and yelling at each other over the din of the flames. Guthrie was bellowing frantic instructions, and I saw Kinross emerge from the workshop with a heavy fire extinguisher, hunching against the heat as he ventured as close to the flames as he could.

A hand fell on my shoulder. I turned and saw Brody, face jaundiced by the yellow light.

'What happened?' I asked.

'No idea. Where's Fraser?'

'Guess.'

We broke off, coughing as a sudden shift in wind sent the smoke over us. The wind was shredding the flames into a wildly flapping sheet. It seemed like most of the village was there now, either watching helplessly or trying to fight the blaze. Buckets were being passed along a line, and a hose had been rolled out, its thin jet vanishing ineffectively into the flames. It was obvious they couldn't save the boat, but the priority now was making sure the fire didn't spread.

Across the yard, I caught a glimpse of Maggie's distinctive red coat as she stood with a group of onlookers. Standing by himself, a little way from everyone else, was Cameron, his face hollowed and shadowed as he stared at the flames. I looked around for Ellen, but couldn't pick out her face in the crowd. I'd assumed she'd come down to the harbour, but now I thought about it, it seemed odd that she hadn't woken Fraser or me first.

Brody saw me looking round. 'What's wrong?'

'Have you seen Ellen?'

'No, why?'

'Her car had gone from the hotel. I thought she must have come down here.'

'She wouldn't have left Anna,' Brody said, scanning the crowd. There was a note of anxiety in his voice.

Even now I can't remember when I became aware of a sudden

tension in the air. It was like a ripple of communal unease, spreading as quickly as the flames themselves. I looked back towards the boat, already feeling a dawning presentiment of disaster without knowing why. It was fully ablaze now, flames funnelling into the gap formed by the missing hull timbers. And then the wind gusted, lifting the veil of smoke to reveal something moving inside.

Cocooned in fire, a human arm was slowly lifting, as though in salute.

'Jesus Christ,' Brody breathed.

Then, with a flurry of sparks, the deck collapsed and buried the awful sight from view.

Pandemonium broke out. People were crying and yelling instructions, shouting for someone to do something. But I knew better than anyone there that there was nothing anyone could do.

I felt a sudden grip on my shoulder, strong enough to hurt even through my coat. Brody was staring at me, his face etched with an unforgettable expression. He uttered just one word, but it was enough.

'Ellen.'

Then he was barging people aside as he ran towards the burning boat.

'Brody!' I yelled, going after him.

I doubt he heard. Only when the flames beat him back did he stop. I grabbed hold of him, flinching from the heat. We were close enough for our coats to steam. If the boat collapsed now we'd be caught in it.

'Come on, get back!'

'She was moving!'

'It was only a reflex! It was the fire, that's all!'

He pulled away from me, staring into the flames as though trying to find a route into them. I grabbed him again.

'Whoever it is, they're dead! You can't do anything!'

What we'd seen wasn't a sign of life. If anything it was just the opposite, a blind, mechanical motion caused by the arm's tendons contracting in the intense heat. There was no chance anyone could have survived the fire for this long.

The truth of what I was saying finally penetrated Brody's frenzy. He allowed me to pull him away, stumbling like a man caught in a nightmare. What was left of the boat looked as though it could collapse any second. Shutting out thoughts of who the victim might be, I ran to where Kinross was still futilely spraying the fire extinguisher on to the flames. His face was savage and angry as he edged as close as he could. Nearby Guthrie's meaty face was streaked with tears, either from the smoke or the sight of his dream going up in flames.

'We need to get the body out!'

'Get the fuck out of my way!'

I grabbed his arm. 'You can't put it out! Get some poles! Now!'

He wrenched free, and for a second I thought he might take a swing at me. Then he bellowed to the other men battling the fire, shouting for them to fetch scaffolding poles and long pieces of timber from the building supplies stacked nearby.

Feeling helpless, I could only stand with Brody and watch as they began using them to try to snag the body from the flames. Guthrie and another man skittered back as part of the fire collapsed, sending sparks gyrating crazily into the sky. There was no way the body would survive such rough handling unscathed, but there was no alternative. If it wasn't recovered now, the fire would destroy any forensic evidence that might be left anyway.

More than that, though, it would have been unthinkable to simply wait until the fire had burned itself out.

Brody's face was haggard. *It can't be Ellen*, I told myself, feeling an awful hollowness. I tried to think of where she could be, of another reason for her car to be missing. But that only raised even worse questions. *Dear God, what about Anna? Where's she?*

I knew I should go back to the hotel to see, but I was afraid of what I might find. Across the other side of the yard I caught a glimpse of Maggie's bright red coat. Seeing her, I felt my anger start to rise. Whatever she'd kept from me earlier might not have been able to prevent this, but she'd hidden behind her profession for long enough.

Skirting the burning boat, I started across the yard, and as I did I almost bumped into someone coming the other way.

It was Ellen.

She was carrying Anna on one shoulder. The little girl was half asleep as she stared at the flames.

'What happened?' Ellen asked, staring past me to the fire.

Before I could answer Brody came running over.

'Thank God you're all right!'

He seemed about to hug her but stopped, suddenly embarrassed. Ellen was looking bewildered.

'Why wouldn't I be? I've been at Rose Cassidy's. Look, why are you both staring at me like that? What's going on?'

'You were at Maggie's grandmother's?' I asked, recognizing the name. Something dark and unsettling began to twitch in my subconscious.

'Aye, she had a fall, so one of her neighbours came to fetch me. Rose isn't fond of Bruce Cameron,' she added, wryly. A crease of concern appeared between her eyes. 'Poor woman's worried more than anything. Maggie went out earlier and hasn't come back.'

The sense of foreboding was growing stronger. 'I just saw her. She's down here,' I said, looking round.

There was no longer any sign of Cameron, but Maggie was still where I'd last seen her, watching the boat burn with Karen Tait and a group of other islanders. She had her back to me, an unmistakable figure in her oversized coat. I went across, driven by an apprehension I still couldn't name.

'Maggie?' I said.

But at that moment a cry went up from the boat. 'Over here. We've got it.'

250

I looked over, saw that the men had succeeded in dislodging a still-burning shape from the fire. Kinross and the others pawed at the blackened object with poles, trying to drag it further away from the flames. It could almost have been a log, its smoking surface still licked by tongues of flame.

But it wasn't.

I'd actually started to go over when Maggie turned round, and shock rooted me to the spot.

The face gazing back at me from inside the red hood wasn't Maggie's. It was a teenage girl's, blank and uncomprehending.

Mary Tait. The girl I'd seen outside my window.

22

An eerie silence had descended in the boatyard, a collective hush as people saw what had been pulled from the blaze. Then the spell broke. A fresh clamour erupted all around me as people jostled to either get away from the sight, or to get a better look.

But I was still struggling to recover from the shock of seeing Karen Tait's daughter wearing Maggie's coat. Because it obviously *was* Maggie's. The distinctive red coat had seemed huge on the reporter, but Mary Tait was much bigger. Large as the coat was, it looked almost too small for her heavy frame.

Karen Tait, Mary's mother, had turned to glare at me, but by now Brody had followed me over.

'What's wrong?' he asked.

I found my voice. 'That's Maggie's coat.'

'He's lying!' Karen Tait bridled drunkenly. But there was a shrillness to the accusation that didn't ring true.

Kinross had broken away from the group of men by the fire and was pushing his way towards us. His son trailed behind, the firelight cruelly highlighting his pockmarked features with shadowed craters. At the sight of Kevin, Mary's face broke into a beaming smile, but it wasn't returned. When the teenager saw where his father was heading he dropped back. Mary's smile faded as he slunk away into the crowd.

Kinross was blackened and stinking of smoke, still clutching the charred pole he'd used to drag the body from the fire. He hawked and spat a glob of sooty phlegm on to the floor.

'We've got it out, like you asked.' He looked from me to Karen Tait. 'What's going on?'

'It's them, they're calling Mary a thief!' Tait cried.

Brody didn't react to the accusation. 'That's Maggie's coat Mary's wearing.'

Tait's face contorted. 'That's a lie! Don't believe him!'

But Kinross was staring at the girl's coat with recognition. I remembered how he and Maggie had bantered on the ferry. There had been real affection there. He looked back at where the other firefighters had gathered to stare at the smouldering body they'd pried from the flames, and I saw him make the same connection I already had.

'Where is Maggie?' he asked sharply.

No one answered. Something in Kinross's expression seemed to close down. He swivelled his gaze back towards Karen Tait.

'We don't have time for this now,' I said quickly, trying to ignore my own fears for Maggie. 'We need to get this place secured, and get the body somewhere safe.'

Brody nodded. 'He's right, Iain. This can wait. We have to get everyone out of here. Will you help?'

Kinross didn't respond. He continued to stare at Karen Tait, but she wouldn't meet his eyes. He levelled a finger at her.

'We haven't finished,' he warned. Then, turning his back, he began yelling instructions to clear the yard.

Leaving Brody to watch Karen Tait and her daughter, I pushed my way through to the body as Kinross and a handful of other men began herding people away. It lay charred and twisted on the dirty concrete floor of the yard, a sight that was both pitiful and horrific.

Rain had puddled nearby, and in the light from the burning boat oil glistened on the water like a dead rainbow. Tendrils of steam rose from the cooked flesh, and I could feel the heat still radiating from it, like a joint left too long in the oven. The mouth had pulled open as though in a rictus of agony. I knew that was fanciful, that it was an inevitable effect of the tendons contracting in the fire, but somehow I couldn't shake the image.

Please, let me be wrong.

I turned to Guthrie as he went past, ushering a huddle of people from the yard. 'Can I have a sheet of plastic or tarpaulin?'

I thought he either hadn't heard or was ignoring me. But a few moments later the big man returned with a bundled-up piece of dirty canvas. He thrust it out at me.

'Here.'

I started to open it out, struggling in the high wind with only one arm. To my surprise Guthrie came to help. As we wrestled with the flapping canvas, a figure emerged from the shadows. In the flickering light from the flames, I saw it was Cameron. He stared down at the body.

'Dear God,' he whispered. His Adam's apple bobbed as he swallowed. 'What can I do?'

There was none of his usual bombast, and I wondered if he was only now starting to realize what was at stake. I might have accepted his offer, but Guthrie didn't give me the chance.

'Fuck all, as usual,' he rumbled dismissively. 'You think a bandage is going to do any good here?'

Cameron looked as though he'd been struck. Without a word he turned and made his way out of the yard with the rest. At another time I might have felt sorry for him, but there were more urgent matters just then.

A decision would have to be made eventually about what to do with the body, but for now it needed to be covered. Without asking, once we had the tarpaulin open Guthrie helped me start to spread it over the blackened form.

'Who do you think it is?' he asked.

I might have imagined it, but I thought there was an almost fearful note in his voice. I just shook my head as we lowered the canvas and hid the body from sight.

But the heaviness in my heart told me that Maggie finally had her front page story.

The fire had all but burned itself out. What had once been a boat was now a mound of glowing ash and embers, still guttering fitfully with flame. The wind kept it alive for the time being, but it was rapidly dying, beaten by its own fury as much as the efforts of the islanders. The entrance to the boatyard was now cordoned off with a pitifully inadequate strip of police tape, the last that Fraser had left. Tied to two posts, it thrummed like a live thing in the wind, little more than a token obstruction.

Most of the islanders had gone home. Brody had asked Ellen to wake Fraser when she got back to the hotel, and the police sergeant had appeared not long afterwards, sheepish and rumpled. He'd tried to grumble that I should have tried harder to wake him, but no one was in the mood to listen to either his complaints or his excuses.

We'd eventually decided on taking the body into the workshop. There was still no way of knowing when SOC would arrive, and the protocol that said a crime scene should be left undisturbed hardly seemed to apply here. Dozens of people had been milling around the boatyard, and after it had been manhandled from the fire there was no longer any point worrying about contaminating the body. I would have to take a look at it later, but in the meantime the best we could do was make sure it was kept safe.

The body was far too badly burned to be recognizable, but I don't think anyone really doubted any more who it was. There had still been no sign of Maggie, and for all her faults she wouldn't have abandoned her grandmother like that. Guthrie and Kinross had carried the body inside using the tarpaulin as a stretcher, and set it at the back of the workshop. Guthrie had gone straight home, subdued and sombre-faced. But Kinross had flatly refused to leave.

'Not until I've heard what she's got to say,' he declared, jerking his chin towards where Karen Tait waited miserably with her daughter.

Brody hadn't argued, but I thought I knew why. Tait might not respond to pressure from him or Fraser, but Kinross was a different matter. He was one of her own, and I didn't think she'd be able to hold out against him.

Mother and daughter were sitting at the same table where the men had been playing cards that afternoon, out of view of where the body now lay. Mary's features bore the same vacant expression as when she'd looked up at my window from the street. She'd been persuaded to take off Maggie's coat. Wrapped in a bin-liner, it was now locked out of sight in the back of the police Range Rover. There had been nothing in its pockets, and no visible bloodstains or signs of damage, but Forensics would still need to examine it for trace evidence. Perhaps it was my imagination, but as I'd watched the girl take it off it already seemed to have lost some of its brightness, the vivid red starting to look faded and worn.

Kinross had given Mary his heavy oilskin to wear instead. Apparently oblivious to the cold, he'd helped her on with it almost tenderly. But there was no tenderness in his face as he stared at her mother.

Karen Tait stared resolutely down at the table's cigarette-burned Formica, refusing to look at any of us. Brody took the chair opposite her, and I noticed that Fraser no longer made any objection to him taking over. The retired detective looked tired, but there was no hint of it when he spoke.

'All right, Karen. Where did Mary get the coat?'

She didn't answer.

'Come on, we all know it belongs to Maggie Cassidy. So why is Mary wearing it?'

'I told you, it's hers,' she said dully, and flinched as Kinross suddenly slammed his hand down on the table.

'Don't lie! We've all seen Maggie wearing it!'

'Easy,' Fraser growled. But he backed off when Brody gave a small shake of his head.

'You saw what was on the fire, Karen!' Kinross's voice held part warning, part entreaty. 'For Christ's sake, tell us where Mary got the coat!'

'It's hers, Iain, honestly!'

'*Don't fucking lie to me!*'

Tait's resistance abruptly collapsed. 'I don't know! I only saw it tonight! I swear, that's the God's honest truth! She must have found it.'

'Where?'

'How do I know? You know what she's like, she wanders all over the island. She could have got it anywhere!'

'Jesus, Karen,' Kinross said in disgust.

'It's a good coat! Better than I can afford! You think I'm going to throw it away? And don't you look at me like that, Iain Kinross! You never worried about Mary being out on the nights you've wanted to come round!'

Kinross started towards her, but Brody put out a restraining arm.

'Calm down. We need to find out where she found it.' He turned back to Tait. 'What time did Mary go out?'

She gave a sullen shrug. 'I don't know. She was out when I got back from the hotel.'

'Which was when?'

'Half past eleven . . . twelve o'clock.'

'And what time did she get in?'

'How should I know? I fell asleep.'

'So when did you see her again?' Brody asked, patiently.

Tait gave an irritable sigh. 'Not until all the commotion with the fire woke me up.'

'And she had the coat then?'

'Yes, I've already told you!'

If he felt any contempt for the woman, Brody didn't show it as he switched his attention to her daughter.

'Hello, Mary. You know who I am, don't you?'

She looked at Brody without comprehension, then went back to the small torch she'd been playing with. It was a child's, plastic and brightly coloured. A few flyaway strands of hair had fallen down across her eyes, but she didn't seem to notice as she shone the torch beam into her face, switching it on and off.

'You're wasting your time,' Kinross said. Despite his words, his tone wasn't unkind. 'She probably doesn't remember where she got it herself.'

'No harm in trying. Mary? Look at me, Mary.'

Brody spoke gently. Finally, she seemed to notice him. He gave her a smile.

'That's a nice coat, Mary.'

Nothing. Then, suddenly, a shy smile lit her face.

'It's pretty.' Her voice was soft, like a little girl's.

'Yes, it's very pretty. Where did you get it?'

'It's mine.'

'I know. But can you tell me where you got it from?'

'From the man.'

I felt rather than saw Brody stiffen. 'Which man was that? Is he here now?'

She laughed. 'No!'

'Can you tell me who he is?'

'The *man*.'

She said it as though it were obvious.

'This man . . . Will you show me where he gave you the coat?'

'He didn't *give* it to me.'

'You mean you found it?'

She nodded, absently. 'When they ran off. After all the noise.'

258

'Who ran off? What noise, Mary?'

But he'd lost her. Brody continued to try for a while, but it was obvious that Mary had told us as much as she was going to. He told Fraser to drive them home, and then come straight back. Kinross also left, but before he did he gave one last look towards the back of the workshop where he and Guthrie had laid the body.

'She always was one for getting into trouble,' he said, sadly. Then he went out, letting the workshop door bang shut behind him.

Outside, the wind's banshee wail seemed louder than ever. The rain had started again, thundering against the corrugated roof and almost drowning out the chug of the workshop's generator. Brody and I went over to the body. Covered by the tarpaulin, it looked like a primitive sarcophagus as it lay on the concrete floor.

'You think it's her?' Brody asked.

I'd told him about Maggie's visit to my room earlier that night. How she'd known Janice Donaldson's first name, but wouldn't say who had told her. I remembered the pensive smile she'd given me as she'd left my room. *Tomorrow, I promise.* Except there wasn't going to be a tomorrow for Maggie.

I nodded. 'Don't you?'

Brody sighed. 'Aye. But let's see if we can be more sure.' He glanced at me. 'You ready?'

The honest answer would have been no. You never can be, not when it's someone you know. Someone you liked. But I just nodded and pulled back the tarpaulin. A waft of warm air greeted me, carrying with it an odour of overcooked meat. The way we respond to smells is largely a matter of context. Given its source, this one was nauseatingly out of place.

I crouched down beside the body. Shrunken by the fire, it looked pitifully small. Whatever clothing it had worn had burned away, as well as much of the soft tissue. The flames had twisted and warped it, exposing caramelized bone and tendons, drawing up the limbs into the characteristic boxer's crouch.

It was a sight that was becoming sickeningly familiar.

'So what do you think?' Brody asked.

An image of Maggie's gamine grin rose up in my mind. Almost angrily, I pushed it away. *Compartmentalize. This is work. Save the rest for later.*

'It's female. The cranium's way too small to be a man's.' I took a deep breath, looking at the smooth bone of the skull that was exposed beneath the blackened scraps of flesh. 'Also, the chin is pointed, and the forehead and eyebrow ridge are both smooth. A man's would be much heavier and more pronounced. Then there's the height.'

I indicated where the thigh bone was showing through the burned muscle tissue, aware of the awful intimacy of what we were doing.

'It's hard to be precise when the body's drawn up like this, but judging by the length of the femur this was someone quite short, even for a woman. Five foot, perhaps a little less. Certainly no taller.'

'Could it be a child?'

'No, it's definitely an adult.' I peered into the silent scream of the mouth. 'The wisdom teeth have broken through. That means she was at least eighteen or nineteen. Probably older.'

'Maggie would have been what? Twenty-three, twenty-four?'

'About that, I expect.'

Brody sighed. 'Right height, right age, right sex. There's not much doubt, is there?'

I found it hard to speak. 'No.'

Somehow, admitting it made it seem worse, as though I were letting Maggie down in some way. But there was no point in pretending. I forced myself to continue.

'For what it's worth, she was at least partially dressed when she was put on to the fire.' I pointed to a tarnished metal disc that was embedded in the charred flesh between the hipbones. It was the size of a small coin. 'That's a trouser button. The fabric's burned away, but it's melted its way into the flesh. By the look of it I'd guess she was wearing jeans.'

Just like Maggie had been, the last time I'd seen her.

Brody pursed his lips. 'So she probably wasn't raped. That's something, I suppose.'

It was a fair assumption. Few rapists would bother to put their victim's jeans back on before killing her. And certainly not afterwards.

'Any idea about cause of death?' he asked.

'Well, from what I can see there's no trauma to the skull. They got the body off the fire before cranial pressure caused a blow-out, which simplifies things a little. There's no sign of any head injury as there was with both Janice Donaldson and Duncan. I suppose it's possible that she just wasn't hit as hard, although . . .'

I trailed off, bending forward for a closer look. The fire had stripped away the skin and muscle of the throat to expose burned cartilage and tendon. I scrutinized it, then did the same to the arms and legs, and finally the torso. The soft tissue was charred enough to disguise the signs, but not hide them altogether.

'What is it?' Brody prompted.

I pointed to the throat. 'See here? The tendon on the left-hand side of the throat's been severed. Both ends have contracted right back away from each other.'

'Severed, as in cut?' Brody asked, leaning forward to see.

'Definitely as in cut. The fire might have caused them to snap eventually, but the ends are far too clean for that.'

'You mean someone slit her throat?'

'I can't be sure without carrying out a proper examination, but that's how it looks. There are what look like other puncture wounds as well. Here, on the shoulder. The muscle fibres are badly burned, but you can still make out a cut running across them. Same with the chest and stomach. I'd guess when I take X-rays we'll find blade marks on the ribs, and probably other bones as well.'

'So she was stabbed to death?' Brody asked.

'The fire's made it hard to say if she was stabbed or hacked, but she was certainly attacked with a bladed weapon. I'll need to examine the cuts to the bones in a lab before I can say for sure what type. But it's more complicated than that.'

'Complicated how?'

'Her neck's broken.'

I kneaded my eyes as a wave of tiredness washed over me. Tired or not, though, there was no doubt about what I'd seen.

'Look at the angle of her head. I don't want to disturb the body too much, but if you look you can see the third and fourth vertebrae are visible. They're splintered. And the left arm and right shin are broken as well. You can see the bones protruding through the burned tissue.'

'Couldn't that have happened when the boat collapsed in the fire, or when she was dragged out?'

'That might have caused a few breaks, but not this many. And a lot of these look like compression fractures, so they were caused by an impact . . .'

I stopped.

'What?' Brody asked.

But I was going to the grubby window. It was too dark to see much, but in the dying light from the burning boat I could just make out the dark bulk of the cliff face, towering above the boatyard.

'That's how he got her body down here. He threw her off the cliff.'

'You sure?'

'It'd explain the fractures. She was attacked with a knife, and either fell or was thrown off the top. Then her killer came down and dragged the body from the foot of the cliff into the yard.'

Brody was nodding. 'There are steps at the end of the harbour that lead to the cliff top. With a torch you could just about manage them in the dark, and it'd be a lot quicker than taking the road back down through the village. Less chance of being seen, too.'

That didn't explain why Maggie would have been up there in the first place. But at least now we were starting to form a picture of what had happened, if not why.

Brody rubbed his face wearily, his hand rasping on the grey stubble silvering his chin. 'Do you think she was alive when she went over?'

'I doubt it. Fall victims almost always have what are called Colles' fractures in their wrists, where they've put out their arms to stop themselves. There's nothing like that here. Only one arm's been broken, and it's above the elbow, in the humerus. That suggests she was either dead or unconscious when she fell.'

He glanced out of the workshop's window. It was still pitch black outside. 'It's too dark to see anything up there now. Soon as it's light we'll go up to the cliff top and take a look. In the meantime—'

He broke off as there was a sudden commotion outside. There was a yell, then something clattered to the floor as we heard the un-mistakable sounds of a struggle. Brody jumped up and ran for the door, but it was flung open before he reached it. A blast of icy wind roared into the workshop as Fraser burst in, dragging someone with him.

'Look who I found snooping at the window!' he panted, thrusting the intruder ahead of him.

The figure stumbled into the centre of the workshop. Shocked and pale, the acne-scarred face of Kevin Kinross stared at us fearfully.

23

The teenager stood in the workshop, dripping water on the concrete. He was shivering, his eyes downcast, shoulders hunched in a posture of abject misery.

'I'm only going to ask you once more,' Fraser warned. 'What were you doing out there?'

Kevin didn't answer. I'd covered the body with the tarpaulin again, but not before he'd seen it lying on the floor when Fraser had dragged him inside. He'd immediately jerked his gaze away as though scalded.

Fraser glowered at him. This sort of policing was more his territory, an opportunity to assert his authority.

'Look, son, you don't cooperate, you're going to be in a whole world of trouble. This is your last chance. This place is taped off, so what were you doing out there? Trying to listen in, is that it?'

Kinross's son swallowed, as though he were about to speak, but no sound came out. Brody interrupted.

'Can I have a word with him?'

He'd been silent so far, letting Fraser handle the questioning. But the sergeant's bullying clearly wasn't working. It was just intimidating the already cowed teenager still further.

Fraser flashed him an irritated look, but gave a terse nod. Brody went and fetched a stool from the table where Mary Tait and her mother had been earlier. He set it down next to Kevin.

'Here, sit down.'

He perched himself on the corner of a workbench, his manner far more relaxed than Fraser's confrontational interrogation. Kevin looked down at the stool uncertainly.

'You can stand up if you'd rather,' Brody told him. Kevin hesitated, then slowly lowered himself on to the stool. 'So what have you got to tell us, Kevin?'

The angry mounds of Kevin's acne looked worse than ever against his pallor. 'I . . . Nothing.'

Brody crossed his legs, as though the two of them were having a friendly conversation. 'I think we both know that's not true, don't we? I'm pretty sure you haven't done anything wrong, except for sneaking around outside. And I'm fairly sure we can persuade Sergeant Fraser here to overlook that. Provided you tell us exactly why you were doing it.'

Fraser looked tight-lipped at Brody's assertion, but didn't contradict him.

'So, Kevin, how about it?' Brody asked.

The tension in the teenager was obvious as he fought between answering and maintaining his silence. Then his eyes went to the tarpaulin-covered body. His mouth worked, as though words were trying to force their way out.

'Is it right? What everyone says?'

He sounded agonized.

'What are they saying?'

'That that's . . .' He darted another quick look at the tarpaulin. 'That that's Maggie.'

Brody paused, but then answered. 'We think it might be, yes.'

Kevin started to cry. I remembered the way he'd behaved around Maggie, how he'd blushed whenever she'd acknowledged him. His crush had been painfully apparent, and I felt more sorry for him than ever.

Brody fished in his pocket for a handkerchief. Wordlessly, he went over and gave it to him, then returned to the workbench.

'What can you tell us about it, Kevin?'

The youth was sobbing. 'I killed her!'

The statement seemed to charge the air with an electric current. In the silence that followed, the stink of burned flesh and bone seemed stronger than before, overlying the smell of fuel oil, sawdust and solder. The workshop's walls reverberated under the gale's assault, rain clattering like tin tacks against the corrugated roof.

'What do you mean, you killed her?' Brody asked, almost gently.

Kevin wiped his eyes. 'Because if not for me she wouldn't be dead.'

'Go on, we're listening.'

Having come this far, though, now Kevin seemed to balk. But I was thinking about his reaction when Brody had revealed that the body found in the crofter's cottage belonged to a prostitute from Stornoway. Not just shocked. Stunned. As though he'd only just made a connection. What was it Maggie had said about her anonymous source? *It's not like it sounds. The person who told me . . . It was in confidence. And I don't want to make trouble for them. They're not involved.*

'You told Maggie the dead woman's name, didn't you?' I said.

Both Brody and Fraser looked at me in surprise, but that was nothing compared to Kevin. He stared at me, open-mouthed. He seemed to search for a way to deny it, then his will buckled. He nodded.

'How did you know what the woman was called, Kevin?' Brody asked, taking over.

'I didn't for sure . . .'

'You were sure enough to give Maggie the tip. Why?'

'I . . . I can't tell you.'

'You want to spend time in a cell, lad?' Fraser cut in, oblivious to the angry look Brody shot him. 'Because I can promise you that's where you'll be heading if you don't talk.'

'I'm sure Kevin knows that,' Brody said. 'And I don't think he wants to protect the person who did this to Maggie. Do you, Kevin?'

The teenager's gaze involuntarily twitched towards the tarpaulin again. His expression was anguished.

'So come on, Kevin,' Brody coaxed. 'Tell us. Where did you get the name from? Did someone tell you? Or do you know someone who knew her? Is that it?'

Kinross's son hung his head. He mumbled something none of us could hear.

'Speak up!' Fraser barked.

Kevin's head jerked up angrily. 'My dad!'

The cry rang out in the confines of the workshop. Brody's face had stilled to immobility, masking any emotion.

'Why don't you start at the beginning?'

Kevin hugged himself. 'It was last summer. We'd taken the ferry across to Stornoway. My dad said he had some business to see to, so I walked into town. I thought I might go and see a film, or something . . .'

'We don't care what you watched,' Fraser interrupted. 'Get to the point.'

The look Kevin gave him suggested he might be his father's son after all.

'I cut through some back streets, near the bus station. There were these houses nearby, and when I got nearer I saw my dad standing outside one of them. I was going to go over, but then this . . . this woman opened the door. She was just wearing a short bathrobe. You could see nearly everything.'

Kevin's pocked face had gone crimson.

'When she saw my dad she grinned . . . sort of a dirty smile. And then he went inside with her.'

Brody nodded patiently. 'What did she look like?'

'Well . . . like she was a . . . you know . . .'

'A prostitute?'

That earned a shamed nod. Brody looked as though this new development was as unwelcome as it was unexpected.

'Can you describe her?'

Kevin's fingers went unconsciously to rub the livid bumps on his face. 'I don't know . . . Dark hair. Older than me, but not that old. Pretty, but . . . like she didn't look after herself.'

'Was she short, tall . . . ?'

'Tall, I think. Big. Not fat, but not skinny.'

He could be shown photographs later to see if he recognized Janice Donaldson. But his description fitted her so far.

'So how did you know what she was called?' Brody asked.

The teenager's face flamed an even deeper red. 'After he'd gone in, I . . . I went over to the doorway. Just to see. There were a few buzzers, but I'd seen he'd pressed the top one. It just said "Janice".'

'Did your dad ever know that you'd seen him?'

Kevin looked appalled. He shook his head.

'So did he go to see her again?' Brody asked.

'I don't know . . . I think so. Every few weeks he'd say he'd got some business to see to, so I . . . I guessed that was where he was going.'

'Some business,' Fraser muttered.

Brody ignored the interruption. 'And did she ever come to see him here? On the island?'

The question was met with another quick shake of the head. But I was recalling the curt way Kinross had silenced Cameron in the bar earlier. At the time I'd thought he'd simply been irritated by Cameron's officious manner, but now the way he'd effectively ended the meeting was shown in an altogether more sinister light.

Brody kneaded the bridge of his nose, wearily. 'How much of this did you tell Maggie?'

'Only her name. I didn't want her knowing my dad went with . . .

you know. I just thought . . . her being a reporter, she'd be able to write a story saying who the woman was. I thought I was doing her a favour! I didn't know it would end up like this!'

Brody patted the youth's shoulder as he started crying again. 'We know you didn't, son.'

'Can I go now?' Kevin asked, wiping his eyes.

'Just a couple more questions. Do you have any idea how Mary Tait might have got Maggie's coat?'

Kevin lowered his head, avoiding anyone's eyes.

'No.'

The denial was too rushed. Brody regarded him expressionlessly.

'Mary's a pretty girl, isn't she, Kevin?'

'I don't know. I suppose.'

Brody let the silence build for a few seconds, waiting until Kevin had started to shift uncomfortably before asking the next question.

'So how long have you been seeing her?'

'I haven't!'

Brody just looked at him. Kevin dropped his gaze.

'We just . . . meet up. We don't do anything! Not really. We haven't . . . you know . . .'

Brody sighed. 'So where do you "meet up"?'

The teenager's embarrassment was painful. 'On the ferry, sometimes. The kirk ruins, if it's dark. Or . . .'

'Go on, Kevin.'

'Sometimes out at the mountain . . . At the old cottage out at the croft.'

Brody looked surprised. 'You mean where the body was found?'

'Yes, but I didn't know anything about that. Honest! We haven't been there for ages! Not since summer!'

'Does anyone else go out there?'

'Not so far as I know . . . That's why we use it. It's private.'

Not any more. I thought about the empty cans and remains of campfires we'd found. Nothing to do with the murdered prostitute

269

after all, only the detritus of sneaked encounters between a handi-capped girl and a scarred and frustrated boy.

Fraser's contempt was plainly written on his face, but at least he'd the sense to keep quiet. Whatever Brody was thinking was impossible to tell. He kept his expression professionally neutral.

'Is that where Mary goes when she wanders off? To meet you?'

Kevin stared down at his hands. 'Sometimes.'

Brody thought for a moment. 'Was she at your house when we called round to see your dad?'

Until then I'd thought nothing of how Kevin had peered out through a gap in the front door, holding it closed so we couldn't see inside. He bowed his head, his silence confirmation enough.

'And how about tonight? Did you meet her then, as well?'

'No! I . . . I don't know where she went! I went home after I told Maggie! Honest!'

He seemed on the verge of tears again. Brody considered him for a few seconds, then gave a short nod.

'You'd better get on home.'

'Now, just wait a second . . .' Fraser objected.

But Brody had anticipated him. 'It's all right. Kevin's not going to say anything about what he's told us. Are you, Kevin?'

The youth shook his head, earnestly. 'I won't. I promise.' He hurried to the door, then stopped. 'My dad wouldn't have hurt Maggie. Or the other woman. I don't want to get him into trouble.'

Brody didn't respond. But then there wasn't much he could say. There was a brief glimpse of lashing rain as Kevin went out, then the door swung shut and he was gone.

Brody went over to the table and pulled back a chair to sit down. He looked drained. 'Christ, what a night.'

'You think we can trust the lad to keep quiet?' Fraser asked doubtfully.

The former detective passed his hand across his face. 'I can't see him running home to confess this to his father, can you?'

Fraser seemed about to concede the point, but then he suddenly looked aghast. 'Christ, what about the girl? Kinross knows she was a witness! No wonder he was so keen to stay while we questioned her!'

His words sent a chill through me. But Brody didn't seem concerned.

'Mary's not in any danger. Even assuming Kinross is the killer — and we still don't know that he is — he's going to be satisfied that she didn't see anything that could incriminate him. He knows she's no threat.'

Fraser looked relieved. 'So what now? Arrest him? Be a pleasure to slap cuffs on that bastard!'

Brody was silent. 'Not yet,' he said at last. 'All we have against Kinross is the fact he knew Janice Donaldson. That's not enough to arrest him. We'd only be tipping our hand, and giving him time to prepare his story before Wallace's team get here.'

'Oh, come on!' Fraser exclaimed. 'You heard what his own son said! And that bastard probably killed Duncan as well! We can't just sit on our arses!'

'I didn't say we should!' Brody rapped back, suddenly heated. He made an effort to calm himself. 'Look, I've worked murder investigations before. You jump in half-cocked, you risk letting the killer walk. Is that what you want?'

'We've got to do something,' Fraser persisted.

'And we will.' Brody looked across at the tarpaulin-covered shape, thinking. 'David, do you still believe Maggie's body was thrown off the cliff?'

'I'm sure of it,' I said. 'Hard to see how she could have got all those injuries otherwise.'

He looked at his watch. 'It'll be light in a couple of hours. As soon as it is, I say we take a look up there. See if there's any sign of what happened. In the meantime, I suggest you two go back to the hotel and try to get some sleep. We've got a busy day ahead of us.'

271

'What about you?' I asked.

'I don't sleep much. I'll stay here and keep Maggie company.' He gave a smile, but his eyes looked haunted. 'I couldn't stop her from getting killed. Seems the least I can do for her now.'

'Shouldn't one of us stay with you?'

'Don't worry about me,' Brody said, grimly. He picked up a crowbar from the workbench and hefted it, testing its weight. 'I'll be fine.'

24

Dawn rose almost as an afterthought next morning. There was no daybreak as such. Just an imperceptible lightening that crept up on you unawares, until you realized that night had been replaced by a murky twilight, and that it was officially morning.

I'd not gone straight to bed from the boatyard. Instead, I'd had Fraser take me to Maggie's grandmother's. Ellen had said earlier that she'd gone to the old woman's because she'd had a fall. I doubted I'd be able to do much for her, but I felt I ought to see her anyway.

I owed Maggie that much.

Rose Cassidy lived in a small, semi-detached stone cottage rather than a prefabricated bungalow like most of the neighbouring houses. It was ramshackle, with net curtains and an antiquated look that hinted at an elderly tenant. There was the flicker of candles in a downstairs window, and also one upstairs. *Candles for the dead.*

The house had been full of women, gathered to keep vigil with Maggie's grandmother. Walking in, I'd been struck by the smell of old age, that particular fustiness that seems equal parts mothballs and boiled milk. Maggie's grandmother was as frail as a baby bird, a scribble of blue veins visible under the parchment-thin skin. She already knew that her granddaughter was dead. The body still had to

273

be formally identified, but it would have been wrong to offer that as false hope.

Surprisingly, Fraser had elected to come in with me to find out what the old woman knew of the hours leading up to Maggie's death. Her granddaughter had seemed excited earlier, she'd told him, in a quavering voice. But she hadn't explained why. After cooking them both an evening meal – like most of the other houses, the oven used bottled gas – Maggie had left the house to go to the meeting in the hotel bar.

'It was after half past nine when she got back,' Rose Cassidy recalled, gesturing with a shaking hand to a clock with oversized numerals on the mantelpiece. Her reddened eyes were opaque with cataracts. 'She seemed different. As if there was something on her mind.'

That fitted what we already knew. This would have been after she'd been told the dead woman's name by Kevin Kinross, and then visited my room at the hotel.

But there had also been something else troubling Maggie besides whether or not to betray Kinross's son's confidence. Whatever it had been, she hadn't revealed it to her grandmother. The old woman had heard her leaving later, at around half past eleven, and called to ask where she was going. Maggie had shouted upstairs that she was taking the car, that she was meeting someone to do with work, and that she wouldn't be long.

She never came back.

By two o'clock her grandmother had known that something was wrong. She'd fallen from bed as she was banging on the wall to rouse her neighbour. It was another indication of Cameron's standing on the island that Ellen had been sent for rather than the island's nurse. Not that there was much anyone could do for her anyway. She hadn't been badly hurt by the fall, but like many other old people I'd seen, her body was slowly winding down, trapping her in a life that was no longer wanted. And now she'd outlived her own granddaughter.

It seemed an unnecessarily cruel longevity.

It had been after six before I'd got back to the hotel. Still dark, but there was no point in going to bed. I sat on the hard chair, listening to the moaning of the gale until I heard sounds of movement downstairs and knew Ellen was up. Feeling more tired than I could ever remember, I plunged my head into cold water in an effort to wake myself up, then knocked on Fraser's door and went down to the kitchen.

Ellen insisted on cooking a full breakfast – a steaming plateful of eggs, bacon, toast, and sweet, scalding tea. I hadn't felt hungry, but when it came I ate ravenously, feeling energy slowly seep back into my limbs. Fraser came downstairs after a few minutes and sat opposite me, his face pouchy from lack of sleep. But at least this morning he was sober.

'Radio's still out,' he grunted, without being asked.

I'd not expected otherwise. I was long past optimism or disappointment. Now all I wanted to do was see this through.

Dawn had broken, and light was seeping into the sky as we drove back down to the boatyard. It was another filthy day. Waves pounded the shingle and cliffs, flinging sheets of spray high into the air to be carried inland. Kinross's ferry was still moored in the harbour, bucking violently on the angry sea. At least its owner wouldn't be taking it anywhere this morning, no matter how badly he might want to. Beyond it, white-tops crashed against the pinnacle of Stac Ross, foaming against each other as though frustrated by their failure to smash its dark rock.

And over it all, the wind ruled. Far from dying down, the storm had gained in intensity. Elemental in its savagery, it buffeted the Range Rover, flinging the rain against the windscreen in such torrents that the wipers struggled to clear the glass. When we climbed out of the car it harried us over to the boatyard. The ashes and skeletal spars of the burned fishing boat stood like a remnant of a Viking funeral, a stark reminder of the night's events.

Inside the workshop, Brody was sitting in an old car seat. The crowbar was laid across his lap as he faced the door, coat collar turned up against the chill. Behind him, Maggie's tarpaulin-shrouded body looked childlike and pathetic on the concrete floor.

He smiled wanly when Fraser and I went in. 'Morning.'

He seemed to have aged overnight. His face was haggard, the flesh more tightly stretched over the bones; new lines were etched in the skin round his eyes and mouth. A frost of silver stubble clung to his chin.

'Any problems?' I asked.

'No, it's been quiet enough.'

He stood up, joints cracking as he stretched. He gave a little sigh of appreciation as he took a bite from the bacon sandwich Ellen had sent for him. I poured him a mug of tea from the Thermos flask she'd also packed while I told him what we'd learned from Maggie's grandmother.

'If Maggie took the car that should make it easier to find where she went. Assuming it hasn't been moved,' he said when I'd finished. Neatly dusting crumbs from his fingers and mouth, he drained his tea and stood up. 'Right, let's take a look at the cliff.'

'What about . . . about that?' Fraser asked, jerking his head uneasily at the body. 'Shouldn't one of us keep an eye on it? In case Kinross decides to do anything.'

'Are you volunteering?' Brody asked. He smiled thinly at the reluctance on Fraser's face. 'Don't worry. I found a padlock in one of the drawers. We can lock the doors, and I can't see Kinross – or anyone else – risking anything in broad daylight anyway.'

'I don't mind staying,' I offered.

Brody shook his head. 'You're the only forensic expert we've got. If there's any evidence up there, I'd like you to see it.'

'That sort of thing isn't really my field.'

'It's more yours than mine or Fraser's,' he said.

There was no arguing with that.

Brody hurried home to check on his dog while Fraser and I secured the doors with the oil-smeared padlock. The metallic snick brought an unwelcome flashback of being trapped in the burning community centre. I was glad when Brody returned a few minutes later, and we could set off for the foot of the cliffs.

At their closest point, they lay only thirty or forty yards from the boatyard, but the rain battered us relentlessly as we crossed the open ground.

'Christ on a bicycle!' Fraser exclaimed, hunching against it.

The cliffs themselves afforded some protection once we reached them. A strip of shingle ran along their base, broken with jagged outcrops of rock. Leaning into the wind, we made our way along it, treading carefully as we scanned the rain-slick pebbles.

After a few yards Brody stopped. 'Here.'

He pointed to a rock protruding from the shingle. It had been sluiced almost clean by the rain, but a smear of something dark clung to it. I crouched down for a better look. It was a clot of bloodied tissue, veined and torn. The shingle around it was disturbed, a depression that could have been left by the impact of something heavy. What might have been drag marks ran from it towards the boatyard, disappearing where the shingle gave way to firmer ground.

I'd brought more freezer bags from the hotel to use as stand-ins for evidence bags. Taking one from my pocket, I used the blade of my penknife to scrape up a sample of bloody tissue. If the rain kept up it would have washed most of the blood away by the time the police got here, and the gulls would have scavenged what was left.

Brody was looking up at the top of the cliff, about a hundred feet above us. 'The steps are further along, but there's no point all three of us climbing up.' He turned to Fraser. 'Makes more sense for you to take the car and meet us at the top.'

'Aye, you're right,' Fraser hurriedly agreed.

Giving him the plastic bag to take back to the Range Rover, Brody and I crunched along the shingle to the steps. They were cut into the cliff face, steep and winding. There was an old handrail, but it didn't inspire confidence.

Wiping the rain from his face, Brody regarded them, then looked at my sling. 'Sure you're up to it?'

I nodded. I wasn't going to back out now.

We started up. Brody went first, leaving me to follow at my own pace. The steps were slippery with rain. Seabirds huddled against the cliff, feathers ruffling in the wind. The higher we climbed, the more exposed to it we became. It shrieked and flailed at us, as though wilfully trying to fling us off.

We were only a few yards from the top when Brody's foot slipped on a broken step. He skidded back into me, knocking me out against the handrail. I felt the rusted metal give under my weight, and for a moment looked directly down into the open drop. Then Brody grabbed me by the scruff of my coat and hauled me back to safety.

'Sorry,' he panted, letting go. 'You OK?'

I nodded, not trusting my voice. My pulse was still racing as I started after him again. But as I did, I noticed something on the rock face a few yards away.

'Brody,' I called.

When he turned I pointed to where another dark smear tufted a bulging outcrop on the cliff face. It was too far out of reach for me to get a sample, but I could guess how it got there.

This was where Maggie's body had struck the rock on its way down.

We reached the top of the cliff a few minutes after that. Emerging on to it, we were hit by the full force of the gale. It tore at our coats, filling them like kites and threatening to fling us back over the edge.

'Bloody hell!' Brody exclaimed, bracing himself against it.

Below us, Runa's harbour was revealed as a shallow horseshoe of churning water, hemmed in by cliffs. The view was vertiginous, wind-lashed grey sea and sky blurring together on an indistinct horizon. One or two lone gulls braved the wind, their plaintive caws coming to us as they futilely tried to ride the currents before being swept away. Inland, the brooding slopes of Beinn Tuiridh loomed in the distance, while a hundred yards away Bodach Runa, the island's standing stone, rose from the turf like a crooked finger. Other than that, all there was to see was the treeless moor, grass flattened by the wind. There was nothing to suggest that Maggie, or anyone else, had ever been up here.

The rain slashed against us like buckshot as we made our way to the spot where Maggie must have fallen from. I was beginning to think we were wasting our time when Brody pointed.

'Over there.'

A couple of yards in front of us the ground had been disturbed. The turf was flattened and torn, and when I looked more closely I could see gouts of viscous black clotting the grass.

Even after all the rain, there was a lot of it.

'This is where she was killed,' Brody said, wiping rain from his face as he bent down to examine it. 'The amount of blood that's here, she must have practically bled out.'

He stood up, scanning the ground around us.

'There's more over there. And there.'

The patches were smaller than the one by the cliff's edge, already almost washed away. They formed a trail of blood that led away from the drop. Or, more likely, towards it.

'She was running away,' I said. 'She was already injured before she got to the edge.'

'Could have been trying to reach the steps. Or just running blindly.' He gave me a look. 'You thinking what I'm thinking?'

'About what Mary Tait said?' I nodded. *They ran off. After all the noise.* Perhaps the people she'd seen hadn't just run off. Perhaps one of them had been chasing the other.

But where had they come from?

Brody looked round the empty cliff top, shaking his head in frustration. 'Where the hell's her car? It's got to be around here somewhere.'

279

But I'd been considering the windswept cliff top myself. 'Remember when you asked Mary where she'd got the coat? What did she say, exactly?'

Brody gave me a puzzled look. 'That a man gave it to her. Why?'

'No, she didn't say a man. She said *the* man.'

'So?'

I pointed at the standing stone, now no more than fifty yards away. 'You told me Bodach Runa meant the Old Man of Runa. Perhaps that's the man she meant. Mary had a torch. She could have got up here using the steps, the same as us.'

Brody stared off at the standing stone, thinking it through. 'Let's take a look, shall we?'

The police Range Rover was visible perhaps a quarter of a mile away, snaking its way towards us as we set off for the stone. The road dipped out of sight occasionally, but Bodach Runa itself was hard to miss. Fraser would be able to see where we were heading and meet us there.

Brody walked at a fast pace across the uneven terrain. Shivering from the cold and rain, the ache already beginning to make its presence felt again in my shoulder, I was hard pushed to keep up with him. The ground rose up in a ridge between us and the standing stone, so that we could only see its upper half. But as we drew nearer I could make out something in a dip behind it. Gradually, the roof of a car came into view.

Maggie's old Mini.

It was parked in a hollow just beyond the stone. A couple of sheep huddled against it out of the wind, adding to the car's air of abandonment. They bolted as Brody and I slithered down the grassy bank towards it. The sound of a car engine came from an overgrown track that ran from the hollow, and a few moments later the Range Rover came bumping into view.

Fraser parked at the end of the track and climbed out. 'That hers?'

'Aye,' Brody told him. 'That's Maggie's.'

Both doors hung open, swinging slightly as the wind pushed them back against their hinges. The front seats were soaked from the rain, but it wasn't water alone that darkened them. Splashes and smears of blood dappled the dashboard and windscreen as though flung there by a mad artist.

'Jesus,' Fraser breathed.

We approached a little closer but still stayed well back, so as not to contaminate the ground around the car. Brody peered through the open driver's door at the blood-spattered interior.

'Looks like she was attacked through her side and managed to scramble away out of the passenger door. What do you think, a knife or axe?'

It seemed unreal, discussing what weapon had been used to kill Maggie, when only the evening before I'd sat next to her in this same car. But sentiment wasn't going to catch her killer.

'Knife, I'd say. Not enough room to swing an axe, not without leaving marks on the inside of the car.'

I looked around the hollow. At night, beyond the arcs of a car's headlights, it would have been impenetrably dark. Dark enough for Mary Tait to watch, unobserved. And to hear.

I imagined there would have been a lot to listen to.

Fraser was looking behind the car. 'There's more tyre tracks back here. Don't look like the Mini's.'

Brody clicked his tongue, exasperated. I knew he was thinking that either rain or sheep's hoofs would have churned the tracks into mud by the time SOC got here to take casts. But there was nothing we could do about it.

'She told her grandmother she was meeting someone. Looks like this was where. Mary must have been up here already, and close enough nearby to hear the commotion.' He frowned, staring at the car. 'I still can't see how she came by the coat. It wasn't damaged or bloodstained, but how come Maggie wasn't wearing it on a night like that?'

'Perhaps she took it off for Kinross,' Fraser suggested. 'Along with a few other things, if you get my drift. No other reason for them to be up here. Then they had a lovers' tiff, or whatever, and Kinross lost his rag.'

'This was no lovers' tiff!' Brody snapped. 'Maggie was an ambitious young woman; she'd have set her sights higher than a ferry captain. And until we can prove it was Kinross she met last night, I'd try not to jump to conclusions.'

Fraser coloured up at the rebuke. But something he'd said had sparked my own train of thought.

'He's probably right about Maggie taking off her coat,' I said. I told them about the car heater being stuck on full. 'Both times Maggie gave me a lift she put it on the back seat. That'd explain why there was no blood on it.'

Brody was trying to see into the back of the car. 'Could be. There's hardly any spatter back there. If the car doors were left open when Maggie tried to get away, Mary could have just walked up and looked inside. Even if she noticed the blood in the front I doubt she'd realize what it was.'

Still keeping his distance from the Mini, he began to circle it. When he got to the other side he stopped.

'Over here.'

Fraser and I went round to see what he'd found. Maggie's shoulder bag was lying on the ground below the passenger door, its contents spilled on the muddy grass. Scraps of wind-blown tissue and paper littered the ground around it, snagged by grass stalks and turned to pulp by the rain.

Lying amongst the make-up and other artefacts of Maggie's life, its muddied pages fluttering like trapped moths, was a ring-bound note-book.

'Let me have a plastic bag,' Brody said to me.

'You sure about this?' Fraser said uncertainly.

Brody opened the bag I'd given him. 'Maggie was a reporter.

Crime scene or not, if she made a note of who she was meeting, it's not going to survive long out here.'

Treading carefully, he went to the car and crouched down by the open passenger door. Taking a pen from his pocket, he slid it into the notebook's ring binding. Then he carefully lifted the book and slipped it into the bag. Even from where I stood I could see that the pages were disintegrating, the writing on them reduced to an illegible colourwash of ink.

Brody's mouth compressed with disappointment. 'Well, whatever was in it, it's not much use any more.'

He started to get up again, then stopped.

'There's something under the car.' There was a new excitement in his voice. 'Looks like her dictaphone.'

I thought about all the times I'd seen Maggie brandishing her tape recorder. Like many modern journalists, she'd relied on it more than a notepad and pen. So if she'd kept some sort of record while she'd been on the island, it didn't have to be a written one.

Brody could barely contain his impatience as I peeled off another plastic bag. 'Don't worry, I'll tell Wallace this was my decision,' he said, giving Fraser a shrewd glance.

For once the police sergeant didn't argue. Evidence as potentially important – and vulnerable – as this could hardly be left until SOC arrived. Putting his hand into the plastic bag, Brody reached under the car sill and picked up the dictaphone. Then, retracing his steps to where Fraser and I waited, he reversed the bag so the muddied recorder was enclosed in it.

He held it up so we could get a better look. The voice recorder was digital, a Sony model similar to the one I'd lost in the fire.

'Wonder how long the batteries last on these things?' Brody mused.

'Long enough,' I told him. 'It's still recording.'

'What?' He stared at it. 'You're joking.'

'It started when you spoke. Must be voice activated.'

He studied the recorder's LCD display. 'So this could have been running when Maggie was killed?'

'Unless it was turned on accidentally when it was knocked out of the car, then yes.'

The wind wailed around us as we all considered that. Brody rubbed his jaw thoughtfully, staring at the small silver machine in the plastic bag. I knew, even before he spoke, what he was going to say next.

'How do I play it?'

25

The dictaphone hissed into silence after the last recording had finished. None of us spoke. The memory of what we'd just heard was still resonating, as devastating as a shell burst. Brody clicked off the machine, then stared into space, motionless as a statue.

I wanted to say something to him, but I'd no idea what.

The police Range Rover rocked in the wind, rain beating a tattoo on its roof. We'd retreated back to its warmth to play Maggie's dictaphone. Each of the recordings she'd made were stored in its memory as a separate file, which in turn were arranged into folders. There were four folders in all, one titled *Work*, two blank and empty. The fourth was headed simply *Diary*.

The entries were ordered by date. About a dozen of them had been made since Maggie had arrived on Runa.

Brody had selected the most recent. According to the logged time and date, it had been made just before midnight. Around the time that Rose Cassidy had told us that Maggie had gone out.

'Here goes,' Brody had said, and pressed the play button through the plastic bag.

Maggie's dead voice had issued eerily from the speaker.

Well, this is it. No sign of him yet, but I'm a few minutes early. Just hope he turns up after all this . . .

'Hope who turns up? Come on, tell us the bastard's name,' Fraser muttered. But Maggie had other things on her mind.

God, what am I doing here? I was actually excited about this earlier, but it all seems a bit pointless now. Why the hell did Kevin Kinross have to tell me the woman's name? I'm a hack on a local newspaper, not an investigative journalist! How did he know it anyway? And that stupid stunt with David Hunter. 'Is the victim called Janice?' Really slick, Mags. Now he thinks I'm withholding information. But I can't just drop Kevin in it. So what do I do now?

There was a sound it took me a moment to place – Maggie was drumming her fingers on the steering wheel. She gave a sigh.

First things first. Right now I need to get my head cleared. Don't want to make a hash of things now, not when I've pushed so hard for this. Christ, this car's still like a bloody oven . . . There was a rustling noise: she was taking off her coat. *Must admit, I'm starting to feel a bit spooked. Probably just all this other business, but I can't help but wonder if I'm being stupid. I mean, there's a killer loose on the island, for Christ's sake! If I heard about anyone else doing this I'd . . . Hang on, what was that?*

There was a long pause. The only sound was Maggie's breathing, quick and nervous.

I'm getting jumpy. Can't see anything now. Looked like a flash, like a torch. Probably a shooting star, or something. It's so dark out here I can't tell what's land and what's sky. Still . . .

There was an audible clunk.

Right, very safety conscious. Drive out to the middle of nowhere and then lock your doors. I mean, I'm not really worried. Not really. The man just wants to talk in private, that's all, and the way tongues wag on this island you can hardly blame him. Even so, I'm starting to wonder if this is such a good idea. Better be worth it. I'll give him five more minutes, and if he's not here then— Shit!

We could hear that her breathing had become fast and ragged.

286

There's that flash again. That's no bloody shooting star, somebody's out there! Right, that's it, I'm going . . .

There was a coughing whine as the car's engine turned over but wouldn't start. Over it we could hear Maggie's voice, further away now, as though she'd just thrust the dictaphone aside in her haste to start the Mini.

Come on, come on! Oh, don't do this! I don't believe this, come on, car, don't be such a fucking cliché! Oh, you fucking heap of junk, come on!

Calm down, you're flooding it! I found myself urging her, even though I knew it wouldn't do any good.

Then she gave a laugh of pure relief.

Oh, thank Christ! There's headlights. He's here. Bloody late, but I'll forgive him that! There was another laugh, stronger this time, then a snuffle of eyes being wiped and nose being blown. *God, some bloody reporter he's going to think I am! Come on, Mags, get your act together. You're supposed to be a professional. Shit, I can't see a bloody thing for his head-lights. How about turning them off, eh? Right, here he comes, let's hide this thing out of the way . . .*

We heard more rustling as she moved the dictaphone somewhere out of sight. There was the clunk of the door locks being taken off, then the creak of a door opening. When Maggie spoke again, she sounded bright and cocky.

Hi. What time do you call this, then? Thought you said midnight? Look, how about turning off the headlights? I can't see a . . . Oh, sorry, I didn't . . . Hey, what are you . . . Oh, Jesus! JESUS!

I bowed my head as Maggie's screams and pleas began to shrill out of the speaker. The dictaphone had dutifully recorded everything. There were thumps and crackles as it was buffeted during the struggle, but they didn't drown out the awful soundtrack of Maggie's murder.

The confusion of cries and scrambling reached a climax, then there was a sudden silence. It was broken only by a faint noise, like rushing water. We were listening to a recording of the wind, I realized. The dictaphone had been knocked from the car as Maggie made her short-lived escape. With nothing louder to activate it, the machine soon shut off. There was a brief lull, then Brody's voice emerged.

Wonder how long the batteries last on these things?

I heard my own voice answer, *Long enough. It's still—*

Brody stopped it there.

None of us looked at each other. It was as though, by listening to the recording of Maggie's killing, we'd colluded in something shameful.

'Why couldn't she have just said the bastard's name?' Fraser said. Even he sounded shaken.

I stirred. 'She'd no reason to. The recording was for her own benefit. Whoever it was, she didn't think she was in any danger from him. She was only nervous while she was waiting, not once he'd arrived.'

'Got it wrong, didn't she?' Fraser said. 'All that business with the headlights. What's the betting he left them on to dazzle her, so she wouldn't see he'd got a knife?'

Brody had been listening without comment. 'What about the flash she saw before the car arrived?'

'Mary Tait,' I said.

He nodded, his face pulled into a mask of fatigue as he ran his hand over it. 'Wandering around with that toy torch of hers. If it weren't so bloody tragic it'd be funny. Maggie gets spooked by a harmless teenager, and opens her car door to a killer.'

'Aye, but who the hell was it?' Fraser said in frustration.

Brody turned his attention back to the dictaphone. 'Let's see if there's anything else on here that might tell us.' He gave a gallows smile. 'Might as well be hung for a sheep as a lamb.'

The wind rocked the car, flinging rain against it as though trying to force its way inside. Having played the last file first, Brody now went back to the start to play them in order. Maggie's voice came from the speaker once again.

288

Well, this is turning out to be a better trip than I expected. Just wish my gran had access to the Internet, but the information age has passed her by, bless her. Have to get someone at the newsroom to check out spontaneous whatever-it's-called. And do a search on David Hunter's background while they're about it. I'll bet there's something interesting there. There was a chuckle. *Aye, and in his background as well. What's an expert from London doing out here, and with Sergeant bloody Neil Fraser, of all people? Jesus, of all the bloody cops to run into. Still, good news for Ellen's bar takings, I dare say . . .*

I glanced at Fraser. His expression was thunderous.

Got a real bruise on my arm where he threw me out of the cottage. Serve him right if I really did file a complaint. Too shocked to do much when it happened, though. God, the state of that body! I'd love to get a better look. Perhaps I should think about taking another trip out there tonight. Fraser's bound to be in the bar by then . . .

The back of Fraser's neck was burning crimson. Brody kept his face impassive as he played the next file.

Maggie sounded bad-tempered and out of breath. *Well, a right waste of time that was. And I still didn't manage to get a proper look at the body. Last time I try to play at commandos.* It was possible to hear a smile enter her voice. *Still, gave me quite a rush, I have to admit. I've not been that scared since I wet myself playing hide-and-seek at junior school. God, when that young PC jumped out at me! What was his name? Duncan, I think they called him. Keen bugger, but at least he seemed human. Cute, too, come to think of it. Wonder if he's single?*

The next two entries were mainly concerned with her personal musings on family and work. Brody skipped through them until a familiar name jumped out.

Went out to the Strachans' earlier, hoping to get an interview. Fat chance. David Hunter was there with his arm all strapped up. Learned the hard way about going out at night on Runa without a torch. She gave a snort. *Bruce Cameron was there as well, sniffing around Strachan's wife, as usual. Creepy sod. Can't see why the Strachans put up with him. Grace is nice enough, even though she's so good-looking I should hate her. But can't make up my mind about her husband. All charm one minute, frost the next. Mind you, I wouldn't say no . . .*

The recording ended on her mischievous laugh.

The next entry was another personal one, with Maggie worrying about her career prospects. Brody skipped through to the next. I felt a jolt of recognition when I realized what it was about.

Bit of a turn-up for the books this afternoon. Took a short cut to my gran's down the alleyway behind the hotel, and who should come rushing out of the back door but Michael Strachan. Looked guilty as hell when I said hello. Don't know who was more surprised, me or him. Never even occurred to me there might be anything between those two. I mean, Ellen's attractive, but the man's married to a goddess, for God's sake! But there's definitely something going on there. Perhaps I should sound out my gran, see if any tongues have been wagging . . .

So that had been who Ellen's anonymous visitor had been, when I'd discovered her crying in the kitchen. The date and time of the recording confirmed it. After everything else I wasn't altogether surprised, but the knowledge gave me no satisfaction. I glanced uneasily at Brody. A furrow had appeared between his eyebrows, but he made no comment as he played the next entry.

Well, you live and learn. Here's me thinking I'm the seasoned reporter, unearthing some big secret, and it turns out to be old news. Course, my gran's sworn me to secrecy anyway, bless her. Sounds like practically everyone knows, but just keeps quiet about it. Can't help but wonder if it would have stayed a secret if it had been anyone else. People here know which side their bread's buttered on, I expect. She gave a cynical laugh. *The thing is, it's obvious once you look for it. The little girl's got Ellen's colouring, the same lovely red hair, but if you ignore that you can see that Strachan's her father . . .*

Oh, hell, I thought. Fraser gave a low whistle. 'So Strachan's been playing away from home? Some people are never satisfied.'

Brody looked startled, as though he couldn't quite believe what he'd just heard. But it made all too much sense to me. What was it

Ellen had said about Anna's father the night she'd treated my burns? *Let's just say there was never any future there.*

Now I knew why.

The planes of Brody's face had hardened. Ellen wasn't his daughter, but she might as well have been. Tight-lipped, he stabbed at the machine with a blunt finger to play the next file.

It was immediately obvious from Maggie's voice that something was wrong.

God, what a lousy bloody day. Seemed like a good idea, trying to get an interview with Strachan and his wife after she'd been attacked. Awful business, but they're the most glamorous couple in the Western Isles, and this is a big story now. Thought I was being clever, dropping the soup all over the floor and batting my eyes at Strachan. Then Dr David bloody Hunter comes out with that Campbell's crack. God, I just wanted the ground to swallow me up.

And as though that wasn't bad enough, he tells me the young policeman's been murdered. Duncan. What was his surname? That's awful, I can't remember. Some bloody journalist I am. He was really nice, helped me on the ferry with my bag. Even that night he caught me at the cottage. Doesn't seem possible that someone on this island – Christ, someone I know! – must have killed him. I mean, what's going on? I don't even want to talk about it any more . . .

The file ended abruptly. Our breathing had misted the car windows, so that it seemed as though we were enclosed in a sea of fog. The world outside might have ceased to exist as Brody selected the next entry.

'Two left.'

This time I thought there was something wrong with the recorder. The noise that came from its speaker was unintelligible at first, an indistinct babble of sound. It was only when I recognized Guthrie's booming voice ordering a drink that I realized we were listening to a recording made in the bar before the meeting. Snatches of conversation came and went, then Brody's voice came from the speaker. It sounded tinny and far away as the dictaphone struggled to pick up his speech from across the room.

We listened once more to Kinross's vehement refusal to believe the killer was an islander, Maggie's own question about the dead woman's identity, and Cameron's abortive attempt to assert himself. The recording became unintelligible again as the meeting broke up.

When it finished the tension in the steamed-up interior of the car seemed unbearable. Then Brody spoke.

'Last one.'

This time Maggie's voice sounded much more upbeat.

Finally, some good news! Almost missed it, too. I'd no idea the note was there, it was stuffed so far down in my coat pocket. It'd have been a real sickener if I'd not found it in time. Although why he wants to meet me at midnight, and out at Bodach Runa, I don't know. Man's got a sense of the dramatic, I'll give him that. Anyone else but him, I might have second thoughts, but I dare say he just wants to wait till his wife's asleep. Either way, no way can I pass this up. I've been trying hard enough for an interview, and if Michael Strachan wants to keep it private, I'm not going to argue.

There was a sudden, exuberant laugh.

Glad I didn't break my granny's third-best bowl for nothing after all. God, I just hope he isn't setting me up. Be a real anticlimax if he doesn't show . . .

The recording finished. The only sound was the drumming of the rain on the car roof, and the mournful bluster of wind. Wordlessly, Brody played the last section again.

. . . if Michael Strachan wants to keep it private, I'm not going to argue . . .

Fraser was the first to find his voice. 'Jesus Christ! She went to meet *Strachan*?'

'You heard her.' Brody spoke quietly. He sat very still, as though unwilling to move.

'But . . . Christ, it doesn't make any sense! Why would Strachan kill Maggie Cassidy? And the others? What about his *wife*! He can't have attacked her himself?'

'People do anything when they're desperate,' Brody said. He slowly shook his head. 'I didn't see this coming either, but Strachan makes more sense than Kinross. We thought Janice Donaldson might have been killed because she tried to blackmail a client, and who'd make the best target? A widowed ferry captain, or a wealthy married man who's the pillar of his community?'

'Aye, but . . . why would Strachan bother with a low-rent tart like Donaldson when he's got a wife like that?'

Brody gave a weary shrug. 'For some men it's the sordidness that provides the kicks. As for the rest . . . The more someone has to lose, the harder they'll try to keep it.'

I didn't want to accept it, but it made an awful sort of sense. First Janice Donaldson, then Duncan had been killed as Strachan tried to cover his tracks. And even though Maggie's persistence in trying to interview him was innocent, to a killer who wasn't prepared to take any chances it would have appeared in a very different light.

'He planted the note yesterday,' I said, slowly. 'While I was out there. He left Grace and Maggie with me while he went to clean her coat.'

Even the stalker that Grace thought she'd seen had no doubt been engineered by Strachan, a means of distracting her so he could slip a hastily written note into Maggie's coat pocket. A note that was now probably lost on the moorland near the Mini, scattered with the rest of the contents of Maggie's bag. I felt shock begin to give way to anger; outrage at the extent of Strachan's crimes. His betrayal of everyone who'd trusted him.

Including me.

The Range Rover lurched as a gust of wind savaged it. The gale seemed to have grown worse while we'd listened to Maggie's recordings.

'So what do we do now?' Fraser asked.

Moving with the deliberation of a crash victim, Brody slowly opened the glove compartment and put the dictaphone inside.

He closed it again, pressing the door shut with a deliberate click.

'Try the radio.'

Fraser tried first his own, then the car's fixed set. 'Still dead.'

Brody nodded, as though that was only what he'd expected. 'We can't afford to wait for the mainland team any more. We need to bring him in. Strachan's going to be off this island the second the weather clears. There's not only his own yacht, there's a dozen or so other boats he could try for. We can't watch them all.'

'We don't know for sure he'll run,' Fraser countered, but he didn't sound as if he believed it himself.

'He's killed three people, including a police officer,' Brody said, implacably. 'Maggie wasn't even a threat, he just thought she was. He's losing it, getting desperate. We give him the chance, he'll be gone. Or kill somebody else. You think Wallace will thank you if that happens?'

Fraser gave a reluctant nod. 'Aye. Aye, you're right.'

Brody turned to me as the police sergeant started the car. Something seemed to have gone out of him after he'd heard the recordings, but I wasn't sure if it was the revelation about Strachan's being the murderer, or the father of Ellen's child.

'What about you, David? I can't ask you to come with us, but I'd appreciate it.' A corner of his mouth twitched in an attempted smile. 'We need all the help we can get.'

I wasn't sure how much help I'd be with only one good arm, but I nodded. I'd come this far. I wasn't going to back out now.

Strachan had hurt enough people.

Both Strachan's Saab and Grace's Porsche SUV were parked outside the house. Fraser pulled up behind them – blocking them both in, I noticed. The wind clubbed at us as we climbed out of the Range Rover, as though eager for violence. The temperature had dropped, threatening to freeze the rain that was being flung wildly in all directions. Brody paused by the Saab, bending to examine its tyres. He looked at me to make sure I'd seen as well.

They were thickly caked with mud.

He stood back, letting Fraser take the lead as we approached the house. It towered above us, its granite walls sheer and unforgiving. Seizing the iron knocker, the burly sergeant began pounding on the front door as if trying to break it down.

From inside we could hear the dog barking, then the door was opened. Grace looked out at us from behind a security chain. She smiled, relieved when she saw who it was.

'Just a second.'

The door was closed again so she could slip off the chain. She opened it and stood back so we could enter.

'Sorry about that. But after yesterday . . .'

The bruising on her cheek somehow only accentuated her beauty. But I noticed there were shadows under her eyes that hadn't been there before the attack. An attack carried out by her own husband, to divert attention from himself.

I felt my outrage towards Strachan tighten into a hard knot of resolve.

'Is your husband in?' Fraser asked.

'No, afraid not. Gone off on one of his jaunts again.'

'His car's still here.'

Grace looked startled by his brusqueness. 'He doesn't always take it. Why, is something wrong?'

'Do you know where he is?'

'No, I'm sorry. Look, would you mind telling me what's going on? Why do you want to speak to Michael?'

Fraser ignored the question. The dog continued to bark madly from the kitchen, claws scrabbling on the door.

'Do you mind if we look round the house?'

'But I've already told you he isn't here.'

'I'd still like to see for myself.'

Her eyes flashed at his tone, and for a moment I thought she would refuse. Then she gave an angry toss of her head.

'I don't like being called a liar. But if you must.'

'I'll look in here,' Brody told Fraser. 'You check the outbuildings.'

Grace watched them go, still angry but also bewildered. 'David, why are they looking for Michael? What's wrong?'

My hesitation must have been answer enough. For the first time she looked worried.

'This isn't something to do with what's been happening, is it? The murders?'

'I can't say. I'm sorry,' I said, hating the fact that her world was about to be shattered.

The dog was becoming hysterical at the sound of our voices. 'Oh, for God's sake, Oscar, be quiet!' Grace said, impatiently opening the kitchen door and pushing the golden retriever back in. 'Come on! Outside!'

The dog wagged its tail, oblivious to the tension as she tugged it towards the back door in the kitchen.

Brody came back downstairs. He gave a quick shake of his head. 'Not there. Where's Grace?'

'Quietening the dog. She's scared. I think she's started to guess why we're here.'

He sighed. 'Strachan's got a lot to answer for. Bad enough finding out your husband's a murderer, let alone got a child by another woman.' An expression of pain creased his features. 'Christ, what the hell was Ellen thinking of . . . ?'

'Brody,' I said quickly, but it was too late.

Grace stood frozen in the kitchen doorway.

'Mrs Strachan . . .' Brody began.

'I don't believe you,' she whispered. She'd gone white.

'I'm sorry. You shouldn't have had to hear like that.'

'No . . . You're lying! Michael wouldn't. He *wouldn't*!'

'I'm very—'

'Get out! Get *out*!' It was more a sob than a shout.

'Come on, let's go,' Brody said, quietly.

I didn't like leaving her like that, but there was nothing I could do, or say, that would make any difference to Grace. As we went outside, she was hugging herself, her perfect face now a stricken mask. Then Brody had closed the door behind us, shutting her off from sight.

'Christ. I didn't mean that to happen.'

'Well, it has.' I felt unaccountably angry. 'Let's find Fraser.'

I pulled my coat hood tight as we made our way towards the out-buildings. It was much colder now. The wind seemed to be trying to push us back, flinging rain in icy blasts against us. Fraser was just emerging from the barn when we rounded the side of the house.

'Find anything?' Brody asked.

'You'd better see for yourselves.'

He led us back into the barn. I'd last been here with Strachan, when Grace had been missing. Or when I'd thought she was miss-ing, I reminded myself. He'd known all along where she was.

Fraser went to where a petrol-driven lawnmower stood in the far corner. Behind it was a large petrol container. There was no lid, only a broken plastic strap to show where one had been attached.

'What's the betting that the top we found near the camper van is from that?' Fraser said. 'Remember when Strachan's wife's car ran out of petrol? I'd put money that's where he got his accelerant from to start the fires. Christ, if I get hold of the bastard . . .'

Brody's jaw bunched as he looked down at the container. 'Let's check the boat.'

The yacht was unlocked. It was as we'd left it, the shattered remains of its comms still lying on the floor. But Strachan wasn't on board.

'So where the hell is he?' Fraser asked, savagely, as we stood in the heaving cockpit. 'Bastard could be anywhere.'

But even as he said it I knew there was only one place Strachan would have gone. Looking across at Brody I saw that he'd realized too.

He was on the mountain. At the burial cairns.

★

The storm was destroying itself. Roaring down from the Arctic Circle, the front had gathered speed and force as it crossed the North Atlantic. By the time it reached the UK mainland its elemental fury would be largely spent, torn apart by its own unsustainable violence.

On Runa, though, it had reached its peak, building into a frenzy as though determined to wrench the tiny island from the sea. As we clambered up the exposed slopes of Beinn Tuiridh, the wind seemed to have doubled its intensity. And the temperature had plummeted. The icy rain had turned to hail, white stones that bounced and skidded underfoot, beating down on my hood like gravel.

We'd left the car on the road as close to the foot of the mountain as we could get, and started up. It was still light, but visibility was poor and the afternoon was already passing. There was another hour, two at most, before the first dimming of twilight. And once darkness fell, then being out here could very quickly go from being dangerous to fatal.

Despite the exertion, my hands, feet and face were numb. The cold made my injured shoulder burn with a dull, strength-sapping ache. To make matters worse, we'd only a vague idea of where the cairns were. It had been night when I'd blindly stumbled up here, following the glow from Strachan's fire, and I'd been delirious with exhaustion and pain. In daylight, the mountainside was a bewildering jumble of boulders and gullies. Its rock-strewn slopes were covered with formations that could be either natural or man-made.

'Never been up here before,' Brody panted. 'But I don't think the cairns are very far. Shouldn't take us too long. If we head straight up we're bound to come to them.'

I wasn't so sure. The slope was treacherous with loose stone and scree, and there was nothing resembling any sort of path. We were forced to make our own route, often finding ourselves faced with rocks that had to be either scrambled over or bypassed. If he'd managed to carry me down here single-handed at night, Strachan was obviously stronger than he looked.

And more dangerous.

We were walking directly into the wind, bent almost double by the effort. We'd started out close together, but as the steep gradient took its toll we'd become strung out. Brody forged on resolutely, but with my balance impaired by my strapped arm I was finding the going harder. Not as hard as Fraser, though. Overweight and unfit, the police sergeant was wheezing for breath and falling further behind with every step.

I was considering calling for a rest when there was a clatter from behind me. Looking back I saw that Fraser had fallen. Loose rocks formed a mini-avalanche around him as he slid backwards on his hands and knees. He stayed on them, gulping air through his open mouth, too exhausted to get up.

Ahead of us, Brody was carrying on unaware. 'Brody! Wait!' I called, the wind throwing my words back at me.

I hurried back down to Fraser. I got my hand under his arm, and tried to pull him to his feet. He was a solid, dead weight.

'Give me a minute . . .' he gasped.

But I could see that a minute, or even longer, wasn't going to make any difference. There was no way he could go any further. I looked up for Brody again and saw him almost lost in the hail. Then a sudden gust peppered my eyes with shards of ice, making me avert my face.

'Can you make it back to the car?' I asked, putting my mouth close to his ear so he could hear me over the wind.

He nodded, chest heaving.

'You sure?'

He waved me on irritably. I left him to it and hurried after Brody. I couldn't see him at all now. My breathing became ragged as I tried to catch up. I kept my head down, staring at the ground directly in front of me, partly to protect my face from the wind's bite, but mainly because I was too tired to do anything else. Whenever I looked up, hoping to catch a glimpse of Brody, the hail obscured the slope ahead like static on a TV screen.

A stone skidded from under my foot, sending me down on to one knee. I sucked in air, not sure how much further I could go.

'Brody!' I shouted, but the only answer was the shriek of the gale.

I clambered to my feet again. It was too exposed to stay where I was. I had to decide whether to carry on or follow Fraser back down, and as I stood there I realized that the tumbles of rock nearby were oddly symmetrical. I'd been so focused on catching up with Brody that I'd not taken notice of the surrounding landscape until now.

I was standing amongst the burial cairns.

But there was no sign of Brody. I told myself that he couldn't have missed them, that he wouldn't have gone straight past, even though that was what I'd almost done myself. As I looked round for him an eddy in the wind created a gap in the swirling hail, like a curtain being drawn back. It only lasted for a moment, but while it did I saw a larger stone structure further off along the slope.

My boots skidded on the hail-covered slope, carving ruts in the sodden turf as I went to take a closer look. The structure was like a round stone hut, partially caved in. Just outside it was the remains of a campfire. The ashes were cold, already half covered with hail, but looking at them I saw the flames leaping up, and remembered the hooded figure emerging into the firelight the night I'd been lost. Strachan's words came back to me. *The broch's a good place to think . . . I love the idea that someone would have been sitting up there by a fire two thousand years ago. I like to think I'm keeping the tradition . . .*

I looked around, not really expecting to see either Fraser or Brody, but hoping all the same. But I might have been the only living soul on the mountainside.

Bracing myself against the wind, I edged closer to the hut. The entrance yawned in front of me. I peered into it, trying to sense if anyone was inside. All I saw was blackness. *Just do it.* Crouching down, I ducked through the low opening.

Silence draped around me like a blanket as the wind was cut off. It was pitch black, the air heavy with loam and age. It was cramped inside, barely high enough to allow me to stand. But no one jumped out at me. As my eyes acclimatized, I made out cold stone walls and bare soil underfoot. Whatever this was, it looked as though it had stood empty and unused for millennia.

Then, from the corner of my eye, I noticed a small, pale blur. I bent down to examine it. Some of the stones had tumbled from the inner wall, forming a small hollow. Inside was a half-melted candle stub, surrounded by dirty yellow pools of solidified wax from countless predecessors.

I'd found Strachan's hide. But where was Strachan?

I straightened, and as I did the grey light coming from the entrance suddenly dimmed. I spun round, heart banging, as a shape rose from the shadows behind me.

'Hello, David,' Strachan said.

26

I didn't speak. My mind still seemed stalled, robbing me of any speech or movement. Strachan took another step away from the wall, so he was silhouetted in the entrance.

He held a knife down by his side, its blade catching the light from behind him.

'Managed to find your way up here again, eh? Told you you'd find it interesting.'

His voice echoed flatly in the confines of the *broch*. He didn't come any closer, but he was between me and the only way out. I tried not to look at the knife. Our breath steamed in the small chamber. His eyes looked hunted and sunken, the dark stubble blue-black against the pallor of his face.

He tilted his head, listening to the wind howling outside.

'Do you know what Beinn Tuiridh means? It's Gaelic for "Moaning Mountain". Pretty apt, I always thought.'

His tone was conversational, as though he'd come here for a stroll. He ran his hand across the stone wall. The other, holding the knife, remained at his side.

'This place isn't as old as the cairns. Probably only a thousand years or so. You get *broch*s like this all across the islands. I've never been able to make up my mind if it was built here because of the cairns or in spite of them. Why build a watchtower in a graveyard? Unless they were watching over the dead, I suppose. What do you think?'

When I didn't answer he gave a small smile. 'No, I don't suppose you're here out of archaeological interest, are you?'

I found my voice. 'Maggie Cassidy's dead.'

He was still studying the hard stones. 'I know.'

'Did you kill her?'

Strachan stood poised for a moment with his hand on the wall. He dropped it with a sigh.

'Yes.'

'And Duncan? And Janice Donaldson?'

There was no surprise at hearing the prostitute's name. He just nodded, and any last doubt I might have had vanished.

'*Why?*'

'Does it matter? They're dead. You can't bring them back.'

He seemed shrunken. I'd expected to hate him, but I felt more confused than anything.

'You must have had a *reason*!'

'You wouldn't understand.'

I tried to see any sign of madness in his eyes. They just looked tired. And sad.

'Did Janice Donaldson blackmail you, was that it? Was she threatening to tell Grace?'

'Leave Grace out of this,' he warned, his voice grown suddenly hard.

'Then tell me.'

'All right, she was blackmailing me. I'd been fucking her, and when she realized who I was she got greedy. So I killed her.' He sounded listless, as though none of this had any real bearing on him.

'And what about Duncan and Maggie?'

'They got in the way.'

'That's it? You killed them just for that?'

303

'Yes, that's it! I butchered them all like pigs, and I got a thrill out of it! Because I'm a sick, twisted bastard! Is that what you wanted to hear?'

His voice was thick with self-contempt. I tried to keep mine steady. 'So now what?'

As we'd been talking, I'd been trying to slowly work my injured arm out of the sling under my coat. Even if I managed it I didn't give much for my chances if he attacked me, but I'd have none at all if I was one-handed.

He was backlit by the light from the entrance, half in shadow as he answered. 'Well, that's the question, isn't it?'

'Don't make this any worse for yourself than it is already,' I said, with a confidence I didn't feel. 'Think about Grace.'

He took a step towards me. 'I told you to leave her out of this!'

I made myself stay where I was, resisting the impulse to back away. 'Why? You *attacked* her! Your own wife!'

There was real pain in his eyes. 'She took me by surprise. I was in the house when the three of you called round. I guessed why you'd come, and I knew you'd be back. I only wanted to stop you using the yacht's radio, to give myself more time to *think*. But the bloody dog knew I was down there, and when I heard Grace coming into the cockpit, I . . . I just spun round and backhanded her. I didn't mean to hit her so hard, but I couldn't let her see it was me!'

'So then you staged everything? Put her through all that?'

'I did what I had to do!'

But he sounded shamed. I pushed on, sensing an advantage.

'You're not going to get off the island, you know that, don't you?'

'Probably not.' He had an odd smile on his face. Seeing it, I felt suddenly cold. 'But I'm not going to give myself up, either.'

He lifted the knife. Its blade glinted silver as he held it up, considering it.

'Do you want to know why I came up here?' he began, but I never heard his reason.

304

Suddenly a bulky shape flew into him from behind. There was a clatter as Strachan's knife flew from his hand, and then I was knocked against the wall. Pain burst in my shoulder as the stones shuddered under the impact. Everything was shadow and confusion as Strachan and another figure struggled on the floor. In the half-light I made out the granite features of Brody. Strachan was younger and fitter, but the older man had size on his side. Using his weight to pin him, he smashed his fist into Strachan's face. There was a meat and bone impact, then another as Brody hit him again. Strachan went limp even before Brody hit him a third time. I thought he'd stop, but he didn't. He carried on, putting all his weight into the blows.

'Brody!'

It was as though he hadn't heard. Strachan was no longer resisting, and as Brody drew back his fist once more I caught hold of his arm.

'You'll kill him!'

He shrugged me off. In the light from the entrance I could see the grim intent in his face and knew he was beyond reasoning. I pushed myself off the wall, driving into him and using my impetus to knock him off the unmoving Strachan.

Fire lanced through my injured shoulder. Brody tried to push me aside, but the pain maddened me. I shoved him back.

'No!'

For an instant I thought he was going to attack me, then the rage seemed to drain from him. Panting, he slumped against the wall as the fit passed.

I knelt down next to Strachan. He was bloody and dazed, but alive.

'How is he?' Brody asked, breathlessly.

'He'll live.'

'More than the bastard deserves.' But there was no energy left in the words. 'Where's Fraser?'

'Back at the car. He couldn't make it up.'

I looked round for the knife. It was lying by the wall. I used one of the remaining freezer bags to pick it up. It was a folding fishing knife, its blade five inches long. Big enough.

But as I looked at it something stirred at the back of my mind. *What is it? What's wrong?*

Brody held out his hand. 'Here, I'll look after that. Don't worry, I won't use it on him,' he added when I hesitated.

A nagging sense that I was overlooking something persisted as I passed it over. There was a groan from Strachan as Brody put the knife into his pocket.

'Help me get him up,' I said.

'I can manage,' Strachan gasped.

His nose was broken, making his voice sound hollow and adenoidal. I went over anyway. So did Brody, but it wasn't until he wrenched Strachan's arms behind his back that I saw he'd produced a pair of handcuffs.

'What are you doing?'

'Souvenir from when I retired.' He snapped the cuffs round Strachan's wrists. 'Call it a citizen's arrest.'

'I'm not going to try to get away,' Strachan said, making no attempt to resist.

'Not now you're not. Come on, get up.' Brody roughly pulled him to his feet. 'What's wrong, Strachan? Aren't you going to plead innocence? Insist you didn't kill anyone?'

'Would it make any difference?' he asked, dully.

Brody looked surprised, as though he hadn't expected him to buckle so easily.

'No.' He pushed him towards the entrance. 'Outside.'

I ducked through after them, blinking as I emerged into the daylight. The freezing wind took my breath away as I went to examine Strachan. His face was a mess. The blood and mucus that smeared it was superficial, but one of his eyes was puffed almost shut. From the way the cheek under it was also swollen, I guessed it wasn't only his nose that was broken.

I felt in my pockets for a tissue and began trying to staunch the blood.

'Let him bleed,' Brody said.

Strachan gave a travesty of a smile. 'Ever the humanitarian, eh, Brody?'

'Can you make it down?' I asked him.

'Do I have any choice?'

None of us did. Strachan wasn't the only one in bad shape. The climb and fight had taken its toll on Brody. His face was grey, and I doubted I looked any better. My shoulder had started throbbing again, and I was beginning to shiver as the wind cut through my fire-damaged coat like icy knives. We all needed to get off the exposed mountainside, fast.

Brody gave Strachan a shove. 'Move.'

'Take it easy,' I told him, as Strachan almost fell.

'Don't waste your sympathy. He would have killed you back there, given a chance.'

Strachan looked over his shoulder at me. 'I don't want any sympathy. But you were never in any danger from me.'

Brody snorted. 'Aye, right. That's why you'd got the knife.'

'I came up here to kill myself, not anybody else.'

'Save it, Strachan,' Brody told him roughly, steering him down the slope.

But the feeling that something wasn't right about this, that I was missing something, was stronger than ever. I found myself wanting to hear what Strachan had to say.

'I don't understand,' I said. 'You've murdered three people. Why suddenly decide to kill yourself now?'

The desolation on his face seemed genuine. 'Because enough people have died. I wanted to be the last.'

Brody's next shove sent him to his knees on the hail-covered grass. 'You lying bastard! All the blood on your hands, and you stand there and say that? Christ, I ought to—'

307

'Brody!' I quickly moved in between them.

He was trembling with anger, all his fury focused on the man kneeling in front of him. With an effort, he made himself relax. His fists unclenched as he stepped back.

'All right. But when I hear his self-pity, after all the lives he's ruined. Ellen's as well . . .'

'I know, but it's finished. Let the police handle it now.'

Brody drew in a long, shaky breath, nodding assent. But Strachan was still staring at him.

'What about Ellen?'

'Don't bother denying it,' Brody told him, bitterly. 'We know you're Anna's father, God help her.'

Strachan had scrambled to his feet. There was an unmistakable urgency about him now.

'How did you find out? Who told you?'

Brody regarded him coldly. 'You weren't as clever as you thought. Maggie Cassidy found out. Seems like everyone on the island knew about it.'

Strachan looked as though he'd been struck. 'What about Grace? Does she know?'

'That's the least of your worries. After this—'

'*Does she know?*'

His vehemence took us both aback. I answered, feeling an awful apprehension start to bloom.

'It was an accident. She overheard.'

Strachan looked as though he'd been struck. 'We have to get back to the village.'

Brody grabbed hold of him as he turned away. 'You're not going anywhere.'

Strachan shook him off. 'Let me go, you bloody idiot! Christ, you've no idea what you've done!'

It wasn't his anger that convinced me, it was what else was in his eyes.

Fear.

And all at once I realized what had been bothering me. Why the sight of the knife had sparked it. It had been what Strachan had said: *I butchered them all like pigs!* It had been a sickening, distracting image, especially after seeing the vicious slashes on Maggie's burned body and the blood spattering her car. But although Maggie had been killed with a knife, had been *butchered* in a very real sense, none of the other victims had. So either Strachan hadn't meant what he'd said, or . . .

Oh my God. What had we done . . . ?

I fought to keep my voice steady. 'Take his handcuffs off.'

Brody stared at me as if I were mad. 'What? I'm not going to—'

'We don't have time for this!' Strachan broke in. 'We need to get back! *Now!*'

'He's right. We have to hurry,' I said.

'Why, for God's sake? What's wrong?' Brody demanded, but he still started to unlock the handcuffs.

'He didn't kill them,' I said, willing him to hurry. The enormity of our mistake was starting to dawn with appalling, bell-like clarity. 'It was Grace. He's just been protecting her.'

'Grace?' Brody echoed, incredulously. 'His *wife?*'

A look of self-loathing crossed Strachan's battered face.

'Grace isn't my wife. She's my sister.'

27

The journey back to the Range Rover was a nightmare. Although the hail had stopped, the mountainside was littered with white pellets of slowly melting ice, turning the slope into a frictionless slide. The light was fading and the wind that had tried to slow us on the way up now chased us back down, making the descent even harder.

Hindsight is the cruellest luxury. We'd been right, and yet hideously wrong. The intruder at the clinic, the wrecked yacht radio and attack on Grace, that had all been Strachan. He'd been stalking us from the first day we'd arrived on the island, watching our progress, even sabotaging us at times. Yet he'd been doing it to protect his sister, not himself. He wasn't the killer.

She was.

I felt sick to think of how much time we'd wasted. The only faint source of hope was that Strachan had taken both sets of car keys with him, deliberately stranding Grace at the house after learning what she'd done to Maggie. If she wanted to go to the village, she would have to walk. Even so, she'd had time to get there by now. I tried to tell myself that she might not have gone to the hotel straight away, but I didn't believe it. I'd seen how distraught she'd been when Brody and I had left her. It wouldn't take long for that to transform to anger. All the unanswered questions would have to wait. Right now our priority was reaching Ellen and Anna before Grace did.

If we weren't already too late.

We didn't talk on the way down. We didn't have the time, or the breath. Once we reached more level ground we broke into a stumbling jog, silent except for the laboured rasp of our breathing. Strachan was easily the fittest, but the way he ran with one arm clamped to his side made me think he might have cracked ribs to go with his other injuries.

Fraser had seen us coming. He was waiting in the Range Rover, engine running and the heater pumping out blessed hot air. He gave a savage smile when he saw Strachan's bloodied face.

'Somebody fell down the steps, did they?'

'Get us back to the hotel. Fast,' Brody gasped, hauling himself into the front passenger seat. 'We need to find Ellen.'

'Why, what—'

'Just drive!'

Still breathless, Brody turned round to confront Strachan as Fraser banged the Range Rover into gear and roared off towards the village.

'Talk.'

Strachan's pulverized face looked almost unrecognizable. His broken nose was flattened, and the cheek under his nearly shut eye was dark and swollen. He must have been in considerable pain, yet he gave no sign.

'Grace is ill. It's my fault, not hers,' he said, dully. 'That's why I wasn't planning on coming back down from the mountain. With me dead, she wouldn't be a threat any more.'

'Why is she a threat anyway?' Brody demanded. 'You're her brother, for Christ's sake! Why's she doing this?'

'Her *brother*?' Fraser exclaimed, throwing us against the side of the car as he swerved into a bend.

Neither of them answered him. Strachan looked like a man staring into an abyss of his own making.

311

'Because she's jealous.'

The barren landscape flashed by outside, but it was almost un-noticed now. I found my voice first.

'She killed Maggie because she was *jealous*?' I said, incredulously.

Strachan's bloodied mouth twitched involuntarily. He swayed limply with the movement of the car, making no attempt to steady himself.

'I didn't know what she'd done until she came back, covered in blood. But Maggie had called to the house twice to see me. Grace might have overlooked the first time, but not the second. She pretended she'd seen a prowler to get me out of the way, and then slipped a note into Maggie's coat arranging a meeting. She even took my car, so Maggie would think it was me.'

So the prowler had been a distraction, after all, I thought. Except it had been Grace's own, not Strachan's.

'You've got to understand how it was,' Strachan said, and for the first time a hint of pleading had entered his voice. 'When we were growing up, there were just the two of us. Our mother died when we were young, and our father was away most of the time on trips. We lived on an isolated estate, with security guards and private tutors. All we knew was each other.'

'Get on with it,' Brody told him.

Strachan lowered his head. The dankness of the *broch* still clung to him, mingling with the smell of stale sweat and blood.

'When I was sixteen I got drunk one night, and went to Grace's room. I'm not going to spell out what happened. It was wrong, and it was my fault. But neither of us wanted to stop it. It became . . . normal. As I got older I thought about ending it, but then . . . Grace got pregnant.'

'The miscarriage,' I said, remembering what he'd told me in his drawing room. It seemed an age ago now.

'It wasn't a miscarriage. I made her have an abortion.' Now there was no mistaking there was pain as well as shame in his voice. 'It was a backstreet clinic. There were complications. Grace almost died. She never admitted who the father was, even when they told her she could never have any more children. But she was changed after that. Unstable. She'd always been possessive, but now . . . When our father died I tried to finish it between us. I told Grace it was over and started seeing another girl. I thought she'd accept it. But she didn't. She went to the girl's flat and stabbed her to death.'

'Jesus,' Fraser said. The tyres skidded on the wet surface as he threw the car into another bend. He was driving as fast as he dared on the winding road, but it didn't seem nearly fast enough.

Strachan passed a hand over his face, oblivious to his injuries. 'No one suspected Grace, but she didn't even try to deny it to me. She told me she didn't want me to see anyone else. Ever.'

'If you knew she was dangerous, why didn't you tell the police?' I asked, holding the grab rail for support as the car bumped over a sudden dip.

'And let everyone know what had been going on?' Strachan shook his head. 'The dead are dead. You can't bring them back. And it was my fault Grace was like she was. I couldn't just abandon her.'

We were all jolted as Fraser braked suddenly. The road ahead was full of sheep. The car fishtailed, throwing up sheets of spray as he hammered on the horn, scattering them in front of us. There were panicked bleats as woolly bodies jostled outside the car windows, close enough to touch. Then we were clear and accelerating away again.

Strachan barely seemed to notice. 'We left South Africa, travelled around the world to places where nobody knew us. Where everyone would assume we were married. I tried to limit the . . . physical aspect between us. I'd still see other women. Prostitutes, mainly. I can't afford to be choosy.' The self-loathing was plain in his voice. 'But Grace isn't just jealous, she's cunning. She always seemed to find out, and when she did . . .'

He didn't need to finish. I willed Fraser to go faster. We hadn't even reached Strachan's house yet. *Too far. It's still too far.*

'Each time it happened, we'd move on somewhere else,' Strachan continued. 'And each time she got that bit worse. That's why we came here, to Runa. I liked this area, its wildness, and on an island like this Grace wouldn't be able to just come and go. We started to feel we were really part of something here. I found myself really wanting to *make* something of the island!'

Brody regarded him with contempt. 'So where did Janice Donaldson fit into your little paradise?'

A spasm of pain etched itself on to Strachan's face. 'She blackmailed me. I'd been seeing her for a while, but hadn't told her my real name. Then one day Iain Kinross showed up at her flat while I was there. I'd no idea he was another of her clients. He didn't see me, but my reaction tipped Janice off. She checked up, found out who I was. The next time I went she threatened to tell Grace. I paid her off – Christ, I even gave her more than she asked for. But it can't have been enough.'

'Did you know all along your sister had killed her?' Brody asked, roughly.

'Of course not! I'd no idea she'd come to Runa! Even when I heard a body had been found, I didn't know it was anything to do with Grace. The whole burning thing, the fires, that was new. She just used a knife with the others. But when the constable was killed . . . I couldn't kid myself any longer.'

I thought about his reaction when he'd seen Duncan's body. It had been genuine after all. But it hadn't been the shock of seeing a body, it had been the realization that his sister had started killing again.

'Why did she kill him?' Fraser demanded without turning round, his voice cracked. He was slewing the car round the bends almost recklessly, throwing us from side to side.

'I don't know. But in the past whenever Grace . . . had an episode, we'd always moved on. This time we couldn't. And when she realized there was going to be a murder investigation she must have panicked and tried to get rid of anything that might incriminate her. Duncan must have just been in the way.'

'In the fucking *way*?' Fraser snarled, the car swerving as he started to turn round.

'Easy,' Brody warned him. His face was like stone as he turned back to Strachan. 'How many people has she killed?'

Strachan shook his head. 'I don't know for sure. She doesn't always tell me. Four or five before this, perhaps.'

I don't know which was worse, the number or the fact that Strachan hadn't even kept track of his sister's victims.

'Tell me about Ellen,' Brody grated.

Strachan closed his eyes. 'Ellen was a mistake. There always was that . . . *tension* between us. I tried to avoid her, I daren't make Grace suspicious. But a few months after we'd arrived here, I found out Ellen was going to visit college friends in Dundee. So I made an excuse to be there as well. It only happened that once, Ellen insisted on that. When I found out she was pregnant, I tried to pay her to go away somewhere. Somewhere safe. But she refused. She said she wouldn't take a penny off me, because I was married. Quite an irony, eh?'

His bitterness quickly faded.

'I've lain awake at night, terrified what would happen if Grace ever found out . . .'

He tailed off. Now his house was visible up ahead. Both cars were still outside, and the lights still burned in the window. Seeing them I felt a faint hope.

'Should we see if she's still there?' Fraser asked.

'She won't be,' Strachan said with certainty.

Brody looked at the approaching house, torn. If Grace was still here we could end this now. But if she wasn't we'd have lost even more time.

'What's that on the drive?' I asked. A pale yellow shape was lying motionless in the driveway. I felt cold as I realized what it was.

The body of Oscar, Strachan's retriever.

'She killed his *dog*?' Fraser exclaimed. 'Why the hell would she do that?'

No one answered, but Strachan's face was bleak as we left the house behind.

'Drive faster,' Brody told Fraser.

Within minutes, the first houses had appeared ahead of us. The light had almost gone as we entered the village. Its streets were ominously empty. Fraser barely slowed as he flung the Range Rover into the side road leading up to the hotel.

The front door stood open.

Strachan leaped out of the car even before it had stopped moving. He ran up the hotel's steps to the entrance, but then stopped dead, his battered face suddenly leached of colour.

'Oh, Christ,' Brody breathed, staring inside.

The hotel had been wrecked. Broken furniture littered the hall. The grandfather clock lay face down and smashed, the mirror torn from the wall and smashed into crazed shards of glass. It was frenzied, wanton destruction, but that wasn't what had stopped Strachan.

The hallway was covered with blood.

The metallic stink of it thickened the air with a slaughterhouse taint. It was pooled on the wooden floorboards, spattered in abstract splashes across the panelled walls. It had sprayed highest just inside the doorway, jetting up the walls almost as far as the ceiling. This would have been where the attack first took place, but its progress afterwards was easy enough to follow. The blood formed a trail, big round splashes at first, then smeared tracks as its source had stumbled down the hallway.

The trail disappeared into the bar.

'Oh, no . . .' Strachan whispered. 'Oh, please no . . .'

There was hardly any coagulation, which meant the blood was still fresh. Not very long ago it had been pumping round a living body. Both Strachan and Brody seemed paralysed by the sight of it. I forced myself to go past them and hurried down the hall, trying to avoid treading in the splashes on the floor. A bloody handmark stood out on the white doorframe, where someone had clutched it for support. It was too smudged to say how big or small the hand had been, but it was low down on the frame, as though whoever had made it had been crawling.

Or a child.

I didn't want to see what was inside. But I'd no choice. I took a breath, trying to prepare myself, and stepped into the bar.

Nothing in it had been left intact. Chairs and tables had been tipped over and smashed, curtains slashed, bottles and glasses shattered in a frenzy. In the middle of it all was Cameron. Limbs splayed out in the relaxation of death, the schoolteacher lay slumped against the bar. His clothes were soaked through with blood that had only just begun to dry. A wide gash had opened a second mouth in his throat, slicing across his trachea as though trying to free the bulging Adam's apple.

The teacher's eyes were wide with shock, as though unable to believe what Grace had done to him.

Fraser appeared behind us. 'Oh, Christ,' he mumbled.

The air was a nauseous cocktail of alcohol and blood. There was another odour as well, but even as my stunned senses began to recognize it, a sudden sound tore through the silence.

A child's scream.

It came from the kitchen. Strachan was running even before it had died. Brody and I were just behind him as he burst through the kitchen's swing door, but the scene inside halted us all in our tracks.

The devastation we'd found before was nothing compared to this. Broken crockery crunched underfoot, while spilt food littered the floor in dirty snowdrifts. The kitchen table had been upended and its chairs smashed, the tall pine dresser pushed over on to the floor. Even the ancient cooker had been wrenched away from the wall, as though someone had tried to tip that over as well.

But right then none of that really registered.

Ellen was backed into a corner, terrified and bloodied, but alive.

317

She clutched a heavy saucepan, gripping it white-knuckled in both hands, ready to ward off or swing.

Standing between her and the door was Grace. She clutched Anna tightly to her, one hand clamped over the little girl's mouth.

The other held a kitchen knife to her throat.

'Get back, don't go near her!' Ellen screamed.

We didn't. Grace's clothes were mud-spattered and wet from the walk to the village. Her raven hair was wild and windblown, her face puffy and streaked with tears. Even dishevelled as she was, she was still beautiful. But now her madness was all too apparent.

So too, was something else. The smell I'd noticed in the hallway and bar was instantly identifiable in here, thick enough to clog the throat.

Gas.

I looked again at how the cooker had been pulled away from the wall, and glanced at Brody. He gave a barely perceptible nod.

'The cylinders are round the back,' he murmured to Fraser, not taking his eyes from Grace. 'There should be a valve. Go and turn it off.'

Fraser slowly backed out, then disappeared down the hallway. The door swung shut behind him.

'She was waiting when we came back from Rose Cassidy's,' Ellen sobbed. 'Bruce came in with us, and when he tried to talk to her she . . . she . . .'

'I know,' Strachan said, calmly. He took a step closer. 'Put the knife down, Grace.'

His sister stared at his bloodied face. She looked taut as a bow-string, ready to snap.

'Michael . . . What happened to you?'

'It doesn't matter. Just let the girl go.'

Mentioning Anna was a mistake. Grace's face grew ugly.

'Don't you mean your *daughter*?'

Strachan's poise faltered. But he quickly recovered. 'She's done nothing to you, Grace. You've always liked Anna. I know you don't want to hurt her.'

'Is it true?' Grace was crying. 'Is it? Tell me they were lying! Please, Michael!'

Do it, I thought. Tell her what she wants. But Strachan hesitated for too long. Grace's face creased up.

'No!' she moaned.

'Grace . . .'

'*Shut up!*' she screamed, the tendons in her neck standing out like cords. 'You fucked this *bitch*, you chose her over *me*?'

'I can explain, Grace,' Strachan said, but he was losing it. Losing her.

'*Liar!* All this time, you've been lying! I could forgive you the others, but this . . . How *could* you?'

It was as though no one else existed any more except her and her brother. The smell of gas was growing stronger. What the hell was Fraser doing? Brody began edging nearer to Grace.

'Put the knife down, Grace. No one's going to—'

'Don't come near me!' she screamed.

Brody backed off. Chest rising and falling, Grace glared at us, her face contorted.

The silence was suddenly broken by a metallic clatter. Ellen had let the saucepan drop. As it bounced on the floor, the sound of it shockingly loud, she stepped slowly towards Grace.

'Ellen, don't!' Strachan ordered, but there was more fear than authority in his voice.

She ignored him. All her attention was fixed on his sister.

'It's me you want, isn't it? All right, I'm here. Do what you like to me, but please don't hurt my daughter.'

'For God's sake, Ellen,' Brody said, but he might as well not have spoken either.

Ellen spread her arms in invitation. 'Well, come on! What are you waiting for?'

319

Grace had turned to face her, a tick working one corner of her mouth like broken clockwork.

Strachan broke in, desperately. 'Look at me, Grace. Forget her, she's not important.'

'Stay out of this,' Ellen warned.

But Strachan took one pace forward, then another. He held out his hands as if he were trying to soothe a wild animal.

'You're all that matters to me, Grace. You know that. Let Anna go. Let her go, and then we'll get away from this place. Go somewhere else, start again. Just me and you.'

Grace was staring at him with such naked yearning it felt obscene to see it.

'Put the knife down,' he told her, softly.

Some of the tension seemed to drain out of her. The smell of leaking gas seemed to grow heavier as the moment hung, poised to go either way.

Then Anna chose that moment to wriggle free of Grace's hand.

'*Mummy, she's hurting—*'

Grace slapped her palm back over Anna's mouth. The madness was a white heat in her eyes.

'You shouldn't have lied, Michael,' she said, and pulled back Anna's head.

'*No!*' Strachan cried, flinging himself at her as the knife swept down.

Brody and I lunged forward as Strachan struggled with his sister, but Ellen was faster than either of us. She snatched Anna away as Grace screamed, a cry of pure fury. Leaving Brody to help Strachan, I rushed to where Ellen was clutching her daughter.

'Let me see her, Ellen!'

She wouldn't let go. She hugged Anna to her, both of them smeared with blood and weeping hysterically. But I could see that the blood was from Ellen's cuts, that the little girl wasn't hurt. *Thank God*. As I sagged with relief, Brody's voice came from behind me.

'David.'

He sounded odd. He had hold of Grace, pinning her arms behind her back, but she wasn't struggling any more. They were both staring at Strachan. He stood nearby, looking down at himself with a faintly surprised expression.

The knife handle was jutting from his stomach.

'Michael . . . ?' Grace said, in a small voice.

'It's all right,' he told her, but then his legs gave way.

'*Michael!*' Grace screamed.

Brody held her back as she tried to go to Strachan. I managed to reach him, trying to take his weight on my good shoulder. 'Get Anna outside. Take her to a neighbour's,' I told Ellen, as he sank to the floor.

'Is he . . .'

'Just take her, Ellen.'

I wanted them well away from here. The stink of gas had become so thick it was nauseating. I glanced at the portable heater that lay on its side nearby, relieved that at least it wasn't still on. With so much propane leaking into the room the last thing we needed was a naked flame. I wondered again what was taking Fraser so long.

Grace was still being restrained by Brody, sobbing, as I knelt by Strachan. His face had gone shockingly white.

'You can let go of my sister now,' he said, voice hoarse with pain. 'She's not going anywhere.'

I gave Brody a nod when he hesitated. As soon as he released her Grace dropped down beside Strachan.

'Oh God, Michael . . .' Her face was a mask of anguish as she turned to me. 'Do something! *Help* him!'

He tried to smile as he took hold of her hand. 'Don't worry, everything'll be all right. I promise.'

'Don't talk,' I told him. 'Try to keep as still as you can.'

I started to examine his wound. It was bad. The knife blade was fully lodged in his stomach. I couldn't even begin to guess what internal damage it had caused.

'Don't look so grim . . .' he told me.

'Just a scratch,' I said, lightly. 'I'm going to help you lie down flat. Try not to move the knife.'

Its blade was the only thing preventing him from bleeding to death. As long as it stayed where it was, it would act as a plug to slow his blood loss. But not for long.

Grace was weeping more quietly now, the violence drained from her as she cradled her brother's head on her lap. I tried to keep my anxiety from my face as I quickly ran through my options. There weren't many. There were none of the facilities here that Strachan needed, and the only nurse on the island was lying dead in the other room. Unless we could get him evacuated, and soon, he was going to die whatever I did.

Fraser rushed back in, skidding on the broken crockery and spilled food on the floor.

'Jesus!' he panted, seeing Strachan, then gathered himself. 'The gas canisters are locked in a cage. I can't open it.'

Brody had been struggling to move the heavy pine dresser that was lying in front of the back door, partially blocking it. Now he abandoned the attempt, staring round the wrecked kitchen.

'The keys for the cage must be here somewhere,' he said, frustrated.

But even if we'd known where Ellen kept them it wouldn't have done any good. Every drawer had been pulled out and smashed, their contents scattered amongst the rest of the debris. The keys could be anywhere.

Brody had reached the same conclusion. 'We don't have time to look. Let's get everybody out while we break into the cage to turn off the gas.'

There was no way Strachan should be moved, but the gas left us no choice. It was so thick now I could taste it. The atmosphere in the kitchen would soon be unbreathable. And propane was heavier than air, which meant it would be even worse on the floor where Strachan lay.

I gave a quick nod of assent. 'We can use the table to carry him.'

Grace was still weeping as she cradled her brother's head. Strachan had been watching us in silence. Even though he must have been in agony he seemed remarkably calm. Almost peaceful.

'Just leave me here,' he said, his voice already weakening.

'Thought I told you to be quiet?'

He grinned, and for a moment looked like the man I'd met when I'd first arrived on the island. Grace was keening, an almost animal sound of grief as she stroked his face.

'I'm sorry, I'm so sorry . . .'

'Shh. Everything's going to be fine, I promise.'

Fraser and Brody were struggling to right the heavy table. I went to the kitchen's window, hoping it hadn't been painted shut. Even a little ventilation would be better than nothing. But I'd only taken a few steps when I saw Strachan grope for something lying in the broken crockery nearby.

'Get away from there, David,' he said, holding it up.

It was the lighter for the gas range.

He had his thumb poised on the ignition button. 'Sorry, but I'm not going anywhere . . .'

'Put it down, Michael,' I said, trying for an assurance I didn't feel. There was so much gas in the kitchen that one spark would set it off. I glanced uneasily at the portable heater that lay nearby. It had its own propane supply, and the cage containing the big cylinders was stored right against the kitchen wall. If the gas in here ignited they would all go up.

'I don't think so . . .' Strachan's pallid face shone with sweat. 'Go on, get out. All of you.'

'Don't be bloody stupid,' Brody snapped.

Strachan raised the lighter. 'One more word from you, and I swear I'll press it right now.'

'For fuck's sake, Brody, shut up!' Fraser said.

Strachan gave a death's head grin. 'Good advice. I'm going to count to ten. One . . .'

'What about Grace?' I said, stalling for time.

'Grace and I stay together. Don't we, Grace?'

She was blinking through her tears, as though only now becoming aware of what was going on.

'Michael, what are you going to do . . . ?'

He smiled at her. 'Trust me.'

Then, before anyone could stop him, Strachan wrenched the knife from his stomach.

He screamed, seizing Grace's arm as blood gushed from the wound. I started forward, but he saw me and raised the lighter.

'Get *out!* *Now!*' he hissed through clenched teeth. 'Oh, *Jesus!*'

'Strachan—'

Brody grabbed hold of me. 'Move.'

Fraser was already running for the door. I took one last look at where Strachan lay, teeth gritted in agony as he held the lighter raised in one hand and gripped his sister's hand with the other. Grace's expression was one of dawning incredulity. She looked across at me, her mouth opening to speak, and then Brody had hustled me out into the hall.

'No, wait—'

'Just run!' he bellowed, giving me a shove.

He kept hold of me as he pounded down the hallway, half dragging me outside. Fraser had reached the Range Rover and was fumbling for the keys.

'Leave it!' Brody snapped, without stopping.

The nearest houses were too far away to reach, but there was an old stone wall much nearer. Brody dragged me behind it, Fraser throwing himself down beside us a moment later. We waited, panting.

Nothing happened.

I looked back at the hotel. It seemed familiar and mundane in the twilight, its front door banging forlornly in the wind.

'Been more than ten seconds,' Fraser muttered.

I stood up.

'What the hell are you doing?' Brody demanded.

I shook him off. 'I'm going to—' I began, and then the hotel exploded.

There was a flash, and a wall of noise almost knocked me off my feet. I ducked, covering my head as pieces of slate and brick rained down. As the thuds began to peter out, I risked a look back up the hill.

Dust and smoke swirled around the hotel like a gauze veil. Its roof had been blown off, and bright yellow flickers were already visible inside the shattered windows, quickly spreading as the fire took hold.

People were running out of the nearby houses as the hotel began to blaze. I could feel the intensity of the heat even from where I stood.

I turned on Brody angrily. 'I could have stopped him!'

'No, you couldn't,' he said, tiredly. 'And even if you could, he was a dead man as soon as he pulled out the knife.'

I looked away, knowing he was right. The hotel was an inferno now, its timbered floors and walls reduced to so much kindling. Like everything else that had been inside.

'What about Grace?' I asked.

Brody's face was shadowed as he stared into the flames.

'What about her?'

28

Two days later, the sky dawned bright and clear over Runa. It was approaching midday when Brody and I left his car on the road above the harbour and walked up to the cliff top overlooking Stac Ross. Seabirds soared around the tall black tower, while waves shattered against the rock's base, flinging slow-motion sheets of spray high into the air. I breathed in the fresh salt air, savouring the thin warmth of the sun on my face.

I was going home.

The police had arrived on Runa the previous morning. As though finally sated with the chaos it had overseen, the storm had blown itself out within hours after the hotel had burned down. Before the night was out, while the hotel ruins still smoked and smouldered, the phone lines had started working again. We'd finally been able to get word to Wallace and the mainland. Although the harbour was still too rough to allow anything in or out, the sky was still lightening when a coastguard helicopter clattered above the cliffs, carrying the first of the police teams that would descend on Runa in the next twenty-four hours.

As the island found itself at the epicentre of frenzied police activity, I'd finally got a call through to Jenny. It had been a difficult conversation, but I'd reassured her that I was all right, promised I would be home in another day or so. Even though the island was swarming with police and SOC, I couldn't leave straight away. Not only were there the inevitable interviews and debriefings to endure, but I still felt there was unfinished business. It would take days or perhaps even weeks to recover the bodies of Strachan, Grace and Cameron from the ruins of the hotel, assuming anything identifiable had survived its destruction. But there had still been Maggie and Duncan's remains to attend to, and I wanted to be on hand while SOC examined them.

It wouldn't seem right to leave without seeing things through to the end.

And now I had. Maggie's body had been taken back to the mainland the evening before, while Duncan's remains had been removed from the camper van in the early hours. So had his Maglite, bagged up ready for laboratory analysis. Not only was it the right shape to have made the injury to his skull, but SOC had found what appeared to be traces of blood and tissue baked on to its casing. It would have to be tested to make sure, but I was more convinced than ever that Grace had used his own torch to kill him.

I'd done as much as I could. There was no reason for me to remain on Runa any longer. I'd said what few goodbyes I had to make; shared an awkward handshake with Fraser, then called to see Ellen and Anna. They were staying at a neighbour's house for the time being, bearing up surprisingly well after what they'd been through.

'The hotel was only bricks and mortar. And Michael . . .' There were shadows in Ellen's eyes as she watched Anna play nearby. 'I'm sorry he's dead. But I'm more thankful for what was saved than what was lost.'

Another coastguard helicopter was due within the hour, and once it had discharged its cargo of police officers it would take me back to Stornoway. From there I'd fly to Glasgow and then London, finally completing the journey I'd started a week ago.

Not before time.

Still, I didn't feel as elated as I'd expected. Even though I was looking forward to seeing Jenny, I felt oddly flat as Brody and I walked up to the cliff where the helicopter would put down. Brody, too, was silent and lost in his thoughts. Although I'd been sleeping in his spare room, I'd not seen much of him since the mainland police teams had arrived. Ex-inspector or not, he was a civilian now, and he'd been politely excluded from the investigation. I felt sorry for him. After all that had happened, it must have been hard for him to be brushed on to the sidelines.

When we reached the cliff top we rested. The stone monolith of Bodach Runa stood some distance away, the Old Man of Runa still keeping his lonely vigil for a lost child. The dip where we'd found Maggie's car was out of sight, but the Mini itself had since been moved. Gulls and gannets wheeled and cried in the bright winter sunlight. The wind still gusted, but less strongly, and the clouds that had seemed a permanent cover were gone, replaced with high white wisps of cumulus that skated serenely across the blue sky.

In some regards, at least, it was going to be a beautiful day.

'This is one of my favourite views,' Brody said, looking out at the sea stack that rose like a giant chimney from the waves. The wind ruffled his grey hair, mirroring the movement of the waves two hundred feet below. He reached down to stroke his dog's head. 'Been a while since Bess has had a chance to stretch her legs up here.'

I rubbed my shoulder through my coat. It was still painful, but I'd almost grown used to it. I'd be able to get it X-rayed and properly looked at once I was back in London.

'What do you think will happen now? To Runa?' I asked.

At the moment the island was still in a state of shock. In the space of a few days it had lost four members of its community, including its main benefactor; a tragedy made all the harder to accept because of the shocking manner of their dying. The gale, too, had added to the tally, swamping a fishing boat in the harbour and causing Strachan's yacht to slip its chain. Wreckage from the beautiful boat would be found days later, but that was the least of the island's losses. It was the others from which it would struggle to recover.

Brody turned down his mouth. 'God knows. Might keep going for a while. But the fish farm, the new jobs, the investment, all that's gone. Can't see it surviving without them.'

'You think it'll become another St Kilda?'

'Not for a few years, perhaps. But eventually.' His mouth quirked in a smile. 'Let's hope they don't drown their dogs when they go.'

'Will you stay?'

Brody shrugged. 'We'll see. Not as though I've any reason to go anywhere else.'

The border collie had crouched at his feet, head down on its paws as it stared up at him, intently. Smiling, he took an old tennis ball from his pocket and tossed it for the dog. It trotted after it, legs too stiff to run, then brought it back, tail wagging.

'I just wish we'd been able to talk to Grace, find out why she did what she did,' I said, as Brody threw the ball again.

'Jealousy, like Strachan said. And hate, I expect. You'd be surprised how powerful that can be.'

'That still doesn't explain everything. Like why she clubbed Janice Donaldson and Duncan, but used a knife on Maggie and Cameron. And the others that Strachan told us about.'

'Means and opportunity, I expect. I don't think she really planned anything, just acted when she got the urge. Duncan's Maglite was probably lying to hand, and I dare say something similar happened with Donaldson. But we'll never know now.'

The collie had dropped the ball at his feet again. Brody picked it up and threw it, then gave me a rueful smile.

'There aren't always answers to everything, no matter how hard we look. Sometimes you have to learn to just let things go.'

'I suppose so.'

He took out his cigarettes and lit one, drawing on it with satisfaction. I watched as he put the pack away.

'I didn't know you were left-handed,' I said.

'Sorry?'

'You threw the ball with your left hand just now.'

'Did I? I didn't notice.'

My heart had begun to thump. 'A few days ago in your kitchen you used your right hand. It was when I told you and Fraser that whoever killed Duncan was left-handed.'

'So? I'm not with you.'

'So I just wondered why you used your right hand then, but your left now.'

He turned to look at me, quizzical and a little exasperated. 'Where are you going with this, David?'

My mouth had dried. 'Grace was right-handed.'

Brody considered that. 'How do you know?'

'When she had hold of Anna, the knife was in her right hand. I'd forgotten about it till I saw you just now. I knew something still jarred, but I didn't know what. And when I saw Grace preparing food earlier she used the same hand then. Her right, not her left.'

'Perhaps your memory's playing tricks.'

I wished it was. For a moment or two I even allowed myself to hope. But I knew better.

'No,' I said, with something like regret. 'But even if it was, we can check to see which hand the fingerprints on her paintbrushes and knife handles are from.' Even if the prints weren't clear, their angle would reveal that much.

'She could have been ambidextrous.'

'Then we'll find equal numbers of both.'

He took a long draw of his cigarette. 'You saw what Grace was like. You can't seriously think Strachan was lying?'

'No. I don't doubt she murdered Maggie, and God knows how many others before they came here. But Strachan just assumed she'd killed Janice Donaldson and Duncan as well. He might have been wrong.'

I was still willing Brody to laugh it off, to point out a fatal flaw in my reasoning. He just sighed.

'You've been here too long, David. You're looking for things that aren't there.'

I had to moisten my mouth before I could get the next words out.

'How did you know Duncan was killed with his own Maglite?'

Brody frowned. 'Wasn't he? I thought that's what you said.'

'No, I never mentioned it. I'd wondered, but only to myself. I didn't say anything about the Maglite until SOC got here.'

'Well, I must have heard it from one of them.'

'When?'

He gestured with the cigarette, vaguely irritated. 'I don't know. Yesterday, perhaps.'

'They only removed the torch during the night. And no one's going to know for sure that's what killed him until lab tests have been carried out. They wouldn't have said anything.'

Brody stared out across the sea at the black pinnacle of Stac Ross, squinting in the bright sunlight. Two hundred feet below us I could hear the waves crashing on the rocks.

'Let it go, David,' he said softly.

But I couldn't. My heart was banging so hard now I could hear it.

'Grace didn't kill Duncan, did she? Or Janice Donaldson.'

The only answer was the crying of gulls, and the distant crashing of the waves below the cliffs. *Say something. Deny it.* But Brody might have been carved from the same stone as Bodach Runa, silent and implacable.

I found my voice. 'Why? Why did you do it?'

He dropped the cigarette to the ground and crushed it out with his foot, then picked up the stub and put it in his pocket.

'Because of Rebecca.'

It took a moment for the name to register. Rebecca, the estranged daughter who had gone missing. Who Brody had spent years trying to find. His words came back to me now, clear and awful in their implication: *she's dead*. And suddenly everything sprang into focus.

'You thought Strachan had murdered your daughter,' I said. 'You killed Janice Donaldson to try and frame him.'

The pain in his eyes was confirmation enough. He took out another cigarette and lit it before he answered.

'It was an accident. I'd been trying to put together evidence against Strachan for years. That's the only reason I moved out to this godforsaken island, so I'd be close to him.'

A gull soared overhead, wings tilting as it caught the air currents. Standing there in the cold winter sun, I felt a rush of unreality, like plunging too fast in a lift.

'You *knew* there'd been other deaths?'

The wind whisked away the smoke from his cigarette. 'I had a good idea. I'd already started to think Becky was dead. I'd been able to follow her trail so far, but then it just stopped. So when I heard rumours about her seeing some rich South African before she'd vanished, I started digging. I found out that Strachan had moved around, lived in different countries but always for short periods of time. So I looked at newspaper archives of places where he'd settled. I found reports of girls being murdered or disappearing around the same time. Not in all of them, but too many to be coincidence. And the more I looked, the more convinced I was that Becky was one of his victims. Everything fitted.'

'And you didn't tell the police? You used to be a detective inspector, for God's sake! They'd have listened to you!'

'Not without proof they wouldn't. I'd pulled in every favour I could when I was looking for Becky. A lot of people thought I'd lost the plot as it was. And if I'd confronted Strachan he'd have just gone to ground. But Rebecca had been using her stepfather's name. There was no way he could connect us. So I decided to play the long game and came here, hoping he'd slip up.'

I was shivering as I listened, but the chill I felt had nothing to do with the cold.

'What happened? Did you get tired of waiting?' I asked, surprising myself with my own anger.

Brody flicked the ash from his cigarette, letting it disintegrate in the wind.

'No. Janice Donaldson happened.'

His face was unreadable as he told me how he'd followed Strachan on his trips to Stornoway, inventing business and meetings of his own, taking the ferry to arrive first whenever Strachan had gone on the yacht. To begin with he'd been worried that Strachan had been preparing to select another victim. But when nothing happened to any of the women he spent time with, Brody's relief turned first to puzzlement, then frustration.

Finally, he'd approached Janice Donaldson in Stornoway one night after she'd left a pub. He'd offered to pay her for information, hoping to learn more about Strachan's habits, perhaps discover a tendency towards violence. It had been the first time he'd shown his hand against his enemy, a calculated gamble, but he reasoned that the risk was worth it. It wasn't as if Donaldson knew who he was.

Or so he'd thought.

'She recognized me,' Brody said. 'Turned out she used to live in Glasgow, and I'd been pointed out to her when I'd been searching for Becky. Donaldson had known her. She'd been thinking about claiming the reward I was offering for information, but she'd been picked up for soliciting before she had the chance. By the time she was back in circulation I'd gone. So she offered to sell it to me now.'

He drew down a lungful of smoke, blew it out again for the wind to take away.

'She told me Becky had been a prostitute. I suppose on some level I'd already guessed, given the way she'd been living. But actually being told it, by someone like that . . . When I refused to pay her, she threatened to tell Strachan who I was, that I'd been asking questions. Then she started saying things about Rebecca, things no father wants to hear. So I hit her.'

333

Brody held out his hand, considering it. I remembered how easily he had battered Strachan senseless in the *broch*. I was conscious of the constriction of my sling under the coat, and of the cliff's edge only a few yards away. It took a conscious effort not to look at it, or to step away from him.

'I always had a temper,' he went on, almost mildly. 'That's why my wife left. That and the drinking. But I thought I'd got it under control. Nothing stronger than tea these days. I didn't even hit her very hard, but she was drunk. We were down at the docks, and she fell backwards, cracked her head on a stanchion as she went down.'

Not a club after all, then, but an impact all the same. 'If it was an accident why didn't you turn yourself in?'

For the first time there was heat in Brody's eyes. 'And be sent down for manslaughter, when that murdering bastard was still free? I don't think so. Not when there was another way.'

'You mean frame him.'

'If you like.'

It made a twisted sort of sense. There was no link between Brody and Janice Donaldson, but Strachan was a different matter. If she was found dead on Runa, when it emerged that he was one of her clients – and Brody would have made sure that it did – then suspicion would quickly focus on him. It wasn't ideal, but it would have been a justice of sorts.

For Brody that was better than nothing.

Something else had occurred to me as I'd listened. I thought again how the cracks had crazed Janice Donaldson's skull without actually breaking it.

'She wasn't dead, was she?'

Brody stared across at Stac Ross. 'I thought she was. I'd put her in the car boot, but I wouldn't have risked bringing her over on the ferry if I'd known. It wasn't until I opened it over here and saw she'd thrown up that I realized. But she was dead then, right enough.'

No, I thought, she wouldn't have survived the ferry crossing with

an injury like that. At the very least it would have caused haemor-
rhaging that would have been fatal without fast medical attention,
and perhaps even with it.

But she hadn't been given the chance.

So Brody had gone ahead as planned. He'd planted evidence at the
crofter's cottage that would further incriminate Strachan: dog hairs
from his retriever, an imprint from one of Strachan's wellingtons that
Brody had taken from their barn one night, and which he'd then
hidden back there for the police to find. Then he'd set fire to the
body, not only to destroy any traces that might link him to it, but also
to hide the fact that Janice Donaldson hadn't died in the cottage, as
an examination would otherwise have found. He'd even sold his car
and replaced it with a new one, because he knew there would be
microscopic evidence left in the boot no matter how thoroughly he
cleaned it. Using all his experience as a police officer, Brody had
tried to anticipate everything.

But with murder, as with life, that's never possible.

His cheeks hollowed as he drew on the cigarette. 'I was going to
let someone else find the body. But after a month of waiting, knowing it was just lying there, I couldn't stand it any longer. Christ, when
I went in again and saw it . . .' He shook his head, mutely. 'I'd not
used much petrol, just enough to make it look like a botched attempt
to torch the body. I *wanted* it to be identified, to obviously be murder,
that was the whole point. But all I could do then was report it and
hope that SOC did their job properly.'

But instead of SOC, he'd got a drunken police sergeant and an
inexperienced constable. And me.

I felt physically sick at the extent of his betrayal. He'd used us all,
playing on our trust as he'd steadily pointed us towards Strachan. No
wonder he'd been so loath to accept Cameron or Kinross as suspects.
An acid sense of bitterness rose up in my throat.

'What about Duncan?' I asked, too angry to care about provoking
him. 'What was he, collateral damage?'

Brody accepted the accusation without flinching. 'I made a mistake. When the cottage collapsed, it wiped out all the evidence I'd planted. I was starting to worry that there wasn't enough to incriminate Strachan even if the body was identified. I'd been sounding out Duncan, knew he was a smart lad. So I decided to use him.'

He shook his head, annoyed with himself.

'Stupid. Should have known better than to complicate things. I didn't say much, only that I'd got my suspicions about Strachan, and that someone ought to look into his background. I thought I could steer bits of information his way, let him take the credit for it. And then I cocked up. I told Duncan that Strachan had been visiting prostitutes in Stornoway.'

Brody studied the glowing tip of his cigarette.

'First thing he asked was how I knew. I told him it was just gossip, but I knew that wouldn't hold up. No one else on Runa had any idea, you see. Lousy timing, too, because right afterwards you announced that the victim was probably some prostitute from a big town. I could see Duncan was already starting to wonder how I'd known. I couldn't risk it.'

No, I realized, he couldn't. Now I understood the reason for Duncan's distraction the last time I'd seen him alive. Perhaps his suspicions were already taking root even then. Brody couldn't allow that. He couldn't afford to let anyone suspect he might have been stalking Strachan, that he had a motive for bringing him down.

Even if that meant keeping quiet about his own daughter's murder.

He sighed, regretfully. 'It's the little things that trip you up. Like that bloody Maglite. I'd taken a crowbar with me to the camper van, but Duncan must have seen my torch while I was outside. I could have jumped him when he came out to check, but I waited until he was back inside. Putting it off, I suppose. He left the Maglite on the table when he let me in, so I picked it up and hit him with it.' He gave a shrug. 'Seemed the thing to do at the time.'

The disgust I felt only fuelled my anger. 'The fires were just a distraction, weren't they? Torching the community centre and the camper van, it wasn't to destroy forensic evidence. You just wanted us to think it was, so Duncan's death would look incidental. And you could incriminate Strachan at the same time, planting the broken petrol cap—'

I broke off, staring at him as another missing piece fell into place.

'That's why Grace's car ran out of petrol. You siphoned it off to use to start the fires.'

'I had to get it from somewhere. If I'd taken his it might have tipped him off.' Brody had been gazing out at the horizon, but now he turned to me. 'For the record, I didn't realize you were still in the medical centre when I started the fire. There were no lights on, and what with the power cut I thought it'd be empty.'

'Would it have made any difference?'

He flicked ash from his cigarette. 'Probably not.'

'Jesus Christ, didn't you ever think you could have been *wrong*? That there was something else going on? What about when the yacht radio was smashed and Grace was attacked? Didn't you wonder *why* Strachan would do something like that when he hadn't killed anybody?'

'Anybody *here*, perhaps,' he said, and for the first time there was an edge to his voice. 'I assumed he was panicking. I thought he wanted to get off the island before the police started questioning everyone. He wouldn't have wanted them looking too closely into his past.'

'But it wasn't his past that was the problem, was it? It was his sister's. You picked the wrong Strachan!'

He sighed, looking out at the horizon again. 'Aye.'

There was an appalling irony to it. Because of Brody's attempts to frame her brother, Grace had believed along with everyone else that there was a killer loose on Runa. She'd even believed she'd almost been a victim herself. So she'd taken advantage of the situation, murdering Maggie and burning her body so it would appear that the

337

killer of Duncan and Janice Donaldson had claimed another life.

Full circle.

'Was it worth it?' I asked quietly. 'Duncan and the rest. Was it worth all those lives?'

Outlined against the cold blue sky, Brody's hewn features were unreadable in the morning wind.

'You used to have a daughter yourself. You tell me.'

I had no answer to that. The anger was ebbing from me now, leaving in its wake a leaden feeling of sadness. And a chilling awareness of my own situation. For the first time I realized how careful Brody had been to put the cigarette stubs back in the packet. He'd left nothing to show he'd been here. Even if I'd had both arms free he was bigger and stronger than me. He'd already killed twice. I couldn't see him balking at a third time.

I took a quick look at the cliff edge, only yards away. *You won't be leaving Runa today after all*, I thought, numbly.

A dark fleck had appeared on the horizon. It was too still to be a bird, hanging apparently motionless in the sky. The coastguard helicopter was early, I realized, but the surge of hope quickly died. It was still too far away. It would take it another ten or fifteen minutes to get here.

Too long.

Brody had seen it too. The wind ruffled his grey hair as he stared at the approaching speck. His cigarette had burned almost down to his fingers.

'I used to be a good policeman,' he said, casually. 'A lousy husband and father, but a good policeman. You start off on the side of the angels, and suddenly you find out you've become what you hate. How does that happen?'

I glanced desperately at the helicopter. It didn't seem to have grown any bigger. At this distance no one on board would even be able to see us. I began trying to work my arm from the sling under my coat, knowing as I did that it wouldn't do any good.

'So what now?' I asked, trying to sound calm.

Something like a dry smile touched his mouth. 'Good question.'

'Janice Donaldson was an accident. And what happened to Rebecca will be taken into account.'

Brody took one last draw on his cigarette, then ground it out carefully on the sole of his boot. He put the stub in the packet with the rest.

'I'm not going to prison. But, for what it counts, I'm sorry.'

He turned his face up to the sun, closing his eyes for a moment, then reached down to stroke the old border collie.

'Good girl. Stay.'

I took an involuntary step back as he straightened. But he made no move towards me. Instead he began walking unhurriedly towards the edge of the cliff.

'Brody . . . ?' I said, as his intention began to dawn. 'Brody, no!'

My words were carried away. I started after him but he'd already reached the edge. Without hesitating he stepped out into space. For an instant he seemed to hang there, borne up by the wind. Then he'd gone.

I halted, staring at the empty air where he'd been a moment before. But there was nothing there now. Only the cry of the gulls, and the sound of the waves crashing below.

Epilogue

By summer the events that had taken place on Runa had started to recede, faded by the blunting effect of memory. The post-mortem into what had happened had produced little that wasn't already known. At the end of it, as Strachan had said, the dead were still dead, and the rest of us got on with the business of living.

A search of Brody's house turned up the file that he'd put together on Strachan. It was a good, solid piece of police work, which was no less than I'd expect. He just hadn't dug quite far enough. Like everyone else, Brody had never thought to question whether Grace might not be Strachan's wife.

It had proved to be a fatal omission.

But the file still provided a chilling roll call of victims, although there was no way of knowing how many Brody – like Strachan – might have missed. It was probable that the fate of some of Grace's victims would never be known.

Like Rebecca Brody.

Her father's body had been recovered from the sea by a fishing boat a week after he'd thrown himself from the cliff. The fall, and the salt water, had carried out their usual disfiguring transformation, but there was no room for doubt. That loose end, at least, could be securely tied off, which I thought Brody would appreciate. He'd always hated mess.

Not everything had such a neat resolution. Fuelled by spirits from the bar and oil for the generator, the fire had completed the destruction started by the exploding gas canisters and razed the hotel to the ground. A few charred pieces of bone, too damaged by the heat to yield any DNA, were identified as Cameron's because of their location in the bar. But Grace and Michael Strachan had been together in the kitchen when they'd died. What few calcined bone fragments were recovered were impossible to differentiate.

Even in death Strachan hadn't been able to escape his sister.

Ironically, for the moment at least, Runa itself still seemed to be prospering. Far from becoming another St Kilda, the publicity it received had brought an influx of journalists, archaeologists and naturalists, as well as tourists drawn by its new-found notoriety. How long it would last remained to be seen, but Kinross's ferry was suddenly very much in demand. There was even talk of building another hotel, although it wouldn't be Ellen McLeod who was running it.

I'd met Ellen again at the inquest into Brody's suicide. She carried herself with the same steel-tempered dignity I remembered, but while there were still shadows in her eyes, there was also a new optimism. She and Anna had moved to Edinburgh, living in a small house paid for by the hotel's insurance. Both Strachan and Brody had left them well cared for in their wills, but Ellen put everything they left her into a fund to help rebuild the island. It was blood money, she'd said, with a flash of her old fierceness. She wanted nothing to do with it.

But there was one thing they had brought with them from Runa: Brody's border collie. It had been either that or let her be destroyed, and, as Ellen said, it wouldn't have seemed right to punish the old dog for the crimes of its owner.

I thought Brody would have been grateful for that.

As for me, it was surprising how quickly life slid back to normal. There were still days when I'd wonder how many people would still be alive if I'd never gone to Runa, if Janice Donaldson's murder had been dismissed as an accident. Oh, I knew that Brody's poisoned obsession with Strachan would have driven him to try again, and that Grace's madness would have resurfaced eventually. But the butcher's bill still weighed heavily on my conscience.

One night as I lay awake thinking about it, Jenny had woken and asked what was wrong. I wanted to tell her, wanted to exorcize the ghosts that had followed me back from the island. Yet somehow I couldn't.

'Nothing.' I'd smiled to reassure her. Knowing as I did that it was the small lies that eroded a relationship. 'I just can't sleep.'

Things had been tense enough between us anyway after my return. What had happened on Runa had only served to reinforce her dislike of my profession. I knew she thought it was too much of a link to the past, that it tied me to my own dead in a way she mistrusted. In that she was wrong – it was because of what had happened to my family that I'd once tried to give up my work. But Jenny remained unconvinced.

'You're a qualified GP, David,' she said, during one of our not-quite-arguments. 'You could find a job in any number of practices. I wouldn't care where it was.'

'And what if that's not what I want to do?'

'It used to be! And it'd be about life, not death!'

I couldn't make her understand that, as I saw it, my work was already about life. About how people had lost it, and who had taken it away. And how I might help keep them from taking anyone else's.

But as the weeks passed, the friction between us eased. Summer came, bringing hot days and balmy nights, making the events on Runa seem more distant than ever. The questions about our future still remained, but they were shelved by mutual, if unspoken, consent. Yet the tension was still there, not yet gathering into a storm, but never far below the horizon either. I'd been invited for a month-long research trip to the Outdoor Anthropology Research Facility in Tennessee, the so-called Body Farm where I'd learned much of my trade. It wasn't until autumn, but so far I'd put off making a decision. It wasn't just my being away that would be a problem, although Jenny wouldn't like it. It was the statement of intent that making the trip would represent. My work was a part of me, but so was Jenny. I'd almost lost her once. I couldn't bear losing her again.

Even so, I continued to stall, putting off the moment when I would have to decide.

Then, late one Saturday afternoon, the past caught up with us.

We were at my ground-floor flat rather than Jenny's, because it had a small terrace at the back, big enough for a table and chairs during summer. It was a warm, sunny evening, and we'd invited friends round for a barbecue. They weren't due to arrive for another half-hour, but I'd already started the fire. Cold beers in hand and the scent of charcoal in the air, we were enjoying the weekend. Barbecues had good associations for us, a reminder of when we'd first met. Jenny had brought out bowls of salad, and was feeding me an olive when the phone rang.

'I'll get it,' she said, when I started to put down the tongs and spatula. 'You're not getting off cooking that easily.'

Smiling, I watched her go inside. She'd grown her blonde hair longer recently, long enough to tie back. It suited her. Contentedly, I took a drink of beer and turned my attention back to the charcoal bricks. I was squirting lighter fuel on to them when Jenny came back out.

'Some young woman for you,' she said, arching an eyebrow. 'Said her name was Rebecca Brody.'

I stared at her.

I'd never told Jenny what Brody's daughter was called. I knew she wouldn't want to know such details, and hearing the name from her, now, after all these months, left me speechless.

'What's wrong?' Jenny asked, looking worried.

'What else did she say?'

'Not much. She just wanted to know if you were in, and said she'd like to call round. I probably didn't sound very enthusiastic, but she said it would only take a few minutes. Look, are you OK? You look like you've seen a ghost.'

I gave an uncertain laugh. 'Funny you should say that.'

Jenny's face fell when I told her who the caller was.

'I'm sorry,' I said when I'd finished. 'I thought she was dead. God knows what she wants. Or how she found out where I live.'

Jenny was silent for a moment, then gave a resigned sigh. 'Don't worry, it isn't your fault. I'm sure she's got a good reason.'

The door buzzer sounded from the hallway. I hesitated, looking at Jenny. She smiled, then leaned forward and kissed me.

'Go on. I'll leave you in peace while you talk to her. And you can ask her to stay for something to eat, if you like.'

'Thanks,' I said, kissing her before going inside.

I was glad Jenny had taken it so well, but I wasn't sure I wanted Brody's daughter as a guest. I couldn't deny I was curious, but I felt oddly nervous at the prospect of coming face to face with her. Her father had died believing she was dead.

And five other people had died because of it.

But she could hardly be blamed for that, I reminded myself. *Give her a chance.* At least she'd made the effort to come and see me. She wouldn't be doing that unless she felt some responsibility for what had happened.

I took a deep breath and opened the door.

A red-haired young woman stood on the doorstep. She was slim and tanned, a pair of dark sunglasses perched on her face. But neither they, nor the unflattering loose dress she wore, could hide the fact that she was startlingly attractive.

'Hi,' I said, smiling.

There was something familiar about her. I was trying to place it, looking for something of Brody in her without being able to find it. Then I smelt the musky scent she was wearing and the smile froze on my face.

'Hello, Dr Hunter,' Grace Strachan said.

Everything suddenly seemed both slowed down and pin-prick sharp. There was time to think, uselessly, that the yacht hadn't slipped its chain after all, and then Grace's hand was emerging from her shoulder bag with the knife.

The sight of it freed me from my shock. I started to react as she lunged at me, but it was always going to be too late. I grabbed at the blade, but it slid through my hand, slicing my palm and fingers to the bone. The pain of that hadn't even had time to register when the knife went into my stomach.

There wasn't any pain, just a coldness and a sense of shock. And an awful sense of violation. *This isn't happening.* But it was. I sucked in air to shout or scream, but managed only a choked gasp. I clutched hold of the knife's handle, feeling the hot sticky wetness of my blood smearing both our hands, gripping it as tightly as I could as Grace tried to pull it out. I held on even as my legs sagged under me. *Keep hold. Keep hold or you're dead.*

And so is Jenny.

Grace was grunting as she tried to tug the knife free, following me down to the floor as I slid down the wall. Then, with a last frustrated gasp, she gave up. She stood over me, panting, her mouth contorted.

'He let me go!' she spat, and I saw the tears running in parallel tracks down her cheeks. 'He killed himself but he let me go!'

I tried to say something, anything, but no words would form. Her face hung above me for a moment longer, ugly and twisted, and then it was gone. The doorway was empty, the sound of running feet a fading echo on the street.

I looked down at my stomach. The knife handle protruded from it, obscenely. My shirt was soaked through with blood. I could feel it under me, pooling on the tiled floor. *Get up. Move.* But I no longer had any strength.

I tried to shout out. All that emerged was a croak. And now it was growing dark. Dark and cold. *Already? But it's summer.* There was still no pain, just a spreading numbness. From a nearby street, the chime of an ice-cream van drifted cheerfully on the air. I could hear Jenny moving around on the terrace, the tinkle of glasses. It sounded friendly and inviting. I knew I should try to move, but it seemed like too much effort. Everything was growing hazy. All I could remember was that I couldn't let go of the knife. I didn't know why any more.

Only that it was very important.

Acknowledgements

Embarking on a sequel is a daunting task for any writer. A number of people helped bring *Written in Bone* to fruition. DC Iain Souter of Shetland Police gave invaluable background on the difficulties of policing remote Scottish islands, as well as insights into island life – thanks, Iain. Dr Tim Thomson, lecturer in Forensic Anthropology at the University of Teesside (formerly of the University of Dundee), generously shared his expertise on fire deaths, and Dr Arpad Vass of Oak Ridge National Laboratory in Tennessee once again fielded queries promptly. Further forensic background came from several non-fiction works: *Death's Acre*, by Dr Bill Bass and Jon Jefferson; *Introduction to Forensic Anthropology*, by Steven N. Byers; *Flesh and Bone*, by Myriam Nafte; and *Corpse* by Jessica Snyder Sachs. Barry Gromett of the Met Office advised on winter storm conditions in the Outer Hebrides, while the South Yorkshire Community Fire Safety office and the press offices of South Yorkshire Police, Northern Constabulary and the Nursing and Midwifery Council were extremely helpful. Any factual errors or inaccuracies should be laid firmly at my door, not theirs.

I'd like to thank my agents, Mic Cheetham and Simon Kavanagh; Camilla Ferrier, Caroline Hardman and the rest of the Marsh

Agency; my editor Simon Taylor and all at Transworld, and my US editor Caitlin Alexander. Thanks also to Jeremy Freeston for grabbing his video camera at short notice, to Ben Steiner for his suggestions, to Kate Hurley and SCF for their read-throughs, and to my parents, Sheila and Frank Beckett for their continued support and enthusiasm. Finally, thank you to my wife Hilary for her sometimes painful editorial insights, and above all her patience.